THE BEADED NECKLACE

A NOVEL BY

A. TRAURING

This edition published in 2014 by
AT Press, Atlanta, Georgia

ISBN 978-0-9915291-2-4

© AT Press 2014
v 5.6

Cover photograph copyright Vasilchenko Nikita,
licensed from Shutterstock

This is a work of fiction. Names, characters, places, and
incidents either are products of the author's imagination or
are used fictitiously. Although the main setting is the
University of New Orleans Lakefront campus, all persons and
events depicted are FICTIONAL. Any resemblance to actual
persons (living or dead), events, or locales is so unlikely that
you have got to be kidding.

Thanks to Sue Sandell for editorial support. This is a much better book because of her work.

Thanks to Noelle for putting up with years and years and years of hearing me go on and on and on about Amy and Paul.

Thanks to the EPC Book Club for fellowship, good reading, and wonderful support.

Amy and Paul live at
http://atrauring.weebly.com

✄ 1 ✄

Monday, September 13, 2021 -- UNO campus, New Orleans

The scream jolted both of them awake. Before Amy had a chance to think, another cry pierced the pre-dawn quiet of the Pontchartrain Hall dormitory. Paul said, "You okay?"

"Must be, I'm not the one screaming," she answered, rubbing their face and sitting up.

There were more shouts and yells and rushing feet in the hallway outside their door. Amy pulled on her terrycloth robe and tied the sash, and stuck her feet in flip-flops. "Let's see what's going on," she thought.

The hall was full of women in various sleeping attire -- nightgowns, robes, yesterday's shirt grabbed at the sound of excitement and danger. Paul thought, "I have never seen so many hair curlers in one place before." She snickered.

The yelling was coming from just outside the dormitory's front door. Amy pushed into the crowd and let it make their way to a chilly morning with the barest hint of dawn in the east. Some of the women had flashlights. It took a few moments to grasp the scene: a pile of clothes on the ground, the sobbing Resident Advisor sitting on the grass beside it with her hands over her mouth, one of the senior women talking into her cell phone. The crowd of UNO students stood in a big semi-circle.

"What's going on?" Amy asked the woman next to her.

"Laura Adams," she said.

Amy shook their head. "No, that's our RA, Greta."

"Next to her."

It dawned on Amy that the woman meant the pile of clothes. "What happened?"

"I hear she's, like, hurt or something."

Paul thought, "This can't be good. Can we --" but Amy already was elbowing their way to the front of the crowd. When she began to walk toward the crying RA, the senior girl stopped talking into her phone long enough to shout, "Get back!" It was Paul who flipped her a bird and crouched next to Greta.

"Are you okay?" Amy asked, touching the woman's shoulder.

Greta nodded, eyes wide in her wet face. "It's awful," she whispered. "Awful."

Amy patted her, then turned to the pile of clothes. Finally she could see it was the woman who lived down the hall, Laura Adams. She was lying on her side, eyes open and seeing nothing. Reflexively, Amy did what she had seen her surgeon father do a thousand times, press the carotid artery in the neck for a pulse. There was none. The woman's flesh was cold to the touch.

The senior with the phone reached down and grabbed Amy by the arm, awkwardly yanking her up. "Don't touch anything!" she shouted. The morning chill and her own self-important excitement made her face a bright red, inches away from Amy. It made Paul angry. He took the lead to say, in Amy's voice, "Do you know if Laura needs help?"

"I don't know!" she shouted. "I called campus security; they'll be here soon. They'll know what to do! Now don't touch anything; get away."

Paul thought, "For all she knows Laura is alive, but she's still keeping anyone from doing anything to help her." He sat down next to the shocked RA and put their arm around her. Cellphone woman flashed an expression of anger and distaste, and went back to telling someone on the line how dreadful it all was, simply dreadful.

❦ 2 ❧

Sometime in 2014 -- New Orleans

It started when Amy was eleven years old. Paul's mind woke up in the little girl one morning, and it was months before her father and two doctor friends were able to deduce what happened. Amy was not crazy; Paul's personality was transferred to her when the gurney holding his comatose body brushed against her, spreading a small amount of fluid from a bedsore onto her. Paul Owens' body died on that gurney, but his mind lived on in Amy. From that moment on, his only existence was from inside Amy Clear.

It took time for Paul to come to grips with his new type of existence, just like it took Amy awhile to set boundaries and keep control of her body. They became buddies; he became part of Amy's family. Wholeheartedly and unreservedly, they loved each other. Paul was totally dependent on the girl for his very existence. She counted on Paul for sanity when adolescent hormones turned her life inside out.

There was a big change when Amy was fourteen. Paul was sound asleep when he discovered what a female orgasm felt like; Amy had an erotic night dream that culminated in a body-shredding climax. It took his breath away. The release she experienced was thrilling and exhausting.

Quietly, Amy thought, "Are you awake?"

Paul thought back, "I am now. Wow!"

She was embarrassed. "I don't know what happened," she stammered.

"You don't?" he thought, incredulous. After a long pause, he said out loud, "Do you want me to explain it?"

"No, I know what it is. I'm just embarrassed," she whispered.

"No need to be embarrassed," he said, "it's okay. We can't be shy with each other." Then, "I hope you enjoyed that as much as I did." He moved their arms to hug their body.

Paul felt a smile on their face. "Oh, yes," she said out loud. "I don't know about not being shy, but thanks. I think I'm going back to sleep. I'm exhausted."

A few days later Amy asked if there were a way to plan dreams. "I'd like to have another one like the other night," she said.

Paul remembered a time when he had hoped for lucid dreaming, and for the same reason. "I never figured out how," he said, "and I tried for years. Let me know when you come up with a way."

Three nights after that, Amy turned on the light at their night table. "Can you help me?" she asked out loud.

"Sure," he thought back. "What do you need?"

"Our hand holding," she said. She took a deep breath. "I'd like you to do something else with that left hand of ours."

Paul moved their left arm, and he put their palm on their right breast.

"Oh God yes," fourteen-year-old Amy said out loud. "Please."

And so Paul made love to her. She retreated; he was able to use both hands. He did not have to ask what she liked, because he felt exactly the same sensations that she did. It was wonderful to Paul -- to share a sexual intimacy with a woman and a girl he absolutely and totally loved, and to feel the added closeness of literally sharing every touch, every shudder, every joy. What sleep they had was deep and dreamless. It was entirely too soon when SpongeBob SquarePants woke them up by shouting "Yaaaaayyy!!!" from the bedside alarm clock.

ੴ 3 ੴ

The sky showed pink and lavender streaks of dawn by the time campus security arrived. The brown and white SUV with the flashing yellow light rack stopped in front of the walkway that went from the parking lot to the dorm entrance, and two men in light brown uniforms alit, armed with batons and walkie-talkies. The senior woman ran to them, shouting, "My sorority sister is over there! Please help her!" She took one of the security men by the arm to make him hurry, but he shrugged her hand off and said, "Please."

They walked past Amy and the RA, and knelt in the grass on either side of Laura Adams. One of the men made the same check Amy had done, and reached the same conclusion. He stood up and whispered something to the senior woman, who stepped back in horror. Then the man faced the clot of students and shouted, "Who found this woman?"

Greta the RA raised her hand silently.

"Roommates? Anyone here a roommate of this woman?" A small woman standing toward the back of the crowd raised her hand, as students will. She was five-foot-one, with a very slight frame. Everything about her posture screamed 'timid' as she walked up to the security guard.

"The rest of you, go inside. Everyone. Get! Get!" Senior girl rushed back to the security man to protest, but he said, "Thanks for your help. Now go back inside. Now!"

All the women were talking excitedly as they slowly made

their way back inside the dormitory. The two security men went to the Resident Advisor. One said to Amy kindly, "You can go inside now. This is no place for a young woman."

Amy shook their head. "I want to stay with Greta, if that's okay."

Paul thought, "Wait -- you don't like Greta."

The security man nodded and turned back to the Resident Advisor. Amy thought to Paul, "I don't. But the poor woman's shell-shocked. She can use someone to sit with her. Besides, I want to hear what these guys have to say."

Laura's roommate silently sat with Amy and Greta. The RA put her hand on the woman's arm and said, "I'm so sorry, Leslie." The roommate nodded.

The two men who made up the security team hunkered side-by-side for a short conversation. One said, "God. My Margaret is the same age as this girl." The other said, "I'll call NOPD."

The first one sidled to Greta and asked, "Are you okay, honey?" Silently, she nodded. "Is there anything you need? Can I call anyone?" She shook her head. Amy tightened her grip on the woman's shoulder and she wept again, still shaking her head.

"I'm sorry, but I have to ask you some questions. Is that okay?" A faint nod. Her eyes were focused on something miles away, as the morning birds came out in loud force.

"What happened? You're the one who found the woman?"

"Y--Yes," she stumbled. Amy patted her shoulder. "I was going out for a run before class. It was 5:15. I saw a pile of clothes so I went to look, and that's when I saw Laura." She inhaled sharply. "I -- I --" and fell silent.

"Did you see anyone else?" the security man asked, softly. His partner was on his walkie-talkie, trying to get through to the Parish police.

Greta shook her head.

"Anything unusual? Something that might have been a weapon?"

Still shaking her head, Greta said, "It was still dark. I saw Laura and I saw her eyes and I screamed." She finally aimed her eyes at the man. "Is she -- is she going to be okay?"

Amy hugged the woman from the side. The security man

looked down, then turned to the roommate. "What's your name?" he asked.

Barely audible, she whispered, "Leslie. I -- I'm Leslie Roper."

"And you're this woman's --" he was pointing at the pile of clothes nearby "-- roommate?" She nodded. "Does -- Did she have more roommates than just you?" A shake of the head. "Okay, Leslie. When's the last time you saw her?"

The security man had to ask her to speak up, her whisper was so soft. Finally she said, "She was in the room when I came back from dinner last night, around 6:30. Then I went to the library. I got home around eleven. She wasn't there, and I went to bed."

He nodded, he said "Okay, thank you," and he got up to join his co-worker.

Everyone waited for the police to arrive. Paul and Amy carried on a silent conversation while Greta and Leslie stared at the ground and the two security men rehashed the Zephyrs' miserable minor league baseball season. "I don't like this," Paul thought to her. "I'm not a six-one manly man anymore. This is scary."

"Did you ever see a dead person before?" she asked. "I mean, before you came to me?"

She felt him shrug inside. "Funerals, that's all. Everyone saying how good Uncle Louie looked, and me thinking, 'No, he looks like hammered shit.'"

"I'm glad Dad dragged me to his ER so often. I got used to seeing dead people. You remember? After a week I quit throwing up."

"Death is a part of life," Paul pontificated. "It's weird how we think the Victorians were prigs because they didn't talk about sex, but they kept their dead relatives in the parlor until it was time to get them to the cemetery. "

She thought back, "Now people won't shut up about sex, but we're terrified of dead people."

"Zombie apocalypse."

She laughed, which made one of the security men turn to look. "Something like that," she thought back.

"You're good about locking our door," he thought. "We're going to have to be even more careful. All the girls are. Hell, maybe even the boys."

"I know you studied security before you came to me, so tell me what we need to do."

Almost two hours passed before a New Orleans police detective arrived with a medical examiner and a photographer. Greta had gotten up long enough to fetch a blanket from her room and spread it over Laura's body. Amy had decided her two morning classes weren't as important as witnessing a police investigation that was more real than anything she'd ever seen on television, but she did go back to her room to dress in jeans and a sweatshirt. She even felt good about being supportive of the RA whom she didn't like.

The police detective was young, barely thirty years old. He had a full head of curly black hair over a particularly handsome face. His black suit seemed one size too big, and his necktie was tight but pulled to one side. As he got out of the unmarked car, he put on a hat -- not a patrolman's cap, but an old fashioned felt fedora. Amy couldn't remember the last time she saw one outside of a movie. The detective wore an appealing half smile as he walked toward the security men. He lit a cigarette before he hailed them.

"People still smoke?" Paul thought. Amy's doctor father would be horrified, but she found it just a minor bump in the detective's otherwise attractive demeanor. "Swoon," she thought, and she heard Paul laugh inside.

Trailing the detective was the medical examiner. He was a balding man, mid or late fifties, in a shiny gray suit and an out-of-date skinny black necktie. He was breathing hard as he walked up the path, lugging his medical bag. With him was the photographer, a woman in her thirties, with three cameras strung around her neck.

Amy heard the detective offer, "That the body?" Security man two said, "Yep."

"What do you think?"

"I know she's dead," he answered. "I don't get paid $16 an hour to think nothing about this shit."

"Did you secure the area?"

The same security man said, "Did we what?"

He shook his head and muttered, "No wonder it looks like the circus was here. We'll take pictures anyway, but --"

The tall senior girl with the cell phone ran out of the dormitory lobby to the detective, shouting "Thank God you're here! What are we to do?"

"Who are you?" he asked bluntly.

"I'm Laura's sorority sister." Pointing to the campus security men, she went on, "They said she's," and whispered dramatically, "dead." Then she was talking in her normal excited tone, "What do we do? Tell us what to do!"

Amy thought the smile that spread across the detective's face was charming. "Sure. First you calm down. Will you do that for me?" The woman nodded vigorously. "Good. And now go inside and get out of our way. We've got a lot of work to do out here."

"But -- but -- but!" she sputtered. The detective suddenly feinted as if he were going to jump at her, and she ran back to the dormitory lobby.

"Who found the body?" he asked the three women sitting on the ground.

"I did," Greta said, holding up her hand.

"And one of you is the roommate?" Wordlessly, Leslie raised her hand.

"And who are you?" he asked Amy.

"I live in this dorm. Greta needed a friend, so I sat with her. My dad is a doctor, I'm curious about this."

"I'll bet you are," he said. "Why don't you go back inside? Your friend will be okay now."

"No!" Greta barked, her eyes suddenly wide. She grasped at Amy's arm and pleaded, "Let her stay, please?"

The detective smiled and shrugged. He said to Greta, "Tell me how you found the victim."

The RA tensed visibly at the word, but after a moment she answered, "I told the campus policemen. I was going for a run before class. It was 5:15. I saw a bundle of clothing on the ground, and I went to look at it. Then I saw it was Laura --" Amy held the woman's shoulder tighter "-- and, and, and I started screaming."

He nodded kindly as he knelt beside her. "The rent-a-cop said you didn't see anyone? Nothing that looked like it could have been a weapon?" Greta shook her head.

"What can you tell me about the dead girl?"

Paul spoke up, sounding like Amy, "Officer, her name was Laura Adams."

"That's 'detective'," he said, but he heard the suggestion to be less *noir*. "What can you tell me about Laura?" he said.

"She's a Zeta; her sisters probably know her better. She's a senior, so she's twenty or twenty-one. She's from upstate somewhere, I think it's Monroe. Education major. She's got a boyfriend from home; I don't remember where he's in school." She looked up at the detective, who was smiling kindly. "She dated a couple of men here, you know, for fun. Nothing serious."

"Do you know their names?" he asked, pen poised over his notepad, and cigarette ashes dropping onto it.

Greta took a deep breath. "She was hanging out with Ronnie Kimmel. And she spent time with Reggie Young."

"Very good," he said, trying to encourage her. "Was the -- was Laura well liked? Did she get along with the people in the dorm?"

"I guess. No one ever complained to me about her, and it's my job to hear the complaints."

"Did she drink? Use drugs that you know of?"

Greta shrugged. Amy offered, "Not that I ever knew about."

The detective turned his attention to Leslie. He noted how vulnerable and weak she looked, and thought she would be a life-long target for male predators. Despite himself he sighed. "You're the roommate?" A nod. "What's your name, Sweetheart? When did you see her last?" Leslie repeated her story.

"Was that typical? Her being gone at bedtime on a Sunday night?"

"I guess. I didn't think anything of it."

"Did she have a boyfriend?"

For the first time, Leslie sounded animated. "Yeah. Her hometown beau. He's in school at Alabama. I got to meet him; he's a great guy."

"But he's not here? Was she seeing anyone here? A special friend, maybe?"

She sounded listless again. "Yeah. She was friends with Ronnie Kimmel. And she spent some time with that Reggie creep."

The detective raised his eyebrows. "Tell me about the creep," he asked.

"Reggie. I think it's Reggie Young. He's awful. He's a nasty, dirty, disgusting man."

This time he only raised one eyebrow.

"Manipulative. Charming until he doesn't need you anymore, and then he's mean."

"And they were friends?" She shrugged. "Any idea where Laura went last night after you went to the library?" A shake of the head. He wrote something in his notebook, and flicked his cigarette butt onto the walkway.

The detective turned to Amy. "Were you friends with the de - - with Laura?"

"I don't know her well. We say 'hey' in the hall, or chat in the laundry room. We don't socialize. She's a year ahead of me. Was."

He bounced the back of the pen off his lower lip while he thought. Then he asked, "Any of you ever see signs of injury on her before? Bruises? Black eye?"

Leslie raised her hand. "She broke her leg on a ski trip out west two winters ago," she whispered. Greta added, "She must have had a hundred signatures on the cast by the time they took it off."

The detective put his notepad in an inside jacket pocket, and pulled out a card case. "Thank you, ladies. I've got your contact information. If you think of anything we didn't go over, please call me." He gave each of them a business card. "Even if it seems trivial, it might help us find who did this." He smiled, then stood up. "Let me see what my medical examiner is up to."

Amy said, "Officer, if I keep my hands in my pockets, can I watch? This is fascinating to me."

He shook his head. "It's 'detective.' Really, Sweetheart, I'm sure you've got better things to do. You don't want to be around a dead body."

"I'm used to it," she said, and she heard Paul laugh inside. "My dad is an ER surgeon; he made sure I saw lots of dead people."

He stared. He made a motion to his jacket, then resisted the impulse to take his notepad out. "Do you like being around dead bodies?"

"I don't mind it," she answered. "If that's what I have to do to learn stuff, it's okay. Please?"

She heard Paul think, "Why don't you kiss him and get it over with?" She stamped her foot, which startled the detective, but her face continued to smile and plead.

"Look," he finally said, "I'll make a deal with you. Don't touch anything. Don't interrupt me or the medical examiner. Don't get in the photographer's way. And understand that if my boss shows up I'm going to say I don't know you. Okay?"

Amy felt a wave of excitement. "Sure thing! Uh, what do I call you?"

"Your Majesty. Or Detective Riordan. But don't call me Joe."

"Okay, Your Majesty. What's wrong with Joe?"

He grinned. "My name is Steven. Come on," and he led her to the earthly remains of Laura Adams.

The photographer was focusing some extreme close-up shots of Laura's neck, while the medical examiner held a portable light. Her other two cameras were hanging from a tree branch behind her. The detective whispered to Amy, "She's taking ultraviolet pictures now. She's already got the color and infrared shots. Each of them can show something different." Amy nodded.

Paul thought to her, "This is better than CSI."

"What's CSI?" she thought back.

"Oh. A TV show from before I knew you. Never mind."

When the photographer finished, the medical examiner picked up the ruler she had placed on the dead girl. Instead of returning it, he used it as a pointer as he said to the detective, "She was strangled. Here's the ligature mark." The detective peered from a few inches away, and Amy tried to see over his shoulder.

"What do you make of these?" Riordan asked, using his pen to point at things on the girl's neck, along the ligature mark.

"The things that look like scratches," pointing, "are probably from the girl's fingernails, trying to get at the thing around her neck. I'll scrape under her nails." The detective nodded, while Paul whispered -- out loud -- "Oh! I see." Riordan turned to glare at Amy for a moment, but the doctor was highlighting something else. "These marks, along the ligature line. Maybe we can get more at the morgue, but I'm guessing she was wearing a necklace with some ornaments, like beads. That was the weapon."

"Hmmm. Then where is it?"

The examiner said, "She may be lying on it. Now, look here - -" he had grasped the body's right upper eyelid by the lashes and pulled it back, a sight that made Amy flinch. "See these little red marks on the inside of her eyelid? And in the sclera? Petechiae. They come from increased venous pressure. She wasn't choked -- it wasn't lack of air that killed her. The garrote blocked her jugulars, depleted blood built up in her brain." He let go of the eyelid, then worked at smoothing and closing it. "She would have been unconscious in ten seconds. If the killer kept up the pressure, she'd be dead in five minutes. I'm told it's not painful."

Riordan was taking notes. "Signs of a struggle?" he asked.

"Just the fingernail marks. I don't see anything on the neck to show the perp used their hands."

Amy blurted, "Laura is six feet tall. How big does a man have to be to do this?"

Both men looked at her. The medical examiner said, "Riordan, when did you go back to teaching forensics?"

"It's a fair question, Jermaine," he said, then whispered to her, "I told you not to interrupt!"

"You might be surprised, young lady," the doctor answered. "Either by accident or with knowledge, it only takes maybe five pounds of pressure on the right spots to obstruct the jugular veins. Even a small woman can strangle a large man."

She nodded. Then it was Paul who asked, "What does this mean?" They were pointing to the ligature mark. "In front it's right under her jaw, but it slants down on the sides, and in back it's even with her shoulders." They looked up.

Riordan hissed, but the examiner raised his eyebrows. "Good point," he admitted. "Maybe she was leaning forward. Or it might indicate that the perpetrator was shorter than the victim." To the detective he said, "At least you picked a clever student this time."

Paul thought to Amy, "This time?"

"Any doubt of the cause of death?" Riordan asked.

Doctor Jermaine shook his head. He began fitting paper bags over the woman's hands.

"Time of death?"

He looked at his watch. "Superficial body temperature is 86 degrees. I'd say she died between midnight and one o'clock." The examiner rocked forward onto his knees and said, "Steven, give me a hand turning her over." Amy scrambled to get out of the way while the two men rolled the body onto its back, and then onto the other side.

The detective said, "What is -- did you fart, doc?"

"Post mortem defecation," he said absently as he patted the ground the body had been on, "dead bodies do that. Damn, I don't see that necklace."

Riordan stood, and Amy did as well. "Get with me after you do the autopsy," he told the examiner. "Thanks for your help."

Ignoring the detective, the doctor spoke to Amy: "Go home, young lady. This is no place for a nice woman like you."

He waved at two orderlies who placed the body on a stretcher and eased it into the back of an ambulance. They would be out of the public's sight when they placed Laura Adams in a black plastic body bag.

"Now what?" Amy asked Riordan. Paul thought, "Ask him about the bags on her hands."

"Now nothing, Clear," he answered. "I go talk to the dean so I can get some phone numbers, and you go to class."

"Wait!" she cried. "I've got all these questions. And -- and I'm a junior here, I know the deans, I know the students. I'm sure I can help you."

He stared at her, with his half smile and his wavy hair and his fedora. Paul thought, "Oh, please."

Riordan said, "Tell you what. Get me contact information on those men she dated," he opened his notepad, "Ronnie Kimmel and Reggie Young. And the people at her sorority. Call me this evening with what you find."

She smiled, she grinned, she felt like dancing. "You bet, Your Majesty," she said. Then Paul jumped to lead and said, "What's with the paper bags on her hands?"

"Sometimes there are forensic clues on a victim's hands -- signs of a struggle, maybe a perp's skin under the nails. The bags prevent contamination until Jermaine there gets her to the autopsy table."

Amy's mouth fell open, then she said, "I learned more today than I have in four weeks of biology class."

"Call me this evening," Riordan said, and went back to the unmarked car where the doctor and photographer were waiting.

Back in their dorm room, Amy was poring over the student directory at her desk, looking for names and phone numbers. Paul said, out loud, "I love being a pretty girl. It's amazing what we get away with."

"Hmmm?" She was trying to find the K's for Ronnie Kimmel's phone number.

"That detective Riordan. He must have broken half the rules of police procedure by letting us hang with him."

"Wasn't that great?"

"And how!" he said. "You called it, you said it was fascinating. He's smart. And that doctor, what a hoot. I like him."

She wrote down a number, then found the page for sororities. "Zeta Tau Alpha president is Madison Parker." She wrote the name down. "I wonder who Laura's little sister is? Was?" She stopped, twirling the pencil in her right hand. "He's a hunk."

It took Paul a moment to follow her. "Got a crush on Riordan?"

She smiled, bashful. "Hey, you have crushes on half the women in this dorm; let me have one."

That evening, Amy called the detective. "Riordan," he answered. "What?"

"It's Amy Clear, Your Majesty," she said. "I have those phone numbers you wanted."

"Well, well. Good job. What are they?" Amy dictated the names and numbers.

When he began to dismiss her, Amy said, "Can I come with you when you interview them?"

"What? God, no. Have you any idea how against the rules that is?"

"Probably not a lot more than you letting me look over your shoulder today. Look, you'll get lost trying to find your way on campus. I can help. Really." She heard Paul think, "You don't want to study for Psych, do you?"

There was a pause. Finally Riordan said, "Okay, tell you

what. I'll meet you at your dorm; I know where that is. Eight-thirty tomorrow morning. These people will be in classes, but the dean gave me their schedule. You help me find them, I'll let you watch. But remember, don't interrupt!"

Paul felt her smile wrap all the way around to the back of their head. "Sir, yes Sir, Your Majesty, Sir!" she said.

The next morning Amy dressed all in black -- jeans, long-sleeve turtleneck, and shoes. She was sitting in the dorm lobby at 8:05, bubbling with excitement. She thought to Paul, "Maybe I'll become a cop. That sergeant years ago told me to go to the police academy."

"I hate cops," Paul thought back. "They make me nervous. I did too many, uh, wrong things when I was your age. Cops make me feel guilty."

"That's what you get for being bad."

"Hey! I wasn't -- okay, I was bad, but I wasn't evil." He thought a moment, then added, "Maybe being a detective is different. A beat cop's job is to intimidate people into behaving, but I'll bet detectives are more about problem solving."

"Can we be a detective and also join the circus?" she said silently, "You know that's my real goal in life."

Amy pretended to read her Psych assignment, but she spent more time looking at the big clock behind the information desk. It was still five minutes fast, left over from the days when the residents had curfews and the administration liked to hand out demerits.

༰ 4 ༰

Monday, September 13, 2021 -- UNO campus, New Orleans

As they walked to the Chemistry Annex to talk to Ronnie Kimmel, Detective Riordan explained what he wanted from Amy. "You take notes. Good notes, very complete notes. How's your handwriting?" Before she could answer, he handed her his pocket notepad and went on, "Notice their posture, any physical reaction they have to questions -- do they get nervous, do they blush, do they wet themselves? These are going to be interviews, not interrogations. At this point I'm just looking for information. Everyone is a suspect --" he turned his head to look at her, "-- even you, because you insisted on staying at the crime scene and you like dead bodies --"

"I never said that! I said I can put up with them!"

He smiled, then turned forward as they continued to walk across the UNO campus. "Yeah, yeah, I've heard it all. Once I have real suspects, then it's time for interrogation."

"Where did you learn all this?" she asked.

"Nine months at the Police Academy, and getting bawled out five times a day by my COs ever since. What room is his class in?"

They entered the Chemistry Annex -- clean, brightly lit, with textured wallpaper and marble design in the linoleum. "205," she said, and the detective looked around. "This way. I had a class there last semester." They walked up a broad stairway, then halfway down the hall. Through the square glass window in the closed door they saw the teacher -- probably a second year grad student -- lecturing.

"Wait here," the detective said, and opened the door.

The teacher and students were used to latecomers, and they all ignored Riordan until he walked up to the instructor and waved his badge case. "Excuse me, Doc," he said. "I need to speak to Ronnie Kimmel." He heard some whispering from a back corner of the room.

"Class will be over in fifteen minutes," the teacher said, "you can talk to him then."

Riordan faced the class and called, controlled but loud, "Ronnie Kimmel! Front and center. Now!" There was some rustling, and a puzzled young man picked up some books and walked to the front. When he reached the detective, Riordan took him by the arm. He turned back to the irate instructor and said, "I'll remember you." Then, "C'mon, Mister Kimmel, we need to talk," and he led him from the classroom.

"What's this all about?" Kimmel asked, looking back and forth between Amy and Riordan. "Who are you?"

Riordan turned on his charming smile. "I'm Detective Riordan. I'm with Orleans Parish police. This is my intern, Miss Clear. You are not in trouble, but I hope you have some information that can help me."

"Umm, okay," he said tentatively, his head still swiveling between the two people.

Amy volunteered, "We passed an empty room when we got off the stairs. Will that work?"

"Excellent, Miss Clear, well done. Come on, Ronnie, this won't take long."

Once inside the vacant room, Riordan waited until the student picked a seat. Then he pointed to a place across and sideways for Amy, so she was not facing Kimmel directly, and he sat in a chair aimed 90 degrees from the student. Paul thought, "Interesting seating geometry. It's got to be deliberate; let's ask later." She nodded, and opened Riordan's notepad. She leafed through several pages of his scrawl until she found a blank page, then sat with pen poised.

The detective began. "I'm sure you've heard about Laura Adams," he said, softly.

"That's so awful! I was with her on Friday night. I can't believe she's dead."

"How well did you know Laura?"

"We were pretty good friends. We'd hang out a lot -- she's got a boyfriend at Alabama; we were just buddies."

"Did you ever sleep with her? Or expect to?"

"What? No. I mean, when I first got to know her last year I thought maybe, you know. I didn't know about the boyfriend then."

"Did you want more from her than just being friends?"

"Doesn't every guy? But I got used to it. She's good people; I like her. I dated some other women for, uh, romance."

Amy wrote furiously to keep up with the interview. Paul thought, "I don't think he did it," and she thought back, "Hush! I'm busy!"

"Did she date anyone else here that you know about?"

"She said she was friends with Reggie Young, which surprised me. He's such a cockhound, I can't imagine him just being friends with a woman."

"Oh, really?" the detective responded. "Was that current? Or how long ago?"

"I guess she told me about him last spring. I got the idea it was current, but I didn't ask. I don't want the details."

"Anyone else?"

"Not that I knew about."

"Tell me, Ronnie, did Laura drink? Did she use drugs?"

After a moment he said, "I don't know about drugs," and looked up and to his left, moving his hands in front of his mouth. "But we drank. We're both twenty-one."

"Since you knew her pretty well, do you know if there was anyone who disliked her? Maybe a guy who wasn't as understanding as you about the boyfriend?"

He shook his head.

"Did she wear a necklace?"

"Did she --" Ronnie repeated. He looked up, thinking. "A silver cross, that's all I ever noticed. Simple thing, on one of those plain skinny chains."

"Where were you last night around midnight?"

"In bed. This class started at 7:30."

"Your roommate vouch for you?"

"Both of them, yeah."

"Okay, Ronnie. I think we're done for now. Is there anything else that might help us? Anything at all?"

When he shook his head again, Riordan handed him a business card. "If you think of anything, call me. It doesn't matter how trivial you think it is, it may be the key to solving this. Okay?"

Kimmel nodded. "Can I go now?"

"Sure, kid. Stay out of trouble, you hear?"

As soon as Ronnie had left the room, the detective said, "Let me see your notes." Amy leaned over to hand them to him, and watched while he thumbed through them. Four pages. She was holding her breath.

"Not bad, Clear. I wish you had noticed what he did when I asked if they used alcohol or drugs. My guess is they smoked dope together. Jermaine's autopsy report will let me know."

Paul thought the same words Amy said: "What? What did he do?"

Riordan grinned and stood up, and offered his hand to Amy. "He brought his hands up to cover his mouth and he broke off eye contact with me, and he looked up and to the left. He was lying. Let's go find your sorority queen."

On their walk to the Liberal Arts building, Riordan lit a cigarette and automatically held the pack out. Amy shook her head. "You are the only person I know that smokes."

"You don't get out much, Sweetheart. The real world is a little different from your campus. This Madison girl, is she the tall one who had her cell phone glued to her head yesterday? She was a pain."

Amy shook her head, "I don't know. I know who you're talking about, but I don't know who she is."

"Self-important twerp," he muttered. "She was getting off on electing herself an Important Person and making sure everyone knew it. How far to the building she's in?"

"Down there," Amy pointed. "I had an English class there last year."

He looked at papers on his clipboard. "She's taking French.

Ooh la la."

Once inside, the woman leading the class listened when Riordan introduced himself and explained why he was interrupting. "Madison isn't here today," she said.

"Any idea where she might be?" he asked. Amy hid her face while the instructor explained that senior women, all the women at University of New Orleans, are considered adults and do not have to explain their absences. He thanked her and turned away.

In the hall he muttered, "Okay, Clear, where is she?"

It was Paul who said, "If she's the drama queen you think she is, we'll find her in her dorm room."

Riordan snickered. "Lying in state, no doubt. Receiving her loyal sorority sisters. Okay, where is --" he looked at the clipboard "-- Privateer Place?"

"Just over there," she pointed, "toward the canal. I have friends over there, I know my way around it."

Privateer Place was an apartment complex owned by the university. It was for students who wanted more freedom than a dormitory allowed but still needed the convenience of living on campus. The fenced-in swimming pool was the first thing they saw. Riordan said, "This beats the hell out of the dive where I live. I may move here."

Amy grabbed the clipboard to steady it in Riordan's hand and read the building and room number. "She's got three roommates," Amy said. She waved her student ID card at the swipe pad and they entered the roomy lobby. A student working the desk said, "Can I help you?"

"Sure, Sweetheart," the detective said, showing his badge. "I need to visit Morgan --" he looked at the clipboard, "-- no, Madison Parker. Where's her room?"

"Let me buzz her," the woman said. "I can't let you go up there."

"Do you always interfere with a police investigation?" he asked. The woman slowly put the handset back on the phone cradle. She swallowed and said, "Uhh. Up those stairs and down a hallway."

"We'll find it, thanks. And don't call her, okay? That's a good girl." He turned to Amy and said, "Lead on."

Amy thought to Paul, "Isn't he great? He doesn't let anyone

push him around. I wish I could do that."

"All you need is a badge and a gun," Paul thought back. "He is impressive, though."

"Oh, good! We agree."

"That much, anyway."

They went up the carpeted concrete stairs to the second floor. "Her room is down this way," Amy said, and they walked down a long hall, both of them turning their heads at each door to read the room numbers. As they walked, Riordan said, "That swipe card thing you did to get us in here. Do all the dorms use that system?"

"My dorm uses them from eight at night to six or seven in the morning -- I'm not sure which. I try very hard not to be up that early. This place uses it all the time. I think the family housing uses it 24/7, too."

"What is it? Your student ID?"

"Yeah, I mean, yes. They do something to it each semester at registration. If you're not enrolled, it quits working."

"I'll bet campus security has a timestamp of who swipes themselves in everywhere. Do you swipe something to leave the building?"

Amy shook her head as they finally came to Madison Parker's room. High-pitched squeals of female conversation came out of the open door. Riordan tugged his suit jacket down, then beat a tattoo on the door frame. The voices fell silent, until one woman, her voice getting louder as she neared the doorway, called, "Yes? Who is it?"

The detective stepped inside the small entryway, with Amy close behind. They were met by a woman wearing a dark blue dress with a Zeta Tau Alpha pin. She was exceptionally well dressed and groomed. "Can I help you?" she asked.

Riordan showed his badge. "I'm looking for Madison Parker. Is she in?"

She turned her head to look back where she had left the other women, then faced him and said, "I don't believe she is up for entertaining." A smile flashed across her tan face for half a second.

"Good," he said as he started walking past her. "I'd hate for entertainment to interrupt my business with her."

"No, wait!" she called, grabbing at Amy, "You can't go in there." Amy, feeling brave from watching Riordan, shook the woman's hand off her arm and followed him. "Too late, Sweetheart," he said, not bothering to look back, "I'm already there."

Five women were in the suite living room. Four were dressed like the one who had welcomed them, in the sorority uniform dress, pearls, hose and high heels. They were seated or standing around the room. Reclining on the sofa, in a flowing pink dressing gown, was the same woman who had acted as ringmaster at Amy's dormitory the morning before. Riordan noted she didn't look nearly as tall lying down. She was every bit as well groomed as the other women in the room, but appeared to be suffering -- no, enjoying -- a bout of the vapors.

"Miss Parker," he said to the prone woman, "I'm Detective Riordan. We met yesterday."

Amy opened Riordan's notebook and thumbed to a blank page.

"I think I remember you," she said, the back of one hand pressed to her forehead. "It's all so confusing."

"Yes, it is. Look --" turning to look at the sorority sisters around the room, "-- this is official police business. Give us fifteen minutes."

There was a general grumbling. One woman said, "Well, I never! I'll talk to my daddy --"

"You do that, Sweetheart," he interrupted. "Tell him my name is R-I-O-R-D-A-N. But do it from somewhere else. Everybody out!"

Madison Parker whispered, "I'm so tired. I don't know if I can talk to you now."

The detective put his fists on his hips. "You'll talk to me now, or you'll talk to me at the station house." He waited to let his words sink in. "Any questions?"

Slowly she sat up and waved her retinue away. They were talking softly as they left. The detective said, "Clear, shut that door." She followed the last sister and locked the entrance door.

When she got back to the living room, the detective was sitting across from Madison, facing her side. He patted another chair he'd dragged over for Amy.

"You know why I'm here," he began. "I hope --"

"It's awful," she whispered. "It's just awful."

"Yes, Madison, it's awful. And it will be more awful if more girls turn up murdered. I want you to tell me everything you know about Laura Adams. Like, how long have you known her?"

"Oh, I don't know, nothing --"

"Madison. Please. You can help save lives. Tell me about Laura."

A deep breath. "Laura pledged Zeta a few weeks before I did, our freshman year. She's active in some of our charitable efforts -- we're supporting a pediatric AIDS foundation this year. Zeta believes --"

"Laura," the detective reminded her.

"I'm sorry. Yes, Laura." A sigh. "She was a sparkplug on our intramural softball team. All the women love her. I don't know what to tell you."

Amy spoke up. "Who's her little sister this year?" Riordan clenched his eyes shut and rubbed his temples. "Now it's Rashika Johnson. Last year it was Courtney Lowe. Both of them have said a lot of nice things about Laura."

"Any of the girls she was especially close to?" he prodded.

"Mister Riordan, the members of Zeta Tau Alpha are women."

He somehow maintained a smile as he said, "Any of the women she was especially close to?"

There was no answer.

"Miss Parker? Are you all right?"

"What I tell you, that's just between you and me, right? And her," pointing at Amy.

"For now, yes, but I cannot promise secrecy. A police investigation goes where it goes." He shifted in the chair and tried to look kindly as he looked at her. "What is it you want to tell me, Madison?"

The woman became agitated, looking anywhere but at the detective, picking non-existent lint off the sofa, straightening the already plumped pillows. "Laura was on probation," she finally said, looking at the floor. "We had an intervention with her about her drinking -- it was April or May. She was twenty-one, she was legal to drink, but she was drinking too much and not holding it well. Laura disrupted a couple of chapter meetings, and that's what made me act." She took a sip from a glass of something on the coffee table. "We gave her until the end of fall semester to get her shit together or we were going to kick her out of the sorority." Then, with puppy dog eyes, "Please don't embarrass our chapter by telling anyone."

"I understand," he said. "You said she was disruptive. What was her behavior outside of the sorority? Were her grades suffering? Other self-destructive behavior?"

Madison shook her head. "Maybe Rashika, her little sister, knows. Laura kind of distanced herself from us after the intervention."

Amy was writing notes furiously, trying to keep an eye on the woman to notice her reactions to Riordan's questions.

"Did she disrupt any more of your meetings?" Another shake of the head. "Did she stop drinking?"

"I don't know, officer."

"That's detective," he smiled. "Did Laura have enemies? Was there anyone in the sorority who disliked her? Wished her harm?"

"Some of the women resented her when we did the intervention, but I would think that went away when Laura seemed to straighten up."

"Miss Parker, what is your major?"

She blinked at the unexpected question. Even Amy looked up at the detective. Madison said, "I'm a theatre major. Why?"

He shrugged. "I heard Laura was majoring in education. I was curious if you were on the same track."

Riordan looked at Amy and said, "Any questions you want to ask, Clear?"

Paul thought, "He just promoted you." She said, "Yes. Was there anything that happened in Laura's personal life before the drinking? Boy trouble? Family problems?" She was relieved to see a fleeting smile cross the detective's face.

"She had a boyfriend from home, he's at Alabama," the sorority president said. "I got the impression something might have happened during Spring break, but she still talked about him. I don't know anything about her family."

Riordan was tapping his index finger against his cheek.

"Where were you last night around midnight?"

"Zeta had a charity fundraiser off campus last night. I got home around two."

Paul was the one who asked, "Was Laura at the fundraiser?"

Madison seemed to be searching her memory. "No. I mean, I didn't see her there."

The detective stood up as he pulled his card case from an inside jacket pocket. "If you think of anything else that might help us, I want you to call me," and he handed her his card. "It can be profound, it can be trivial; until we hear it we don't know if it's the missing key to solving this. Uh, we'll let ourselves out."

Amy followed the detective out, through the gaggle of Zeta sisters waiting in the hall outside Madison's door. Riordan tipped his hat and said, "Ladies," as they walked by them.

When they walked out the lobby door they both blinked and squinted in the sun. He took her by the arm long enough to lead her to a cement bench outside the fence surrounding the swimming pool. "What did you think of her?" he asked.

"Drama major, drama queen." Paul added, out loud, "Emotionally she dropped Laura at the intervention."

Riordan nodded. "You asked a good question," he said. "If Laura and her boyfriend had trouble, that may have caused her drinking. And if they broke up recently, he might be a suspect."

"Maybe the roommate knows what happened. Or the little sister."

"Show me your notes," he said. He took the notepad from her and leafed through the three pages devoted to Madison Parker. Something made him smile, but he returned the notepad without comment. "Next up is the cockhound friend. He's not in class right now, so where do you think we'll find him?"

"If I knew him I might have an idea," Amy said. "His dorm room? The Cove? The library?" Paul added, "When's his next class, it might be easier to find him then."

The detective smiled at the good idea. He glanced at notes he had taken when he spoke to the dean before meeting Amy that morning. "Three o'clock."

"So... how about Laura's roommate?"

Riordan pulled a sheaf of papers out of a different jacket

pocket and worked through them until he found "...Leslie Roper, here we go." He glanced at his watch. "She'll be in the chemistry lab. Okay, where's that?"

She held one hand up to block the sun and turned her head, searching for a landmark. Finally she pointed south. "See that big modern tower? That's engineering. The chem annex is just this side of it."

"Ace. Let's go."

As they walked, Amy asked, "Don't we want to look at their dorm room?"

"'We'?" he laughed. "A few hours and it's 'we'?"

Paul was surprised to feel blood rush to their face. He couldn't remember the last time Amy blushed. He was more surprised when he felt Amy stick out their tongue and blow, "Pttthhhhh!" Riordan laughed again. "Yeah, we do want to look at her room. Can we do it now? Do the girls lock their rooms?"

"Ever since yesterday morning, yes, we lock our rooms."

He was still laughing. "The roomie might be able to tell us if Laura's had any trouble at home, or with that Alabama boyfriend. I'm curious if she stopped drinking, or if she just stopped doing it around the sorority."

Paul said, "Or if Laura ever had a drinking problem. That might be some fantasy of Madison's."

"Sweetheart, you watch too much TV."

They walked further. Amy asked, "Did you get the autopsy results from Doctor Jermaine?"

"Oh, I didn't tell you?" He glanced at her while they were walking. "Time of death between midnight and one AM. Blood alcohol consistent with having a beer at dinner, something like zero-point-zero-five percent. Preliminary says no recreational drugs, but detailed toxicology findings take a little longer. And no recent sexual activity." He shook his head, "What a wimp."

"Wimp? Laura? Or who?"

"Kimmel. Who dates a girl who's got a steady, and doesn't, uh, extend benefits?"

Amy thought to Paul, "Does that make him wimpy?"

Paul thought, "I'd guess it makes him not the killer. If that's wimpy, I'm all for it."

"But, wimpy? Because he's friends with a woman?"

Paul spoke up. "Your Majesty, are you friends with any women? Friends that you're not trying to get in bed?"

"None of your beeswax, Clear. Let's keep it professional, shall we?"

Paul thought to Amy, "I take it his answer is 'no.' Hey, I wonder if he's planning on sleeping with you. Oh, crap, with us."

"What are you laughing about?" Riordan asked.

"None of your beeswax, Your Majesty. Chemistry is that building there."

The lab rat pointed them to Leslie Roper's work area. She was wearing safety goggles, a plastic apron, and what looked like oven mitts as she used an extended clamp to turn a test tube very, very slowly, and let just a few grey pellets plop into a beaker of clear liquid, which began to bubble and steam. Riordan and Amy stepped back, trying not to startle the woman while she was performing the task. But when she returned the test tube to the tube rack, Riordan cleared his throat and said, "Miss Roper." It was not a question.

"Please let me finish," she said. Leslie dipped a cotton patch in alcohol and rubbed it against a glass slide caked with something the color of rust. Then she dropped it into the beaker. Instantly the liquid in the beaker glowed a cool blue. By the time she finished writing something in her lab book, the glow had faded.

"You're the policeman, right? And you -- you live in my dorm. What?"

Riordan said, "Detective. If you can spare a few minutes, I'd like to talk to you in a more, uh, conventional environment."

She slid the goggles up to her forehead, then fumbled to set her rimless eyeglasses back in place. "This is the usual for me. But there's a desk across the hall." She removed the apron and gloves, but still had the goggles when they all sat in the room opposite the lab.

Amy said, "How are you doing, Leslie? I didn't think you'd be in class today."

"I didn't know what else to do. If I stayed in the room I'd start crying again."

"When's the last time you saw Laura?" the detective asked. Leslie repeated what she had said the day before.

"Why did he ask that?" she thought to Paul, "She already told him this."

"How close were you and Laura?" Riordan asked. Amy rushed to find a blank page in the detective's notepad.

"I'm not a Zeta, so we didn't hang out a lot. But we got along well. She took me home for Easter last year."

"Ah. Tell me about her family."

The woman became animated, "Her mom is real sweet, her dad is nice and seems very young. She's got a younger sister who -- well, she's in high school, she hates everything. And I got to meet her boyfriend, Tyler. He's great, I really liked him."

"She got along well with everyone?"

"Even with the sister. God, she was miserable."

"Did Tyler ever visit Laura here? At UNO?"

She thought. "Umm, maybe once a semester. He's at Tuscaloosa. He calls her all the time."

Amy said, "Leslie, someone told us they thought Laura and Tyler may have had a falling out. Did she say anything to you about that?" Riordan pursed his lips but kept his eyes on the roommate to see her reaction.

"Yeah. She said it wasn't all that big a deal, they still talked on the phone almost every day."

"Did she say what it was about?"

For the first time, Leslie smiled. "Kids. She wants 'em, he doesn't."

"That can be a deal breaker," Riordan observed. "Do you know this Tyler's last name? How we can contact him?"

"It's in Laura's stuff. She was always doodling her first name and his last name."

"Ah. When can we look at your room?"

Amy added, "Her side of your room."

She looked up at the wall clock in the classroom, and said, "I don't want to miss my Psych lecture. I'm not doing well there. Three o'clock?"

Amy looked at the note she had written on the inside of her left wrist: 'R Young 3 PM'. "Can we meet you around four?"

"Excuse me," Riordan said to the roommate, and turned to Amy. "What's wrong with three, Clear?"

"Reggie Young. Three o'clock class. Remember?"

"I do now," he said, smiling. Then to Leslie, "She's my appointments secretary. We'll see you at four."

When they were standing outside, on Founders Road, the detective said, "It's almost one. What do we do now, Clear?"

It was Paul who said, "You buy us lunch, Your Majesty."

Amy led him to The Cove. They stood on line to order, then took a small table away from the front door. "You're doing good, Clear," he volunteered. "Some decent questions. When you probed the roommate about Laura and her boyfriend, you said 'Someone' told you instead of saying who told you. That's smart. And you kept me from overbooking."

"Why did you ask Leslie when she last saw Laura? She told you yesterday."

"I'll probably ask her again. If the story essentially stays the same, and no one else contradicts it, I assume it's true. If she's lying, the story will be different each time. And sometimes when they re-tell the story, a lost fact comes out."

She heard Paul think, "I told you!" and she smiled.

"You're a happy camper, Clear," he observed. "What's your secret?"

"I talk to myself a lot. I amuse me. How about you?"

A snort. "What makes you think I'm happy?"

"Oh, come on! You're mega-good looking, you've got a great job, you're so smart and you know all this stuff." Another bite of her burger, and then Paul added, "Plus, you've got me as a minion. Of course you're happy."

"Thanks, Clear. I wasn't so sure, but you explain it great. Now if only you could do something about my checkbook."

"I'll work on that," Amy said.

"Why are you doing this?" the detective asked. "I'm all for minions, but usually they're nowhere near as smart as you. Do you want to be a cop? Or are you avoiding a class?"

"When I was a kid, me and my dad and some friends of his collared a guy who killed someone we knew. I don't want to be a policeman; what I really want to do is join the circus. But this stuff fascinates me. And it's so different from my normal life, it's exciting."

They finished their meals, but it was too early to leave for their three o'clock appointment. Amy asked, "How long have you been a detective?"

"Six years," he said. "And a beat cop for two years before that."

"What did you do before that?"

He laughed. "Went to school. Got a degree in business administration at Centenary."

"Business? Is that a requirement to become a policeman?"

He smiled, "I didn't like it. Sometimes you have to do things to discover that. So, yeah, I became a cop. My father was career military."

He got up to refill their drinks, then returned to the table to say, "Time to move on. Let us meet Reggie Young and see what his story is."

She took her limeade. "What class is he in?" she asked as they walked back into the afternoon sun.

"Privateer Hall? What's that?"

"Oh, East campus. That's our glorified gym. Are you going to sneak me into the men's locker room?" She laughed when she heard Paul think, "Ah, the ultimate man cave."

"You think you'd enjoy that. We'll see what the smell does to you. Lead on."

They found the junior class inside the building, working on basketball skills. Riordan spotted the older man with the whistle and explained what he needed. The coach blew the whistle twice at ear-splitting volume, and then yelled even louder, "Reggie Young. Up here. Now!" He blew the whistle again, and the rest of the class went back to drills.

The student was wearing shorts and a cutaway tank top, both drenched in sweat. He was five foot nine, about one hundred seventy five pounds. Amy saw the curly brown hair and the blue eyes, and she said to Riordan, "He's in my math class. Huh."

The man approached the coach, who pointed him to Riordan. He was smiling as he walked over, giving Amy an obvious once over. He winked at her before turning to the detective. "Coach says you want to talk to me?"

Riordan introduced himself and Amy, and said, "Where can we talk privately?"

"Locker room is empty now." When there was no objection,

he led them through the portal behind one of the baskets and into the humid, smelly sanctum. When Reggie straddled the bench in front of his locker, Paul thought to Amy, "I wonder how Riordan will set up the interview geometry." The detective sat the same way on the bench across the aisle so he was not facing the student head-on. He motioned Amy to sit on the same bench but behind Reggie's line of sight. She found the next blank page and was ready for the interview to begin.

"Some people have told me you were friends with Laura Adams," Riordan began.

"Uh-huh."

"How long have you known her?"

He frowned and bent over his left shoe, fooling with the laces. "Three, four months. It was spring semester."

"Tell me about your friendship."

"Nothing to tell. We hung out some. Went to some movies. Drank some. No big deal."

"Was it a big deal to Laura?"

"I don't know."

Paul thought to Amy, "What's with the two-word answers? He smells worse than the locker room."

"Did you sleep with her?"

"No."

Riordan raised his eyebrows. "Why not?"

"She said 'no.' She had a boyfriend back home."

Amy sneezed three times; the last one was a prolonged 'ah-ah-ahh-ahhh-CHOO.' "Excuse me!" she said, "I'm sorry."

Reggie turned to look. He smiled and winked again. "What are you doing back there? Come on up here where I can see you." He held out his hand to her.

Automatically, Amy began to raise her arm to take his hand, but Riordan said, "She'll stay there. Look at me, Reggie. I was about to ask you if you have any other platonic lady friends ."

He turned back to the detective. "No way. It's so easy to be non-platonic."

"Then what was so different about Laura?"

He shrugged. "I guess I liked her."

"You've got quite a reputation, Reggie. Seems you are a well known cockhound."

He smiled broadly. "You bet!"

"Look, guy to guy, tell me -- what's your average?"

"Twice a week. And about eighty percent. Which do you mean?"

"I'm impressed. Ever get angry with the twenty percent?"

He nodded and said, "Nah. No point." Riordan kept his head steady but swiveled his eyes to Amy and made a face. He hoped she would write up the inconsistency of words and body language. "If Sue says no today, Mary will say yes tomorrow."

"What did Laura tell you about Tyler?"

"Who's Tyler?" The man looked puzzled.

"Her boyfriend. His name is Tyler."

He laughed. "She never said his name. Once she explained herself, we never talked about him."

"What did you talk about?"

"Movies. Our families." He shrugged. "What does anyone talk about?"

"Did Laura wear a necklace?"

"Not that I noticed. Other than that dumb cross. I used to give her shit about it, too."

Amy asked, "What do the women you've gone out with say about you?" Rirodan frowned as Reggie twisted to look at her. Suddenly she felt her heart racing.

The man smiled. "Most of them say I'm dynamite in bed. A few of them think I'm a man slut. And one pesters the crap out of me."

Amy was relieved when Riordan followed up, asking, "Pesters you how?" She heard Paul think, "Amy? What just happened?" She thought back, "I don't know!"

"She emails me and calls me all the time. We went out twice last year, we had a good time, and that was that. But not for her. My own little stalker."

"Are you worried? Is she dangerous?"

Reggie said, "She's just some chick. I can deal with her; I don't need police help."

Riordan let silence fill the locker room for a long moment. Then he said, "Where were you Sunday night? Around one o'clock Monday morning?"

"I think I was still drinking at the frat house. I don't remember when I went back to my dorm."

"Guys there will vouch for you?"

"Sure. And my roommate."

"Give me some names," and he pointed at Amy.

Reggie turned toward her and rattled off the names of three fraternity brothers. Again, he winked, and said, "I'm assuming they remember anything, we were working on tequila. And my roommate is Bruce Weeks."

"I'll find out. And in case you don't know, it is a felony in Louisiana to tamper with a witness. Do not discuss this with those people."

Reggie squinted. "Am I under arrest, officer?"

"Detective. Not yet."

"Heavy. If we're done, can I get back to practice? We have a game against the KAs this weekend."

Riordan waved to dismiss the student. Once he was gone, the detective said, "Let me see your notes." Amy passed the notepad to him and waited for his evaluation.

Shortly he held it in his lap and asked, "Did you see what he did when I asked about the women who said no?" She shook her head. "His mouth said he didn't get mad at them, but he nodded his head yes. I'd like to talk to some of the ones who turned him down."

He handed the notepad back to her. "What do you think about him?"

"He's fairly repulsive as a human being," Paul said. Amy continued, "But he is a looker. There's something attractive about his confidence."

"Clear! Don't tell me you're one of those women who likes bad boys."

"I never thought I was before," she said. Paul asked, "Is it that obvious?"

Riordan laughed. He stood up, holding his hand out to Amy, and said, "Time to visit Laura's room."

As they worked their way out of the locker room and Privateer Hall, Amy and Paul held a silent conversation. "Were you trying to embarrass me?" she asked, angry. He thought back,

"No way! I could feel how you were turned on. I wanted to see if Riordan could tell."

"Well, he can. Am I that easy?"

"Ummm, transparent, maybe. You don't have much practice lying."

"Practice? Are there exercises? Do they give on-line classes?"

"We'll start with Deceit 101, and move up to Mendacity. By the time we get to Treachery, we'll have a great poker face."

"You are so not helping."

Paul thought, then said, "If he gives you any crap about it, slam him. None of his beeswax, you know?"

She laughed, "I won't have to lie to do that."

"What?" Riordan asked.

"Amusing myself," she said aloud. "That's why I'm such a cheerful person."

"When do you think you'll go out with Romeo?" the detective asked as they walked toward Pontchartrain Hall.

"When do you think you'll mind your own business?" she retorted.

"I'm a detective. That's what I do, mind other people's business."

"And who minds yours, hmmm?"

Riordan stopped walking and looked at her. "Okay. Truce. You just seem too nice to get messed up with that Reggie."

She smiled at the complement from the detective who had taken her under his wing, and who she thought was an exciting man. "Thanks. Truce."

The Resident Advisor was standing with a student when they walked into the Pontchartrain Hall lobby. She quickly came to them and threw her arms around Amy. It took her by surprise, and it was a moment or two before Amy returned the hug. Greta stepped back and said, "You were a lifesaver yesterday. I will never forget what you did. Thank you."

Amy smiled, and said, "You looked like you needed a friend. I felt so bad for you."

Riordan said hello. "Have you thought of anything else we should know about Laura Adams?"

"Officer, no. Have you arrested anyone yet?"

"It's detective. Not yet. Any ideas who we should nab?"

Amy explained why they were in the dorm, and they left Greta in the lobby. "She seems nice," the detective observed.

"I guess," she said. "I don't much like her."

He turned his head toward her as they walked down the hall. "Then why did you sit with her? The security man said you were there for hours."

"You don't have to like someone to feel bad for them over something like this."

He cocked his head. "You're nicer than I am," he laughed.

Amy stopped and knocked at Leslie's door. The woman opened the door quickly. She had changed into shapeless slacks and an oversized T-shirt, and clearly had been crying. "I'm glad you're here, Amy," she said; then she greeted Riordan.

"Tell me how you're doing," Amy said, while the detective began to walk around the room. Even the two-person dorm facilities were not very big.

"I was okay, and then Laura's mother called. They're driving down from Claiborne tomorrow. She said they'd be taking Laura home --" Abruptly she sat on the edge of her bed. Leslie managed a half smile as she began to weep, and she said, "-- and I started doing this."

Amy sat next to her. "Some things are worth feeling bad about. Your roommate's dead. Nobody will hold it against you that you're crying."

Leslie forced another half-smile onto her face. She sniffed and looked down at her shoes, and softly said, "Thanks."

Riordan was pulling latex gloves on as he said, "Miss Roper, is it alright if I look through Laura's desk?" When she nodded, he said, "Come on, Clear, we've got work to do." He held out a pair of gloves for her. Amy smiled and touched Leslie on the shoulder, then left her by herself, sitting on the bed.

"What are we looking for?" Amy asked, donning the gloves.

"A calendar or date book. A diary. That necklace." He stopped and called to Leslie, "When they found Laura, she didn't have her purse or cell phone. Where did she keep them in the room?"

Still sitting, the roommate said, "She kept her purse in one of the desk drawers. There were some thefts at the beginning of the semester and she started being careful."

Amy opened drawers until she found the purse -- a large, multicolored cloth bag. The detective said, "Give it here," and he spilled the contents onto the desk top. Amidst the detritus of Laura Adams' purse were her wallet, her keys, and her cell phone.

First, Riordan went through the wallet. There was forty two dollars in cash, three credit cards, a driver's license, and Laura's student ID. "No robbery," he mused, "and she must have thought she was only going outside for a minute to see someone she knew. Clear, see if she's got a datebook in this junk."

While the detective scrolled through Laura's cell phone, looking for recent calls, Amy patted down the purse debris. Gum, Kleenex, two matchbooks, various pens, loose change, and safety pins, but no datebook. Amy began to open other desk drawers, then cabinets. She stopped when she found a locked metal box that looked like a small cash drawer. She put it on the desk, and tried Laura's keys until there was a loud 'click'. The lid bounced up.

Riordan slipped the cellphone into a pocket, and looked over Amy's shoulder as she swung back the top of the box. They saw a plastic bag with what Paul assumed was marijuana, and a package of Zig-Zag cigarette rolling papers. There were some condoms, some currency, some jewelry, and two small books. Amy called, "Leslie, did you ever see any of this?"

The late Laura's roommate walked over to the desk. "I don't know what you're talking about," she said, quickly looking at her shoes.

"The books, I mean," Amy said. Meanwhile, Riordan stuck his hand in to look at the jewelry, trying to find the necklace that the medical examiner thought might be the murder weapon.

"Sometimes she had that one out," Leslie pointed to the one with the plain black cover. "I think that's her address book."

Even as he looked at the jewelry, Riordan said, "Why keep that locked up?"

"How about this one?" Amy lifted the one with a dull red quilted cover. Leslie shook her head, and Amy opened it. "Dear Diary," page one said, and she closed it.

Paul thought, "This might have the answer. Where did she go Sunday night?"

Amy thought back, "I feel dirty looking at someone else's diary."

"She won't hold it against you," Paul replied silently

"What do you have, Clear?"

She handed it to him. "A diary. Please don't make me read it."

He stared at her. "You have got to be kidding. She may name her killer in this and you don't want to read it?"

"I guess it's all the unrelated stuff I'd have to read until I got to the killer's name. My sister found my diary when I was fifteen and, uh, there was some trouble."

Riordan held up a string of chain and bead. "Jermaine said he thought a necklace might have been the weapon. I wonder if this is it."

"Your Majesty. If the killer used that yesterday morning, how did it get back inside this locked box?"

There was a pause, until Riordan said, "Just testing you, Clear." Still, he dropped it in his coat pocket. Amy heard Paul laugh.

Riordan gave Amy the address book, and handed her a legal pad that had been on the desk. "Anyone who sounds useful, write it all down. I want that Tyler guy's information. Her family. And anyone on campus, okay?"

Amy worked her way through the alphabet. Tyler's surname was Rouelle, there were numbers in Tuscaloosa and in Claiborne. The four or five people named Adams, she assumed were relatives. The contact information for Ronnie Kimmel and for Reggie Young were in the book. Other entries were in towns Amy recognized as being around the woman's home in north Louisiana.

Riordan leafed through the diary. The last entry was from Saturday, just a day before her death. He read aloud,

"Ronnie is still such a sweetie. How many guys would spend time with a girl who said she was engaged to someone else, and just wanted a friend? Maybe once a month he tries to kiss me -- I pretend I don't like it, but of course I do. We went to the campus movie and drank vodka-and-coke. I don't remember the name of the film, but Brittney Spears was in it, haven't heard from her since middle school! We're going hiking across the lake next weekend, I can't wait.

"Tonight Reggie is supposed to take me out to dinner. I don't know why my sisters say he's so awful. They say he's a pig, but not to me. When I told him about Tyler, he stopped trying to feel me up and hasn't tried again. Good. I gotta say, he's a lot of fun. After dinner we'll probably go up to Pontchartrain Beach and watch the submarine race."

Leslie said, "What's a submarine race?"

Paul remembered a radio DJ from when he was a kid who had a gimmick about submarine race watching. "It's a code phrase," he said as Amy. "It means making out."

"Really?" the detective said, surprised.

Amy thought, "You know some of the strangest stuff." Aloud, trusting Paul, she said, "For real and for true. But that doesn't make sense. First she wrote she didn't want Reggie to touch her, then she says she's going to fool around with him?"

"From what Reggie told us," Riordan mused, "it would come as a surprise to him, too."

Amy finished writing out the relevant contacts from Laura's address book. She opened a few more drawers and cabinets, but nothing struck her as unusual or noteworthy.

"Can I ask you something?" Leslie said to Amy. "What -- how -- are you a policewoman? Why are you working with the officer?"

Riordan absently said, "That's detective," as he continued to peruse the diary

"Combination of curious and pushy. I offered to help and Steven said yes, so here I am. I don't know what I'll tell my professors."

"Are you done, Clear?"

"I guess so. Now what?"

Riordan pulled off the latex gloves. "Now I go home and eat dinner. In the morning I should have the reports on the body. With luck I'll have an idea of who to browbeat tomorrow afternoon."

"Will you let me play with you tomorrow? Please, Your Majesty? Pretty please?"

"Sweetheart, you are impossible." He winked at her. "I'll call you after I talk to Jermaine."

✿ 5 ✿

Tuesday, September 14, 2021 -- UNO campus, New Orleans

"It's so exciting!" she told her friend Florence while she sat in the woman's desk chair. "I have learned so much in the last two days. And the detective is going to let me hang with him tomorrow, too."

"Aren't you upset at all?" Florence was Amy's tennis buddy and pal. She was sitting on her dormitory bed in Privateer Place. "A dead body? Outside your dorm?"

"I always lock my door," she sniffed. "The doctor said even a small woman can strangle a big man. He told me how."

"Remind me to be nice to you."

"He's a real hunk, too."

"The doctor?"

Amy laughed. "No, he's older than my dad. The detective! Real good looking, he's got all this wavy hair, he wears a hat. And he smokes."

"You have some strange taste in guys," Florence shook her head. "And meantime, I'm scared. There's some killer on campus."

"You're right. Let's go into town for supper. Uh, how are you fixed for gasoline?"

"Half a tank. Let's go."

❦ 6 ❧

Wednesday, September 15, 2021 -- UNO campus, New Orleans

On Wednesday, Amy sat in the last row of her classes, near the door. Her phone was set to vibrate. She was vibrating herself, waiting to hear from Detective Steven Riordan.

"You're entertaining," Paul thought, "but you're too busy daydreaming. Give me the pen and I'll pay attention to class." She nodded, and watched as Paul moved their left hand to pluck the pen from their other hand. He opened their notebook, and started scribbling as the Psych lecture continued. This was a benefit of the physical relationship Amy shared with Paul: with her permission, either one of them could control her body. She thought of a driver's education class she had in high school, where the teacher in the passenger seat could commandeer gas, brakes, and steering. At times like this, where she was too excited to concentrate on anything as mundane as school, Paul could take notes and pay attention. Later he'd explain to her what she had missed.

The call didn't come until Amy was in her Sets and Symbols math class; she felt her phone rumble. She backed into the hallway and took the call. "Hello?"

"Clear! Meet me at your dorm in an hour; we have work to do."

"Of course, Your Majesty. Any update from Jermaine?"

"The toxicology report is consistent with smoking a little marijuana in the twenty four hours before death. He still thinks the perp used a necklace to kill her."

"Did you let him look at the one that was in Laura's lock box?

"Damn," he said, "you weren't supposed to notice that I took it. He said it doesn't match the marks on her neck."

She was tapping her foot while she stood in the hall. "So who are we interviewing today? Or are you ready to interrogate?"

"The roommate, that mousy girl, she was the last to see her alive. And because of that last diary entry, I want to talk to your lover boy again."

"Hey!" Amy shouted. "Don't blame him on me."

"See you in an hour," Riordan said, and hung up.

Paul thought, "May as well sit in for the rest of the lecture. Maybe you can make an appointment with Reggie, he's in the --"

"I know where he is," Amy interrupted, aloud. "He winked at me when we got to class. I think I'll wait until Riordan's here to protect me before I talk to him." She walked back into the classroom and took her seat.

Paul thought, "Protect you? From him?"

She wrote in her notebook, "From myself."

☞ 7 ☜

Wednesday, September 15, 2014 -- UNO campus, New Orleans

She got back to her dorm fifty minutes later, but Riordan was waiting in the lobby. "Don't keep me waiting again," he said. "Let's talk to Leslie."

"Hey! I'm early!"

"If I'm here first, you're late. Get with it, Clear." He was smiling as he began to walk her to the hallway.

As they got close to Leslie's room, there was a commotion. The door was open, and there were voices -- not loud, but several. Riordan knocked on the door frame and stepped inside.

Leslie was weeping again, her eyes bright red. A couple in their forties was going through Laura's bureau and desk. The detective said, "Is this a private party or can we join?"

Amy said, "Mrs. Adams -- Mr. Adams -- I -- I'm so sorry." She waved at Leslie, who waved back and managed another half smile.

"Are you one of Laura's little friends?" the man asked. His wife continued putting clothes into a big cardboard box.

"Actually," Riordan said, "I'm a New Orleans police detective. Steven Riordan. I am sorry to meet you under this circumstance." He held out his hand. After a moment, Mister Adams shook it.

"I'm Tom. This is my wife, Rebecca. What --"

The wife dropped the sweaters she had been holding and said, "Have you caught him?"

Riordan shook his head. "We are still in the very early stages of this investigation. And if you have a moment, I'd like to ask you some questions." Amy pulled out the notepad and opened it to the post-it she'd used to mark the next blank page. Leslie retreated onto her bed, leaning against the wall and holding a pillow in front of her chest.

Tom looked at his wife, and then put his hands in his front pockets. Rebecca stood beside him with one hand on his shoulder. "All right."

"When was the last time Laura was home?"

Rebecca answered, "Six or seven weeks ago. She had a dental appointment."

"And the last time you visited her here?"

Rebecca again, "We drove her down at the start of the semester."

"Did you talk on the telephone? Send emails?"

"Of course," Tom said. "We talked once or twice a week. There were lots of emails. Why?"

"Was there anything that made you think something wasn't right? Tone of voice, missed appointments, things she talked about?"

"What a horrible thing to suggest!" the woman said. Riordan said nothing, but turned to her husband, with a question mark on his face. Tom said, "She told us she was having some trouble with her sorority. Seems after three years they were deciding they didn't like her."

"Did she say why? What the issue was?"

"Just that they were turning against her."

Amy said, "Tell me about Laura and Tyler."

Tom looked at the detective and didn't respond until Riordan nodded. "They were engaged. They've been a couple since high school. Good kid, good family. He's at Alabama."

"Did she talk about some, uh, disagreement they had over the summer?"

Tom looked at his wife. The woman sighed, "Laura told me he didn't want kids. They had words when she was home at Easter. She loves children. I told her he was only twenty, he'd come around eventually."

"So there wasn't any interruption in their relationship?"

The woman shook her head.

"Did Laura ever mention any boys she knew here at UNO?"

Both her parents shook their heads. "She was engaged," Rebecca said tartly.

Riordan took over. "We're not suggesting anything unseemly. We know she made friends with two men here, but there is no reason to think it was anything but innocent. Still, we haven't ruled them out as suspects. Did she ever mention a Ronnie or a Reggie?"

"No, officer," Rebecca said.

"Detective," Riordan and Amy said in unison. Riordan went on, "Have you spoken to Tyler yet?"

"Yesterday, after the school called me," Tom said. His wife turned back to packing up Laura's clothes.

"How did he take it?"

"How do you think he took it?"

The detective frowned and said, "Mister Adams, this is a police investigation. I want to know how you perceived him when you told him about Laura."

"He screamed 'No!' a bunch of times. He was very upset."

Riordan nodded at Amy, then said, "I imagine this was difficult. Thank you for your time. Again, I am very sorry for your loss."

The husband nodded and turned away. Riordan said to Leslie, "Can you come with us to Amy's room for a couple of minutes?" He walked toward where she still sat on her bed. "I'm sure your things will be safe with Laura's parents here."

"Uh, okay." To the parents she said, "I'll be back in a little while. If you need me I'll be in --" and she turned to Amy. "Room 217," she said, and Leslie repeated it.

As soon as they were in the hallway, Leslie whispered to Amy, "Thank you for rescuing me. I like Laura's parents fine, but they're so angry and sad, they've been making me cry all day."

"Didn't make it to the chem lab today?"

"I wish!"

Amy unlocked her door, and tried to be as hospitable as her single room allowed. She cleared some books off the desk chair for Riordan, and threw a pile of clothes -- she thought they were clean but she wasn't sure -- to one side of the bed to make room for Leslie.

"This is how you live, Clear?"

"Impoverished Undergraduate Revival," Amy replied, "it's very *chic*."

He turned to Leslie and began. "Miss Roper, you are the last person we've found to see Laura alive. Please tell me again about seeing her Sunday."

Leslie repeated the same story she told him earlier.

"What was she wearing?"

The woman thought for a moment. "The same blouse, but she was wearing a skirt when I saw her after dinner. When they found her in the morning she was wearing jeans. I didn't notice what shoes she had on."

"Did she say anything about what she had done the day before, the evening before? Saturday?"

"Umm," looking up while prodding her memory, "That she might not eat for a week, she was still stuffed from eating catfish with Reggie."

"Anything about what she did after dinner?"

"Sorry," she said, apologetically.

"Plans for that evening? For Sunday?"

"That she was going to study, that's all."

Amy asked, "Leslie, anything else? What was Laura's mood the last time you saw her? Was she doing anything unusual?"

Her eyes got wide. "Now that you mention it, she kept washing her hands. We've got one like yours," she pointed at Amy's room sink.

"Did you ask her about it?" Riordan probed.

"Yeah. Yeah, I did. She said she had gotten some gunk on her hands and it felt like it was still there."

"Did you see anything on her hands? Stains? Abrasions? Missing fingers?"

"That's the strange part," Leslie said, shaking her head. "Her hands looked fine to me."

Paul thought to Amy, "I wonder if that had anything to do with watching the submarine race with Reggie?"

A puzzled look came over her face as she thought back, "Huh? How?"

When he saw Amy's expression, Riordan barked "What? Clear?"

"A voice inside me wonders if the handwashing might not be related to the submarine race watching."

The detective's jaw dropped "Someday you have to introduce me to that voice inside you, she's brilliant. In fact, I think it's time we go shake down Reggie Young a little. Miss Roper, you have been very helpful. I'm sorry I have to send you back to Laura's parents, but if you think of anything else, call me or let Clear here know. Clear, why aren't you ready yet? Let's go!"

While they walked to Privateer Place, Amy asked, "What's the connection between Laura making out and washing her hands?"

"What's your major?" he asked.

"Math. Statistics, actually. Why?"

"Ever read Macbeth? Lady Macbeth goes all psycho over washing non-existent blood off her hands after she helps her husband kill the king. It's a psychological projection." He was walking faster.

"I still don't see what that has to do with Laura. Was she feeling guilty that she was going to strangle herself?" She was having trouble keeping pace with the detective.

"Think sideways, Sweetheart."

"I can't think and run at the same time. Slow down!"

Riordan smiled when he turned to look at her, and he made himself walk slower. "You're not going to have a heart attack on me, are you? I'll never be able to explain that to the CO."

"Laura and handwashing," she panted, "sideways?"

"Wait 'til I talk to Reggie. That voice of yours may have solved this case."

Amy thought to Paul, "What is he talking about?" He decided to play dumb, and thought back, "I don't know, but it's probably going to be good."

She rolled her eyes and gasped, out loud, "You're no help."

"Watch and learn," Riordan responded, "watch and learn. What's his room number?"

Amy used her student ID to open the front door of the apartment dorm. The detective waved at the same woman behind the desk, then led Amy up the stairs and down a different hall. As they stood outside Reggie Young's room, Riordan said, "Take notes. And for God's sake keep your mouth shut! Okay?" She was still pulling out the notepad when he banged on the door and shouted, "Police! Open up!"

Several doors down the hallway opened. After a while Reggie opened his. He looked as if he'd been sleeping. "What the fuck?" he said.

"Good to see you, too, Mister Young. May we come in?"

"I guess --" and Riordan had pushed passed him, clearing a path for Amy to follow.

The room was messier than some, better than many. What clutter there was showed on the side of the room with the rumpled bedclothes, which the detective took to be Reggie's half. The other side looked positively vacant. "You live alone?" Riordan asked. Amy took a desk chair and opened the notebook. "No," Young said, "but Bruce isn't here much. He sort of lives in the computer lab."

"IT major?"

"Total geek. God, what a loser."

Riordan took another desk chair, leaving Reggie standing. He took off his fedora to fan his face, then held it in his lap. He tapped his cigarette pack and took one out, and stuck it behind his left ear. Amy heard Paul think, "I'll bet he's waiting for Reggie to get nervous and start blabbing." They watched the detective hold his feet out, one at a time, examining his shoes.

"Can I sit down?"

"Nobody's stopping you, Reggie. It's a free country." The detective wore a huge, obviously false smile.

When the student finally sat on the edge of his bed, arms folded in front of his chest, Riordan said, "Tell me about the last time you saw Laura Adams."

"I already did."

"Then tell me again."

"Why?"

"Because I asked you nicely, asshole," Riordan said, calmly. "Or would you rather go downtown to talk?"

"I don't like how you barge in here and order me around."

"Duly noted and under advisement. Now, the last time you

saw Laura?"

Reggie put his hands flat on the bed beside him and pushed himself back, so his legs were sticking out straight. "I took her to dinner. It was at Jaegers."

"What did she order?"

"I don't remember. I had fried shrimp. We had rum and cokes."

"She had catfish," Riordan said. "What did you do after dinner?"

"Uh, we hung out and talked. We drank more."

"Where?" The student did not answer, and Riordan said, "What's that? I'm sorry, I didn't hear you."

He mumbled, "Pontchartrain Beach."

"Let's see, you went to the number one make-out spot in Orleans Parish with a woman who wouldn't let you touch her. Am I getting this right?"

"It was her idea."

"And what happened while you were there?"

"We just talked, and stuff."

"Nothing else?"

He shook his head.

"Well, I heard you were watching a submarine race," the detective grinned.

"Who told you that?" Reggie demanded, leaning forward.

"Never you mind who. Who won the race?"

"Do you even know what that means?"

"Why don't you tell me, Reggie."

There was a long pause before he responded. "Laura surprised me when she said she wanted to go there. And then she said she felt sorry for me and wanted to do something for me."

"Why did she feel sorry for you?"

"She said it was because she never let me touch her. At first I was pissed that she felt pity for me, and that it hadn't registered on her that I like her. Laura is the only girl I actually like to hang out with. Uh, did."

Amy thought to Paul, "Steven said the autopsy showed no recent sexual activity. How does this work?" She heard him reply, "Watch and learn, I guess."

"So, what happened?"

Suddenly Reggie was smiling. "She unzipped my pants and got me off."

"How?"

"She used her hands."

Despite herself, an "Oh!" of understanding escaped Amy's mouth.

"I don't understand something," the detective said, as he began to fool with the cigarette that had been parked behind his ear. "On Tuesday I asked you about this, and you said you never had sex with Laura."

"Yeah?"

"Why didn't you tell me this then?"

"This? This was a hand job, it wasn't sex."

Amy heard Paul think, "You mean I wasted half my life as a man?"

"Reggie, you seem to come from a different planet than I do. Why was this not sex?"

He smiled again. He made a circle with his left thumb and index finger, then stuck his extended right index finger in and out of it several times. "That's sex. A hand job -- hell, I never touched her, she didn't even pull up her shirt. She wouldn't let me do anything for her. That's not sex."

"Ah," Riordan said. "Did that make you mad?"

"What's to be mad about? I had a happy ending. Made me sleepy, though."

"Tell me something, Reggie. Is that when you first thought about killing her?"

"What on -- Fuck that. I never thought about killing Laura. I liked her!"

The detective leaned back, and arranged the fedora on his head. "A couple of things, Mister Young. People don't commit murder without some kind of motive. You have a rather obvious one, even though that doesn't mean you're the killer. There are some other people we're talking to. Last time you said there was a woman stalking you? Give me her name and contact information." He stood up, and held an extended hand out to his left for Amy. "In the meantime, don't leave New Orleans. We'll be talking again, I promise you."

When Reggie gave him a piece of paper with the woman's name, Riordan tipped his hat, and left with Amy.

They heard his dorm door slam behind them, and shouted curses from within. Amy saw the detective was grinning. "I think he knows we're serious," he said.

"Do you really think he killed Laura?" Amy asked, in disbelief.

"No idea," he said. "He could have. Ronnie Kimmel could have. Stalker girl could have. It may be someone we haven't stumbled on yet."

"But you were such a bully with Reggie. How come?"

They were outside the dorm apartment buildings, standing on the other side of the fence that surrounded the swimming pool. Riordan stopped and looked at her as he answered. "First off, he's a grade-A asshole. But second -- if you think that was bullying, you'll never make it as a cop. The idea is to piss off innocent people, and trip up guilty ones. If I --"

His phone went off. The detective lifted it out of his coat pocket and pushed the accept button. "Riordan. What?" He listened. He asked, "Where?" He listened some more. "Well, fuck. Okay, give me forty-five minutes." He thrust the phone back in the pocket and said, "Great, I just got called onto another case. And no, Clear, you can't come with me."

"I wasn't --"

"But there is something you can do for me." He handed her the piece of paper with the stalker girl's information. "Go talk to her. Don't pretend you're a cop, but it's okay to say you're helping the police." He took some business cards out of his case and gave them to her, too.

"Are you sure --"

"You've seen me, so now it's sink or swim time. Find out what she's doing to Reggie, why she's doing it, and where she was when Laura Adams got killed."

"But what --"

"I don't know how late I'll be tied up," he began leading them back to her dorm, where his car was parked, "so no point in trying to call me."

"But tell me --"

"I'll call you when I can -- Christ, it might be two in the

morning. But you college --"

"WILL YOU SHUT UP!" Amy yelled. Riordan froze in mid-word, staring in disbelief. Amy smiled as sweetly as she could, and said, "That's better. I'll take care of this. Uh, I guess you better take your notebook," and she held it out to him.

"Too much coffee," he muttered. "Thanks for doing this. We'll go over it tomorrow, hear?"

Amy stood at attention and saluted, "You bet, Your Majesty. Now get out of my way, I have some police business to do."

She watched Riordan drive off, then went back to her room. Paul said, "You're more than a pretty face or he wouldn't let you do this."

"This is going to be fun," she said back as she took a notebook off her desk. "Alexandria Scruggs," she mused. "She's in Pontchartrain Hall South. Let's see if she's entertaining visitors."

"What are you going to ask her?" Paul thought as they took the walkway to the other dorm building.

She smiled. "Ask her about Reggie. And where was she Sunday night."

The South building was only three stories, and Alex Scruggs lived on the top floor. It was a quick walk up the stairs. Amy stood outside her room and whispered, "Here goes nothing." She rapped on the door.

"Hey," a short, dark woman said when she opened her door. Alexandria was five foot three and about one hundred pounds. Her complexion was almost albino, it was so pale, while her hair, in a peculiar upswept style, was jet black. Her eye makeup was excessive. Amy heard Paul think, "Hello, nurse!"

"Hi. Alex?" The woman nodded. "I'm Amy Clear. I'm a junior; I live in North hall. Can I come in?"

"Sure. It's nice to have company," she said, stepping aside.

Amy was not prepared for what she saw. Alex appeared to live in a single, and her suite was filled with dozens and dozens of pictures of Reggie Young. "My God," she said. She turned to Alex and said, "Who's the hunk?"

The woman grinned. "That's my boyfriend. Isn't he yummy?"

Paul thought, "Perfect opening..."

Amy said, "Tell me about him."

"He's a doll," she said, hands clasped in front of her stomach as she stared, smiling, at one of the pictures. "We started going out last year." She turned to Amy and said, "You can sit over there. Can I get you something? Water? A coke?"

Amy shook her head and sat in the desk chair. There were photos of Reggie, torn from the campus newspaper, thumbtacked at the desk. She saw a few framed ones on walls, and another one on the produce crate that served as a night stand.

Looking back at Alex, she thought, "There's something odd about the way she looks." Aloud, she thanked her for her hospitality. Paul thought back, "Something about her eyes."

"He's in my math class," Amy said. "I didn't realize he has a steady."

"Oh, you know Reggie. What do you think about him?"

Amy said, "He's very handsome," and Alex nodded. "And his self-confidence is something else." She thought to Paul, "She's wall-eyed."

"He is those things," Alex gushed. "And between you and me, he is a wonder in bed. He really is great."

Amy paid attention to the woman's face. When Alex moved her head, her left eye took a few seconds to look forward. "A glass eye?" she thought. It was unsettling, watching a person who was looking at you and also not looking at you at the same time.

"Alex, where are you from? Are you local?"

"Almost. New Iberia. Do you know where that is?" She was smiling.

"Isn't that on the way to Lafayette?" The woman nodded.

"Do you go home on weekends? Are you close to your family?"

"Excuse me," Alex said abruptly. "You're Amy? Amy what? Why are you here?"

She handed one of the detective's business cards to her. "Amy Clear. I live in the north building. I've been working with Detective Riordan about the girl who was killed this week."

"That was so awful!" she exclaimed. "I've been double-locking my door ever since I heard."

"A good idea," Amy said. "We don't have much to go on, so

we're talking to a whole lot of people. We even interviewed Reggie."

"Why? Surely you don't think he would do something like that?"

Amy smiled and crossed their legs. "We started with the woman's roommate and sorority sisters and friends. Did you know Laura Adams?"

"I know all of Reggie's friends." The look of pain on her face was pitiful.

"Can you tell me anything about her? Did she have any enemies?"

Silently, she shook her head.

"Alex, Reggie gave us your name. He said you email him and call him a lot."

"Sure. He's my lover boy."

Amy sighed and plunged ahead. "That's not what he told us."

"Oh, that silly. He's such a kidder. What did he tell you, that I'm stalking him?"

"Uh, yes. He said he went out with you a few times last year and that was all."

The woman's left eye swung out toward the window when she squinted. "I don't know why he would say such a thing."

Amy heard Paul think, "I hate to burst her bubble, but we've got a job to do." She thought back, "I'll try to be kind."

"Listen to me, Alex. I'm not here to pass judgment on you or on Reggie. I'm just trying to find out what happened." She leaned forward, facing the woman sitting on her bed. "I told you we don't have any leads yet. So we're working on potential motives. You have a huge emotional investment in Reggie, and Laura Adams was a friend of his. We have to consider the possibility that, uh, someone in your position might be jealous of Reggie's other female acquaintances. Do you follow me?"

Alex held on to a grim smile and nodded, while her eyes continued to look in different directions.

"So I have to ask you this. Where were you Sunday night around midnight?"

"I was right here," she said. "Reggie was with me. I have an eight AM class on Monday, we were in bed by eleven."

Amy scribbled in her note pad. "This is too strange," she thought to Paul, "but I know I'm not supposed to challenge them on a first interview."

"Okay. Do you live alone here?" She nodded, still with the forced smile.

"Can I talk to any of your friends?" Amy asked, really at a loss.

There was a long pause, before Alex said, "I don't have a lot of friends."

Amy felt out of her depth and stood up. "I hope I haven't made you uncomfortable, Alex. That was not my intention. If --"

She stood up as well and interrupted, "Not at all. It really is nice to have some company." Her smile looked more natural, more sincere. "Come back any time."

"If you think of anything about Laura, or about Reggie, that might help us, please call Detective Riordan. Or come find me, I'm in 217 North."

Alex stood in the open door and watched Amy walk all the way down the hall to the stairwell. On the stairs, Paul thought, "She is one good looking woman. And messed up? Whooo."

"I feel bad for her. She is weird. And she has no friends, she was even glad to see me."

"Although -- What if she's sane and Reggie is lying? What if they really are a number and for some reason Reggie doesn't want anyone to know?"

Amy sat down in the building lobby to write up notes. "I wonder," she thought, "if we talk to Reggie's roommate, see if he tells us where Reggie spent Sunday night."

"Her eyeball creeped me out," Paul thought. "I'm a bad person, I know it's not her fault, but it still gives me the willies. But aside from that, she is one pretty woman."

"You think we're all pretty."

"Guilty as charged," Paul thought. "Trapped in your wonderful female flesh, but I am still a MAN."

"Down boy," she muttered out loud, and finished writing her notes.

Walking back to her room, she thought to Paul, "I think I'm going to the computer lab. Reggie said his roommate practically lives there."

"More fun that reading your Psych assignment?"

"Which, in turn, is more fun than a root canal."

While they walked in the September sunshine, Paul thought, "Tell me again why you took psychology."

"If all I took was math classes I'd never get out of school. And Psych was at ten o'clock, I wouldn't have to get up at the crack of dawn."

"Riordan seems to know a lot about it. The way he questions people, even the way he sits to do an interview. If you do want to become a cop, keep up in Psych. And let me off, okay?"

She smiled as she walked, "You're stuck with me, geezer. If I were a cop, I'd work you over with a rubber hose and have my way with you."

Paul said aloud, "Promises, promises."

Amy walked down the one flight of stairs in the computer center to the lab. It was a large room, with thirty work stations, and lit with appalling yellow fluorescent light. Everything about the below-ground room screamed 'lack of sunshine.' The person she imagined was the lab prefect was a grad student, a few years older than her, wearing a tight T-shirt that did not adequately cover his considerable midsection. "Practice Static Safety," the shirt proclaimed, "Hack Naked." If there was a joke behind it, she didn't get it.

"I'm looking for Bruce Weeks," she told him. With a fat index finger he pushed his eyeglasses up his nose. "Back row," the man said in a squeaky voice, "red shirt. Go for it."

She thanked him and walked to the back of the lab. Only one person was in the back row, and indeed, he was wearing a red shirt -- with a collar and long sleeves, and a logo over the pocket that said "Optium."

"Bruce?" she offered. He turned to look at her, and immediately became nervous in close proximity to a member of the opposite sex. She held out her hand. "I'm Amy Clear, I'm working with Detective Steven Riordan. Can I ask you some questions?"

Bruce was just under six feet tall. He had unruly brown hair over an unexpectedly pleasant face. Paul laughed inside when he noticed how uncomfortable he was with the need to interact with a stranger, and a female girl woman at that. He finally pushed the adjoining chair toward Amy, and cleared his notebook out of her way. He still hadn't said a word. "A deer in headlights, poor guy," Paul thought. Amy replied silently, "Hush. I need to draw him out."

"Thank you, Bruce," she began. "I'm sure you've heard about Laura Adams, the woman who was killed on campus?" He nodded. "Did you know her?"

He shook his head, and finally made himself speak. "I met her once, but I didn't know her."

"Oh. How did you two meet?"

"She was a friend of my roommate." His hands were on the desk top, completely still.

"I'm helping the police with their inquiries," she went on. "We don't have a clue what happened, so we're talking to a lot of people. Can you tell me about Reggie Young?"

Bruce smiled. "Oh, yeah. He's my roomie."

"Have you known him long?"

He nodded. "We've roomed together more than a year, since fall before last."

"Do you two get along well?"

"Yeah, I think so." He obviously was considering the question. "We don't spend a lot of time together; he's in a fraternity and I'm always here. But, yeah. He lets me do stuff for him sometimes."

Paul was the one who asked, "Do stuff -- what do you mean?"

"Sometimes he lets me get his dry cleaning, buy books or clothes for him." He was smiling. "Stuff like that."

"And you enjoy that?"

He nodded. "I like Reggie. He's so cool, and does he ever get the girls. It's a big deal that he lets me do things for him."

Amy thought, "Bruce has a thing for macho man Reggie." Paul thought back, "In some strange way or another. For his sake I hope it's not a gay thing. That's a non-starter with Reggie."

She took over the questioning. "Do you know Reggie's friend Alex Scruggs?"

"Reggie says she's a troublemaker," he wrinkled his nose. "He says she's crazy, she won't leave him alone."

"Really? How's that?"

"He says she calls him all the time and texts him and emails and like that."

Amy nodded, and asked, "Does Reggie ever see Alex?"

"Not since last year, best I know. He says he doesn't like her anymore."

"Who does Reggie like, Bruce?"

Again, the man paused to ponder the question. "He said he liked Laura, he says he spent a lot of time with her. They met -- oh, I guess the end of last year."

"Anyone else?"

"No one special." Bruce shook his head. It seemed sad to Amy. "He's always out with girls, but it's always a different one."

"Does he tell you what he feels about the women he dates?"

"Not usually. In all honesty, I don't think they much matter to him. It's what they let him do that he cares about."

Paul thought, "Cockhound."

"Do you remember what Reggie did Sunday night?" Amy asked. "When did he get back to the dorm?"

"I think it was -- I'm guessing around midnight. He was -- I mean, he had been drinking at his fraternity."

"He told us he got home late that night. Midnight?"

He shrugged. "All I know for sure is that he got home after I did."

He was silent. Amy thought to Paul, "Anything you want to ask him?" He took the lead and said, as Amy, "What part of IT do you like best?"

His face brightened and he became animated. "Programming is fun because it's satisfying to solve a problem. But I'm thinking that might get boring after a few years. I really like hardware architecture. I want to build the computer that makes a Cray look like an 8080."

"I have no idea what that means," Paul said. "Help me."

"Cray makes the supercomputer. The 8080 was about the first consumer computer processing chip, fifty years ago."

"Ah! Deep Thought. So you like to develop hardware, then wire it up?"

Bruce wore a serene smile. "Exactly."

"I'm done," Paul thought to Amy. She stood up and said, "Thanks, Bruce. I appreciate you giving up some of your lab time to talk to me."

She saw his ears turning red as he looked down. "Really," she said, "thank you." She touched him on his forearm and left the lab.

As they walked up the stairs to ground level, Paul thought, "He's a nice guy, just insecure as all get-out. And he's got a man-crush on Reggie."

"Do you think he's jealous of the women Reggie sees?"

"It's possible. Let's go over that when Riordan calls you."

She walked out into the sunshine and headed back to her dorm. "Crap," she said out loud. "I've got six chapters of Psych to read."

℘ 8 ৶

Thursday, September 16, 2021 -- UNO campus, New Orleans

"Hello?" Amy said, after she finally found her ringing telephone and mashed the accept button. It was six-ten in the morning.

"Clear! I didn't wake you, did I?"

She sat up in bed and heard her Psych book hit the floor. "Actually --"

"Never mind about that. Tell me what happened with stalker girl."

"Give me a second to think," she said. It actually took four seconds before she was able to say, "Harmless wacko. She's got pictures of Reggie all over her dorm room. She's convinced he's her boyfriend, and she even said he spent Sunday night with her."

"Hmmm," Riordan said. "I wonder if --"

"Ha!" Amy cried, "it's my turn to interrupt you. I went to visit Reggie's roommate in the computer lab. He says Reggie hasn't seen Alex Scruggs since last year, and that Reggie got back to the dorm around midnight Sunday night."

"Who sounds more believable?" the detective asked.

"Neither one of them," Amy answered. "Stalker girl is delusional, and the roommate has an enormous man-crush on Reggie. It's pretty embarrassing to watch."

"Okay, Clear, you did good."

"What about your new case? Is it coming together easier than this?"

"Domestic violence jobs are the pits. You're looking at a man and a woman and three little kids, and the only question is which one was the gutless wonder that shot everyone else and then themself. Usually it's the husband, not always. In any event, it's depressing."

"Do you get any time away from all this death and dismemberment? Or is it just one right after another?"

"Usually it's two or maybe three at the same time. I earn my pay, miserable though it is."

"So, what's next, Your Majesty?"

"Nothing. I want to talk to Reggie's frat brothers about their drinking together that night, see if they know when he left for home. And I may talk to Ronnie Kimmel again, although he seems to be in the clear. Maybe you ought to take in a few classes."

"Don't leave me out!" she cried. "This is too much fun. I mean, this is too exciting. I mean --"

She heard Riordan laugh. "It's okay, Sweetheart. I'll call you when I need something on campus again. Call me on Monday if you don't hear from me by then." And then she heard him hang up.

"What a letdown!" Paul said out loud.

"Yes. Why do I feel like all the air got sucked out of the room?"

He rubbed their left hand up and down their right arm, trying to comfort Amy. She went on, "We were special for three days. Now it's back to school. That blows."

"We can get another hour of sleep," Paul suggested.

"I'm too pissed and depressed." She threw the bedcovers back and sat on the side of the bed, rubbing their face. Then she fell back on the bed and was snoring in minutes.

When she awoke, she was surprised to find herself seated in a back row of her psychology class, hearing the lecture. "What the hell?" she said, out loud. Paul thought back, "And a gracious good morning to you, too. Feeling any better?" On those few occasions where Paul woke up and went into the world while she still slept, it always disoriented Amy. She imagined it was what an alcoholic felt, coming to after a blackout. What had she done? What had Paul done that anyone watching would have thought SHE had done?

She saw the pen in their left hand, and Paul's terrible handwriting in her notebook. "How much did I miss?" she thought. She looked down and saw her socks did not match.

"Forty one minutes. Fascinating stuff about why Freud was wrong about the superego."

"Did we eat breakfast?"

She felt him smile inside her. "One egg sunny side up and three strips of bacon." Paul loved runny eggs and Amy hated them, and the only time he got to eat one was the rare instances when she slept in. She somehow swallowed her gorge and muttered, "It's a good thing I like you. Otherwise I'd hate you."

Paul continued to take notes on the lecture, while Amy thought about how dull her day would be without Riordan, without the excitement of being involved investigating a murder. Math was next. Maybe she'd talk to Reggie -- for police business, of course.

When class broke up, Amy took back control to pick up her books. Paul thought, "Are you doing any better?"

"I'm still bummed," she said, aloud. A student near her said, "About what?" It jerked Amy up. "About talking to myself," she said with a half smile, and she left for her Sets and Symbols class.

"It's dull," she sighed. "School is not exciting. Having Riordan boss me around is."

"Yeah," he thought back, "that has been a lot of fun. I think he'll be back in touch. He accepted your take on talking to Alex and Bruce. He obviously trusts you."

They were almost done with the short walk from the Geology and Psychology building to the Math building. The sun was bright despite the ever-present haze. Paul added, "I'm impressed with Riordan; he seems to know what he's doing. But he has to be breaking all sorts of rules by using you like this."

She thought back, "I don't care about the rules. I care that he thinks I'm good at this and he's letting me play with him. Do you think he's attractive?"

She felt Paul's laugh on their face. "I can't get past the fact that he's a guy, you know?" he thought. "Besides, it's trouble to mess around with co-workers or bosses like I guess you're thinking."

"Mister Bringdown," she muttered aloud. Paul was her friend, not her father or big brother or conscience. But his opinion mattered to Amy. She was thinking about pouting over his disapproval. It was fun to think about Riordan -- Steven -- that way.

When she got to the classroom, she saw Reggie was sprawled over three chairs in the second row. Before Paul could notice, she had taken a seat next to Young.

The man looked up at her and smiled, and gave her a wink. "Where's your chaperone?" he asked.

"Cleaning up after a five-person murder-suicide," she said. "How are you?"

"Better now that you're here."

Amy heard Paul snicker and think, "Tell me about my eyes!"

"Well," she said, "aren't you the king of flattery."

The instructor stood behind the podium desk and began the lecture. Amy and Reggie each opened their books and took notes. After awhile, Amy heard Paul think, "He's going to ask you out, you know."

"Good!" she thought back.

"You really want to be alone with a possible murderer?"

"Him? And how!"

"Not very professional, fraternizing with a suspect."

"I'm a third year math student, not a cop."

"This is dangerous. And stupid. And --"

"And I'm going to say 'yes'," she thought back. "Now hush, I've missed two classes this week, I have to catch up."

When the professor left the dais, students began to make noise, collecting their books and talking among themselves. Reggie put his hand on Amy's arm and said, "Would you like to come with me to the school movie Saturday? It's some comedy, it should be fun."

She smiled up at him. "I'd like that," she said. "Come get me. I'm in 217 North Pontchartrain."

He smiled back and said, "See you in class tomorrow," and left the room.

Amy sat back down, surprised that she needed to catch her breath.

"You are out of our minds," Paul thought to her.

"Right now," she whispered aloud, "I am one happy camper."

"But he may be a killer!"

"Stuff it!"

"Look," Paul began, "I'm in here too. If something --"

"I said, 'Stuff it!' You can beat me up tomorrow, but let me enjoy how good I feel right now, okay?" She added, aloud, "He asked me out."

৫ 9 ৡ

For seven years, Paul and Amy had been lovers.

Amy melted when Paul touched her. She knew him so well and trusted him so totally that she was able to retreat completely, to allow Paul absolute control of her body. In all these years, never once did Amy want to say, "Don't do that, do this instead;" because he felt what she felt, he always, always, always touched her in the right place, at the right time, in the right way.

As much as anyone might fantasize about that sort of closeness with a lover, there were dissatisfactions for each of them.

Both of them wanted a physical touch that didn't include feelings from both sides of their shared skin. Paul missed feeling a woman in a way that didn't also include feeling being touched -- feeling a woman's breast without the breast that now was part his also feeling the hand. And Amy wanted to know what it felt like to be caressed without her hands also feeling her body. She wanted to feel something hot and alive and manly inside her, not just her own fingers, even when Paul was controlling them.

They both wished for the impossible: a man and a woman, very much in love, sharing the same body, they wanted to be able to kiss each other.

Their physical play quickly taught Paul that sexual sensation was more intense for a woman than a man. It also allowed him to continue to think of himself as a man, even though the woman's body he loved was now his own body, too.

In Amy's sophomore year at UNO, Paul was mad with jealousy and disgust and fear over her dates, her kisses, and her few affairs. He was jealous that she wanted the attention of any other man. He was disgusted and afraid over witnessing and experiencing sex with another man. Intellectually he knew he had no choice but to get used to it, but emotions use a different logic.

Amy was excited after Reggie asked her out. And, as happened when she was excited about anything, she talked to Paul about it.

"This is going to be more fun," she thought to him as she walked back to her dorm. "I'll mix a little business with a little pleasure. If he's the killer, I'll get it out of him."

Her words solidified what he had felt as he watched the man ask her out: jealousy and disgust, but also a basic fear for safety. "I may have to do what I can to chase him away," he thought back

She stopped where they were, in a pile of red and yellow leaves under a huge oak tree on the campus. "You WHAT?" she asked, out loud. A couple glanced at her as they walked by.

"I'm worried that he may be the killer, damn it! Plus, I'm jealous," he thought to her.

"Oh, come on! We went through this last year. You don't have to be jealous; you know I love you."

"So what if you think I don't HAVE to be jealous. I AM jealous. Not only are you interested in another man, I have to watch from close up."

They were climbing the stairs to her second floor room. "You're overreacting," Amy thought. "Whatever I do with anyone else, you are inside me. I always will be closer to you than to anyone else."

He sighed, and waited for her to unlock the door so they both could speak out loud in the privacy of their room.

"I've told you this a million times," he said as she took off her light jacket and kicked off her shoes. "You are my existence. I'm not talking about some hippie co-dependency shit. My only eyes are yours, my only ears are yours. Now that my sister is gone, I do not have a single friend independent of you."

"That's how it's always been," she said. She was rubbing their feet, and Paul was trying to concentrate on their conversation.

"Since I've been with you, yes," he said. "But for 55 years I had my own body, I could walk to the corner without asking permission, I had friends, I did stuff. Lots of stuff. I miss that."

"I'm sorry," she said softly, "but there's nothing I can do about that. We have one body, and it's mine. Do you not like the stuff we do?"

"That's not the point," he sighed. "I like most everything we do. I even like it when you shop for shoes -- although I will deny it if you ever tell anyone I said that."

She waited while Paul tried to battle his fear and get his thoughts in order. "You do realize this is about sex, right?"

"I don't know why," she said, "it's --"

She coughed, the sound they made when they both tried to talk at once.

So he thought to her, "I don't want to sleep with a man again. I don't want to watch you do it again."

She smiled at his words. "They have a seminar here for men like you, Stop Homophobia. Shall I sign you up?"

"Does that mean you'll sleep with a woman?"

"No!"

"Now that we've cleared up our prejudices --"

"What? What did we just clear up? What are you talking about?"

He paused, and then said seriously, "If I'm not interacting with you, I barely exist." He led them to the sink and took a few handfuls of water. When he could speak again, he said, "I can't walk around the block or go home and read if you're on a date. I'm still inside you. Please, please don't do this to me again."

They both were quiet, sitting at the tiny desk in the dorm room. Amy used the fingers of their right hand to trail up and down their left arm, part of a physical language they had developed to show concern, or support, or even acknowledgment.

Finally, Amy whispered, "What do you want me to do?"

"I don't know." He paused. "Yes, I do -- swear off men, they're just the devil's spawn. They only want one thing, you know." Amy laughed. "Really, have you considered taking vows?"

"You're crazy," she said, still laughing.

Paul moved their left hand to rub their right shoulder and arm. "Crazy about you," he said. "And jealous."

She sat for a long moment, then took a deep breath. "I'm going out with him," Amy said, firmly. "Close your eyes if you want. I think he's good looking, and maybe I'll find out something about Laura's murder, and..." she trailed off.

"And?" Paul said.

She laughed, "You know."

"Yeah. That's the problem."

They sat for a minute. Finally, Amy said out loud, "The world may be ending, but I've got to catch up on my Psych." She pulled the textbook to the center of the desk, then reached for another book -- the novel Paul was reading. She opened her book; then, below it, she opened Paul's. Years earlier they had figured out a method that allowed each of them to read separate things at the same time. As she was arranging the books, she said, "This ought to keep us busy until dinner time. Then we can go to The Cove for a burger. Some of my friends will be there."

"Mumble, bitch, gripe," he said, then repeated it: "Mumble, bitch, gripe."

"I am so far behind," she said out loud, and opened her textbook.

An observer would have been curious to see the two books in front of Amy. They would have been astounded to see her right hand occasionally turning pages of the top book, while her left hand periodically turned pages of the lower one. Every now and then a laugh came out of her mouth, as one of them found a funny phrase.

When Amy finished her assignment, she closed her Psych text. Paul thought, "Let me finish this section, okay?" The two of them read to the end of the chapter. "My God," Amy said aloud, "she KILLED him?"

"It's okay," Paul thought to her as he replaced his bookmark, "d'Urberville deserved it."

"Are you doing okay?" she thought to him as they sat a little longer.

"Mumble, bitch, gripe," he said out loud. "I lived through it before, I'll live through it this time. But I am worried that he just might be Laura's killer."

"How come I'm not? Am I too stupid to see he might be dangerous?"

She felt Paul shrug. "Maybe you're just so excited about working an honest to God murder case." A smile spread across their face. "I know I am."

She nodded, feeling relief. He was on board with her going out with a maybe killer.

"You hungry? I am." Amy said. She put on their jacket, and headed for The Cove, the student grill and hangout where Riordan had bought them lunch. Amy thought Reggie would be there, and hoped Paul would be more comfortable if their meeting were informal.

On a Thursday night, four weeks into the fall term, The Cove was dimly lit, with the annoying throb of a bad PA system playing generic AltRock music. About half the tables and seats were taken. Amy spotted her tennis friend, Florence, sitting with a girl she didn't know, and she went to join them.

"Well, look who the cat dragged in," Florence Draper said, taking her feet off an adjoining chair so Amy could sit.

"What's for dinner?" she asked, and nodded at the other woman at the table.

"The bad news is that it's the usual," Florence answered. "The good news is that it's cheap. Amy, this is Carol Rogers. She's in my textile design class. Carol, meet Amy Clear. She's as bad at tennis as I am."

They exchanged greetings, then Amy excused herself to get her meal. "I like Florence," Paul thought to Amy. "It's nice how she doesn't take herself seriously, but she's pretty good at tennis."

"We're the one who're bad at it," Amy thought back. "Do you want cheese on our burger? And... oh, look, they've got limeade again."

When they returned to the table, Florence and Carol were talking about their academic major. "The color wheel in the design lab blew my mind," Florence said. "All of a sudden I could see how colors come in families; certain ones just go together."

Amy nodded, but it was Paul who said, out loud, "Like french fries and ketchup."

Amy thought, "What are you doing?" Carol said,

"Metaphorically speaking, I suppose so."

Florence laughed. "I was thinking more along the lines of blue, green, and gray."

"I mean how they seem incomplete without each other," Paul went on, while Amy swore at him. "Nobody eats a spoonful of ketchup, and fries are just so much better with that red tomato-y goodness."

He heard Amy shouting, "Stop! Stop!" but he went on. "Is it just me, or do men not know the names of colors?"

Carol nodded vigorously, while Florence laughed. "Get beyond primary colors," Florence said, "and they're all the same to a guy."

"That's why there are two men in the whole design department," Carol said. "And I'm sure they're both gay."

Paul laughed out loud. Amy stood and said, "Will you excuse me? I have to yell at myself again," and stepped outside the door, in the hallway to the vestibule.

"What are you doing?" Amy yelled at Paul in her mind.

"Just trying to have a life," he thought back.

"Florence is my friend. She doesn't know you exist."

"Maybe she should."

"Yes, right, UNO will ship us off to Uncle Lazlo's Funny Farm. You know we can't tell people about us!" She walked into the ladies room and hid in a stall while they continued their silent conversation. "And I don't want you to mess up my friendships."

"I just want to be part of them," he thought, "even if they never know about 'Paul.' Remember what I said about wanting to interact."

Amy tapped their foot while she thought. "I can stop you, you know. I can keep you from talking."

She felt him shake their head. "No, you've said how that wears you out. The only way to shut me up is to withdraw, and neither of us wants that. Just -- just let me share."

"Things have been so great with us for years. Why this? Why now?"

"You know why. Reggie. Sex."

She rolled their eyes. "Will you behave tonight? I'm really hungry. I hope Florence hasn't eaten all the french fries. Can we talk about this later?"

"I guess," Paul finally said. "But I'm not going to shut up, if that's what you mean." A pause. "I'm not going to, uh, expose us, you know."

She walked back to the table in The Cove. Carol was gone. "I was afraid you'd eat my fries," Amy said as she sat down. "Where's your friend?"

"She has a date. Can you believe that? Four weeks into the term and she's got a date."

Amy wiped ketchup off their lower lip. "I've got one, too," she said. It sounded like "Eyef gt unto."

"What's a girl got to do to get any action around here?" Florence asked. "Who's the guy? Did I do him already?"

"What a mouth on you!" Paul said, laughing. Amy pinched her left arm with her right hand, trying to punish him. He retreated and let Amy say, "Reggie Young, he's in my math class. Cute guy. I think we're going to a movie." She jammed a whole handful of fries in their mouth to keep Paul from talking.

"Well, I'm glad I'm a design major," her friend said. "I may not have a date, but I'm going to be the best looking girl on campus this weekend."

Amy had just crammed a huge bite of burger in with the fries, so she raised their eyebrows with a grunt.

"I'm making a dress for class," Florence went on, "and by damn, I'm going to wear it even if all I do is sit on the quad."

Paul thought to Amy, "This doesn't make any sense. She's a good looking woman. It's not like she has running sores. Why doesn't she have a date?"

Amy thought back, "Good question." When she had swallowed enough of her dinner, she asked, "Why don't you have a date? Do you have some weird disease that only comes out when a guy is around?"

"I don't know," she said, thoughtfully. "Some men think I'm too bossy, too outgoing, I know that. And some of them are such mooks, they'll never get a finger on this luscious body."

"But you've got a million friends," Amy said. "Surely one of them? Or they know someone?"

Florence looked down and said, "I get bored easily."

"What does that mean?" Paul asked.

"I go out with a guy maybe three times, maybe we sleep together, and then, I don't know, I just can't stand to be near him anymore."

A cough came out of Amy's mouth when she and Paul both tried to say "Oh" at the same time. Finally Amy asked, "Isn't that -- sad?"

"Sometimes," Florence answered slowly, "if I can't find a steady supply of men." She looked up and smiled. "Otherwise it's a lot of fun."

Paul tried to be gentle as he asked, "Do you like men?" Back before he was married, long before he woke up in Amy's body, he had wondered what drove the few women he'd known who seemed to behave the way Florence described. He heard Amy think, "Please stop, she's my friend."

Florence shrugged. "Sometimes yes, sometimes no. My shrink says it's because my dad abandoned my mom and my sister and me."

"I thought I recognized that voice," a man said. Amy turned to see Reggie standing by her chair. "And you don't have your chaperone with you." A big smile broke out on her face.

"Have a sit down, big boy. I'm Florence, and I'm guessing you are..."

"Reggie Young," he said, barely nodding at Florence and sitting next to Amy, "nice to meet you."

"Crap," Paul thought to Amy. "I was enjoying talking to Florence."

"Too bad," she thought back. "Behave, okay?" To Reggie she said, "Fancy meeting you here."

As Reggie began to speak, Paul said out loud, "I've got to go. Florence, you ready?"

"Bastard!" Amy said out loud, then silently yelled at Paul, "Don't do this! I want to talk to him!"

Florence said, "But you're not done with your dinner."

Paul in Amy stood up and said, "I'm full. Let's go. See you in class, Reggie." Florence mechanically stood up, and the two women walked out of The Cove.

As soon as they were in the hallway, beyond the closed door of the grill, Florence said, "And I thought I was weird about men."

Amy struggled to lead, then realized Paul had cut off her time with Reggie, and trapped her into a longer conversation with Florence. "Damn, damn, damn!" she said.

"I'm in Privateer Place on the lake. Have you met my roommates?" Florence said. Then, "Are you all right?"

How was she going to explain any of this to Florence?

℣ 10 ℧

Thursday, September 16, 2021 -- UNO campus, New Orleans

Amy sat and talked with Florence until near midnight. She met her friend's roommates Patrice, Consuela, and Hillary, although she wasn't sure which one was wearing the biggest hair curlers she had ever seen. After a while Amy said, "Can we go outside for a minute? I want to tell you something and I don't want your roomies to hear."

"Sure," Florence said, and slipped her shoes on. They went out the dorm back door, past the clot of cigarette smokers. Even though it was one of the last nights of summer, the air had turned chilly. They wouldn't stay outside for long.

Amy began, "Look, I'm the craziest person you've ever known. I've --"

"I kind of doubt that," her friend said. "You don't know my sister."

"Sure. I'm not really crazy, I just appear that way. Look, I need for a friend to know some things about me."

Florence took a step back. Amy didn't know how to explain, so she said, out loud, "Paul? Can you do this?"

Florence looked around for someone named Paul, but the women were standing alone. She turned back to her friend, and noticed the smile on her face.

"You know how sometimes I argue with myself? I yell at me?" He saw Florence nod cautiously. "It's like part of me wants to go to the movies, but another part of me wants to sit home and read?"

Another careful nod. Florence was rubbing her upper arms to keep warm.

"I'm like that a lot," Paul in Amy continued. "It's like there are two different people in my head. One of me likes Reggie, but the other me doesn't."

"Which one of you -- youse -- I mean, y'all -- doesn't like him?" Florence asked.

Paul held their left index finger against the side of their head. "The one of me somewhere in here."

"I don't understand. Does this mean you're a lesbian?"

"No, absolutely not!" Paul replied. "And it's not like I'm a virgin. Just that some things -- I'm conflicted, you know?"

"I don't think about it, I just take off my clothes. Sometimes when I wake up I'm not sure what happened until I get in the shower."

"Do you drink a lot?" Paul asked, concerned.

"Well, yeah," Florence said. "Works wonders. I highly recommend it."

"Hmmm, maybe that would help," Paul mused. "But what I'm thinking is I need to spend as much time as I can with my friends. We -- I mean, I need friends more than I need to depend on some guy to sleep with. You know what I mean?"

"You think sleeping with a guy will make you that kind of dependent?" Her rubbing became slapping, trying to chase off the night chill.

He thought about his relative helplessness, living in Amy's head. "I've been in a situation kind of like that. I don't want it to happen again." Paul wasn't sure how to disguise what he wanted to say, but he stumbled on. "It was like I was an invalid or something. I couldn't go out and talk to people. I couldn't so much as get a drink of water myself."

"I can imagine that would suck. Look, can we go back inside?" Florence asked, hugging herself. "I'm freezing,"

Walking up the stairs to Florence's room, Amy thought "I couldn't figure out how to talk to her without telling her all the truth. I guess you did a little better than I would have. But now what?"

Paul thought back, "Let's both talk to her, like friends. I'll try not to say anything that makes her think I'm not you."

"Truce?"

"Truce!"

When they walked home that night, Paul thought, "Was that so bad?"

"I guess not," Amy thought back, "but it's so different from how we usually work, it's uncomfortable."

"I hope we get used to it. This can't be a one-time thing; it's got to be the new normal."

"I guess," she wasn't really convinced.

"It makes a big difference to me," Paul thought. "This is what I need. I'm not crazy uncle Paul locked in the attic, I'm your friend. I participate in your life. I don't care that Florence doesn't know who I am, but I need to be part of your social life."

Amy nodded as they walked quickly, fighting the midnight chill. "Now can I go out with Reggie?"

"Yeah. I'll need to be able to talk to him, too, same as we did with Florence. I still don't know what I'm going to do when you sleep with him."

Amy laughed and said out loud, "It's only a movie!"

"No. It's real life. Our real life."

✆ 11 ✆

The next night Amy was in The Cove, waiting to have dinner with Reggie. She was wearing a light yellow oxford cloth shirt fresh out of the dorm dryer and a pair of new jeans with sharp creases in the legs. Her Psych book was open on the table in front of her, but she was thinking to Paul. "Please, please don't mess this up," she thought. "It's okay to talk to him with me, but please don't turn him off. We don't want to mess up the investigation."

"No promises," he thought back, "but I appreciate you letting me out of my cage. I'll pretend I'm you, okay?"

"If I join you," a male voice asked, "will you still be here in thirty seconds?" Reggie was smiling.

"A sense of humor," Paul thought to Amy, "a good sign."

She blushed. When she tried to stand up her left foot got caught in the chair rung and she sat back down with a 'whump!' "If I don't die of embarrassment," she answered.

Reggie leaned over and hugged her around the shoulders before he sat next to her. It startled her, but she liked the contact. "I think I've got the definitions we went over in math class today," he offered. "How about you?"

Amy closed her textbook and slid it to him. "My Psych professor has us going through two or three chapters for each class. It's keeping me busy." Then Paul said, in Amy's voice, "but I'm almost through with the novel I'm reading."

Reggie glanced at the text book blurb. "What's the novel?" he asked.

"Tess Of The d'Urbervilles," he answered. "Part of me likes

Victorian novels."

"I'm impressed you have time to read for fun," he said.

"Yeah. Sometimes I can do two things at once." Then Amy added, dropping a hint, "But come the weekend, I try to avoid schoolwork. Got to have a life, you know?"

He laughed. "A life, I remember that. I think I had one in high school."

"Why?" she asked, "what do you do on weekends?"

"I've got a job. I work at the campus bookstore all day Saturday."

"Doesn't that get in the way of your social life?"

"I don't let it. What it messes up is my sleep life."

Paul nodded, "I'll sleep when I'm dead."

"Exactly. Do you work?"

The three people in two bodies talked for quite a while. They stood on line and got dinner, then sat and talked more. Eventually Reggie offered to walk Amy back to her dorm, and she accepted, even though Paul was thinking to her, "Just say no!"

It was a chilly evening, too uncomfortable to stand outside to talk. Paul was relieved that Amy didn't invite Reggie inside, but he was dreading the inevitable: the good-night kiss. Finally Reggie smiled and hugged Amy. "Thanks for a fun evening," he whispered. He leaned back to look at her, then moved forward to press his lips on hers.

Paul hurriedly slammed his inside eyes shut. He was fighting a combination of fear and disgust, slightly easier to deal with when he could not see the perpetrator.

Paul wasn't ready for the intensity of Amy's feelings, flooding her and spilling over him. There was fear, and excitement, and relief. Paul managed to stand back mentally to let himself experience Amy's emotions, and he began to smile inside. She was scared because she liked Reggie, she wanted him to like her, and she was afraid she wasn't any good at kissing; she was excited because she liked kissing; and she felt relief that the man liked her enough to do this.

Reggie hugged them, and broke the kiss to move his head alongside Amy's. His sandpaper stubble brought Paul back to his own feelings of displeasure and jealousy.

"See you tomorrow night," Reggie said in their ear. "We'll have fun at the movie."

Amy looked up at Reggie. All she could make herself do was nod. She wanted the kiss to go on, but was too timid to initiate a new one. "Yes," she whispered.

Reggie waved and left for his dorm. Chilly though it was, Amy leaned against the wall of her dormitory, next to the doorway, and she worked to remember every single second of her kiss with Reggie Young. Her heart was racing with excitement.

Paul wanted to yell insults at Amy to make her abandon thoughts of the man, and keep her from getting involved with a murder suspect. At the same time he wanted to hug her, his best friend, and tell her how glad he was for her happiness. He compromised and said nothing.

Eventually Amy calmed down. She let herself in the dorm with her swipe card, and floated up the stairs to her room. Inside, she shrugged off her jacket and her shoes and threw herself down on her bed. Paul waited.

Eventually she spoke. "More!" she shouted at her ceiling, then hugged herself, and thrashed her legs as if she were running while lying on her back. Paul felt her smile take over their face.

"Amy?" he said out loud, tentatively.

"There's no way he's a murderer. Killers can't kiss worth a damn; it's a scientific fact."

"I missed that study, but I'll take your word for it. He seems to like you."

Shyly, Amy asked, "Are you just a little happy for me"

"Part of me is," he answered truthfully. "The rest of me, not so much. Can you make him shave?"

Amy laughed. "I know what you mean," she teased, "but I don't know, that felt so, so masculine."

"I'm glad that makes one of us happy."

"Good. Because it does, it makes me happy. Paul Owens, this is my body and it's going to do what I want it to. Get with the program or shut up. There's no third option."

Paul sputtered. Experience had taught him that Amy was no weak-minded pushover. Their disagreements over autonomy and leadership had been going on for years. But never before had Amy ended a discussion so imperiously. One more thing to worry about, along with the inevitability of her sleeping with Reggie.

℘ 12 ℮

Saturday, September 18, 2021 -- UNO campus, New Orleans

"Come on, the movie will be fun," Amy said.

"I'm sure it will," Paul replied. "It's the after-party I'm worried about."

They were sitting on the bed in Amy's dorm room, waiting for Reggie to pick her up for their date. Amy was nervous. Paul was a wreck.

"I promise I won't leave you behind," she said. "In fact, I'll never let you out of my sight. But I need you to behave."

"I guess," he said. "You made preparations?"

"Flask of vodka in my purse," she said. "Florence said alcohol helps." Her smile faded, and she went on, "You know, this might not happen. He might decide he doesn't like me. He'll notice my tooth is crooked. He may think I'm ugly. Maybe I smell bad," and she stuck their head down, trying to get their nose close to their armpit.

"No such luck," Paul muttered. "He's going to knock on the door with his dick while he's still in the lobby."

"That would be a bad thing?"

Paul whimpered. And there was a knock on the door.

Amy opened it to find Reggie, holding a sorry bouquet of asters and clematis that he had found growing in a yard he passed on the way to her dorm. "Hi, Amy," he said, holding the flowers out as if they were an admission fee.

"How nice," she said, and took them. "Come in, find a place to sit." She filled a drinking glass with water and stuffed the flowers inside. She put the improvised vase on the desk, between her textbooks and Paul's novel.

She turned back to him and he hugged her. "You look nice," he said, and sat in the desk chair.

Paul thought a laugh to Amy and said, "Translation: I want to do you."

She smiled. "Thank you, you do too." He was wearing faded khaki pants, tennis shoes with no socks, and a T-shirt with a graphic of a clown with a big red nose and a caption that said "Squeeze the Wheeze."

"He does?" Paul thought to her.

She thought back, "Euwww." Then, aloud, she asked Reggie, "When's the movie start?"

"8:30. It's at the student center; it'll take us maybe ten minutes to get there. Are you much of a movie fan?"

"I see so few, but I always like them," she said. "The best ones, nobody I care about dies and the good guys win."

"Not very realistic," he smiled.

"Reality is bad enough without paying money to see more of it."

"I like the car chases and the crashes. And the things that go boom."

"Hey, I may like this guy after all," Paul thought to her. Out loud, he asked, "Jackie Chan? Schwarzenegger? Steven Segal?"

Reggie nodded emphatically. "Totally! And Chuck Norris. And The Bourne Supremacy, awesome."

Amy thought to Paul, "You two have a good time. I'm going to the movies." "Let's go," she said out loud to her date, "we can get a good seat and talk there."

As they left, Reggie said, "Wait a minute. I would have thought you didn't like action movies."

"I'm of two minds about it," she said. "Just depends which half of my brain is doing the talking."

Reggie squinted at her, then shrugged. They chatted about their math class, about upcoming Halloween, about some campus politics.

The film was being screened in a conference room in the student center, with folding chairs set up for about sixty people;

but not even two dollar admission had attracted more than twenty. As they settled into their seats, Amy said, "I brought some booze. Can you get us some Cokes?"

"That's my kind of woman," he said, and headed for the vending machines.

"I don't like this," Paul thought to Amy. "I'm all nervous and queasy. How's your stomach?"

"Fine," she thought back. "Don't you make us sick. He's okay, isn't he?"

"He likes the same kind of movies I do. And he's not opposed to alcohol. I'm still -- I don't know, kind of freaking. I never went to bed with a killer before."

Remembering Paul's history, how he killed one of the men who beat his body into a coma before he came to her, Amy thought, "I do it every night. It's okay."

Reggie came back with two cans of Coca-Cola and two big paper cups. "Let's wait 'til the lights go down to spike 'em," he whispered, handing her a Coke and a cup. She smiled up at him.

Reggie opened his soft drink, then sat back and put his arm around Amy's shoulder. She started to lean toward him when Paul spoke, quietly but firmly: "Don't fucking touch me."

Paul heard the word "What?" in stereo, as Reggie said it at the same time that Amy thought it.

Paul shook their head and muttered, "No, no, no, no, no."

"Are you okay?" Reggie asked. "Did I do something wrong?"

"My Tourette's is acting up," she said, flailing for an excuse. "I'm sorry. Try to ignore it."

He stared at her, and Paul said out loud, "Fucking ignore this, jackass."

"Uh, how do I know what to ignore and what to pay attention to?"

"If it sounds like I like you, pay attention. If I tell you to go away, ignore me. How's that?"

She hissed at Paul, "Great. Now I can't change my mind. Happy?"

"I'm working on it," he thought to her. Out loud he softly sang, "I'm a Yankee Doodle dandy..." If being negative wouldn't work, he'd try being weird.

Amy clasped both hands over their mouth. She moved her

eyes to see Reggie, still staring, with his mouth open. To keep Paul from speaking, she tightened her throat muscles; in a flash she moved her hands and quickly whispered, "Vodka in my purse," then covered their mouth again.

Reggie picked up her handbag and looked inside as Amy reviewed what was in it. Wallet, tampon holder, cell phone, condoms, hip flask -- oh crap, the condoms! "I swear," she thought to Paul, "I will figure out how to kill you and you will die a thousand deaths for this." She heard him laugh.

Someone from the Student Government Association walked to the front of the room and made an announcement about the film, about the movie series, and about student activities fees. Reggie rifled through Amy's purse during the presentation, duly noting the Trojans, until he found the plastic flask. "All right!" he whispered, dropping her purse back at her feet. The ceiling lights went off, and the movie began while Reggie livened up his cup of Coke and offered to spike Amy's.

"Please don't embarrass us during the movie," she thought to Paul. "Will you be quiet?"

"If I like it," he thought back.

Slowly, carefully, Amy lowered their hands. She was relieved that Paul didn't speak. She turned to Reggie and smiled in the flickering light reflected from the movie screen. "Yes please," she said, holding out her cup.

The film was more than half over before Reggie risked putting his arm around her again, and this time Paul remained silent. Amy leaned against her date, feeling warm and comfortable at the touch. "Yes," she whispered. Paul was silent.

A little later, Paul thought to her, "Hello! What happens next?"

"I don't know," she thought back, "I don't know what I'm going to do. I don't know what he's going to do."

"He's going to walk you home. If you invite him in, you're inviting him to stay. That's the way it works."

"It's that easy? Why does Florence have so much trouble?"

"Florence complains if she goes two nights without getting laid. I think she's a fuck machine. A very good one."

"Hush!"

"I mean it as a complement," Paul added.

"No, I want to watch the movie. Hush!"

It was a routine romantic comedy: funny, with many silly obstacles finally overcome when all the right young people ended up in bed. It would fall off the actors' resumes in maybe two years, but it was an inspired choice for a first date. Paul felt a sense of doom increase as they walked back to her dorm with Reggie.

"I liked the scene where the guy hasn't locked the bathroom door and she opens it," Reggie offered. Paul translated: "He wants you to see him naked."

"I'm still stuffed from dinner," he went on. Paul explained, "No, he doesn't want to go get something to eat; he wants to get you in bed right now."

"Not a problem," Amy replied out loud, "I don't eat much." Paul groaned, "You just told him YOU can't wait."

She thought to Paul, "Well, maybe I can't."

When Paul in Amy began to shiver, Reggie asked, "Are you cold?" and put his arm around her. It infuriated Paul that Reggie was fondling their left arm, 'his' arm, so he shrugged it off. Amy stopped to pretend to fix a shoe, then went to Reggie's right to continue walking with him. She liked the feel of his hand rubbing her.

As they got back to Amy's dorm room, Paul said out loud, "Don't touch the merchandise, buster."

Reggie looked puzzled. Tentatively, he said, "I'm supposed to ignore that, right?"

"Right," Amy said. She put her arms around Reggie's neck and pulled his head close for a kiss.

Her head suddenly was full of Paul yelling and making barfing noises. It was hard to maintain the kiss while she was laughing at him. "Take a walk around the block," she thought to him, "I'm busy." She held Reggie tighter, in the hall outside her room. This time she would make the kiss last.

Paul closed his inside eyes tightly. He knew the pressure on their mouth was from Reggie kissing Amy, and it made him want to gag. But another part of him, eyes closed but heart open to Amy's happiness, felt pleasure and comfort from the physical closeness. Paul decided to keep his eyes closed and worry about things later.

He heard Amy think to him, "You almost ruined this."

"Sorry," he said out loud, muffled into Reggie's mouth.

"You're too pretty to be sorry about anything," Reggie said, setting to work on the buttons of her shirt.

Amy elbowed open her door and backed into her room, pulling Reggie with her. "I'm not sorry about anything," she said with a smile. His eyes were aimed at what his fingers were doing, but Amy was staring at his blue eyes, flecked with gray. She thought he was the sexiest man she had ever seen in her life, and she was going to devour him.

༒ 13 ༙

Sunday, September 19, 2021 -- UNO Campus, New Orleans

Amy woke with a full bladder and an empty bed. She was disappointed that Reggie was gone. As she swung her legs around to stand, she was surprised at how sore she was. Their lovemaking had been frantic, if brief, and it had been a while since she had done this. She slipped her feet into flip-flops and covered her nakedness with a sweatshirt before padding down to the bathroom.

Paul had not slept at all. Amy was his best friend -- at this point in his life, his only friend -- but he didn't know where to begin. Complain about the soreness? About having to touch a man? Or talk about how good it felt? About the sense of physical closeness that didn't -- and couldn't -- exist between him and Amy? She was seated in a stall when he finally said, "So... what do you think?"

"I'm tired. Uh, did you have a good time?"

"The part of me that is your body had a blast," he admitted. "My brain, not so much. But I survived. How about you?"

"That was too long a dry spell. Damn, I hurt. I hurt so good." She left the stall and washed her hands. "What the hell?" she said out loud when she looked in the mirror, "My hair? Oh, gross."

She heard Paul laugh.

When they were safe back in Amy's room, he said out loud, "Did the earth move for you?"

"Close enough," she said. "I keep forgetting how weird guys can be;" she thought of places Reggie insisted on licking.

Amy was gathering towels and her toiletry bag, preparing for a shower. Not that she wanted to wash Reggie and sex off her skin, but she did have morning plans.

"You're talking to my friends now, are you better about that at least?" she demanded.

"Yeah, I really am. It makes a huge difference. And I think it will give us more to talk about, too."

"I'm glad it's doing some good because it's hard to get used to it. We didn't want to risk anyone finding out about us for so long that now it feels wrong when you talk in front of outsiders. And the lip you were giving Reggie..."

"It's a work in progress," he replied. "I'm sure I'll say the wrong thing to the wrong person sometimes. You might, too. We'll survive. We've got a plan if they throw us in a nut house."

As she tied her robe and picked up her supplies, Amy thought to Paul, "I was hoping Reggie would be here in the morning, but part of me is glad we can talk."

"You like him?" hoping the answer was no.

"Yeah. I mean, yes. The things I let him do to me, I must like him."

She heard Paul laugh. "You got the logic backwards on that. I'll tell you, unless there was some disaster, every time I slept with a woman for the first time I was convinced I was in love, L-U-V."

"What kind of disaster?" She checked the shower's temperature and entered the stall.

"One girl threw up. I fell right out of love. Another one said she wanted to have my baby. I couldn't handle that on a first date. And one gave me a Bible."

The soap stung as it washed down their body and encountered abrasions on the back of their left arm and between their legs. They thought "Ouch" to each other, then laughed.

"This is Sunday," Amy mused to Paul, "I should hear from Reggie on Wednesday or Thursday, right?"

He groaned out loud. "Yeah, the three-day rule is in effect."

"What would you like us to do next weekend?"

"You and me?"

"Well, you and me and Reggie."

"Right now, I like the idea of sitting down in a tub of ice."

Amy turned off the water. She reached past the shower curtain and grabbed a towel to wrap around her hair like a turban.

Back in her room, she said "I had a good time last night. I'm so used to us not being able to kiss that I forget what a big deal it is. And being touched by someone I like." She was dressing for a Sunday morning tennis match with Florence. "I think my favorite parts were him holding me. Just putting his arm around me. You know?"

"I noticed the same thing," Paul replied, "that Reggie hugging us felt good to me, too." He was quiet for a minute, then said, "God, that hurts to admit. Will you still like me if I'm gay?"

"The stuff we do together? No way you're gay. And if you get any enjoyment out of a guy I date, that's going to make everything a little easier. Hmmm?"

Amy checked her clothes in the mirror behind the door of her single dorm room. She -- she and Paul -- was five-six, and weighed 109 pounds. Smooth brown hair to their shoulders, a shock brushed over their forehead. Grey eyes, heavy eyebrows, little nose, and a crooked front tooth. They wore a light blue polo shirt with a UNO logo on the chest, and a short white tennis skirt that really was wrap-around shorts. Lots of pale legs. She heard Paul whistle and say, "You are so pretty! Want a candy bar, little girl?"

Amy patted their left arm with their right hand as she said out loud, "Thanks, you're the best." She grabbed their tennis racket and a jacket and headed out the door.

℘ 14 ℈

Sunday, September 19, 2021 -- UNO campus, New Orleans

Amy's phone went off before she got to the tennis court. "Clear, it's Riordan. You awake?"

"Sure enough, Your Majesty. Any news?"

"Unfortunately, yes. They found another student on your campus."

She stopped walking. "God, no, not again. Where? Who was it?"

"I'll meet you in, umm, an hour or so. It's at Privateer Place, but a different section from where we talked to the sorority queen. Lakefront? You kids have lakefront dorms?"

"Some of us do, but you've seen my hovel. What --"

"I need you to make those bonehead rent-a-cops set up a perimeter. Don't let people tromp around her. Let's see if we can salvage some clues. Hold it together until I get there."

The detective hung up before Amy could say a word. Alas, she could not hang up on Paul, who said, out loud, "Great. We're Reggie's alibi."

Amy punched Florence's number into her phone and changed direction. "I hope you check your voicemail fast," she said. "There's been another murder on campus. The detective drafted me. I'll be on the lakefront by your dorm, how's that? Sorry about blowing our tennis game."

Amy used her swipe card to get into the complex, and headed for the group of buildings facing Lake Pontchartrain. When she got behind them she saw a clot of students and security people near a pavilion in the large grass verge that separated the dorms from Lakeshore Drive. She ran the rest of the way.

"Hey!" she called to the same two security guards she had dealt with before as she closed on them, "Hey!"

They turned toward her voice. One began to smile. When Amy got close enough, he said, "We've got enough people here. Stay away."

When she reached them, she was short of breath. "Steven Riordan sent me," breathe, "He said we need to," breathe, "secure a perimeter." Breathe. "Last time, he said forensics couldn't find anything," breathe, "because the area got trampled."

"And who is Steven Riordan?" the second one asked.

She didn't have his business card with her. "He's the Parish detective. Cigarettes and hat?"

They recognized the description. The first security man said, "And who are you?"

"I'm his assistant," she said, "Amy Clear."

"Well, Assistant Amy Clear, I guess we ought to start -- what was that? Secure a perimeter?"

Paul thought, "Condescending bastard. You're the real Amy Clear."

Amy heard the patronizing tone without Paul's prompt. She dropped her tennis bag and began counting things on her fingers. "Has anyone checked the victim? Is she alive?" Both men shook their heads. "Okay, get everyone away from the body. Maybe thirty feet. Have everyone walk away from the body that far before those who have to circle around back here. That'll minimize the damage that's already been done."

The men were looking at her, impressed by her authoritative speaking, but still skeptical of a campus co-ed telling them what to do. Amy looked back and forth between them, then pointed to the second man. "You. Get those people away from the body. And check the woman for a pulse." When he didn't move, she said, "NOW!" He ambled off toward the victim and the gaggle of spectators.

She turned back to the other guard. "Who found the body?"

"One of the women over there," he nodded toward the crowd. "She was running on the verge around seven-thirty this morning."

Amy bobbed her head. "Good, well done. I'll need to talk to her until Riordan gets here; don't let her get away. Do we know the victim's name yet?"

"Yvonne Washington. Somebody recognized her. They said she lived in one of the Privateer buildings."

"What was with the body? Purse? Phone? Take-out pizza box?"

"We didn't move the body; we didn't look for things. That's NOPD's job."

"I suppose it is. Did any of these people volunteer anything? Anyone see anything?"

He shook his head. "Apparently the deceased had been out here for some little while. No one reports seeing anyone, or hearing anything, nothing."

"Okay, thanks." She touched the man's chest with her index finger and said, "Her name is Yvonne. Please call her that. Words like 'deceased' and 'victim' upset these people. Let's try to make it easier on them, okay?"

The other guard returned, and the students who had been around Yvonne now congregated around Amy and the security men. Amy asked him, "Well?" The guard shook his head; there had been no pulse. She thought to Paul, "Help me remember what Riordan did last time!"

Paul took the lead and addressed the group, of course with Amy's voice. "Who found Yvonne?"

"Me," a woman said, raising her hand. Paul waved their hand to summon her.

"Who identified her?" Two people in the crowd, a man and a woman, raised their hands. Paul motioned them over.

"Is anyone here Yvonne's roommate?" People turned heads, but no one responded. "Does anyone know where Yvonne lived? Her room number?" One of the men in the back shouted, "Yo!" Paul called, "Please come up here."

Paul thought, "Now we tell them to disperse. You want to, or shall I?"

"I'll do it," she thought. "Listen up, people," Amy began. "Yvonne Washington was our friend, our sister, our fellow UNO Privateer. So was Laura Adams. Everyone, be aware of your personal security. Lock your doors. Walk in groups, not alone. Tell friends where you are going and when you expect to get home. Notice any suspicious activities and let your prefects and advisors know. Please be careful! And now, please, please leave this crime scene so we can begin the investigation. Go to your classes, do whatever you were planning to do before we found Yvonne. But please do it anywhere but right here."

She heard Paul snicker. "You are so much nicer than I am. I'd have told them all to get off my lawn."

"Doesn't cost extra to be nice," she thought back. "Besides, if I'm freaked out, I'm sure they're all upset."

"I wonder if you slept with the killer last night?"

Amy said "Arrgh" out loud. There were six people left around her: the guards, the people who identified the body, the woman who found it, and the person who said he knew where the woman had lived. "Does anyone have paper? A notebook?" One of the men waved a spiral bound book. "Please let me borrow it for a few minutes and take a few pages, okay?"

She opened the book to the back, where she found blank paper. "You said you found her," pointing to a woman in running shorts and a UNO sweatshirt. "What's your name?"

"Melissa Fontenot," she answered. "I live in Pontchartrain South."

Amy wrote it down, and her contact information. "I was on my morning run. I do this three or four times a week. Usually I like this section; it's pretty and they keep the grass mowed, and you can smell the lake. It was around seven-thirty. I saw something on the stone bench by the pavilion, so I went over to look. I saw it was a woman. I thought maybe she was asleep, so I called, but she didn't move. I poked her with my shoe, but she still didn't move, so I called security."

"Well done," Amy said. "Did you look around at all? Did you see anyone? Did anything look unusual?" Melissa shook her head and murmured, "Sorry."

"What about our tennis?"

Everyone turned to see Florence Draper, slowly batting her racket against her left fist.

"Kind of busy here," Amy said in a peculiar, high-pitched voice. "Check your voicemail, okay?" Florence frowned but she turned her back and pulled out her phone.

"Now, you two identified Yvonne," talking to two others.

"What are your names?"

"Jasmine Williams," the woman said. "Yvonne is my sister in Sigma Gamma Rho." Amy wrote it down, and turned to the man. "I'm Darius Nanko, I am exchange student from Kenya. Yvonne was part of your welcoming committee. She helped me get used to your college life."

"Holy Jesus fuck!" Florence yelled. Mouth hanging open, she turned back to look at Amy. "Not another one!"

"Afraid so. We need to reschedule tennis. The detective asked me to start the investigation. He'll be here soon to take over."

"I'm staying here. I'll feel safer." Amy nodded, then turned back to Jasmine and Darius. "When's the last time you saw her?" Jasmine said it was at the last sorority meeting, Monday night. Darius said it had been a week or so since the last student exchange program. "Any idea what her plans were for last night?" No. Amy took down their phone numbers, and asked them to contact her or NOPD if they remembered anything or found out anything that might help the police.

That left the man who indicated he knew where Yvonne lived. "Are you doing okay?" she asked him, and he nodded. "Yvonne lived in the other Privateer Place complex, by the canal," he said.

"What's your name?"

"Willie Jones. I dated Yvonne a little." Amy wrote it down.

"Were you dating her currently?" she asked him.

He shrugged. "We'd go out maybe once a month. We started doing that last year. We weren't a couple or anything."

"But you were friends?"

"I guess," he answered. "Sometimes we'd do stuff together."

"Was she dating anyone in particular?"

"I don't think so. She dated around, a little. Yvonne was wrapped up in school; she wanted to become a nurse. And she sang in the chorus. They traveled some."

"When's the last time you saw her, Willie?"

"A couple of days ago. She was frantic about an organic chemistry test that was coming up."

"Any idea what her plans were for last night?" He shook his head.

"Do you know if Yvonne had any enemies? Anyone who might want to hurt her?"

"Yvonne? You've got to be kidding."

"I hope I'm wrong, but I'm not kidding. Jealous man? Angry rival? Someone she owed money to? Anything?"

Another shake of the head. Amy got Willie to describe where Yvonne lived -- he knew the way, but not what the building or room number were. And she took down his contact information. She finished with the sort of closing she had seen Riordan use: "If anything occurs to you, even if it seems trivial, call NOPD. We need everyone's help to solve this crime. In the meantime, I advise you to increase your personal security. We've got two dead Privateers now." She tore the notes she had taken out of his notebook and thanked him for the loan.

As Willie left, Amy turned to Florence and hugged her. She heard her friend whisper, "What the hell are you doing?"

Amy held up her index finger to ask her to wait, then turned to the security guards. "Thanks for your help, guys. Now we wait for Riordan."

They all sat on the grass to wait. The guards talked among themselves, some campus politics and some home life. Florence grabbed Amy's arm and said, "What is going on here?"

"Another dead student. The detective called me and asked me to handle things until he gets here."

"This is too creepy," Florence said. "I don't scare easy, but I'm scared now."

"You should be. Until we get a handle on this, we're all in danger."

"I'm a little confused," she wrinkled her face. "I understand 'we' as in you and me, or all of us students. Who is the 'we' that have to get a handle on things?"

"Ah, that would be me and detective Steven Riordan and the New Orleans police."

Florence raised one eyebrow. "When did you become a cop?"

"I'm not -- Florence, I told you about this. I conned the detective into letting me help him, and I must be doing a good job because he's doing things like telling me --" she lowered her voice, "-- to boss around the campus security."

They heard a car horn. A black-and-white and an ambulance

had come through a parking lot and were slowly driving on the grass verge, heading toward Amy and the security guards. "Do we get to play tennis after this?" Florence asked.

"I hope not," Amy said, staring at the approaching cop car. "I hope Riordan teaches me how to do the investigation." After a while she turned to Florence and said, "That came out wrong."

"Thanks for making me laugh," her friend said. She stood up, and brushed loose grass off the seat of her tennis shorts. "Call me when you're done and tell me what happened. We'll play tennis another day. And solve this so I don't have to be scared anymore!"

When the cars came to a stop, Amy and the campus security men stood up. Riordan got out, cigarette dangling, and he arranged his fedora. Jermaine emerged from the passenger side, struggling with his medical bag. A different woman from before got out of the back seat with a big case, and only two cameras hanging around her neck.

Riordan waved at Amy, but went to the security men. Amy couldn't hear their conversation, but she saw Riordan laugh, and slap one of the men on the shoulder. The guards turned to leave; one waved at Amy, and they were gone.

The detective was laughing as he came up to Amy. "You're a wonder, Clear," he said. "The rent-a-cop said you bullied them into securing the scene. How'd you do it?"

"Uh-oh. Was that bad?"

He was still laughing. "That was so not bad, it was amazing. What did you say to them?"

"Ummm, I told them you told me to tell them to secure the perimeter. They weren't taking me seriously, so I told them what to do -- I just made it up. You haven't taught me this stuff yet. I told them to get all the people around Yvonne to come up here. They looked at me like I hadn't said a word, so I pointed at one of them and I said, 'You. Do it.' He still didn't move, so I yelled, "Now!" and he went off like a good little rent-a-cop. So, I did good, Your Majesty?"

"Yes, Clear, you done good. Uh, why are you dressed like that?"

Amy looked down. "What are you talking about?" and she

looked back up at him. "My socks match, what more do you want?"

"You look like you're off to play tennis."

"That had been the plan, until the bat-phone rang. Is this a problem? Or should I have gone back to the dorm and spent an hour deciding what to wear to a murder investigation?"

He laughed again, "No, you're fine. Tell me, who did you talk to?"

Amy gave him her notes, and ran down what she had learned. "Necklace?" he asked.

"I haven't seen the body yet. I was too busy up here."

"Come on," he said, walking toward the dead woman, "I'll show you how to do a proper evaluation."

The police woman was taking photographs of the verge, the back of the dorm apartments, and of Lakeshore Drive and the lake beyond. "She'll take a lot of pictures," he said. "First the general ones, then specific ones of the body *in situ*, and then the close-ups. Jermaine!" he shouted, "What do we have?"

The medical examiner didn't look up. "Another strangulation. Come see this." Riordan and Amy crouched on the opposite side of the body on the stone bench. "Same sort of ligature mark as with the first girl," he said, pointing. "And the marks that I thought might be from a necklace, they look a little different, but - - I'll have to get to the lab and compare them."

Riordan said, "If the perp is bringing his own garrote to the scene, that's less opportunity and more premeditation."

"If you say so," Jermaine said. When he finally looked up he saw Amy and smiled. "Oh, hello, missy. So you won't take the good advice of a kindly old doctor?"

"I'm notoriously hard-headed," she replied. "Nice to see you again."

Riordan asked, "Time of death?"

"Between eleven PM and two AM. The lake-effect wind might make the body cool faster than otherwise, so I'm not sure."

"Struggle?"

Jermaine shook his head. "Just the fingernail scratches. The perp must have gotten both of these women by surprise."

The detective stood up, and offered his hand to Amy to help her up. "First I have to make a sketch. Then I'll show you how we do an evidence search." He shook his head, "I wish you'd gotten here sooner, the ground is almost as churned up as it was at your dorm."

"All you had to do was call me sooner," she said, defensive.

"Whoa, you didn't do anything wrong, Clear. I'm just saying."

Riordan stood behind Jermaine, just a few feet away from the bench that was the final resting place of Yvonne Washington. He made a rough drawing of the scene. "How far do you think it is to the fence behind the apartments?" he asked her.

Amy squinted, she had no idea. "Paul?" she thought. He replied, "I got nothing."

"I don't know," she told Riordan. "Maybe three hundred feet?"

The detective reached in a jacket pocket and came out with what looked like a mini-cell phone. When he pressed a button, Amy saw a red laser dot appear on a dormitory wall. He aimed it at a fencepost, then pressed another button. "One hundred forty six feet," he said, and marked it on his sketch. Then, "Where do you think a perp may have come from, or escaped? Look around." She saw he was scanning the area in all directions, and she followed suit.

Pointing north, she said, "Just about anywhere from Lakeshore Drive, there's no fence. Should we look for tire tracks if a car pulled over?"

"Reasonable," he said. "Where else?"

To the east, the verge and the street swung to the right, eventually separating the campus from the Pontchartrain Beach recreation area. In the other direction, the road went over the canal on a bridge, even though the canal forced the verge to turn south, behind the other set of Privateer Place apartments. Then she looked again at the fence Riordan had measured. There were openings in two places: the parking lot escape that the police had used, and a nearer section where it looked as if construction had recently begun. She told him, "From that part of the apartments, just those two openings. But east or west, they're wide open. The Chinese army could get in."

He nodded, still making notes on his sketch. "Very observant.

But to the west, the only real campus entry is the bridge."

"Excuse me, Your Majesty," she said, "but there's a canal lock down there a little ways. I've walked across it a few times. Scary as hell, but it gets you over to London Park and West End."

"Huh!" he said, and took the eraser end of his pencil to his sketch. "So what does this tell us?"

Paul said, "That we'd need a posse of fifty people to do a search?"

"Not on my budget," he muttered. "No, since the search party is me and you, it means that we have to concentrate right around the crime scene." He put his notebook back in his inside jacket pocket. "We use a spiral technique. We start at the body, and slowly walk around and around, looking for anything. Well, anything more useful than whatever the rent-a-cops dragged through here."

"Like mowing a lawn from the center outward?" Paul asked.

"You got it, Clear. Here," and he handed her latex gloves. "Put 'em on and follow me."

Riordan crouched behind Jermaine, carefully looking at the ground. After a moment he sidled forward. They had done this five or six times when he muttered, "A Choctaw scout couldn't make anything of this crap." He pointed at a clump of grass. "Blades are broken in every direction. One of them may have been broken by the killer, but the clue is lost because we didn't secure the scene."

"I appreciate you not blaming that on me this time," she said, still feeling defensive.

"Get over yourself, Clear. Finding the killer is the only thing that matters." He stood up, but continued his spiral review, going faster this time. "Nothing. Not a thing. Not a God damn thing."

Amy pointed a few yards away. "Cigarette butt?"

The detective looked. "Might be one of mine." He fished a fluorescent orange piece of paper out of a pocket, and wrote a big letter A on it, then placed it on the grass by the butt. He took the compass attached to his ID lariat and noted the direction from the body. Finally, he used the laser tape measure to determine distance. He handed the sketch to Amy and said, "Mark the evidence."

"Distance?" "Twenty-three feet, three inches." "Direction?"

"East southeast, call it two hundred fifteen degrees."

"I label it "A"?"

"If you would be so kind."

She handed the sketch back for Riordan's review. He examined it, then folded it and put it away without comment. The photographer came up behind them to take more pictures. When she was done, the detective worked one of his business cards under the butt and scooped it into a small brown envelope. He wrote something on the outside.

They continued the spiral search for another thirty minutes, but found nothing. Amy was surprised to see they were almost at the fence behind the dormitory apartments. "You covered a lot of ground," she remarked.

"We did," he corrected her. "You found the only thing that might be useful. Let's go back to Jermaine. I need a soil sample from near the bench."

By the time they returned to the body, the ambulance drivers had a gurney ready, waiting only for Riordan's release. The detective looked down at the woman's face and shook his head sadly. He made a sign to Jermaine, and the ambulance people began transferring the body.

Riordan took a close look at the newly exposed bench top. "What's this?" he asked Jermaine, pointing at two stains.

"Pee and shit," he said. "I promise you, they were the girl's. Bodies do that when they die." He was packing up the last of his equipment.

"I'll catch up to you," the detective said, then took Amy by the arm and walked her off a few feet. "You did good with the preliminary interviews. I'm going to the Dean's office, I'll find out who the woman's roommate was; that's the first person I'll interview. Then it'll --"

"You'll interview? Call me when you're ready and I'll come with you."

"I don't know, this is getting more and more serious."

"All the more reason you need help. This is no time to break up the team."

"Break up the team?" he repeated, incredulous. "What are you smoking? You --" He stopped. "Oh. This is how you got the rent-a-cop to behave."

She heard Paul laughing, but she shook her head. "No. If you were the rent-a-cop, I'd be saying, "What do you mean, YOU'll interview? That's WE'll interview, got that?"

"Your mother must have pussy whipped your father nine ways from Sunday for you to have learned all this."

She smiled. "Nope. But I can be the Queen of Wheedle. So don't give me a hard time, Your Majesty. Call me when we're ready to do the interview."

"Go on, get out of here," he said as he bent down to take the soil sample. "I'll call you."

❦ 15 ❧

Sunday, September 19, 2021 -- UNO campus, New Orleans

"Who's there?" Florence's voice came through her uncharacteristically closed and double-locked door.

"It's Amy. Let me in before the boogie man gets me."

There were clicks and thuds, until finally the door opened as far as the inside chain would allow. "How do I know it's you?"

"If I'm not, I'm in more trouble than I think."

The door closed momentarily as Florence loosened the chain; then she opened it and let her friend in. "I hate this paranoid shit," she said, closing and locking the door. "Except there are two dead students, so it's not paranoia."

"Nope," Amy said, "Somebody's really out to get someone."

"Tell me what's going on," her friend asked. "Who's this girl? What's the story?"

Amy related her interviews with the students on the verge, and her lesson from the detective. "I'm not changing my major," she said, "but this is so exciting!"

Paul added, "And it beats studying Psych." Amy thought to him, "Careful!"

"I just want to sit in my workshop and sew pretty clothes all day long," Florence said. "I'm getting scared to be by myself now."

Amy bounced on the edge of a roommate's bed. "Where's Consuela and the rest of your UNO family?"

"They're all staying off campus, some friend of theirs lives across the canal. I don't blame them. I just don't think I could stand that much of them, so I'm still here."

"Keep the door locked, you'll be okay."

"Anything come of that guy you ducked out on at The Cove?" She was standing by the room microwave, waiting for the popcorn to finish.

"Actually, yes. But he disappeared sometime during the night. What are the odds on a return matchup?"

"Did he leave a note at least?" Amy shook her head. "Text you yet?" Again. "Email?"

"Nothing, Florence. We had a nice evening --" she smiled when she heard Paul think, "Speak for yourself" "-- and we clicked in bed, and then poof."

"A mook. If you're lucky you won't ever hear from him again."

After a pause, Amy said, "I have to tell someone this. The guy is Reggie --"

"Yeah, I met him, remember?"

"-- and he's actually one of the suspects in Laura Adams' murder."

"He's WHAT?"

"I said, -- what's that smell? Florence, the popcorn!"

"Oh, shit!" Her friend opened the microwave, letting out a small cloud of white smoke and more of that unpleasant, lingering odor. She pulled the bag out of the oven and threw it into a trash can. "Damn!" she shouted, shaking her hand from the sting of the hot bag.

"Are you okay?" Amy asked. Florence nodded, her throbbing fingers in her mouth. "Can we air the place out and go somewhere else?" Amy was waving her hand like a fan. "That smells foul."

"Yeah, good idea," she said around her fingers; it sounded like "Yerf, guu dee." Amy opened the windows, and they walked downstairs, and out to the quadrangle.

"I don't think anyone can hear us," Amy said. "Yes, Reggie is a suspect in Laura's murder. The new victim is a black woman. I'm waiting to hear from the detective about interviewing roommates and friends. Maybe Reggie is in the clear."

Florence stopped sucking her fingers long enough to say, "You never struck me as this kind of risk taker. Sleeping with a possible murderer?"

"He's a looker," Amy said, "and his self-confidence is

magnetic." She heard Paul think, "Arrogant pissant." To Florence she said, "Your mileage may vary."

"You going to see him again?"

"Three-day rule is in effect. If I don't hear from him by Thursday, I guess not. Damn. I'm hoping I can crib his math notes, I've been missing so much class."

Florence said, "The girl they found this morning was from the Privateer Place complex. Our Resident Advisor called a meeting for tonight, she's going to hand out rape whistles and run down safety precautions."

"Good!" Amy responded. "Go to that meeting." Thinking of Paul, she said, "I have a friend who taught me that stuff. You'll never find my door unlocked; I always have my car keys in my hand when I'm in a parking lot; I'm always looking around. Do it all the time, not just when there's a problem."

Amy's phone rang. "Maybe it's Reggie," she said, eyes wide. She took the call, saying, "Hel-loooow."

"Clear. I got Yvonne's contact information. Meet me at that apartment dorm complex, I'll be there in fifteen minutes." By the time she said, "Yes, Your Majesty," the line was dead.

"Better than sex," she smiled to Florence. "Riordan wants me to help him with an interview. He couldn't do this without me. You know, I was the one who found the only evidence from this morning."

"Can you help me beat a parking ticket?" Florence asked.

"Not yet. I have to go. Sorry about the smell in your room."

"Easy for you to say. You're not the one who has to sleep there."

She left her friend standing on the quad, and headed to Privateer Hall and another interview lesson. "I wish I could tell Florence about you," she thought.

"Me, too," Paul thought. "But the telling I'm more worried about is letting Riordan know you slept with Reggie."

"Oh, it won't matter. I don't see him being friends or anything else with Yvonne. It shouldn't come up."

"If they were my fingers," he said out loud as she walked, "I'd cross them for you."

Amy stood in front of the dorm section she thought had

housed Yvonne Washington, but she made sure she could see the entrance to the lakefront section as well. She didn't want to get scolded again for being late, even in jest. She was holding the detective's notebook.

"There you are, Clear. Get us in this place; we've got people to talk to."

She used her ID card to open the gate. Riordan pitched his half-smoked cigarette into the grass by the walkway. "Any developments?" she asked, trotting to keep up with the detective.

"Jermaine hurried on the autopsy, since this is a second victim. No booze, no drugs, no recent sex. Strangled but not suffocated -- it was forced buildup of depleted blood in the brain, just like the first girl. And the necklace pattern on the ligature -- he says it's similar but not the same as on Laura Adams. He thinks it may be a different weapon, or maybe a different part of the same garrote. Hey!" he shouted to the student behind the reception desk, "Where do I find building A-7?"

"Back outside," she said, "to your right, then alongside the canal."

"Thanks, Sweetheart," he said and turned.

"You won't be able to get in," she called after him. "It's on lockdown."

Without turning, he replied, "That's right. I'm the cop who ordered it."

"Lockdown?" Amy asked.

"No one in or out without ID. If we find another body, the whole campus will be on a partial lockdown."

It was Paul who asked, "But if the killer belongs here -- student, staff, faculty -- then lockdown won't do anything."

"That's no reason not to do what we can. We're going to meet with Yvonne's roommate, who just happens to be Yvonne's older sister."

"Another sorority thing?"

"No. Biological. Her older sister is a senior. From what I hear, she's angry at the world and ready to take it out on the first authority figure who comes through her door. So, look, Clear, I --"

"It'll be great to learn from watching you diffuse the situation, Your Majesty."

Despite himself, he laughed. "That rent-a-cop doesn't know

the half of it."

Amy swiped her ID card to open the gate, and they were greeted by a uniformed policeman. "I need to see -- Oh, Steven, how you doing? She with you?" pointing at Amy.

He nodded and answered, "How the hell are you, Mullinax? Get that flatboat into Chef Menteur Pass yet?"

The officer smiled and shook the detective's hand. "I've taken it for a few runs, but I'm waiting for you to come with me to drag for some redfish."

"I'd like that. We'll do it soon, but first I've got this murder to solve." He put his right hand on Amy's back to push her along while he waved at the policeman with his left.

She asked, "Is that what life is going to be on campus until we solve this?"

"Until we solve it," he repeated. The words struck Amy and filled her with pride and excitement. The emotions were so strong Paul could sense them; he thought to her, "I think you passed the audition."

Yvonne Washington's room was on the third floor of the central section of building A-7. "This one will be touchy," the detective said while they were taking the stairs, "so let me do the talking."

She nodded, following behind. Paul thought, "Dealing with victims' families must be hard. All emotional, understandably. You have to be sympathetic, but you still have to ask all those uncomfortable questions."

Amy thought back, "I'm glad he's the one who has to ask them."

On the top floor of the dorm apartment building, they stopped outside an open door. Riordan knocked on the door frame and called, "Mikayla Washington?"

A deep female voice called, "Yeah. Come in."

Riordan held his hat in his hand as he walked the short hallway to the main room of the unit. The university-supplied furniture was standard -- couch, three chairs, credenza -- but the beige carpet was littered with knick-knacks and books and broken glass. The four-shelf bookcase was almost empty.

Mikayla Washington was sitting in a corner of the sofa. She

was doubled over, her arms in front of her stomach and her hands gripping her sides. "Who are you?" she asked, rapidly rocking.

He opened his badge case. "I am Detective Steven Riordan," he told her. "This is my aide, Amy Clear; she's a student at UNO. I am sorry to meet you like this."

The woman glared up at Riordan for a few seconds. Then she exploded from the couch, screaming and crying, rushing toward the detective. "Where is Yvonne?" she shouted, "What did you do to my sister?"

Amy raced around to put herself between the grieving woman and Riordan. Her attempts at calming Mikayla were slow to work; she continued to keen, to shout insults, to yell syllables of anguish that were beyond words. Amy held her back, and finally was able to push her back to the sofa, and help her sit.

"I am sorry about what happened today," Riordan started, "but I must ask you some ques --"

The screams and shouts resumed. "You let my sister die! My baby, my baby, it's all your doing!" Amy sat beside her and made the cooing sounds she remembered seeing her own sister make when her niece had a skinned knee or a broken doll. "Sshhh, it's going to be okay. You just take a deep breath, will you do that for me?" Gradually the woman calmed to only tears.

"There are some things I must ask you," the detective said. "May I sit down?"

Mikayla's eyes burned at him. "No!" she screamed, then began wailing again.

Riordan crouched before the woman so their eyes were on the same level, and softly he said, "I know this is painful, but I must ask you some questions."

She erupted again.

Riordan stood up and said sharply, "Get your things together. We're going to the station house."

"I ain't going anywhere with you, devil!"

"Then you are under arrest for interfering with a police investigation."

Mikayla's jaw dropped, and the screams resumed. When Amy saw the detective reach for his handcuffs, she put her arms around the woman and said, "It's okay. I'm a Privateer, too. Sshhh. The first girl they found, she was outside my dorm." Tears unabated, the woman curled against Amy and clung to her. "Sshhh," Amy went on, softly, "I'm just a junior, and I'm scared by all this. Please, Mikayla, you can help us. Sshhh, sshhh. Help us. You may have the piece of information that lets us prevent any more attacks. Sshhh, it's okay. Help us make campus safe again."

Head still tucked into Amy's chest, the woman forced words between sobs. "She was my baby, she was my baby."

"I have a kid sister, too. I'd die if anything happened to her. I know."

Mikayla looked up at Amy, and slowly sat back. She seemed embarrassed, so Amy looked away and picked up the notepad she'd dropped on the floor. Riordan had scooted a chair around so he was looking at the woman at an angle, less intimidating than facing her head-on would be.

For the last time, the detective began. "I know this is uncomfortable, but it must be done. Miss Clear is right, you may have the missing fact that will let us protect everyone else on campus. When is the last time you saw Yvonne?"

Her weeping increased, but this time she controlled herself. "It was last night," she said, sniffling. "I was going to bed, she was sitting up to study. She was so worried about that damn chemistry test. She was so smart, such a star --"

Amy saw the sobs on the horizon, and she tried to keep the interview on track. She put her hand on Mikayla's arm to distract her, like she'd seen her sister do to keep her children from starting a tantrum. "She was going to study?" she prompted.

A weak nod. "I didn't hear the phone ring, I didn't hear anybody come to the door. I left for an eight o'clock class, I figured Yvonne just hadn't gotten up yet. I didn't think anything of it." Amy patted her arm and smiled.

"Did your sister have a boyfriend? Any special man friend?"

"No. I mean, she dated some guys, she was no wallflower or nothing, but she was serious about school. She wanted to be a nurse. She wanted to do better than Mama."

"Do you know the names of the men she did date? I'm going to have to talk to them later."

"That Willie Jones was her best man friend." Face wet with tears, she smiled and said, "That is a stand-up man. He doesn't fool around with drugs, he doesn't drink, he's respectful to me and to her."

"Anyone else?"

"Donte, what's his name... Thomas, Donte Thomas. He's a clean man. Not as stand-up as Willie, but he's okay."

"Anyone you didn't like."

She frowned. "That white boy -- excuse me," she said to Amy. "They had some class together. He was devil smooth, he talked sweet. My baby fell for that."

It was Amy who asked, "What was wrong with him?

"He's about as sincere as a politician kissing babies. Made my back shiver. We argued about him, only man she and I ever did that about."

Amy feared the worst as Riordan said, "What was his name?"

"Reggie Young." Her eyes were blazing.

Paul and Amy thought the same thing to one another: "Oh, shit." Paul added, "Is there a single girl here he hasn't done?" Amy made herself write Reggie's name in the notebook.

"What about her sorority? Did she have close friends there?"

"She's a Sigma, like I was, officer, and --"

"That's 'detective,' miss."

"-- It's a pretty good group of women, but they're more social than academic. So Yvonne went to meetings, did some charity stuff, but wasn't all that involved. She spent more time with her books."

"You said you used to be a Sigma?"

She nodded. Softly, embarrassed, she said, "I dropped out last fall. I couldn't afford the dues."

"Tell me about Yvonne's friends."

"We're from Opelousas, we spent time with some other people from home. But me and Yvonne, we were each other's best friends."

"Did she have any enemies?"

"What? No. No way. Yvonne's a good girl. Was." Amy saw her eyes water, but the woman made herself stay calm.

The detective smiled. "Of course. But maybe a man who was, uh, disappointed? A jealous woman?" Mikayla shook her head. She grasped Amy's hand. "Did she owe anyone money?" Another head shake. "Alcohol or drugs?"

"NO!" she shouted. "What do you think my baby was? She didn't do none of that stuff. She's a saint, you hear me? A saint!" She went back to rocking and keening. Amy put her arm around the woman and softly spoke to calm her, "Sshhh, it's okay, it's just a question they have to ask everyone, sshhh, it's not personal, it's okay, really..."

It took a minute before Mikayla had calmed down enough for Riordan to ask more questions. "Did your sister keep a diary?"

"Not that I know. I guess you don't tell folk if you do."

"May we look at Yvonne's things? We never know where the missing piece of information will help us."

Amy felt her tense up, but the woman said, "Yeah, go ahead." Amy flashed a smile at Riordan, then she began talking to Mikayla. She tried to draw her into an innocent conversation about school, about her family, about absolutely anything to keep her distracted so the detective could do his work.

Riordan put on two pairs of latex gloves. Yvonne's cell phone lay on the desk, so he looked at the call register. She had called her sister just before noon the day before, and Mikayla had called back around one o'clock. He scrolled through the phone book, noted entries for Willie Jones, and for Donte Thomas, and for Reggie Young. He fished an evidence envelope from an inside pocket and slipped the phone inside. Next he looked through the purse. Yvonne's wallet seemed undisturbed -- drivers license, student ID, an Optimum debit card, and thirty six dollars in cash.

One of the questions Amy asked while Riordan was busy, was about the arrangements. Mikayla said, "The funeral will be at our Catholic church in Opelousas, on Tuesday. Mama, she's all a mess over this, and my brother, he's only fifteen. So I'm making all the phone calls." She looked up at Amy and said, "It's hard, you know?" and began to weep again.

Riordan stripped off his gloves. He looked over Mikayla's head at Amy with a question mark on his face, and she nodded gently. He approached with a business card in his hand. "Miss Williams, I appreciate you talking to me, I understand how painful this must have been. If you think of anything that might help us, call me or contact Miss Clear here. It doesn't matter how trivial it may seem, it just might be the key to solving this." Dully, the woman took the card.

"You going to be okay?" Amy asked as she stood up. "Anyone you'd like me to call?"

"Nah. I'll be all right."

"I'm in Pontchartrain North 217. Call me when you get back to campus, I'd like to hear about the service."

Mikayla nodded. She bent over as she sat, arms folded and grasping her sides, and went back to rocking as they left.

Amy waited until they were in the stairwell before she spoke. "That was agonizing. Are many interviews like that?"

"Enough," the detective answered. "You did a good job calming her down. I was ready to drag her down to the station. I don't have a lot of patience anymore." They were halfway down to the ground. "You touched her. I'm not allowed to do that unless I have to restrain someone." He sighed. "Glad you're on board, Clear."

The compliment thrilled her. "Maybe it takes a woman to calm a woman down?" She heard Paul think, "When will you learn to take a compliment? Say 'thank you'!"

"Uhh, thank you, Your Majesty."

Blinking in the sun, Riordan said, "Looks like we need to pay a visit to your lover boy."

Shame and fear replaced the pride she had felt from the detective's compliment. She thought to Paul, "Crap! What do I do now?"

She heard Paul say out loud, "You may want to reconsider the nice things you just said."

"Clear! No! Christ, tell me you did not fuck him." He was staring at her, hands on hips.

Amy hung her head.

"That is so unprofessional, to get personally involved with a suspect. This can ruin --"

"What, unprofessional?" she interrupted. "I'm not a cop. You told me you'd say you didn't know me if your boss showed up."

"Did he tell you anything?"

"Not about Laura, no."

He shook his head. "Damn, you moved fast. When did this happen?"

She looked at her shoes. "Last night," she mumbled.

"What? I can't hear you."

Amy yelled, "I slept with him last night!" Several students walking nearby turned to look but kept going.

The detective held his chin with his left hand, his right supporting his left elbow. "So he couldn't have killed Yvonne between midnight and one."

"I don't know. I woke up around two and he was gone."

Riordan stared for a moment. "If you were my daughter, Clear, I'd take you over my knee."

It was Paul who responded: "Am I supposed to say 'Daddy, what are you doing?'"

"You kiss your mama with that mouth?"

Amy took the lead back. "No, I kissed Reggie Young with it. Can we talk about something else?"

They began their walk to the East Campus to see Reggie in the gym. Trying to get past her embarrassment, she asked, "Does Jermaine have any word on that cigarette we found?"

Riordan said, "Can we talk about something else?"

The coach recognized Riordan when they entered the gym. "You need Young again?" The detective nodded, and the coach bellowed, "Young! Front!" and blew his whistle. The sixty or so sweaty men went back to basketball and calisthenics

Reggie came straight to the detective, but he said to Amy, "Hi, Lambchop." Amy held her right hand at shoulder height and waved shyly.

"When did you leave Clear last night?" Riordan asked.

"Are you kidding? I was there all night -- wasn't I, Snookums?"

Amy closed her eyes and said, "Can we have this conversation anywhere else?"

Riordan led them outside the gym, where Reggie sat on the ground by the walkway. Amy began to follow suit, but the detective grabbed her arm and pulled her back up. He whispered, "Height is dominance. Don't surrender it."

The detective asked again, "When did you leave Clear last night?"

Amy thought she saw the sun glint off Reggie's front teeth as he opened his mouth. "We fucked all night long. She kept asking for more. It was dawn before we stopped."

Embarrassment and rage filled her. "Bastard!" she cried. "You were done in five minutes!" Riordan was hiding a smile with his hand, watching smoke come out of Amy's ears. She heard Paul think, "What a creep. But calm down, please?"

She took two deep breaths, then said, in clipped, angry tones, "I woke up during the night and you were gone."

Smiling, Reggie asked, "When did you wake up?"

Riordan interrupted to say, "I'm more interested in hearing when you left."

He shrugged, "I don't know. A little after midnight, I guess."

"Where did you go?"

"Home! I was tired." He whistled, then said to Amy, "You're quite a go-er, you know that?"

"Keep it up and you'll be a goner."

Despite the smile on his face, Riordan said, "Clear, I can't let you threaten the suspect, no matter how much he deserves it." Then, to Reggie, "Was your roommate home?"

"That dweeb? I don't remember."

Riordan stared at him for a moment. "Okay, Young, you can go."

Reggie stood up and leaned toward Amy. "See you later, Honey," and he moved to kiss her.

Paul doubled their left hand into a fist and slammed Reggie in the jaw. The man fell back, raising his hands to the pain. Amy screamed; she dropped the notepad and bent over, holding her hurting left hand between her legs.

Riordan watched in wonder, and his smile became a grin. It took a few moments for Amy to straighten up -- flexing her left hand -- and say, "Oh yes, Honeybunch, I'll see you real soon."

Still holding his jaw, Reggie looked back and forth between Riordan's smile and Amy's frown. Without another word, he went back into the gym.

The detective laughed and said, "Ah, young love in bloom. What's the plan, Clear? Three kids, one of each?"

Paul tried to flash their left middle finger, but their hand hurt too much.

"Where do we find the dweeby roommate?"

"I interviewed him in the computer lab, let's try there."

As they walked, Amy thought to Paul, "I appreciate the Prince Charming defense of my less-than-perfect honor, but damn! My hand hurts."

"Bastard has a hard head. Sorry."

"I'm as mad as you are. What a waste of good looks."

A few steps later, Amy thought, "I did have a good time with him." It was a few steps after that that she heard Paul reply, "I'm glad one of us did."

A uniformed policeman was standing outside the entrance to the Computer Center. Amy waved her ID, while Riordan stopped to talk to him. Alone, she walked down the stairs to the computer lab, and headed back to the same area where Bruce Weeks was working. "Hi again," she said as she neared him, startling the man. He smiled nervously and cleared books and a clipboard off the adjoining chair to make room for her. He sat up straight, and she thought he was holding in a widening midsection.

"It's nice to see you again," he said shyly.

"I was hoping you could help me," she said, just now thinking of how to draw him into idle conversation. "My laptop is taking forever to reboot. It didn't used to. What causes that?"

"Can be any of several things." She noticed an unusual look and sound of confidence as he talked about his field of expertise. "There might be a virus on the hard drive. Something in the registry may have gotten corrupted. You may have installed a program that didn't quite finish loading. Or your login may have gone bad."

Paul thought, "I hadn't noticed a prob --"

"There isn't one," she thought back. She nodded at Bruce and said, "Oh. I'll try to troubleshoot those things. Thanks, I know you know your stuff."

The man was blushing as Riordan joined them. Seeing it, he said, "Clear? Am I interrupting?"

She kicked the detective in the right leg, where Bruce couldn't see. "No, not at all."

He introduced himself, showing his badge. "Can I ask you something?"

Bruce looked at Amy, and she nodded slightly. "Uh, okay," her answered.

"Did you see your roommate last night?"

"Yeah, for a few minutes. He got home from a date, he said. He's such a stud," Bruce finished, worshipfully.

"What time was that?"

"It was just before one, an old Big Bang Theory was still on."

"Did Reggie say anything about where he'd been?"

"Only that he had had a good time. His T-shirt was inside out, so I'm guessing he'd been with some girl."

Amy was wishing herself invisible even as she took notes.

"That's astute, noticing his shirt like that. Anything else unusual? His clothes? Did he seem nervous or anything?"

"Nope. He just seemed like Reggie. He spent maybe ten minutes with me before he went to bed, and I didn't stay up much later."

"You've been very helpful," Riordan said. "Now, I'd like you to keep this conversation to just us, okay? And if you think of anything else, my number's on the card." Bruce took the detective's business card and examined it. "Come on, Clear, *andale.*"

Amy touched Bruce on the arm as she stood up. "Thanks for the advice about my computer. I'll let you know how it goes." She waved, and he smiled.

Paul thought, "When did you turn into such a flirt?"

"When it occurred to me that I can make people like me enough to talk to me. It's not serious. God -- you don't think I'm actually, you know, coming on to people?"

He felt some relief, and thought, "A good flirt makes guys think exactly that."

"It's just a new tool in the workbox."

When they were back outside, Riordan asked, "Do you always spend time with killers?"

Thinking of Paul, she said, "Yes. Pretty much. How about you?"

"Only on the job, thank you."

"Do you think that geek is a killer?"

He laughed. "Only in the sense that a boring person kills conversation. Interesting that Reggie said he didn't see Bruce, but Bruce has all this detail."

"I told you he has a man-crush on Reggie. Reggie doesn't

notice Bruce because he doesn't care about him. Bruce probably remembers every nanosecond he's spent around Reggie."

"That's pitiful," the detective said, "but reasonable analysis. Well done, Clear."

"Reggie says he left my room a little after midnight, and Bruce says he got in just before one. Reggie could have killed Yvonne Washington."

"Very good. And you had to sleep with him. Now let's go see Stalker Girl. It's time I got to meet her."

"She's in the south hall of my dorm building. Do you want me to warn you about her? Or would you rather meet her cold?"

"With an introduction like that," he said, "maybe you ought to prepare me."

"She lives in a single room. The main room is plastered with photographs of Reggie. She seems to believe that they are a couple."

"When did UNO become affiliated with Mandeville?"

"Oh no," Amy said, "we're harmless. We may be loony toony, but we don't need bars on our windows."

"Two dead. Maybe you do."

Riordan talked to the policeman outside Pontchartrain Hall South, then walked with Amy up the stairs to the top floor. "It's this one," she said, and she knocked.

Alex Scruggs opened her door. She was dressed in black, wearing an ankle length skirt and a black T-shirt. Her black hair was in the same gravity-defying upswept arrangement. Everything set off her pale complexion and faded blue eyes. "Oh, you again," she said to Amy, with a smile. "Come in, it's nice to have company. And who is your friend?" She followed them into the living room.

Despite Amy's warning, Riordan was not prepared for the level of Reggie idolatry on display. Amy finally said, "Alex, I'd like you to meet a special friend. This is Steven Riordan."

When he heard his name, his attention returned to the woman. He showed his badge case to the woman. "It's good to meet you," she said. "Won't you sit down? It's nice to have some company."

The detective explained why he was there, looking into the deaths of Laura Adams and Yvonne Washington. "Did you know either of those women?" he asked.

"I know all of Reggie's friends," she said. Amy thought she could see Riordan experiencing the same disorientation she had on her first visit. Yes, it was the eyes.

"Tell me about Yvonne," he prompted.

"They went out a little. Not a lot. I was surprised that he was interested in a black woman."

"Do you think the woman had any enemies? Anyone who would want her dead?"

"I don't know how those people think. I don't know." Her eyes were looking in different directions, and Riordan seemed confused.

"When is the last time you saw Reggie Young?"

She smiled and said, "He was here every night this week."

"Miss Scruggs, can you tell me about your, um, decorations?"

"I love my Reggie, that's why I have his picture. Anywhere I look, I see my honey."

Amy noticed Riordan shifting in his seat, clearly uncomfortable. He said, "Please excuse me, Alex, but Reggie has told me some very different things."

"I don't know why he wants to pretend we're not together," she shook her head. "I think he's trying to protect me."

"This may seem odd, but tell me, are you under a doctor's care?"

"Me? Of course not. Whatever for?"

"First off, an ophthalmologist? And a psychologist or psychiatrist?"

Alex froze. She held her face in her hands and pulled something, then held out a hand with her prosthesis. "I lost my left eye in a car accident when I was in high school. People have told me it sometimes makes them uncomfortable, the way the glass eye looks in another direction, but I can't do anything about that."

Riordan's face went pale. "I'm terribly sorry, Miss Scruggs. I apologize for my rudeness. What about any other physicians?"

"You just won't quit!"

"It's my job to not quit," the detective answered. "Other doctors?"

"I take Risperdal." She looked down and replaced the glass eye. She blinked a few times to make sure it was in place, then looked up at Riordan. "It works wonders. I don't have delusions anymore."

Amy heard Paul think, "What was she like before the medication?"

Riordan slapped his hands on his thighs and stood up. "Well then. Miss Scruggs, I appreciate you taking the time to talk to me. You have a pleasant day. We'll see ourselves out."

Once in the hallway, the detective jogged to the stairwell and hid there until Amy caught up with him. "You could have told me about the eye!" he hissed.

"I knew she looked weird, but I didn't know it was fake."

As they clanged down the stairs, he said, "She's loonier than the computer guy. Does -- oh, I don't want to know."

"Does that mean she's not a suspect?" Amy asked.

"Anyone that crazy is always a suspect." He shook his head and made a noise, "Brrrrr."

They walked to the parking lot where Riordan's unmarked car was waiting. "I've got another case I'm working on. I have to put in some time on that. I may be back tonight to talk to the men Yvonne was dating, but it might not be until tomorrow."

Amy stood with her hands in her pockets. "I've been to two classes all week. If I don't catch up on my Psych, my father will kill me. Can you call me and let me know what those guys say?"

"I realize I don't pay you very well, but I still need your help. Don't break up the team?"

Impulsively, she hugged him around the stomach, then stepped back and saluted. "Yes Sir, Your Majesty. You call me."

✇ 16 ৯

Amy was fidgety Wednesday morning, and became more and more anxious as the day wore on. Instead of clues, interviews, and investigation, she was increasingly thinking about Reggie Young. She was in the library when she thought to Paul, "He was supposed to call me yesterday. The three-day rule, right?"

Paul shook their head. Gently, he thought back, "Only if he wants to see you again."

"But he has to! I had a good time; I want more."

"You do? I mean, from him? He's like a used car salesman on steroids. What did Yvonne's sister say -- as sincere as a politician kissing babies?" Paul was feeling relief that it appeared he would not have to endure an encore of Amy snuggling up against Reggie. But he heard the frustration and disappointment in Amy's words. "Look," he began out loud, then stopped. They were in a carrel section reserved for people in the graduate program. Two students at nearby desks looked up at her, then went back to their work. "Wouldn't you rather put him in jail?"

"Sure," she said, then continued silently, "the super-snooper in me wants that. The pissed off woman in me wants that. And the horny girl in me wants something else."

He paused so he wouldn't laugh, then thought, "What if he's a male version of Florence?"

"No," she said out loud, then continued silently, "you're just trying to make trouble."

"I don't know. Maybe where he comes from there's a four-day rule. But I promise, he'll call you Friday if he doesn't have a date lined up. A booty call."

She shook her head. "That -- that might be -- I don't know. Are all men despicable?"

"Speaking as a man," Paul laughed, "yes. Execrable, even. Particularly when they're so young. Reggie is just a child."

"Oh, come on, you geezer. He's my age, he's twenty or twenty-one."

"At any age, women are older than men. Women always are more self-aware, and more sane in their emotions. No matter how hormone-crazed a woman is, a guy the same age is even crazier. Truth."

She sat at the carrel desk with her chin in her left hand, her purse in a heap by the chair.

"Remember what I told Florence?" he thought to her. "About wanting to spend more time with your friends?"

Amy whispered, "Yes."

"You're entitled to feel disappointed and sad," Paul went on. "But if you let yourself feel too crappy for too long, you're letting the son-of-a-bitch control your life. I say we hang out with Florence and her new dress this weekend. She sounded like she'd be glad for the company."

She sat back in the chair. "It's great that you're older and wiser and everything, but it really pisses me off sometimes when you're right."

"Visionaries are never appreciated in their own time," he said out loud as she picked up her purse.

∅ 17 ∂

Friday, September 24, 2021 -- UNO campus, New Orleans

"Hold this, will you?" Florence asked as she reached for her pinking shears.

"He was gone in the middle of the night," Amy continued, "and he hasn't called in a week, and he avoids me in class." She pouted. "What did I do wrong?"

"You didn't kill him when you had the chance," Florence said dryly. "Hold that up, now," and she worked the scissors on the fabric Amy was holding. "Besides, I thought you were all police-girl now. When I found you Sunday, it was scary how efficient you were being. You really acted like you know that stuff."

"Yeah. We're in a lull. Steven is busy with --"

"Who's Steven? Hey! Hold that straight."

"The detective," Amy said, trying to pay more attention to helping Florence make the dress. "He's got other cases, we've interviewed the likely suspects, so he's not around. He called yesterday to tell me about the guys who dated Yvonne, they've both got alibis."

"Alibis," her friend laughed. "We've been friends two years and I've never heard you use that word before."

"Steven made me feel bad when I had to tell him I slept with Reggie."

"Jackass! Trying to impose his bourgeois morality."

"Actually, he said it had the potential of ruining the investigation. Until we got to interrogate him, it looked like I was his alibi."

"There's that word again."

"I told you P--, uh, I slugged him."

Florence frowned, puzzled. "You hit the detective?"

"No! Reggie. Pay attention. When we were questioning Reggie he tried to be, uh, familiar. I socked him in the jaw."

"You are amazing," Florence said. "What happened next?"

"He slunk off like the mongrel he is. Steven laughed. And my hand hurt like hell."

"That should have gotten a lot out of your system."

"I was so angry! And disappointed. And sad. And, and..."

"Mama Flo prescribes ice cream."

It was Friday night, and Amy and Florence were in Florence's dorm room. Amy was helping her friend put together a dress for a design class. Florence also planned to wear it and be beautiful all day Saturday in the absence of a date.

Amy sighed. "A friend of mine told me that if I let myself get depressed about it I was letting Reggie run my life. What do --"

"Your friend is smart," Florence interrupted. "I'll tell you the same thing. If he doesn't care enough to call, you shouldn't care enough to remember his name."

"I told you so," Paul thought to Amy.

"But I slept with him!" Amy blurted out.

"And your point is...?" She had the business end of half a dozen straight pins between her lips, and it sounded like "Nd ur oin sss?"

"Doesn't that matter?"

"Apparently not to he-whose-name-we-have-forgotten," Florence answered. "And therefore, it shouldn't matter to you."

Paul in Amy said, "But that's letting Lizard Breath control my outlook. Florence, I guess there's a part of me that's just an old-fashioned girl. It matters to me." Her friend frowned, concentrating on pinning the hem. It was Amy who added, "Oh, who am I kidding? The bastard hurt my pride."

Florence spit out the pins she was holding. "I can see that. That's what they do. I don't much take that shit." She fiddled with the marking chalk in her hand.

"What do you think I should do?" Paul asked. Amy gratefully withdrew to try to figure out why she felt angry and sad at the same time.

"I still think you should have killed him when you had the chance. Obviously you had a good time. Was he any good?"

Paul decided to give the answers Amy would if she were leading, and he nodded.

Florence took their hand and said, "I want you to listen to me very carefully. This is important. Are you ready?"

Paul nodded.

"You are young and pretty and alive. Your life is in front of you and it will be happy and successful. You don't need what's-his-face to be happy."

"That sounds like it's from a fortune cookie."

"Ah so," Florence said in an oriental sing-song, "wash face in morning and neck at night."

"Not working," he said. "Anything else?"

"You know, that crap didn't work on me the first time I had my heart broken, either."

Amy laughed, and Paul stepped back mentally to let her lead. "What did you do?"

"Revenge. Two nights later I was fucking the guy's older brother. We were an item for a little while."

"How old were -- no, I don't want to know."

"I was sixteen, and to this day I'm convinced I wasted three years of my life before that. Look, my life is my problem. Your life -- you're going to be okay. Do you feel like your life is worthless without a guy? That's just a lie evolution tells women so they'll have lots of babies. It's a crock of shit. Like the old joke says," and she slipped back into the fake Chinese speech, "'You better off.'"

Amy hung her head for a moment, then asked, "How long before I feel better?"

"At the worst, it's not until you're taking your clothes off for your next conquest. But usually --" Florence smiled and looked at her wrist watch with a dramatic flair, "-- usually about three hours. Ice cream makes it go faster, so let's pig out at Creole. I'll drive."

Creole Creamery wasn't all that far from UNO, west on Simon and Lee, a little past City Park. Florence got two scoops of rocky road, and bought a cone for Amy -- lemon custard, swathed in multi-colored sprinkles. They sat at one of the tiny tables in the shop, talking about the dress Florence was working on. Amy had several years of weekly sewing lessons with her mother, so she understood the terms when Florence went on about the bias, the warp, and the gores. But her friend used the words in a more precise way than she was used to; it gave them lots to talk about. Paul was a fan of all things female so he didn't mind a discussion of needlework, and he was glad to feel Amy's spirits improve. The conversation continued in the car back to the dorm. Paul finally said, "Can I help? I think you'll look great in this dress."

"You're already helping," Florence said. "How are you at sewing a hem?"

"Mom complained that they weren't always straight," Amy replied, "but I'm game."

It was after eleven o'clock when Amy's cell phone rang. "Hi, Amy, it's Reggie," she heard. Amy's stomach moved suddenly, she wasn't sure what it meant. And then Paul was leading, and he said, "No, I'm busy. You can't come over because I'm out with a friend."

"What?" Amy thought to Paul. "Stop! Let me talk to him."

Paul continued to lead. "When do you think you might be home?" he heard Reggie say.

"Don't know that I'll get home at all," Paul replied, while Amy continued to protest.

"Oh."

"Look, Tuesday after class, why don't you take me to lunch and we can talk?"

"What are you doing? Let me talk to him!" Still, she did not take back the lead as she could have done.

"I have an appointment that afternoon," Reggie answered.

"Change it," Paul said. "See you Tuesday, Reggie," and he closed the phone.

"I am in awe," Florence said. "I couldn't hear him, but you were amazing."

Amy led, and, distracted, said, "Thanks. Uh, can you excuse me for a minute? I have to have a conversation with myself."

She went into the hallway and yelled out loud, "What do you think you were doing?"

She could hear Paul laughing inside. "You want to get back at him, and I just made old Reggie fall in love with you." Amy was twirling her hair around her right index finger while she listened. "He can't believe how tough you are, but you weren't rude or nasty. He's going to change that appointment that may not have been real anyway. Free lunch on Tuesday."

"But I wanted to talk to him!"

Paul wrapped their arms around themself and softly said, "Talk to Florence. Talk to me. You and I can mess around in bed tonight. Reggie is just poison."

She tried to relax in Paul's hug, imperfect as it was. "I just want -- I want a guy to like me. I want someone to want to be with me." She sniffed. "And asshole though he is, he's here."

"Yes," Paul said. "I understand."

Amy dropped her arms, then wiped her cheek with her shirt sleeve. "I'm still pissed at you for not letting me talk to him," she said out loud. "But I'm glad you did it."

When Amy came back inside Florence asked, "Who were you yelling at?"

Amy was tempted to tell her the truth, about Paul, but decided not to. "Just talking to myself," she said. "I don't always agree with me."

Florence laughed. "As long as you don't throw dishes. Now take the chalk and mark the hemline on this dress."

❦ 18 ❦

Saturday, September 25, 2021 -- UNO campus, New Orleans

It was two in the morning when Amy got back to her dorm. She let herself in downstairs with her ID card, then felt her way up the dim stairs to the even dimmer hallway on her floor. She had just gotten her key in the door lock when a hand from behind grasped her by the wrist.

Paul immediately jumped to the lead. He pushed and tried to run backwards, finally shoving their assailant into the opposite wall. He heard the person go "oof!" but they still held their wrist. He felt Amy's burst of fear, and some of his own.

Paul pushed their arms down, forcing their attacker to bend down. Then he did a ballroom dance twirl, twisting themself until the brute let go. Facing the shadowy hulk, Paul jumped and landed all of their 109 pounds on the assailant's instep. A male cry of pain was ringing in their ears when Paul brought their left knee up to the man's groin. When he bent over in pain, Paul drove their right thigh into his face. There was a crunch; the man fell back against the opposite wall, and slid down to the floor.

The adrenalin was pounding in their ears. "I'm glad you know how to do that stuff," Amy thought to him. "Wow, what a rush!"

"You okay?" Paul thought to her.

"Peachy. Thanks."

Paul fetched his LED flashlight out of Amy's purse. "Let's see who the UNO Strangler is," and he trained it on the moaning lump on the floor.

"Reggie!" she shouted. "Oh god, you didn't kill him, did you?"

"I might have, if I'd known it was him," Paul laughed.

"Let's drag him into my room."

"What? No! Why?"

"I don't want him to get arrested."

Paul unlocked her door but leaned against the door frame, blocking the entrance. "There is a killer on campus. This guy is a suspect. He was lurking in wait for you, and he attacked you. Tell me why you haven't already called Riordan."

Out loud, she said, "You're right." She fished her phone out of their back pocket and auto-dialed the detective.

"Riordan. What?" She felt relieved to hear his voice.

"It's Amy Clear," she said. "You won't believe who is lying on the floor in a bloody but breathing heap at my dorm."

"Don't tease me, Clear. What do you have?"

She was grinning. "Reggie Young attacked me in the dark when I got home a minute ago. I beat him up."

"Yeah, right."

"Please come get him," she said. "Otherwise I might stash him in my closet and keep him as a sex slave."

"An image I will try very hard to erase from my mind," he said. "You're serious?"

"About the attack and the beaten up, yes."

"Let me call the station house; I'll be there soon. What's your room number?

"217 North, Pontchartrain Hall. If he comes to, I'll beat him up some more, okay?"

"I'll be there soon," he said, and hung up.

Amy closed her phone and thought, "NOW will you help me get him inside?"

Amy grabbed Reggie's ankles, and they pulled him into her dorm room. He was still moaning. When she turned on the light she saw what a mess they had made of the man -- and of her clothing. Amy cried out loud, "These jeans will never wash clean." She crouched down, but it was Paul who yelled in Reggie's ear, "Hey, Loser! You got blood all over my pants!"

He shook his head, then cautiously opened one battered eye. "Damn," he said, "all I wanted was a good-night kiss."

"I'm not kissing anything that looks like Freddie Kruger. Here, you want some water?"

He put one hand on Amy's where she was holding the cup, and managed to lift his head enough to sip.

"Looks like a good night's work," Paul thought. "I'm proud of you. I think Riordan will be astounded." He knelt down and yelled in Reggie's ear, "You're lucky I don't carry a gun anymore!"

The man elbowed himself up and looked at his blood soaked shirt. "A gun? My God, did you kill me?" Feebly he struggled to move so he could sit up, leaning against the bed.

"Thought about it," Paul said. "Do you often grab girls in the dark?"

Amy handed him a towel. "What a mess," she shook her head. "Clean yourself up, we're going to have company soon."

"Give me a minute," he said into the towel, trying to staunch the remaining bleeding from his broken nose. "Ow, ow, ow," he muttered.

Amy abruptly asked, "Why did you call me tonight?"

Sheepishly, he said, "I didn't have a date, and you were good in bed. It pissed me off you didn't jump at a booty call. Did I do something wrong?"

Paul laughed. "Not in bed. Everything else, though."

"I don't feel good," the man said. Before Paul could tell him it would be a miracle if he did, Reggie turned his head and threw up on the linoleum floor. Twice. No, three times.

"Oh, crap!" Amy shouted. She turned to yell at him, and saw he was still. "Don't you die on me, you son of a bitch!" she said, poking him. He snorted, but remained unconscious.

Amy stepped into the hall and went down to the janitor's closet to commandeer paper towels, a mop, and a bucket. "What is it about the smell of barf that makes me want to throw up?"

Paul thought back, "Common sense? I'll work the mop."

"Like it matters," she said grimly. Back in the room, she began swabbing the mess. She saw a lot of blood had spilled from Reggie's nose over his shirt, his jeans, and her floor. "Maybe I'll just move out in the middle of the night. It's not like UNO charged me a security deposit."

She was about finished cleaning her floor when she heard footsteps and voices in the hall, coming closer. A moment later Riordan and two uniformed cops were in front of her. "Are you all right, Clear?"

"Yes, Your Majesty," she said, and stepped back to allow them to enter. "He's not," she added, pointing the mop at Reggie where he lay.

"Whew!" from Riordan, "Who blew chunks? It's enough to make me want to throw up."

Amy grabbed her trash can and gave it to the detective. "I've cleaned up his mess, I'm not cleaning yours."

One of the officers doffed his cap and said, "I'm Mullinax. What's going on here?"

"Now, now, Woody," Riordan said, "this is my collar. Clear, what's going on here?"

Amy told them how Reggie surprised her in the dark outside her dorm room, and how she (Paul still being her secret) brought him down. "He said all he wanted was a good night kiss. I hope he likes what he got."

Riordan knelt by the half-conscious man. "You're under arrest for assault," he told him, and read him his Miranda rights. "I'm going to look through your pockets now; do not struggle."

"Wha?" Reggie Young's brain had not yet returned to earth.

"Damn," Riordan said. "No necklace, nothing that could be a garrote." He stood up. "Clear, do you wear anything around your neck?"

"No. I don't have pierced ears, either."

"Too much information." Riordan turned to his pal Mullinax and said, "Let's you and Murphy here hoist Mr. Young up and get him to Charity Hospital." Looking back at Amy, he said, "He walked into a door, right?"

"A door," Paul said, with her voice. "Silly me, I thought they were called knees."

Riordan took the lid off his styrofoam cup of coffee and splashed the warm liquid on Reggie's face. It made the student start. He shook his head, then brought his hands to his nose, muttering, "Ow, ow, ow."

Murphy and Mullinax bent down and pulled Reggie up by his armpits. He swayed, so the officers stood on either side and draped his arms over their necks. "Amy, what happened?" he asked through his swollen face.

"Cheer up," Paul said. "For a few days you're going to have the biggest balls on campus."

The policemen laughed, then walked Reggie out of Amy's room and outside to the waiting squad car.

When they were alone, the detective sat on the desk chair and rubbed his face. "I need sleep!" he said. Then, to Amy, "Now that the cops aren't here anymore, tell me what happened."

Amy let Paul describe their response to Reggie's attack. Part way through, Riordan interrupted to say, "Do you know you have blood all over your pants?"

"There was a lot more on the floor before I mopped up the barf. As soon as you leave I'm going to soak these jeans to see if I can't save them." She sat down on the edge of her bed. "Does this mean we've solved it? Are we safe on campus again?"

"Probably, but not definitely. I'd be more confident if he'd had a weapon with him. Maybe he was doing a copycat thing, after the love tap you gave him outside the gym. Maybe he just exercised some bad judgment."

She nodded, disappointed that Riordan didn't sound more confident that the danger on campus had passed. "Do you need me to make a report or something?"

"Nah. I'll write it up in the morning. I may call you if his side of things is too wacky. Tomorrow I'll get a warrant and search his room." He rubbed his cheeks. "And eventually I'll get some sleep." He stood up to go. "I'm glad you're okay, Clear. I am impressed with the way you walked him into a door. With luck this case is almost over. Thanks." At the doorway he stopped and turned to add, "Don't call me before noon tomorrow. Please?"

As soon as he was gone, Amy emptied her pockets, took off her jeans, and threw them in the sink to soak overnight. She didn't bother to brush her teeth, she just lay on top of the bedclothes.

Amy and Paul both still were wired from the excitement of the battle with Reggie, and the visit from Riordan and the police. "I'm so tired," Amy said out loud, "but I may never get to sleep."

"I have an idea," Paul said, and rubbed their left hand down their right arm, and then down their right leg as far as he could reach. Then he worked his way back up, past their waist, lingered for a moment at their bellybutton, and lightly touched their stomach up to their breasts.

"Nice," Amy whispered, "I like that." She sat up long enough to remove her underpants, then lay back on the bed. "I love you, Paul," she whispered, "I can't imagine my life without you."

Paul used their left hand, 'his' hand by their practice, to gently tease their right breast. He heard Amy sigh, and felt her retreat inside. That gave him both hands to caress themself, to begin coaxing their body and her mind to excitement and surrender. "I'm so glad I'm here," he whispered as he touched their body. "I am the luckiest man in the world."

✄ 19 ✄

The next day Amy met Florence for brunch in The Cove. Her friend was wearing the dress the women had worked on the night before -- red flowered print, low neckline, lower back, skirt just above the knee. The way it draped showed to advantage every curve and swell of Florence's body. The conservative hemline was a contrast to the daring framing of significant cleavage. The color alone drew attention; the cling and display kept it. She was stunning in the dress.

Amy was wearing cut-off jeans shorts and a UNO sweatshirt. The first thing Florence said was, "What happened to your legs?"

Amy looked down. There were ugly black bruises on both thighs and knees from the overnight fight with Reggie. Paul laughed and said, "You won't believe me when I tell you. But that dress -- you look fabulous!"

"I told you I would. If I don't get an A+ in design I'm transferring to Tulane."

Amy and Paul both stared at Florence and her dress. Amy was not the frilliest of women, while Paul had no understanding at all of fashion. But the impact of Florence's body on the dress was riveting. "I can't get over it," Amy said, "you look amazing."

"I made it just big enough so I can eat lunch," she laughed, then stood up. "Let's get on line, I'm buying."

Florence loved the attention she was getting. A woman in front of them on the lunch line praised the dress. Two men behind them were staring. The cook said it was a bit early in the day for wearing that dress. Amy and Paul kept saying "Wow!" to each other.

Back at their table, Florence said, "So what's the deal with your legs? You look like you spent the night in a Cuisinart."

"You won't believe it," Amy said. "I don't believe it. When I got home Reggie was waiting for a good-night kiss."

Florence's eyes bugged out. "Kiss hell, you look like you broke the bed."

"No, just his nose," Amy smiled. "He thought it would be cute to hide and grab me in the dark. I beat him up."

"And then broke the bed?"

"No bed breaking involved. I slammed him into a wall, kicked him in the crotch, and broke his nose." Amy was enjoying dawdling over her burger and fries. "We didn't find out who it was until he was laid out on the floor."

Florence stared. "You -- you really beat him up?" she said slowly. "You are an amazing creature, do you know that?"

"Thank you, thank you very much," Amy said in a fake Elvis Presley voice, and she picked up another french fry. "Ruined the jeans I was wearing; I couldn't get all his blood out."

"So, did you call the police?"

"Dragged the detective out at two in the morning. Reggie's in jail. With luck, no more dead students."

"Remind me never to get on your wrong side," Florence said. "I thought you talked a great game when I heard you on the phone with him last night. But you're the real deal!"

Smiling, Amy drummed her fist on the table in cadence as she said, "Don't - fuck - with - Amy!"

Florence saluted and said, "Sir, yes sir, sir!"

"As you were," she laughed. "Where are we showing off that amazing dress today?"

"I've got it all worked out. We'll go to the East campus around 1:30 to walk around the ball fields. It'll be fun to watch the jocks try to impress me. At 2:30 or 3:00, we'll hang out in front of the library, make them all feel bad about studying instead of knowing *moi*. Late afternoon we'll cruise the dorm complexes, give all of those mooks an eyeful of what they never can have. Then I think we can go into town, get us some oysters or crawfish, and see if we can't fool some bartender into selling us hooch.

What do you say?"

Amy clapped her hands. "Sounds great. Maybe I ought to change clothes -- not that I have anything to compare with your dress."

"That's the idea, Sweetie. Look good, but don't compete with the main attraction."

It was Paul who said, "Meet you back here after I find an outfit that won't embarrass either of us. Assuming you aren't whisked away by some hunk while I'm gone."

"You didn't bail on me for what's-his-mook," Florence said. "I will always love you for that. I'll still be here."

℘ 20 ও

Monday, September 27, 2021 -- UNO campus, New Orleans

Amy was surprised to find she felt guilty about Reggie going to jail. In the privacy of her dorm room, Paul said, "HE's the one who should feel guilty. Hell, he IS guilty. He attacked you. If he's the UNO strangler, we can assume he was going to kill you. And if he's NOT the murderer, he's guilty of extreme stupidity. No, no --" Amy was shaking their head in disbelief "-- you are fine. He's the culprit, not you."

"I hear you," she replied, "I just don't feel it." She was sitting on the edge of her unmade bed, thinking about feeling sorry for herself. Part of her thought it was sweet that Reggie wanted to steal a good-night kiss, but the rest of her was impressed at how decisively Paul had responded to the apparent attack. The difference between a boy and a man, she imagined.

"Feel what you want," Paul said, "but use our brain. You did not do anything wrong. Reggie Young did."

"But -- but if I hadn't slept with him this wouldn't have happened. If I hadn't wheedled my way into the investigation, this wouldn't have happened. If --"

He knew they couldn't both speak at the same time, so he interrupted by thinking to Amy, "And if he hadn't attacked you in a dark hall at one in the morning, this wouldn't have happened. Christ, if your parents had never met this wouldn't have happened. Amy Clear, you deserve to be alive. You don't owe anyone an apology, least of all Reggie Young."

She sat for a moment and patted their left hand -- Paul's by their agreement -- with their right one. "It's going to take me a little while to get my head around this."

"Sure. Meanwhile, the school is safe again and we probably ought to do something about those Psyche lectures we've missed."

ॐ 21 ॐ

Wednesday, September 29, 2021 -- UNO east campus,
New Orleans

Amy and Florence were catching their breath after a particularly long set that finally ended when Florence made a strong return to the left while Amy was racing to the right. "You're getting a lot better at this," Florence gasped.

"Thanks," Amy panted back. "Give me two minutes," breathe, "and I'm taking," breathe, "the next game."

Florence took a long gulp from her water bottle, then poured some of it over her head. She shivered and shook her head. "Tell me, what's it like to be the new Nancy Drew?" she asked.

"Fun," she said. "It feels great that we're safe again, and I won't lie, it feels very nice that I'm the reason."

"You keep amazing me," Florence said. "Are you going to change majors now? Does UNO even have a criminology department?"

Amy shook her head. "Math's what I'm good at. I want to do market research, maybe political polling. Still..."

"Hmmm?" her friend asked, while wiping her neck with a towel.

"Florence, it's over! All that excitement, and now -- poof, it's all gone. I'm bored, I'm depressed. I am dreading my psychology reading."

"Post partum depression. Don't have children."

Amy twirled her racket, then tried to balance it on her index finger. "I like the detective, Steven. He's cute and he's smart and he's successful, and he let me help. He taught me things about crime scenes and interrogations, all that stuff you see on TV shows."

"So why did you sleep with Reggie if the detective is the one you want?"

The racket fell at Amy's feet. "No. He's more like the brother I never had. He thinks I'm smart. He let me do things like take notes, and he was pleased with how I did it. He even liked how I helped when he talked to suspects. Do you have any idea how good that made me feel?"

Florence nodded. "Did your father neglect you or something?"

"What? No! I love my dad. Why?"

"Wanting approval," she shrugged.

"Didn't you like it when your design instructor went gaga over that dress?"

"Good point," Florence said. "He's gay, so I know it was the dress he liked, not what was underneath it."

Amy heard Paul think, "When are you going to introduce me? I like Florence. She's a good friend."

"I don't know," she murmured aloud.

"What?" Florence asked.

Amy shook her head. "Just talking to myself, as usual. Come on, I'm ready to trounce you at this silly game." As they went back on the clay court, Paul thought to Amy, "This is building up. You really have to give me some Paul time. It's getting to me again."

"We'll see," she whispered, then lunged left to return Florence's serve.

☙ 22 ☙

Thursday, September 30, 2021 -- UNO campus Cove, New Orleans

Paul was leading as they looked through the new issue of the UNO student newspaper, *Driftwood*. It was just a four-page tabloid; they'd be finished with it before their hands had a chance to get dirty from the ink. There was a two-column display ad on the back page that grabbed Paul's attention.

"Want to go to a gay bar?" he thought to Amy. They were in The Cove, waiting to get hungry enough to eat dinner. She was putting off some studying.

"Not really," Amy thought back.

"Sappho Rising," Paul thought, "it's just down Elysian Fields, I think we could walk there."

"Why?"

"You've been upset about Reggie since he left in the middle of the night. You know I love you, but aside from me and your dad you have terrible taste in men. Let's go make friends with some women."

"Friends with some -- What? No!"

"Your only friend these days is Florence. You get along with her. And I've been getting antsy about being hidden in the attic of your brain -- you know how I get every once in a while. I say 'dress up and let's go.' I'll lead, okay?"

"There are only two letters in the word 'no,' how can you misunderstand me?"

Paul sighed aloud. "So what do we do tonight? Get a pizza and watch Wolfman Mac's Chiller Drive-In on TV?"

Amy looked away from the paper, but she didn't reply.

"It's just to play," he thought to her. "Something to do to kill an hour or two. Honest, I'll lead."

She put down the newspaper but stayed seated, silent. Even though they shared the same head, the same brain, they had to aim thoughts for the other to know them. Paul waited, but all was quiet.

He took the lead. He grabbed the paper, stood up, and left The Cove, headed for their dorm. Still nothing from Amy. In their room, he opened the closet and looked at their clothes.

"The red blouse," she said out loud. "Forget the camisole. And that little black skirt."

"Want to help?" Paul said as he took the items out.

"No, it'll be more fun to watch you try to put them on."

Paul pulled their UNO sweatshirt off over their head, and then stepped out of their jeans. He walked to the full length mirror so Amy could watch him struggle with her clothes. The red blouse was easy enough. But when he pulled up the skirt, Amy laughed and said, "Zipper goes in the back." He slid it around their waist until she said, "There you go."

"What about shoes?"

"I think the white running shoes will work. In case we get to dance."

Paul found the shoes on the closet floor, and bent over to tie the laces. When he was done he stood in front of the mirror and said, "How do we look?"

"Oh, God," she said, "my makeup is awful!"

Paul said, "I've watched you do it for years and I still don't have a clue. Either you make us beautiful, or I'm just washing our face."

"Move over," she said and took the lead. She leaned into the mirror, and touched up foundation and eyeliner. "That'll do," she said. "I don't want to break too many hearts tonight."

Paul looked at the pretty woman with the shoulder length brown hair. Grey eyes under heavy eyebrows. A small nose. A friendly smile, with a crooked front tooth. "You look great," Paul said. "Be my valentine?"

"You said you'd lead, so let's get going," Amy said.

"*Andale!*"

It was a short walk to the campus bus stop, near the administration building and right by the entrance to the under-used amphitheater. Paul waved at a few people he recognized from Amy's classes. Waiting for the bus, Paul thought, "I've missed this sort of thing. It's even a charge to say hello to that guy from our Psych class."

"I don't know his name," she thought back.

"That doesn't matter. You know him by sight, and he knows who you are. It's the participation in real life. It gets old being cooped up in the back of someone's head."

They got on the southbound bus. Amy showed Paul where she kept her change, in a blue plastic container that opened when they squeezed the edges. "Is that what you've been talking about?" Amy thought as they walked to a seat near the rear exit. "About people?"

"Pretty much," he thought back. "And tonight I'll be able to strike up a conversation with a stranger or two. I expect that'll be fun. Yeah, I've missed it."

"Don't dump me in the parking lot," Amy thought, and Paul laughed.

"I promise. We're going to have a good time tonight. Uh, am I Amy? Or Paulette?"

It was her turn to laugh. "Oh, Paulette! I can't wait to see you like this."

Paul was excited about an evening out, an evening in the lead. He was glad Amy was in good spirits.

They got off the bus at Gentilly Avenue and walked two blocks east. When they were outside Sappho Rising, Amy said out loud, "Here goes nothing."

Paul paid the five dollar cover charge and stepped into the club's large main room. The bar was shaped like a narrow horseshoe, anchored at the back wall, and going halfway to the front of the club. Paul thought it made for a lot more standing room than a conventional design. There were twenty five or thirty tall tables scattered around, with two to four stools at each. The decor was green and pink -- green carpet, pink table tops, and one long accent wall painted the color of bubble gum.

He couldn't tell where the music was coming from -- he

didn't see a jukebox, and the stage in the middle of the pink wall was bare. XM/Sirius, he thought, playing dance music from ten years earlier.

Amy thought to him, "If I didn't know better, I'd say this looks like a normal bar. But where is everyone?"

He looked at their watch: 7:45 on a Thursday night. He saw two bartenders, two waitresses, and no more than a dozen patrons. Paul thought. "No bar with a pink wall can be called normal."

As he sat at the bar, Paul thought, "What do you want?"

"Anything but vodka."

When the bartender came over, Paul said, "Hi, I'm Paulette. I need a big diet Coke, but I promise I'll tip like it's liquor." He laid a five dollar bill on the bar.

The bartender was six feet tall. She looked to be about forty, with short black hair in a pixie cut. She wore a Sappho Rising T-shirt over black waiter pants.

"I'm glad you understand how this works, Honey," she answered. "I'm Maggie. I haven't seen you in here before."

"Yeah, I'm new," Paul said. "Looks like I'm early."

Maggie brought an enormous glass of soda to him. She shrugged. "Never can get the hang of Thursdays. Some weeks the fire marshal would be here by now, some weeks it's so dead I wonder why I bothered to come to work."

"So -- what happens in here?"

"Last night was team trivia, that's always a hoot," she said. "And we finally got the place cleaned up from the Harvest Moon party last weekend."

"You work here long?"

"I'm sorry, Sugar, did you just ask me when I get off work?"

"I might be persuaded," Paul answered, "but what I meant was, how long have you worked here?"

"Ah. Okay. Uh, three, uh, yeah, three years and some."

"Are you from NOLA?"

"Gretna. You local?"

"Metairie. Now I'm at UNO."

A party of seven or eight people came in, and Maggie excused herself to look after them. "You having a good time?" Amy thought. She was drowned out by the young woman standing behind them who said the exact same words.

"I'm sorry?" Paul said as he twisted his bar seat to look at her. He saw a pretty smiling face, streaked blonde hair in a strange variety of lengths. She looked to be sixteen. And he couldn't help but stare at her crooked front tooth.

"Are you having a good time?" she repeated, still smiling.

"Yes," he said, "and suddenly it's even better. I'm Paulette. Wh --"

"Christine," she interrupted. "Can I join you?"

"Please," Paul said. "Let me buy you a drink. What would you like?"

"Oh, whatever you're having."

Paul laughed, "Are you sure? This is just diet Coke."

"Well," Christine crinkled her nose, "maybe a Dixie?"

He turned and waved at Maggie. When the bartender reached them, she said, "I'm glad you met. Christine's been a friend of the bar for forever. What can I get you?"

Paul ordered, then said to Christine, "You don't look old enough to have been coming here more than three weeks. What's your secret?"

"Oh, you're a doll," she said. "But if we're going to talk about looks, I have to tell you, I love that tooth." Christine smiled, showing off her own crooked tooth.

"I think we must be twins," Paul said. "I like yours, too."

Amy didn't say anything, but she was engaged. She was enjoying seeing the world the way Paul usually did, as a hidden observer; and she was seeing Paul in a brand new way, leading. His confidence was infectious, and he wasn't creepy or stupid about talking up Christine. She thought to herself, "What a great guy."

At some point, Paul excused himself to use the bathroom, and Christine said, "Wait, Paulette, I'll come with you." He paused, uncertain, until Amy thought to him, "It's okay. That's what women do." Once inside the restroom, Christine touched them on the arm and said, "Want some?" She was holding an open compact with white powder over the mirror.

Amy gasped and thought, "What is that?" Paul smiled and said, "No, but thanks, I appreciate the offer."

Christine snorted a bit through a sawed off soda straw, then snapped the compact closed and put it away. She looked in the mirror over the sink and kept wiping her nose. Paul said, "I'll be right back," and he let themself into a stall to answer nature's call.

Christine was waiting when he emerged. As he washed their hands, Paul thought the woman was vibrating. "You like that?" he asked her.

She shrugged. "Sometimes. It wakes me up."

When Paul tossed the paper towels into the trash bin, Christine stepped in front of him and smiled. "You're special," she said. Paul began to feel a combination of excitement and fear, wondering if the woman was about to prove herself some kind of crazy. "You drink Coke in a bar, and you turn down coke. And you're nice. I'm not used to girls like you."

Paul smiled at the complement. "I'm not your typical --"

Christine pushed herself against him and kissed him with an open mouth. It was Paul's first erotic touch with a woman in thirteen years, since he woke up in then-eleven year old Amy. His response was totally male: he hugged Christine tightly and returned the kiss. He moved his hand to touch her breasts through her dress, and he thrilled at the barely remembered sensation of feeling a woman without also feeling the hands that were touching her. Christine held Paul's head in both hands and continued the kiss.

Paul heard Amy think, "Check, please." He ignored her. She added, "I need something to drink to survive this. Please, please stop."

And so Paul did. He stepped back, breaking the kiss, then he leaned forward to hug Christine. She whispered, "I'm sorry, but I, I wanted you."

He squeezed her and said back, "No apology needed. That was wonderful. You have no idea what this means to me."

Christine leaned back so she could look at Amy. "I hope it means you like me."

"Yes, Christine." He kissed her again, a quick peck. "Yes, I like you."

The woman hugged him again, and she whispered, "Paulette. Paulette."

"Do you like me?" he asked.

"Oh, yes. I like you lots."

The bathroom door swung open, and two women came in, talking loudly about a movie. When they saw Paul and Christine, one said, "Isn't it a little early for that?" Her friend laughed, and they moved into a stall together.

Paul let go of Christine and smiled at her. She took his hand, and they walked back into the main room of the bar. "Can I have another beer?" she asked him.

Paul said, "Yes, of course. I need a couple of minutes to talk to myself, but I'll be right here. Okay?"

Christine's eyes got wide, and she softly said, "Wow." Then she turned to find Maggie and order another drink.

Paul sat next to Christine, and thought to Amy, "What just happened?"

"Were you trying to teach me a lesson or something?"

"Huh?"

"That was uncomfortable. Why did you kiss that girl?"

"I didn't know I was going to until she kissed me."

Maggie brought the beer. Christine took a long gulp, then took Paul's right hand in her left. She was smiling, waiting.

"You knew this was going to happen, right? That's why you wanted to come here."

"Not quite. I only fantasized about it happening. I expected we'd have a drink, talk to some strangers, and go home. Just the two of us."

"She's pretty forward."

"How old do you think she is?"

"A little older than me, maybe twenty-three or twenty-four."

"Really? I'd have guessed seventeen."

"You boys are so easy to fool."

"You got that right." He shook their head. "What she did, I think she must be lonely."

Amy shrugged. "Talk to her, she's waiting for you. But let's go home in, ummm, thirty, forty minutes? Don't want to wear out our welcome here."

Paul turned to Christine. He lifted her hand and kissed it. "I'm back," he said.

She smiled, the kind of smile a happy child wears. It was a little unnerving in an adult. "Done talking to yourself?"

"Yeah, thanks. Tell me --"

"I do that, too," she said. "I talk to myself a lot."

"How so?"

"There are three of us."

"Uh-oh," Amy thought to him.

"Are all three of you real?"

Christine smiled again. "No," she said, "just me. But the others keep me company."

"I think I understand," Paul said. "I've only got one other person, but she's real."

"That must be great," Christine said. "Are you friends? Or do you fight?"

Amy thought, "Oh, let me," and she took the lead. "We're friends," she said to Christine. "We fight sometimes, but friends do that."

"I wish mine were real," she said.

"Can you make your voices stop?"

"Not really. I have to take pills for them."

"Sounds like they may be real."

Christine's eyes widened. "No," she said, shaking her head. "No, they're not real. They tell me bad things. If they're real, then I'm not real."

It hit Amy and Paul that Christine was not playing; she seemed to be coping with real mental illness. "She's sweet," Amy thought to Paul, "Tell her they're not real."

Paul stroked the woman's arm and said, "Listen to me, Christine. You are real. They are not. You are better than them. You are more important than them. Do you hear me?"

"Thanks, Paulette," she answered. "Sometimes I need to be reminded. How do you do it?"

He shrugged. "I don't know," he said, "I have no idea. I just do."

Christine's mood picked up at that. She began talking about where she lived, and where she worked, and carried on a pleasant and sane conversation. Almost two hours passed before Paul saw Amy's watch and said, "Ohmigod, I've got to go home."

"Can I come with you?"

Paul smiled and shook his head. "Not tonight, Christine. It's too soon. But I hope I see you in here again."

As he stood up, Christine leaned forward and hugged their midsection. Suddenly she pulled their blouse up out of their skirt, and licked their bare midriff. "Paulette," she said.

Paul kissed the top of her head and said, "Take care of yourself. See you."

Outside the bar, Paul looked through the tinted window. He could see Christine was staring out at him. He smiled and waved, then walked up Gentilly to the bus stop on Elysian Fields.

"How did it get to be so late?" Paul asked while they waited for the bus.

"I guess we were having a good time," Amy thought back.

"What a relief! I was afraid you were going to scold me all the way home and then make me sleep on the floor."

"Silly boy," she laughed inside. "There were a few minutes I wasn't crazy about, but mostly I had a good time. Why did you keep kissing her?"

It was Paul's turn to laugh, out loud. "You have to ask?" He nodded absently at an older woman who came to stand at the bus stop.

"I was jealous," Amy thought. "I think I understand now. What you went through when I was with that guy I dated last year, and with Reggie." After a moment, she thought, "I had no idea what a kiss is for you. Christine is the first person you've kissed since we've been together."

He nodded, thought back, "I guess so. You know how much I'd give to be able to kiss you."

Softly, she said, "It would blow me away." Then, "It's not like I'm the Triple Breasted Whore of Eroticon Six, but I've kissed a guy or three. Damn, what you could teach them." He felt their right hand grab their left bicep, squeezing it.

He imagined his smile getting so broad that the top of their head could flip back. "That's the best compliment any woman has ever given me. And I thought Christine had made my day. Can we do this again some time?"

"I don't know," Amy said softly, out loud. She went on silently, "You pretty much promised Christine you'd be back for her. I have to think about it. About all of it."

He nodded their head and said, "Fair enough. Can we talk

about it?"

"About what, Honey?" the other woman at the bus stop said.

"Oh, I'm sorry," Paul said, embarrassed. "I was talking to myself. How are you this evening?"

"You're one of those girls, aren't you? From that club?"

Her words puzzled Paul, so Amy came to the front. "Yes, I guess I am," she answered.

"Are you happy?" the woman asked.

"I think so," Amy said, confused. "I mean, life could always be better, but -- yes, I'd say I'm happy."

Paul added, "How about you?"

The woman said, "You're right, life could always be better. But I've got friends, I've got a job, I've got a place to live, and I've got plans. Pretty sweet, actually."

"Good. What do you do?"

"I'm on my way to work now," the woman said. "I'm a prostitute."

"The way you look," Paul said, "business should be good."

"Oh, you're a sweetheart," the woman laughed. "If some man hits on you, send him to me at the Upstart. I'm there most nights."

The Elysian Fields bus finally came and opened its door. Paul let the woman enter first, and then he sat next to her halfway back. "I appreciate the company," the woman said, patting them on the knee.

Amy asked, "How long have you been at Upstart?"

"I don't know," the woman answered. "My, uh, my manager has a bunch of places, and I go where he says he needs me."

"Pay good?"

"Yup. Even after my manager's cut."

"What'll you do later?"

The woman looked at them, then said, "I don't get off work until six o'clock."

Paul laughed awkwardly. "No, I mean, what will you do for a living later in your life?"

"Oh," she nodded, "I keep up my beautician's license. I'm part owner of a shop in the Garden District. When the time comes, I'll go back to cutting hair."

Paul nodded. "Sounds like you have it worked out. Good."

The woman pulled the bell rope and stood up. "This is my stop, Honey. Thanks for the company. We'll be seeing you." Amy waved and the woman left by the rear door.

"She seemed too nice to be a hooker," Amy thought.

"Whores are people too," Paul thought back.

"Have you -- I mean, did you ever use a prostitute?"

"Nope. I knew a few, though. They were nice enough, but they seemed so tough."

"What makes them do it? Nymphomania?"

"Maybe. I always thought poverty, though. I love the madame in *Mrs. Warren's Profession*. Although I don't think Shaw wanted me to."

"It doesn't bother you? That she's a whore?"

"Nope. I'll bet she's more honest about sex than most husbands and wives. And I don't see any victims."

Amy thought to him, "That class last winter in women's studies said all prostitutes are victims."

"I don't remember this. Victims of what?"

"Uh... Male privilege and patriarchy, I think."

"Pttthhhhh!" Paul stuck out their tongue and blew. "Some guy gets laid, and she gets paid. Win-win, wouldn't you say?"

"You're in a good mood tonight."

Paul stood as the bus approached their stop. "Yes, I am," he said out loud. "I'm with my best friend in the world, and some girl stroked what little is left of my male ego. Life is good!"

"Are you hungry?" Amy asked while they walked toward home. "Let's hit The Cove, get a burger or some soup or something."

"I'm easy," Paul said, and he started whistling. He heard Amy think, "I'm paying attention. I've never been able to whistle."

"I'd offer to teach you," he thought, still whistling, "but I have no idea how I do it."

Before they got to The Cove, Amy took a few stabs at it. She was able to get some sounds out, and Paul tried to encourage her. But she shook their head, "I'll never be as good as you."

"And I'll never be as good as my father was. No reason not to do it when the spirit moves you."

Amy resumed her attempts. She thought to Paul, "Too bad we

can't both do this at the same time. Wouldn't it be neat to whistle in harmony?"

"That's a happy camper," a familiar female voice called out in The Cove.

"Florence!" Amy shouted, "I'm so glad to see you," and she gave her friend a long hug.

"What's this all about?" she asked. "Why is your shirt half undone? Tell Mama Flo, now."

Amy looked down and realized she hadn't readjusted her blouse after Christine pulled it out of her skirt. "I looked like this all the way home?" she said aloud, and she heard Paul laugh inside.

"I hung out in a bar," Amy told her friend as she tucked in her blouse. "Drank a lot of diet Coke and talked to some interesting people. You?"

"Me and a couple of gay boys went to the movies," Florence said. "Fun night." Then, "Wait -- diet Coke? You go to a bar and have soft drinks? No wonder you have trouble getting laid."

"Yes," Paul laughed, "but a fun night. You up for food?"

"I am destroyed with hunger."

Paul looked in Amy's purse and said, "I'm good for burger and fries, but you're on your own for dessert." Then he saw something small and pink, and picked it up to examine. It was a matchbook from Sappho Rising. He opened it and saw Christine had written her name and phone number; her handwriting was feminine and juvenile, with big circles to dot her i's. Amy thought to him, "Does this mean the three day rule is in effect?"

They placed their orders at the counter, then went back to their table to wait for their names to be called. "Who'd you go out with?" Florence asked.

Paul thought, "I wish we could tell her."

Amy thought back, "We can't. Not yet." She answered her friend with "You're never alone with a schizophrenic."

Florence looked up at her.

"I am not crazy," Amy began, "but --"

"There's always a 'but'. How crazy are you, Amy?"

"Pretty damn crazy, but somewhere I have a piece of paper that says I'm sane."

"Draper and Clear!" the PA announced. "I'll get 'em," Florence said, and she went alone to get both meals.

"There was something sad about Christine," Amy thought. "She's ill, isn't she?"

"I think we were good with her, though. She perked right up."

"Soup's on," Florence said as she put down the two trays. "Mine's got mustard."

They began their suppers. "So," Florence said, "you're crazy, right?" It sounded like "yur crethy, ryt?"

Amy nodded. "Yeth, crethy." She swallowed and said, "I told you a little about this. It's like my head is divided in half. I talk to myself all the time."

"I talk to myself too," Florence said.

"So you know I'm not crazy. But I seem to do it different from most people. It's like my favorite color is yellow, but the other half of me likes blue better."

Florence blinked, then took another bite of her burger.

"And until I talk to myself, I don't know what the other half of me thinks."

Florence blinked again, and put down her burger.

"We get along great, both sides of me. It's not a problem, really. Just time consuming sometimes."

"You are great," Florence said, shaking her head. "I have never known anyone like you. God, you are so, so, --"

"Crazy?"

"Well, that too. But you are so YOU."

Amy peered at her friend. "Is that a good thing?"

"Only the best, you silly cow!"

"Mooooooo. Uh-oh -- does that mean I'm a cannibal for eating a hamburger?"

"Yes. The herd will have a midnight meeting and disown you. But I'll sneak away and still be your friend."

"Oh, good." Amy wiped her hands on a paper towel. "You know, that's the second time tonight someone complimented me for being so me." She took more fries.

Florence said, "So I asked you who you went to the bar with, and you spouted this trash about being crazy. Was it with what's-his-face, Reggie?"

"That name is not to enter my ears," Amy answered, "nor

pass my lips. Besides, he's in jail. No, I went with me. And we both had a good time."

"Meet any guys? Do they have friends?"

"Actually...I got to talk to some women." Amy marked each one with another extended finger: "A bartender, a sweet crazy girl, and a hooker."

"Where were you, Mandeville?"

"Some bar down Elysian Fields," she said. "Pretty quiet. And no one gave me any crap about drinking Cokes."

"Perish the thought!" Florence smiled.

"How about you and the movie?"

"Gay guys are great," Florence said, waving a french fry. "You can borrow makeup from them, and they always sympathize when you're on your period."

"Hear that?" Amy said out loud.

Paul -- who, of course, sounded exactly like Amy -- answered, "Check!"

"Talking to yourself?" Florence asked.

"And answering," Amy said.

The women talked and joked until the PA system warned, "For your convenience, The Cove will be closing in fifteen minutes." Amy and Florence finished up their dinners and headed to their dorms. It was late.

Back in their room, Amy and Paul indulged in something they had done for ten years. After she undressed and slid under the bedcovers, she aimed her bedstand lampshade away, and softly said, "Paul?" She danced the fingers of her right hand up and down her left arm. "Paulette?"

"Front and center," he said back, out loud. "If you had half as much fun as I did, it was a great night."

"I did. It was so different. And you were so different."

"I was? How?"

"Have I ever let you lead like this before? For hours and hours? I got to see a different you."

"It's been so long since I got to do something like this! Tell me, how was I different?"

She thought, still touching their left arm. "You were a great guy." Then, "I mean, you're always, you know, a great guy and all that --"

Paul started laughing.

"No, really. You were so confident, and you weren't making ugly passes, you weren't being fresh, you didn't even swear like you usually do, you garbage mouth. You were nice to the bartender lady. And you were really nice to Christine. And even to the hooker on the bus. You talked to them like they were real people."

Still laughing, Paul said, "They weren't real to you?"

She thought more. "The prostitute, I guess not. That's so far from my world. It's like watching a movie or reading a book. I don't know how to act around a whore."

"You surprise me," Paul said. "I forget you're one third my age."

"Oh, don't give me any 'you should have an open mind' crap!"

"No, I won't. You and I have led different lives, there's no reason we should react the same way. But the woman on the bus, she asked us if we were happy."

"You don't think there's something wrong that she wasn't real to me?"

"Nope. You are who you are. Maybe you'll change, maybe you won't. You'll still be you. I like you, so that's fine with me."

"I have to think about Christine," she said. Amy fluffed her bed rest pillow and lay back against it, now sitting up. "That kiss was so... intense."

"She scared me," Paul admitted. "But I'll be honest, she excited me, too. Oh, if only I still had a dick. Was it awful for you?"

"Yes. Well, not totally."

Paul waited for Amy to go on.

"She was so needy, and she picked us. I was flattered, you know?"

"Yes."

"And I like kissing, and I don't get to do it much. It was weird, it was awful, but it was, I don't know... nice, I think. Sweet."

Paul wrapped their arms around themself. "I'm glad it wasn't totally loathsome for you."

After a minute, Amy asked, "Does this mean I'm a lesbian?"

Paul said, "Does Reggie mean I'm gay?"

"No, silly!"

"Back at you." He felt Amy smile, and now she was the one squeezing their arms in a hug. "So, will we be doing this again?"

"I haven't ruled it out. I don't know."

"This was a wonderful night," Paul said, "This was what I've told you I've been missing for so long. Talking to strangers, feeling connected to more of the world than only you. Tonight I felt like a real person, a whole person, not just a dyad personality inside you. And it was so great that you were with me. You talked to Christine and the hooker, too."

"Good," she said. "I think I understand better now what you meant."

"A kiss is always nice," he went on, "but being ME is even better. It doesn't have to be a dyke bar, we can go to the zoo, the laundromat, I don't care, but please let Paulette out again."

"I like Paulette," Amy said. She turned off the desk lamp, then lifted her hips to slip her underpants off. "I like her lots."

℘ 23 ℧

Friday, October 8, 2021 -- UNO campus, New Orleans

Amy was sitting in her psychology class, thinking about ice cream with sprinkles. Paul was taking notes on the lecture. Two rows back, a man Amy did not know but who thought she was foxy was staring at the back of her head, thinking lewd thoughts. It dimly occurred to him that he'd never noticed her writing with her left hand before.

Suddenly Amy's phone let out a ringtone from the "1812 Overture." The instructor stared at her, hands on hips. Embarrassed, Amy got up and ran to the hallway, leaving her things at her seat.

"Hello?"

"Clear? It's Reardon. Meet me in front of the amphitheater. We've got another body."

Amy ducked back into the lecture hall to collect her books and her purse, while thinking to Paul, "Crap. I finally got over feeling guilty, and now Reggie's not the killer?" The instructor again stared at her, hands on hips. Paul smiled and waved as they left.

They took the north path across the campus. The amphitheater was by the school entrance driveway, across from the bus stop they had used the night before; it was a large, raised, empty earthen area that might hold three hundred people standing, and included a bare concrete band shell. The facility was rarely used for more than an ad hoc student gathering place. "He didn't tell me much," she thought.

"I'm guessing another strangulation. I'm really torn about

this."

"You?" Amy asked. "Why?

He thought back, "Being involved in this is just as exciting for me as it is for you. But I was hoping the case was closed. This means we're still in danger."

"And I'll have to deal with Reggie again," she rolled her eyes.

"There's no law that says you have to sleep with him again."

"That's good, 'cause I'd be breaking it. He's smooth, he's good looking, but if I can beat him up that bad, he's not much of a man."

Paul decided to be grateful and say nothing.

Two squad cars were blocking the main driveway turnaround where it met the amphitheater entrance. Amy was a little surprised that the clot of police was across the pavement, in the shadow of the huge UNO marquee. While the moving lights told passersby about some community events on campus, Jermaine was crouched below, examining a body.

"Clear!" she heard, "Over here!" Riordan was waving his cigarette-holding hand, so she ran to him. "Megan Silver. Freshman. Same MO. Looks like you got the wrong man."

"Wait a minute!" Amy said. "I got the right guy -- the one who attacked me."

"Get over yourself, Sweetheart. All that matters is finding the killer."

Amy began to pout, so Paul asked, "Same necklace pattern?" The detective nodded. "Time of death?"

Riordan yelled, "Jermaine! When did she die?"

The medical examiner looked at his wristwatch. "Maybe three this morning."

Paul asked Riordan, "Is that a significant change in pattern? The first two were between midnight and one."

"Maybe," the detective shrugged, "maybe not. Her shirt was ripped open, that may be more significant. It may be a different killer."

"Who found her?"

Riordan was working on the crime scene sketch. "A woman on the maintenance crew. She got out here with a mower around eleven o'clock. She said she thought it was just a pile of clothes and she was going to mow over it, but at the last second she stopped."

Paul's participation pushed Amy past her pout; she didn't want to be left out. She took back the lead and said, "Great. The first time the scene isn't trampled by Privateer elephants, a riding mower cuts it down."

Riordan used his laser rangefinder to measure the distance to Elysian Fields Drive, the big city street on the eastern edge of the campus -- 950 feet, about one and a half furlongs. "We're going to use a strip search. The mower destroyed anything that could have been useful right up to this point, so a spiral search makes no sense. You and I will go over the rest of the area."

Amy stood by the detective as he finished his notes. She watched Jermaine use rubber bands to fasten paper bags over the dead woman's hands. The photographer had finished her work and was standing nearby, chatting with one of the campus security guards. Another woman sat on the curb, with a uniformed policewoman standing by her; Amy guessed it was the maintenance worker who had nearly run over the body.

Finally, Riordan folded his sketch into the back of his notepad, and handed it to Amy. "The spiral search went out from the body in a circle. This time the body is at the edge of the area to be searched, so we'll work like cutting the grass from one side to the other." He put on latex gloves and crouched about two feet from Jermaine, looking east toward Elysian Fields. "We'll go along here, the first area that did not get mowed, up to, oh --" he scanned the grassy neutral ground between the incoming and outgoing roads "-- that first driveway to the University Center building. Then we make right turns when we can't go straight anymore, and eventually we cover everything. Got it?" Without waiting for her reply, the detective began examining the ground. The farther they got from the body, the faster he went, but as they worked their way west, he slowed again. They were in the second pass, even with the body, when Riordan stood up and shouted, "Camera!" The photographer left her conversation with the guard and ran to join him and Amy.

"Look at this," he said to the photographer and to Amy. "Nice even lay of grass everywhere, but here the grass is bent in that direction," pointing toward Megan Silver. "In fact," he slowly walked toward the body, his eyes on the ground, "it looks like she was dragged to where she was found."

He leaned over Jermaine and said, "What's on the heels of her shoes?"

The medical examiner blinked, then took the paper bag off the body's left foot. "Grass stains. A little bit of dirt. Hmmm. Make sure you get earth samples."

Riordan fished the neon orange evidence markers from a pocket and threw them down every five feet or so along the drag marks, until they ended another twenty-five or so feet away. He motioned Amy to the side with him so the photographer could get her pictures. "Take out that sketch, Clear. I want you to update it."

When she had the sketch open and a pencil in hand, she said, "Direction?"

Riordan held up his lanyard compass. "One hundred five degrees."

"Distance?"

"Straight line," and he turned the laser measure back on. "Thirty two feet."

"How do I label it?"

"'A', drag marks."

She handed it back to the detective, who glanced at it, then returned it. "Let's get back to work," he said.

"Back to what? I thought we just found what we were looking for."

"Lazy cops are bad cops," he said. "We're looking for anything, and just because you find one anything doesn't mean there isn't another anything waiting for you." He led her to the first evidence marker, then resumed their strip search.

It took them just over an hour to complete it. Along the way they found and processed a JuicyFruit gum wrapper and a crushed plastic Barq's root beer bottle. Amy updated the sketch each time.

Riordan and Jermaine conferred by the marquee. "The ripped shirt," Jermaine said. "It might have happened incidental to the attack, or it may indicate a sexual motivation."

"In which case, this is a different killer."

"Copycats are not unknown, Steven. When I do the autopsy,

I'll check the clothing for semen. If there isn't any, I'd lean toward non-sexual."

"And possibly the original killer," Riordan added.

"What does the dragging mean?" Amy asked. She saw Jermaine smile.

"The attack began where the first evidence marker is, and the perp dragged her over to the marquee."

Paul asked, "What kind of necklace is so strong you can drag a grown woman by it? Wouldn't most necklaces break?"

Riordan stared at Amy for a moment, a hint of a smile on his lips. Then he looked at Jermaine, who said "I see why you let her follow you around. Resident ignoramus?"

Even though his words were in response to Paul's questions, Amy felt insulted. "Hey! I may not know much about forensics, but I'm not a dummy."

Jermaine laughed, and even Riordan was amused. "Resident ignoramus serves an important function," the detective explained. "You take someone who is smart -- they must be smart -- but doesn't have much knowledge of the professional procedures or expectations. Because they don't have the same viewpoint Jermaine and I have, they will ask questions that wouldn't occur to him and me. And sometimes, those questions are brilliant. You are well named, Clear, you're helping us break through the bullshit."

Amy looked back and forth between Jermaine and Riordan. She knew she had been paid a compliment, but she didn't understand exactly why. Eloquently, she said, "Huh?" even as she heard Paul think to her, "Say thank you." "Uh, thank you," she added.

Doctor Jermaine said, "You are absolutely right, young lady. Most necklaces would break between the weight of the body and the tension being applied by the killer. This one didn't. It hasn't broken over three murders. I don't know what the perp is using, but it's not a typical jewelry store silver chain."

Amy coughed. She and Paul both tried to say the word, "Oh," at the same time.

The detective was musing out loud. "If there is no sexual assault, if the torn shirt is accidental, and if time of death is off a little bit..."

"Your Majesty?"

"I'm thinking it's the same killer. Shit, Young is in jail and another one dies anyway."

Amy thought to Paul, "Great. Now I'm going to have to deal with Reggie in class again." Hoping against hope, she asked the detective, "So, this means we have to let him out of jail?"

"Eventually. The assault on you is enough for us to keep him for now, but not for too long. Shit! I was so hoping we had closed this!" They walked back to the body, now under a blanket by the marquee. "We're done here," Riordan said. "Now we need to find her roommate and see exactly who Megan Silver was."

The student directory told them that the dead woman had lived in a Privateer Place apartment on the Lakeshore Drive wing. Her roommates were Allison Grosse and Brooke Adler. Riordan had Amy call Silver's apartment, and even though it was four o'clock on a Friday afternoon, Allison answered. Amy introduced herself as a junior in the college, then said, "I am helping the police with some inquiries. May we visit you and Brooke in a few minutes?"

"Can you tell me what this is about?"

"As soon as we get to your room. Is Brooke available also?"

"I have some plans for tonight."

"Allison, you can invite us over right now, or I can put the detective on the phone to explain what'll happen if you don't invite us over. Your call."

"Jesus, if you're going to get huffy. Yeah, come over. I'll see if I can find Brooke."

"Thank you, Allison," and the women competed to see who could hang up first.

"Easy with the threats," Riordan said. "They're not under arrest; legally, they can refuse to speak to police."

Amy looked indignant. "I've watched you threaten to take people downtown when they wouldn't cooperate."

"You're funny when you're pissed off," he said. "I make threats if I think I can get away with them. And taking people downtown for questioning -- I'm not going to tell them they're wrong, but most people hear that and they think arrest." He poked the tip of her nose with an index finger, "But you are not police, so you can't follow up on those kinds of threats. And if I ever catch you pretending to be police, you'll be in a heap of pain. Understand?"

"Yes, Your Majesty," she said with a mixture of embarrassment and resentment.

"Let's get going," he said. "Since the lovely and talented Miss Grosse was gracious enough to invite us over, let's not keep her waiting."

Amy had to work to keep pace with Riordan. "What if she used to date Reggie?" she asked.

The detective said, "She was a freshman. She only had, what, four weeks to meet him?" A few steps later he said, "Of course, he didn't wait very long with you. Yeah, it's possible."

"What will that tell us?"

"That Reggie Young is not the killer. It's weird if the one common link we find among these women may just be coincidence, but it happens."

"So if not Reggie... Stalker girl?"

"Oh, please, I never want to sit in the same room with that one-eyed lunatic again. But yeah, she seems to know every move Reggie makes." He snickered, "Maybe we should see her again, let her thank us for putting her imaginary boyfriend in jail."

"Wouldn't it be strange if she and Reggie really were a couple?"

They approached the wrought iron gate to the lakefront complex. Riordan let Amy go ahead so she could pass her ID card over the swipe pad and gain entry.

"Yeah, that would be very strange. And it would be very strange if I won the PowerBall lottery tomorrow night. I think the odds of either happening are about the same. Which way?"

Amy led the detective past the swimming pool, toward the building that had been home to Megan Silver for the last month of her life. Her room was on the ground floor.

Riordan knocked on the door and called, "Police."

Immediately the door opened. They were confronted by a thin, tall woman wearing a sun dress and pearls. "What is this about?" Allison said.

"Please let us in and we'll explain," Amy said.

The woman ignored her, staring at the detective. Riordan

said, "I don't think you want this discussion to take place in the hallway. May we?"

She backed up, letting them in the dorm apartment. In the living room they found another woman on the sofa, leafing through a copy of *Town & Country* magazine. She was wearing a black dress with a short hemline. Her skin was very tan, which set off her string of pearls.

Allison sat next to her roommate, folding her arms in front of her chest. "Please tell me what this is about."

Riordan dragged a chair to one side so he was not looking directly at the women. "I am Detective Riordan with the Orleans Parish Police. This is my intern, Amy Clear." He opened his badge case, and Allison leaned forward to examine it. Brooke was still paging through the magazine, while Amy opened the detective's notebook.

"Your roommate is Megan Silver?" he asked. Allison nodded. "What can you tell me about her?"

Brooke finally looked up. "She should be home any minute. Why don't you ask her?"

Amy cringed at what she imagined would be Riordan's next statement.

"No, Miss Adler, she won't be home. Megan Silver was found dead at eleven this morning."

Both women dropped their facade of sophistication. Brooke let the magazine fall, while Allison jumped up and yelled, "What? What are you talking about?" clasping and twisting her hands.

"Sit down!" Riordan barked. Allison stopped in mid-word. "You'll have plenty of time later to go to pieces, but right now this is a police investigation and I need information."

Allison slowly sat back down. Her roommate was wide-eyed; with the sophistication drained from her seventeen year old face she looked young and vulnerable.

"You're Brooke?" he asked.

"It's pronounced 'BROOK-ee,'" she answered.

"Okay, Brook-ee. Where is Megan from?" He would say the name correctly from then on.

The woman was sitting on the edge of the sofa, leaning forward. "Miami. So am I. We sort-of knew each other there."

Amy was writing in the detective's notepad.

"Sort-of? What's that mean?"

"My daddy and her father do business together, and our families belong to the same Temple. But we never hung out or anything."

"Did that change here?"

"Yeah. I like Megan. She's really cool, her music collection is super."

"How about you?" he turned to Allison. "Where are you from?"

"Mobile. Housing put us together, I didn't know Brooke or Megan until school started."

While Riordan thought about a next question, Amy asked, "Are both of you freshmen?" They nodded, and Amy noted it.

The detective went on, "Allison, what do you think about Megan?"

"Uh, she's okay, I guess. Was."

"Okay? Just okay?"

"The first week we were here, a guy asked me out and Megan gave me shit because he wasn't Jewish."

"You know why she did that!" Brooke interrupted.

Riordan held up his right hand, palm facing the women. "You, Brooke. Why did Megan do that?"

She glared at her roommate out of the corner of her eyes, then said, "Her family is Orthodox. She said her parents made her life hell when she went out with some gentile boy in high school."

"Huh. Interesting," Riordan volunteered. "Are your families like that?"

Brooke shook her head. Allison said, "My parents are more enlightened than that. I understand why Megan tried to lecture me, but it still pissed me off."

The detective took a cigarette out of his pack, and rolled it around in his fingers. Amy saw how both the women stared at it. She heard Paul think, "I don't believe he's nervous. Is that supposed to distract those girls? Hypnotize them?"

"Did Megan have any other friends yet? Guys? A guy?" He continued to fool with the cigarette.

Brooke said "No" as Allison said "Yes."

"Oh, really?"

The women looked at each other. "Who do --" Brooke began, while Allison started, "I thought --"

"You said 'yes,'" pointing at Allison. "Who was she seeing?"

She finally turned her head away from her roommate's glare. "Two boys. One was an AEPi she met during rush; I think his name is Marvin something. And she had a couple of dates with a jock, an upperclassman --"

Despite herself, Amy said, "Oh, no."

Riordan and Allison said in unison, "-- Reggie Young."

"Oh, you know him?" the woman said.

The detective pointed at Brooke and asked, "Why did you say 'no'?"

"Megan went on about Reggie for a week, then she didn't mention him again. They may have gone out twice. It wasn't a thing."

"How about Marvin?"

Brooke laughed. "I'm sure her father would love him. He's a nice enough guy, but such a loser." Riordan saw Allison nod in agreement.

He finally parked the cigarette behind his left ear.

"Allison. Where were you this morning, around two AM?"

"Here. Asleep. Why?"

"Brooke?"

The woman crossed her legs and smoothed her dress. "Are you accusing us of killing Megan?"

"No, what I am doing is asking you where you were at two this morning. Why do you think I would accuse you of murder?"

Paul thought to Amy, "Riordan's about this close to going off all over these girls." Amy nodded, scribbling notes.

Folding her arms in front of her chest, Brooke said, "I was asleep. I had an eight o'clock class."

"Who might have wanted to kill Megan?"

The women looked at each other; one shook her head, the other shrugged.

"Did she owe anyone money? Did she do drugs? Drink? Take on the football team?"

Amy blurted, "We don't have a football team." Allison smiled, while Brooke said, "That's just nasty!"

"I'm sorry if I offended you," Riordan said tersely, "but Megan Silver is dead. Somebody killed her. She is the third victim on this campus, and I want to identify the perpetrator before there's a fourth one. Can either of you tell me anything useful?" Silence. Brooke picked her magazine up off the floor.

He stood up and said, "Show me her room. My intern and I want to examine her things."

A shared look, and Brooke said, "Do you have a warrant?"

"I will need a warrant when I want to look at your room. Megan is a victim, not a suspect, plus she's dead. I don't need a warrant to search her room for clues about her death."

"I don't know about --"

"Clear! Will you talk some sense into these, these lovely ladies, before I say something they will regret?"

Amy went to the sofa and sat on the coffee table, her face only inches from both women. "Three dead. A white woman, a black woman, and now a Jewish woman. I live in Pontchartrain Hall and I'm scared. You knew Megan, so help us make sure she is the last victim. We might learn something important from her cell phone. Her diary. Her wallet. A post-it on her computer. Please help us save lives."

Brooke repeated, "I don't know about it."

"God damn it!" Riordan exploded. "I don't give a flying fuck about the dime bag of grass or the naughty pictures. I'm trying to save some lives. Maybe even your lives!"

Amy saw the women wince. Finally, Allison said, "Okay. What can we do?"

He handed several pair of latex gloves to Amy, and began pulling on his own. "Show us her room."

Allison and Brooke led them to the second bedroom, and one of them reached in through the open doorway and flicked on the overhead light. Even though the university-supplied furniture was in good condition and the accommodations pleasant, the room looked barely lived in. It was too tidy. Amy said out loud, "There's nothing on the walls."

"Good call, Clear. Four weeks; maybe Megan hadn't finished moving in yet. Do you see her purse?"

Allison said, "A couple of my things are in here, let me get them out of --"

"Stop!" Riordan yelled, and the woman froze. "This is now a police investigation area. Do not touch anything in here until I release the room."

"But I need my --"

"Do not make me restrain you," the detective said, low but forcefully. "Out! You can look from the hallway if you want, but I want you out of this room." When Allison continued to stare, he raised his voice: "Now!" She scooted to the doorway and stood next to her short roommate, watching.

Amy was afraid she'd be embarrassed if she looked at the women, so she scanned the room for Megan's purse. It was Paul who asked, aloud, "If she was out at three AM, why wouldn't she have her wallet? Wouldn't she need her ID card to get back in the dorm?"

Satisfied that the roommates were staying out of the room, Riordan turned to Amy. "Excellent point. Maybe she thought she was staying out for the night." Still looking in drawers and cabinets, Amy nodded.

"Shit," the detective muttered, "she's got a desktop computer."

"Problem?" Amy asked over her shoulder.

"Yeah. Only way to get it to the lab is to unplug it, and forensics yells when you do that. Do one of you ladies have a thumb drive I can borrow? The bigger, the better."

Brooke said, "I may have."

"Do us both a favor and erase it before you give it to me. And thanks." He sat at Megan's desk and started by examining the computer monitor.

Allison gasped when Amy opened the top drawer in Megan's clothes bureau. Riordan heard it and turned to see Amy picking up a black rectangle, three inches by two inches. One long edge was sculpted into finger grips. "What's this?" Amy asked. Riordan tried not to laugh while Allison said, "Can I get that out of your way?"

"Toss it to her, Clear," he said. Then, to the roommate, "I told you I don't care about her damn one-hitter. But don't let me see that again." He turned back to the computer.

"Cell phone!" Amy cried. "Wallet!" She poked around the

drawer some more, and said, "What kind of woman doesn't have a purse?"

Brooke returned with the thumb drive. "Thanks, Sweetheart," the detective said, and he plugged it into a USB port. When he rolled the mouse, the screen lit up. Over his shoulder, he asked the roommates, "Tell me about her Facebook page."

"She doesn't have one," Brooke said. "At least, she never mentioned it to me."

Riordan double-clicked the desktop icon, and a browser opened with a "Welcome to your Facebook account." Windows supplied the user name, Larissa. "Password, anyone?"

No response. So he did some right clicking, looked at properties, and chuckled. "There we go. Password is "escape4ME." He entered it and hit enter.

He was looking at the administrator's view of the Facebook site for Larissa. He clicked on the first entry, dated September 6, and read aloud, "Hey everyone, I'm Larissa. I'm starting college today. I don't want anyone I know to know it's me (like my parents LOL), so I'm not going to say where I'm in school, or what my real name is. I'm looking forward to a lot of fun, and maybe even some studying. I haven't met my roommates yet."

"What does she say about us?" Allison asked.

Ignoring her, the detective said, "Miss Clear, let's you and I trade places. I want you to go through this on-line diary thing, and I'll look at the phone."

"Uh, okay. The phonebook has an entry for a guy named Marvin, Marvin Rubin. No listing for Reggie, but there were several calls back and forth to his number. Uh, September 17th," she scrolled through the register, "18th, the 20th, the 21st, and... and that's all."

Riordan was standing in front of her. "You are a quick study." He took the phone. "Experiment on your own phone, see how you can find out what number has the most minutes, and the most number of calls. Usually it's boring answers like mommy and daddy, but sometimes we learn something useful."

"You can get that out of a cell phone?" she asked, incredulous.

"Go through her Facebook stuff. Take notes. If there's anything juicy, read it out loud, okay?" He noticed Allison whisper something to Brooke, and then both women walked away and out of sight.

Amy read silently. On the 7th Larissa met her roommates; she thought they both were great girls. By the next day she had had a fight with Allison -- Amy was surprised she used the woman's actual name -- because she disapproved of a man who asked Allison out. She expressed regret on the 9th. Allison had become standoffish, but Larissa couldn't make herself apologize.

"I have my first date with a college man," she wrote on the 10th. "His name is Reggie. He's a jock, and my parents would hate him, HATE HIM, and that makes it even better. He says he'll take me some place where there's liquor and maybe more (wheeee!). It's tomorrow! Wish me luck!"

There was no entry on the 11th. On Sunday the 12th Larissa said, "I guess college won't be all that different from high school. The boys are all hands, and if you let them think they've won you over, they're finished in four minutes. Reggie's okay and all, but I had to tell him I wasn't done yet and he said he was. So I shoved him off the sofa and he fell on the floor. I told him if that was the best he could do, he could stay on the floor. What Cousin Adam could teach this guy. Anyway, he got pissed at me and told me to get dressed, if I was going to be like that he didn't want to be with me. I told him "With pleasure." I was putting my jeans back on and that little chai pendant daddy gave me fell down -- the loser broke my necklace. When we got back to my dorm I asked him if he was going to call me again. He had a crazy look on his face and he said, 'You mean you want me to?' "Maybe," I told him. I took his hands and pressed them onto my tits and kissed him really hard, then I went inside. He doesn't know which way is up. Boys are so much fun!"

The last mention of Reggie was the next day. "He called me after dinner and asked me what I was doing. I told him I was taking pictures of myself in the mirror for a boy I know at home. He said he has a real camera, he'd be glad to take pictures for me. I told him thanks, but I could take care of that myself. In fact, I could take care of everything myself. He said goodbye. Sayonara, Loser."

Later entries included getting drunk with Brooke and some

other woman, being interested in an English class, and getting angry that her parents wouldn't send her more money until the end of the month. A few entries mentioned Marvin by name, and one mentioned enduring a date with him. With no explanation it said, "I convinced him he didn't want to do me."

"This is so BORING!" Amy shouted.

She heard Riordan laugh. "Strangers' diaries usually are. Anything useful?"

She scooted back in the desk chair and turned it to face him. "Actually, yes. Megan and Reggie went out once. They slept together, she was disappointed, and she seems to have humiliated him."

"Great motivation to kill her," the detective said. "Except Reggie was in jail." He furrowed his brow, chin in the fingers of his right hand. "Does he have a minion? An underling? Someone who would murder people for him?"

Amy laughed, but it was Paul who said, "What was that you said about the PowerBall?"

Riordan opened a document-sized manila envelope and began filling it with things in evidence bags: cell phone, wallet, thumb drive, some photographs, and something she couldn't identify. "We're done here for now," and he stood up. "I'm going to tell the roommates not to set foot in this room, just so I know they'll feel guilty when they come in for the rest of their dope. Maybe they're going to take some clothes. It doesn't matter, but I'll make them think it does."

"You need a vacation," Amy observed. "You didn't used to be this mean."

"Absolutely right, I do need a vacation. And the odds of getting one are like the PowerBall. You have no idea how it screws up your view of the world to deal with a domestic murder/suicide."

When they reached the living room, Riordan shouted, "Allison! Brooke!" There was no response, although Amy was pretty sure they were still in the apartment. "You must stay out of Megan's room. We'll be back." and they left.

They walked back to the parking lot by Amy's dorm, where Riordan always parked. "What happens tomorrow?" she asked.

"Tomorrow?" he mused, "Nothing. Jermaine has weekends

off. I'm going to jump on him on Monday to give me some results. I have to know if there were signs of a sexual attack. And I'd like to know if there's anything useful on the gum wrapper and the pop bottle."

"Who gets to tell Megan's parents?"

He gave a sigh of relief. "We have a communications division now. They get to deliver the news. Poor bastard, I don't envy him."

"Do you think the parents might have some information to help us?"

"No." He took the cigarette from behind his ear and saw the paper had begun to dissolve from his sweat. He pitched it into the grass, then took a fresh one from the pack and lit it with a bright yellow lighter. "Three dead, all from different cities, two different states -- there's nothing about their home life that has anything to do with them getting killed." He exhaled thick plumes of white smoke through both nostrils. "I don't know that the killer is a student, but it's somebody local."

"Marvin?" Amy asked.

"Yeah, Monday I'll talk to him." He saw Amy frown and corrected himself, "We'll talk to him. Maybe he knew Laura or Yvonne."

They were standing next to Riordan's car. "I want to talk to stalker girl, see if she knew about Megan," Amy said. "If she does -- well, she's not in jail."

"As long as you don't make me come with you," he whined.

"And her neighbors," Amy went on. "If we don't believe Alex about her and Reggie being a couple, why are we believing Reggie when he says they're not? Shouldn't we try to find out for ourselves?"

"Absolutely right. But the difference is that stalker girl is delusional, and Reggie is only egotistical."

After a moment, Riordan asked, "Was Reggie as bad in the sack as Megan said?"

Paul felt their face beginning to flush. Still, Amy answered, "He wasn't iron man, but he was okay." She thought for a moment, and added, "Maybe I'm not as demanding as Megan Silver was."

ᛩ 24 ᛪ

Saturday, October 9, 2021 -- UNO campus, New Orleans

Paul was humming an old Beatles song and wishing John Lennon were turning 81 years old, when Amy woke up. "Coffee," she said, weakly, "Must. Have. Coffee." She sat up in bed for a moment, then fell back down.

"I have a great idea," he whispered aloud. "Let's get us some coffee. Then maybe a shower. A nice, lazy brunch, just me and my best friend." He felt Amy's smile spread across their face. "Then maybe we pay a visit to the neighbors of Alex the stalker girl, and to Marvin Rubin. And we can top it off with a call to that Christine woman we met at the club."

"You sweet talking devil," she laughed, "that sounds better than reading six chapters of psychology." They wrapped their arms around themself, the closest they could get to hugging each other. "Are you having as much fun as I am with this?"

"I think so." They stood up and gathered things for the shower. "It's different, seeing how the things on TV really work. And Riordan trusts us." Finally, Amy slipped on her terrycloth robe, and they walked to the dorm bathroom. Paul thought to her, since they were in public now, "It's fascinating to see pieces of these people's lives. I'm so glad we're not them. If you had been like that Allison, I would have throttled you years ago."

Amy turned on the shower. "And if I were like Allison," she thought back, "I'd have let you. Why do you -- Oh God! That's cold!" She hopped out and adjusted the spray, then stuck her hand under the water to sample the temperature before getting back in.

"The necklace," Paul thought. "What looks like what we saw

on the bodies, but is strong enough to hold maybe a hundred and fifty pounds?"

"Plastic," Amy said out loud.

"Only kids wear plastic necklaces," he thought to her as Amy lathered their hair.

"Maybe that's Jermaine's job, to figure it out." Then, aloud, she said, "I love this! The detective, the medical examiner, the photographer, and we're on a first name basis." Paul liked the smile on their face, but not the taste of shampoo.

"When can I call Christine?" he thought.

"I haven't decided that we're going to. Of course, you practically promised her you would, you bad boy."

"I'll beg if you want me to," he thought. "How about, Please? Pretty please with sugar on top? Pleeeze, pleeeze, oh pleeeze?"

"What's so special about her?" Amy asked, rinsing her back.

"It's not just her. It's leading, being in charge of my life for a little while. I've told you how much I miss just talking to strangers. And this one talked back."

She turned off the shower and grabbed a towel before stepping onto the bath mat. "She did more than talk," she snickered.

"Well, that too. I don't much like it when you kiss guys, and that was my first romantic kiss with a woman in a million years. I want more."

"Ugh. I don't like where this is going."

"I understand. Put up with it for me? Like I put up with it for you?"

She was back in her room and answered, "If I do it like you do, I'll be complaining every second of the way."

"Yeah, I guess so. Look, I'll take it!"

"We'll see," Amy said. "Three day rule, we've got until tomorrow to decide. Where are my jeans shorts?"

After a sandwich at The Cove, Amy headed for Alexandria Scruggs' dorm. Her intent was to talk to the neighbors, not Alex. She took out the picture of Reggie that Riordan had given her, and knocked on the door to the right of Alex's.

A young Japanese exchange student stuck his head out and said, "Uh, yes?"

"I'm Amy Clear. I'm a junior, I live in Pontchartrain North. I'm helping the police with their investigation into the, uh, attacks on campus." She held out the photograph. "Have you seen this man visiting one of your neighbors?"

The resident pushed his eyeglasses against his face and squinted at the picture. "No, I don't think so." He looked up. "Sorry."

"Thanks for your time," she said, and moved to the door on the left side of stalker girl's. She heard a woman's voice getting louder as it approached the door; when it opened, a student was holding a cell phone to her ear. "Hang on, Isabel," she told the phone, then said to Amy, "What's up?"

Amy repeated her opening, and held Reggie's picture out.

"Hey," the woman said, "he's cute."

"Have you seen him in this dorm?"

"You know, I think I have."

Amy heard Paul think, "Bingo!" "When?" she asked the student.

"I think...yes, it was about two weeks ago. I heard something in the hall so I looked out. I'm pretty sure it was this man, he was talking to Alex next door."

Amy took the picture back. "Has Alex mentioned this to you?"

She laughed. "Alex doesn't mention anything to anyone. Have you ever tried to talk to her?"

"Oh, really? What's the problem?"

"Well, I don't know if she's stuck-up or fucked up, but she's got the social skills of a parking meter."

Paul thought, "Is there another Alex on this floor? Stalker girl is strange, but I didn't notice anything like that."

"Have you had problems with her?" Amy asked.

"Not really. A couple times I said hello in the hall and it was like I wasn't there."

Amy nodded. "Parish police appreciate your help." She took the woman's name and contact information, and after the door was closed, she wrote up her notes.

Alone in the hall, Amy thought, "Two weeks, that's, uh, September 24th?"

"That's after Yvonne was killed, and before we beat Reggie

up. What was he doing here?"

"Change in plans," Amy said out loud, and knocked on Alex Scruggs' door. "Let's ask."

"I was wondering when you'd get around to me."

"I'm sorry, Alex," Amy replied, off balance. "We've already talked a couple of times."

"I meant now. I heard you snooping about me. Why?" The short woman stood with her hands on her hips, her unseeing left eye looking down the hall.

"It's part of a police investigation," Amy replied. "May I come in?"

There was a long pause before Alex said, "No, I don't think so. Not today."

"O-kay,"Amy drawled. "I want to ask you --"

"No!" she said, forcefully. "I want to ask you why you got my honey arrested."

Paul thought, "How does she know that?" Amy started to say something about the ongoing investigation, but Alex blurted, "You're the bitch that got my man locked up!"

"Uh, actually, I'm the bitch your man attacked in the dark in the middle of the night."

"He was just playing. My Reggie would never hurt anyone."

It was Paul who spoke, of course with Amy's voice. "How about you, Alex? Would you ever hurt someone?"

Alex stared without smiling. Finally she said, "Maybe you better come in," and stepped aside.

"For God's sake," she heard Paul think, "don't let her get behind us!" Amy pivoted to face the woman, and walked backwards into the main part of her dorm room.

"Can I get you anything?" Alex asked. "Water? Coke? It's really nice to have company." She motioned to the sofa, then sat at the other end of it.

Amy's mouth suddenly went dry, but she was afraid to ingest anything from stalker girl's hands. Instead, she said, "One of your neighbors thinks you don't like company."

"Maybe I don't like their company. Besides, it's not against the law, is it?"

Remembering how Riordan had challenged Allison the day

before, Amy said, "You're the only one talking about the law. Why is that?"

She shrugged. "I'm picky. I only like quality people." After a moment she added, "People like you."

Amy heard Paul think, "Uh-oh. Hold on to your wallet."

"What about Laura Adams? Yvonne Washington? Megan Silver? Were they quality people?"

An unmistakable sniff. "Low quality."

"You said Reggie would never hurt anyone. Could you? Maybe people you thought of as low quality?"

"Why would I want to hurt anyone? Uh, what's your name again?"

"Amy Clear. You don't have to look me up in the directory, I'm in 217 North. Tell me, what would it take for you to hurt someone? Them making eyes at Reggie? Them getting naked with him? Them --"

"You're being silly. My Reggie is loyal. He tells me everything. I know about him and these trashy girls. He always comes back to me."

"Doesn't it make you angry when you see them together? When you know they sleep together?"

"Angry?" she said. "No. I feel sad for them. They're wasting their time with him."

Amy heard Paul think, "This woman is living in Egypt. She's in denial." She understood, but wasn't amused. Instead, she asked Alex, "When's the last time you saw him?"

"It was yesterday week," she said quickly. "He spent the night here."

Paul thought, "Not possible," and then Amy said to Alex, "No he didn't. Reggie spent that Friday night in a locked room at Charity Hospital. I watched the police drag him off at three in the morning."

Alex looked down at her shoes and said nothing.

"I'm concerned about you," Amy said. "You've given us statements. Reggie has talked to the detective. Other people have. And all these reports, uh, they conflict. We don't know what to believe."

Alex stood up and fixed her right eye in a stare at Amy, even while the left one seemed to be evaluating the entire room.

"Believe this. Reggie Young is mine. You can keep your harlot hands to yourself. I will never forgive you for getting him in trouble. Do you hear me? Never!"

Reflexively, Amy also stood up. She was thinking of a response when Paul thought, "Maybe we should just leave. No wonder Riordan doesn't want to be in the same room with her!"

Amy held their right hand against their neck, palm out, thinking it might protect her if Alex tried to throw a garrote over them. At the door she turned to face the stalker girl again.

"It was nice to have company," Alex said.

Amy handed her one of Riordan's business cards. "I'm glad you think so."

When the dorm door closed, Amy thought, "We're going back to my room. I need a friendly bathroom." She heard Paul laughing all the way to the outdoors.

Afterwards, Amy wrote up her interview notes for Detective Riordan. Then she looked in the student directory to find Marvin Rubin, the other man the late Megan Silver had dated. He shared a triplex apartment in one of the Privateer Place buildings.

When he answered his phone, Amy introduced herself and said, "I'm working with Orleans Parish detective Steven Riordan. We're investigating the three student homicides at UNO. I understand you were friends with Megan Silver."

"Oh, God, yes," he said in a high pitched voice. "Please, you must find the man who did this!"

"I'd like to visit you in a few minutes to ask you some questions. Is that all right?"

"Oh, I'm about to get dinner." She heard some clucking noises, as if the man were thinking. "Can you meet me at The Cove in a little while? I'll buy you dinner."

Paul thought to her, "Who would have thought that helping a police investigation could help you meet guys? Does *Cosmo* know this?"

Amy laughed, which confused Marvin; then she said, "Sure. Thirty minutes?"

He agreed and was on the verge of hanging up when Amy said, "Wait! How will I know you? What are you wearing?"

"Black slacks, and a pinstriped dress shirt. You?"

"Uh --" Amy looked down to see how she was dressed. "Light blue jeans shorts, a white polo shirt. I have brown hair and a crooked front tooth."

"Smile and I'll find you," he said in his odd voice.

When she ended the call, Paul said, "So, we need to know if Marvin knew Laura and Yvonne."

Amy nodded, and said, "And how did she convince him not to do her. What does that mean?" When Paul didn't respond, she added, "You're a guy, what does that mean?"

She felt him shrug. "Maybe she threw up."

"On purpose? Euuuuwwww."

"I thought they were telling women to piss themselves to stop a rape."

"You're kidding." Amy responded. "Who's telling us that, the tooth fairy?"

Half an hour later Amy walked into The Cove. There were thirty or so people, at tables, on line, and milling around. She felt silly doing it, but she wore an exaggerated smile to show off her crooked front tooth as she looked around.

Amy saw a man in a pinstripe shirt seated with two other men, so she walked toward their table. As she got closer, she saw all of them were wearing skullcaps. "Marvin?"

All of them turned to face her. One said, "Over here." Another said, out of the side of his mouth, "Who's the shiksa?"

The first man stood up and extended his hand, saying "I'm Marvin Rubin." Amy shook it and introduced herself. "Sit, sit!" he said, patting the chair next to him.

"Maybe I didn't make myself clear on the phone. We need to talk privately." One of the men elbowed the man next to him.

"These are my fraternity brothers. It's okay."

She stared at him. He was a few years younger than she was, with a smooth face and short cropped kinky hair. "Marvin, this is an official police matter." She imagined what Riordan would do; then she turned to the other men at the table and said, "You'll have to excuse us for a few minutes. Marvin?" and she motioned to a vacant table nearby. She heard Paul think, "That was pretty damn smooth."

His fraternity brothers made a hubbub, but Marvin made a funny face and stood up, moving to the table Amy had indicated.

"What's the big deal?" he asked, "they're my friends."

She smiled at him and said, "I need to find out what you think, not what they think. This is important."

He stared at her.

"I am not a police officer," she began, "but I am interviewing you on behalf of Detective Steven Riordan of the Orleans Parish police." She opened her notebook on the table. "This is about Megan Silver."

"Ah, yes. Such a shame. I liked her."

"Considering that school began just four or five weeks ago, did you consider Megan a friend?" He nodded. "Did she think of you as a friend?"

"I hope so, but I don't know."

"Tell me about your relationship."

"This is embarrassing," he offered.

"Now you understand why I wanted to speak to you privately," she smiled. "I'm not here to judge you, Marvin, and it's too late to embarrass Megan. Tell me about her."

"We met at a Greek mixer right after school started. She's very pretty, and classy, and she turned me on. So I talked to her. We went out a couple of times."

Amy wrote in the notebook. "Do you know anyone named Larissa?"

A puzzled look. "Should I?"

"The question is if you do. It has nothing to do with 'should'." The man shook his head.

"Did you know a senior named Laura Adams? A woman named Yvonne Washington?" Both times he shook his head.

"Back to Megan. Do you know if she had problems with money? Alcohol? Drugs? Gambling? Any self-destructive or bad habits?"

"Not that I saw," he said. "She told me she was going to call her parents for money. Her family is well off. I don't know about drugs or gambling. One time I tried to get her drunk but she had a good idea when to stop."

"Was there anyone who disliked her?"

Marvin laughed. "Megan was a great girl, but she was very dislikeable. She said she got into a fight with one of her roommates right off the bat. Some of the upper class girls at the mixer resented her because she was pretty and self-confident. I think they were jealous."

"Interesting," she wrote more notes. "Jealous. Enough to want to harm her?"

"God, no," he said quickly. "More like pair her off with someone fast so she'd be out of their way."

"I don't understand that." She put down her pen. "Is it because I'm not in a sorority?"

He laughed again. "Maybe. You're not Jewish, are you?"

"Not unless my parents have been lying to me. Does that make a difference?"

"The short answer is 'yes.'"

She thought to Paul, "Does this make any sense to you?" She heard him think back, "Sorry. I'm from West Virginia. I don't think Jews grow there."

"Whatever," she finally said. Amy picked up the pen again and said, "Megan kept a diary of sorts. How did she convince you not to do her?"

The color drained from Marvin's face for a moment, until a deep red crept upward from his neck. "What a thing to say!"

"'Do her'. Those were her words. What happened?"

"I -- uh -- Look, that's really none of your business." He folded his arms in front of his chest.

Amy smiled to soften her words: "Megan Silver was murdered. It is very much the police's business if you or anyone else had a motive. I already told you, I'm not here to judge you; I just need to know what happened two weeks before her death."

Marvin leaned forward so he could speak softly. "That was the night I couldn't get her drunk. We had been flirting and making out, and I wanted to sleep with her, and I was sure she wanted it, too. It was in one of the upstairs rooms at the fraternity house. We took our clothes off, and we played around. But --" and he stopped.

Amy looked up from her notebook. "But what?" He was staring at the ceiling, mouth open, silent. "Marvin. But what?"

"It was so infuriating. So neurotic."

"Hmmm?"

"Damn it, I'm embarrassed!"

"It's allowed. What happened?"

He seemed shocked by Amy's response. After a moment he leaned toward her again and explained, "I was ready to explode. We'd been fooling around for a while. I got between her legs and I was going to, you know, when she held her hands up against my chest to stop me. She said, "Not again!"

She heard Paul think, "Oh no. You mean stalker girl may not be the craziest person in all of this?"

"What did she mean, Marvin?"

"I have no idea. She never explained. So I didn't go into her. I hoped she just wasn't quite ready. We went on kissing and humping and all that. I tried again later, and she said, 'Only the head, no more than that.' I thought that was pretty strange, but I'm a man, I'll do anything to get laid -- uh, excuse me."

Amy nodded with a smile. "Go on."

She kept saying 'Only the head, only the head,' and she started thrashing around so I couldn't even do that. It pissed me off. Also it was -- no, it pissed me off."

Amy thought to Paul, "Am I missing something? Is this a game I'm supposed to play with guys?"

She felt him shake their head, "I can understand why a horny seventeen-year-old might be mad enough to kill a girl for something like that. I am so glad you're sane."

"So, what? No happy ending?" Marvin nodded. "What happened to your relationship after that? Did you still talk? Were you still friends?"

"Yeah," he said. "We even talked about it a little. She -- one day she told me her father would think I was great."

"What does a woman mean when she says that?"

"I decided it meant something good and said thank you. She had her weird ways, but I really liked her. I wanted to go out with her more."

Amy wrote some more notes. "Did she have other friends? Did she go out with other men?

"I assume so, but I don't know. I didn't -- I was too afraid to ask her."

"Did she wear a necklace? Maybe --"

"Oh, yeah. She had a chai on a silver chain. Actually -- well, she did when I met her, but that night we were together, no, she didn't have anything around her neck."

Amy handed the man one of Riordan's business cards. "I appreciate your time, Marvin. If you think of anything that might help us with our investigation, please call detective Riordan, or me. I'm in Pontchartrain North, 217."

Marvin stared at the card. Without looking up, he said, "I think I promised you dinner."

"It's okay. I've already eaten. Thanks again." As she stood up, the fraternity brothers looked at her. Amy waved at them and left The Cove for her dorm.

As she walked, she thought, "I need to talk to Reggie's roommate again. Alex's neighbor said she saw Reggie over there a couple of weeks ago. Maybe Bruce knows what that was about."

"Can I call Christine?"

"What? Oh, the woman from the club. I still don't know."

"You're having a blast. I'm enjoying this police stuff with you, but I'd like some Paul time. Paulette time."

"I'll decide tomorrow. Oh, dear God, I don't want to read that Psych!"

☙ 25 ☙

Sunday, October 10, 2021 -- UNO campus, New Orleans

"As soon as we get back, I've got to do laundry." Amy was pulling at the front of her T-shirt, trying to hide the obvious lines of her bra. "This is the only thing I've got that's clean."

"Maybe it'll, uh, encourage Bruce to talk to you."

She smiled as she picked up her notebook. "He's already sweet on me. It would be mean to lead him on."

As they walked to the Computer Center, Paul thought, "So, we're trying to find out if Reggie has maybe seen more of stalker girl than he admitted? Maybe even two weeks ago?"

"And I get to tell him my laptop is behaving much better since I took his advice." Notebook in one armpit, she was rubbing her upper arms to warm herself.

"I don't remember, what was the advice?"

"I don't remember what the problem was supposed to be. Am I turning into a horrible person?"

"Nah. Just a flirt, and that's an okay thing. When I was in college I knew a girl who'd rub herself all over me when she asked a favor. I was always quite helpful, as I recall."

A chilly policeman was standing outside the Computer Center. "May I see your ID, miss?" he asked.

Amy gave him the notebook to hold while she looked through her wallet and dug out her student ID. The policeman compared her to the photo, and said, "What's your business here today?"

"I'm looking for Bruce Weeks. He helped me with a computer problem."

The officer swiped her card to unlock the door, then gave it back to her, along with the notebook. She waved while Paul muttered to her, "Nervous! I don't like cops."

Amy went downstairs to the lab. Sunday midday, and Bruce was the only person in the room. She waved and shouted, "Hey, Bruce!" When he heard his name he looked around until he recognized Amy, and then he smiled. He waved back.

By the time Amy reached his work area, he had cleared a stool and swept his computer paraphernalia to one side. "It's nice to see you," he said, shyly, but he touched her arm. Amy took his hand in hers and squeezed. "Thanks for the advice. My laptop is feeling a lot better now." She hoped he didn't ask her what had been wrong with it.

"So, what did you do?" he asked, enthusiastically. "Was it the registry?"

"Uh, I downloaded some utility to tweak the registry, yes. It did the trick."

"Great. What program did you use?"

She shook her head, "I don't remember. I didn't care, as long as it worked."

He was silent. She hoped he was nervous being so close to a woman, but she was afraid he somehow knew she was lying. She asked, "How's the dorm room now with Reggie gone?"

"I miss him," he said. "I never got to see him much, but he's a good guy. A good roomie. I'm mad at whoever got him in trouble." His jaw muscles were flexing, and Amy felt a twinge of fear. Then Bruce blinked and said, "Wait -- was it you -- are you the one who beat him up?"

She hung her head. "Yes. Twice, if you count the punch in the jaw."

"Wow. Wow! I will never mess with you, I promise."

"I'm glad to hear that, Bruce. I'm sure everything will get straightened out soon enough. Look, you've been real helpful with the investigation. Can I ask you some more questions?"

She thought he nodded, so she went on, "Did you know Megan Silver?"

"Oh, sure. Reggie went out with her. I didn't think she was very nice."

"Really? Why not?"

He shrugged. "She seemed, I don't know, kind of smug. And

when Reggie came home after a date he was angry."

"Did he say why?"

"Nah. We had a beer and watched some TV. I had a good time."

"When was that, Bruce?"

He thought. "Three weeks ago? Maybe a month?"

"Hmmm. Do you know if Reggie has talked to Alex Scruggs lately?"

"Yeah! Took me by surprise," Bruce began. "He went to see her a couple of times this term. A few weeks ago he said he was going over there and he didn't come home that night. I think maybe he likes her again. Well, a little, anyway."

"What do you think of her?"

"I only met her a couple of times. Oh, and I sometimes see her at the bookstore. She's okay. If you don't pay too much attention to her eyes." He snorted.

"Who else has he gone out with this term?" she asked, nodding.

"He doesn't bring many of them by the dorm, so I don't know their names. Sometimes he stays at the frat house. He's only home maybe three nights a week."

"My God! What is he doing?"

"He says he's spreading Reggie Joy around. He's so cool."

Amy looked at the detritus on the work bench. A couple of circuit boards, some lengths of wire, a dozen cable ties, some spaghetti, and a soldering iron in a stand. "I'm impressed that you know what to do with all this stuff." She shook her head, then said, "I wanted to thank you for helping me, you rescued my laptop. I'll see you, okay?"

He touched her on the arm again. "Nice to see you. Amy."

They waved as they passed the policeman standing guard outside the Computer Center. Amy mused, "I wonder... Do you think Bruce might have killed Megan because Reggie wanted him to?"

"Ah! The minion hypothesis. He's got such a crush on Reggie, maybe he would."

"And is Alex Scruggs telling the truth? Are she and Reggie a number? I knew we were wrong to assume she was lying."

"Do you think Reggie's reputation has gotten in his way? You know, first two, now three of his conquests dead? Maybe no one will go out with him any more except Alex."

Amy giggled out loud, then thought, "I can't wait to tell Steven what we've found."

Back at the dorm, Amy set up her Psych book at the desk, with Paul's novel underneath it. They each read, although several times Paul had to shout, "Wake up! I can't read if you close our eyes!" After an hour, Amy said, "I've got to do something else for a while."

"Never mind the laundry," Paul said aloud. "I want to call Christine."

"Yes. Okay."

Paul dialed Christine's number from the matchbook she had sneaked into Amy's purse at the bar. She answered on the third ring with a weak and weary, "Hello?"

"Hi, Christine. This is Paulette."

The woman's response grew stronger. "Paulette! I was afraid... Oh, I'm so glad to hear from you. I had such a good time meeting you."

"Me too," Paul said. "How have you been?"

"You told me I was more important than the voices, so I've been taking my pills."

"That's great. Did you have a good weekend?"

She sighed. "I thought about you a lot. But I went to the park yesterday."

"What park do you go to?"

"LaSalle. Do you know where it is?"

"I grew up in Metairie. You know the patch of trees past the playground area? One of them was my climbing tree."

"Let's go there together sometime."

Amy nodded their head, so Paul said, "Yes, let's. I'm thinking of going back to Sappho Rising," he dragged out the words long enough for Amy to think to say "Thursday again." He went on, "Thursday. Do you think you might be there?"

"Definitely! Absolutely! Let me put it on my calendar." Paul heard the noise of the phone hitting the floor. In the distance Christine yelled "Oh, my God!" There was more noise, and then Christine was apologizing for dropping the phone. "I'm so clumsy, I don't know why you want anything to do with a dumbbell like me, I'm --"

Paul interrupted, "Will it make you feel better if I drop my phone, too?" He was glad to hear the woman laugh. "I'll see you Thursday night, Christine. Hey -- thanks for the matchbook."

"Thank you, thank you," Christine said. Before the call was disconnected, he heard her away from the mouthpiece, yelling like SpongeBob, "Yaaayyyyy!"

"What have we done?" Amy asked.

Paul thought to her, "Old Chinese proverb, 'Never fuck anyone crazier than you are.' We may be in trouble."

"Trash mouth! I feel sorry for her. And what she said about thinking about us, and how happy it made her for us to call -- it makes me feel good."

"Hmmm?"

"Some of it is that we're doing something that makes her happy. And that anyone wants so much to spend time with us. Christine likes us."

Paul nodded their head, and said out loud, "I do believe she has a crush on us. Yeah, it is sweet. I just hope she doesn't turn out to be too crazy."

Amy took back the lead, and found her place in the psychology textbook.

Paul said, "What if she wants to kiss me again?"

He felt a smile start on their face. "Feed me liquor this time. I'll deal with it."

✺ 26 ✺

As soon as she answered her phone she heard Riordan talking with no punctuation. "Jermaine says no sign of sexual assault the torn shirt must have been an accident he says the ligature went deep enough to indicate the woman was dragged like we thought the Barq's bottle had been in the sun for weeks and had nothing to do with the woman the gum wrapper didn't show anything the dirt on her heels matched the area"

She waited for a few seconds of silence before she said, "Good afternoon, Your Majesty. How was your weekend?"

"My head feels like a jackhammer. No, like the pavement under a jackhammer. I've got an appointment at LSU for some dent student to fix my toothache."

Paul said, "That's what you get for chewing nails. Hey, we did some work this weekend."

"Who's 'we'?"

Amy heard Paul think, "Shit." She said, "Me and that voice inside me. I interviewed that man Megan went out with, and I went to see stalker girl and talked to her neighbors in the dorm, and I visited Reggie's roommate again."

"Which one are you going to go out with next?"

"Hush!" she said, laughing. "I've got a date with somebody who's not even a student, so there."

"Quick before the pain pill kicks in, what did you find out?"

"Seems that Megan Silver was full of herself. Not only did she humiliate Reggie sexually, she also pulled a similar number on this Marvin guy. However, Marvin didn't know Laura or

Yvonne; he's just a freshman."

"So if he has motive, it's just over her, not the others. Ouch. What else?"

Amy was standing beside a cement bench, on the path between The Cove and the math building. The weather had gotten a little warmer, but it was a gusty day. "Reggie spent a couple of nights with stalker girl. One of her neighbors recognized Reggie's picture, and then Bruce the roommate confirmed it. Alex tried to say the last time she saw him happened to be the night he attacked me, but maybe she was confused about the exact day. Could be she's not quite as woo-woo as we thought."

"You took notes?"

"Professor Riordan taught me well."

"Good --".

"I've developed a minion theory, and what it is, too. Do you think the roommate might have killed Megan on orders from Reggie?"

After a long silence the detective said, "My head hurts too much for this. You come up with some great ideas, Clear, but this one -- it's like the PowerBall thing. Tell me, what's it like on campus?"

"I can't go ten feet without some boy in blue demanding my ID card and asking what I'm doing. Is that really any help?"

"Keeps outsiders out, that's some help. If your non-student date is the killer, he won't be able to get on campus to do any more damage. And if he's not, it's fewer people on campus to get in our way looking for the bad guy."

She heard Paul think, "Can I tell him our date is a she?"

"No!" Amy barked. "Uh, I'm sorry, I mean --"

"I don't need you to approve of police strategy, Clear. It's a lecture, not a dialog."

"I hope the dentist makes you feel better, Steven. Call if you need anything, I know a great Chinese restaurant if you want chicken soup."

℧ 27 ℧

Thursday, October 14, 2021 -- Sappho Rising, New Orleans

Outside Sappho Rising, Amy said, "I'll let you know when I need to lead to take a drink. Otherwise, you'll be the one who gets drunk."

Paul said, "Everything else about us is weird, why not that?" He stepped inside, and paid their cover charge.

"Over here!" Christine shouted from a corner table, standing up. Paul waved, and started over. As he passed the horseshoe bar, he gave a high sign and said, "Hey, Maggie, good to see you." He was pleased at the broad smile that bloomed on the bartender's face.

The club was as empty as the previous week. Only three or four tables were occupied, but Christine had chosen one in a corner, where the pink wall met a green one. As Paul got to the table, Christine gave him a big, long hug. "I'm glad you came," she whispered, and gave Paul a peck on the side of the head.

They were getting seated when the waitress came over. "Christine, introduce your friend, she's so cute!" Paul saw a diminutive woman, barely old enough to be working in a bar, even in Louisiana. She was in the T-shirt and black slacks uniform, but with bright red Keds. Christine grumbled, "Paulette, this is Ashley. She's a waitress."

He heard Amy think, "My god, she's jealous!"

Paul said a non-committal "Hello," then ordered a margarita and a diet Coke. "Sure thing, Sweetheart," Ashley said and went to the bar.

"Two drinks?" Christine asked. She held up her beer glass

and went on, "Who's the other one for?"

"I'm still drinking Coke," he said. "The margarita is for the me I talk to when I talk to myself."

Christine nodded. "You said the two of you mostly get along. That's so nice."

Ashley reappeared bearing booze.

Amy thought, "Drink!" Paul let her lead long enough to start on the alcohol.

"Can I talk to your other half?"

Paul was back in the lead. "We both hear you. Why?"

"I like you. I wonder if I'll like the other part of you."

"What if the other part of me is a man?"

"Oh, how awful. Never mind."

"So you don't just like women, you dislike men?"

Christine was doodling with her index finger in the frost on her beer glass. "I guess. Boys are okay," she wrinkled her nose, "I just don't..." She looked up at Paul. "I never want a boy to touch me again."

"Drink!" He let Amy take another sip. When she withdrew, he had some of the soft drink.

"That's pretty strange to watch," Christine laughed.

"Tastes even stranger," Paul replied.

Paul asked Christine about her voices. She explained her auditory hallucinations began when she was seventeen, about to graduate high school. It was the day after her prom and a disastrous sexual initiation with her boyfriend -- which she described in graphic detail. Another voice turned up when she was in college. She had been diagnosed as schizophrenic, but wasn't all that conscientious about her medication. "I know they're not real," she explained, "but they're my friends. We've been through a lot together. I kind of like them."

"Drink!"

Christine dropped out of college but stayed in the New Orleans area. She was a receptionist for a real estate agency in West End. She made decent money, she had her own apartment, she had an old car. What she didn't have was a lot of friends.

"Why not?" Paul asked. "You're smart, you're pretty, I think you're interesting. Surely other people think so too."

She frowned. "It's hard. Between the voices, and only liking girls, it's hard to make friends."

"I'm amazed. You walked right up to me, so it's not like you're some kind of wallflower."

"Actually, I am. Well, kind of. I saw your tooth. It's just like mine; I had to know you." She finished off her beer and waved at Ashley, holding up the empty glass. "I have trouble getting in the middle."

"The -- the middle?"

"Either I'm so shy I cry, or I'm so forward that I scare girls away. It's hard to find the right balance."

"Drink!"

"Do your friends help? The voices?"

"Sometimes. At least they keep me company when I'm alone."

"I like that about my other person, too."

She frowned. "Even though it's a boy?"

"In a girl's body," he said. "I think he understands women better now. I sure know more about men."

"All boys are gross. They're ugly, they're mean."

"He does have a foul mouth, I'll grant you that," Paul laughed. "But all he has is my body. He insists he's still a man, but you couldn't prove it by looking."

"Drink!"

Ashley brought Christine's beer. "There you go, Honey," she said, but she ran her hand across Paul's shoulders as she walked away. Christine tensed, Paul thought she might jump up to confront the waitress. He said, "I wish she wouldn't do that," and Christine relaxed.

"D--Drink!"

Paul thought, "You want another one?"

"Sure."

"I have to pee," Christine announced. "Come with me." They were talking about her job on the way. Inside, Paul stood by the sink and continued their conversation while Christine took care of business. He heard a snorting sound and some sniffing before she left the stall, rubbing her nose. "Don't you have to go?" she asked.

He shrugged. Christine took his hand as they walked back to their table. On the way, Paul said to Ashley, "Another margarita, please? And Diet Coke?"

The waitress said, "How can you stand that combination?"

"She has help," Christine said defensively, and tugged Paul the rest of the way to their table.

"The park," Paul said. "When shall we go?"

Christine reached across the table to hold Paul's hand. "How about Saturday? I can stand waiting for two days."

Ashley brought their drinks. Amy reached out for the margarita and took two long gulps.

"Your friend likes his alcohol," Christine said.

"You got that right!" Amy said. Paul laughed and said, "Sounds like he agrees. Look, I can pick you up Saturday, we'll have fun at the park, we can find some dinner. It'll be great."

"Let me make dinner for you," she offered. Paul agreed, and they worked out a plan.

It was getting late, and Paul knew he had to leave. He began to make his excuses, and Christine said, "I drove. I'll take you home."

"Oh, you don't have --"

"I want to, Paulette. I want to do something for you."

They settled their tab, with Christine growling at Ashley. In the parking lot, Christine motioned to a ten-year-old Smart Car that was in pristine condition. "I thought this might happen, so I cleaned it out yesterday."

"It's beautiful," Paul observed. "How do you keep it in such great shape? My car is a krewe float of dents."

"Hop in," Christine smiled.

Paul in Amy got in. Before he could find the seat belt, Christine had leaned over and kissed them. "I've been wanting to do that all week," she said.

He thought, "Amy, you okay?"

"I'm drunk," she thought back. "Do what you want."

Paul put his hands behind Christine's head and pulled her closer for another kiss. He could hear her breathing get faster, and realized theirs was, too. Her hands undid the top buttons on their shirt, they were on their legs, they were sliding up under their skirt. The sensation was overwhelming to Paul, he felt like a dry sponge soaking up a sudden rain of emotion and touch. "Paulette," he heard Christine whisper, "I love you, Paulette." The woman grabbed their left hand and shoved it against her chest, then went back to exploring Amy's body.

Lost in the embrace, in the sensations and the feelings of lust and gratitude, Paul noticed a sound. It was Amy, she was moaning to him. He put his hand on their own unoccupied breast, and he thought, "I love you, Amy." The moan rose in pitch, and suddenly he was wracked with an unexpected orgasm. He closed his legs on Christine's hand. He held her, their head tucked under Christine's chin, and he let out a series of cries as Amy's muscles spasmed inside.

"Make love to me," Christine said. "Come home with me. Paulette, I want you so much!"

It didn't occur to him to ask Amy what she thought. He said, "Yes!" leaning against the woman and stroking her breasts through her dress. Christine unsnapped something and the bodice dropped down. Paul touched, he kissed, he rubbed his face on her exposed body. He heard Amy say out loud, "What are you waiting for? Let's go."

"Attagirl!" Christine said. She started the car and left the parking lot, her breasts still exposed. "We'll be at my place in, like, five minutes. Hang on!"

Paul managed to get the seatbelt on, and he straightened their clothes. He looked at Christine's bare breasts, and thought to Amy, "I think we're in for an adventure."

She thought back, "I may need some more liquor for this. You're going to ask her, right?"

"Yup," he said out loud, still eyeing Christine's body. She glanced at him and asked, "Yup what?"

"Talking to myself," he said. "I think I want to introduce you two."

"To a boy? No thanks!"

"The only way you'll know he's a boy is because we say he is. He looks just like me. He sounds just like me."

"Maybe. What will we do in the park?"

Amy answered with a slight slur, "We can climb my tree if no one's looking."

"With you? That'll be great."

Two more turns and Christine drove down an alley, then

pulled into a reserved space behind a triplex. As they got out of the car, Christine said, "Watch out, there are a couple of tricky steps." She took their hand and led them down a dark walk, to a door on the side. In a moment they were inside.

Paul barely glanced at the small apartment before Christine grabbed him by the shirt front and pulled them to her. "I like you so much; you turn me on," she said, and started another long kiss.

Paul was thrilled. That young, pretty, female flesh pressed against him, wanting him. It didn't matter what was or wasn't between his legs, or that the breasts on his body were almost as large as Christine's. In his head, Paul Owens was still a man. He pushed at her, yanked her dress down further, ran their hands everywhere he could reach. Christine's skin was smooth and soft and hairless like Amy's -- but he only felt the outside of her skin. The almost forgotten external feel of an external woman made his pulse pound.

Christine backed away. With a shy smile, she said, "I'd better use the bathroom first. Can I get you anything?"

Amy said, "Got any booze?"

"You really want some? I've got some wine."

"It's for my other half," Paul said. "I'll use your facility next."

While Christine was gone, Paul looked around. A living room, a bedroom, a kitchen, and a bathroom. The apartment was tiny. It was ultra-neat. There was a minimum of furniture.

When Christine emerged she was completely naked, rubbing her nose. "I'll get that wine for your friend," she said, and gave Paul a quick kiss.

"When in Rome," Amy thought to him, and began unbuttoning her clothes. By the time they washed their hands, argyle knee socks were the only things on their body. "Keep a little mystery, huh?" Paul thought.

"Drink!"

When Paul left the bathroom, the bedroom was lit dimly with a pair of flickering candles. The bed was a full mattress on the floor. Christine was on one side, shivering under a sheet. There was a drinking glass full of wine on the other side.

"You're lovely," Christine said. "You're even prettier than I thought you'd be."

Paul crouched down by the bed, and Amy gulped down half the glass. "Can I tell you something?" Paul asked.

"Sure, Paulette. What?"

"I'm scared." He got into the bed and pulled the sheet up, then turned on their side to look at Christine. Their faces were only three inches apart, but neither was touching the other yet.

"How can that be? You're so cool, you seem so together. What are you scared of?"

"It's been so long since I touched a woman," he said, thinking of the wife he had had thirteen years earlier when he still had a man's body. "And I've never done it in this body."

Christine's right hand emerged from under the sheet, and touched their face. "I'm scared, too," she whispered. "But I love you, I know it's going to be okay."

"Drink!"

"Excuse me," Paul said, as he reached behind themself and took the glass. Somehow he brought it forward without spilling it, and Amy drained the glass. He heard her think, "Okay."

Paul reached forward and touched Christine on the shoulders. She closed her eyes and whispered, "Paulette." He ran his hands down her sides, and up her back. All that skin, all that soft, female skin, he wanted it, and the woman in it wanted him. He kissed her and began.

Amy was silent except for one woozy "Drink!" when Paul started to use his mouth on Christine. How could he have forgotten how much he loved the way a woman tastes? And later, Paul was totally unprepared for the feelings of Christine's tongue and lips on the center of their body -- he jerked, he yelled, he opened their mouth silently, and then felt the world explode inside them. The touch was so overwhelming that he grabbed Christine by the hair and pulled her away for a moment, just for a moment, and then pushed their hips back at her face.

He had to rest, to catch his breath. He heard Amy say, "What was that?" out loud. Christine giggled and licked her way up their body, until they were face to face again. The kiss they shared tasted like a woman. They hugged for a long time. Paul rubbed her cheek and her hair, staring at her brown eyes from just a few inches distance. Christine was wearing that childlike smile that had unnerved him at the bar, but now it seemed to radiate contentment.

"Amy," he thought, "are you okay?" There was no answer. He guessed she had passed out from all the alcohol. Maybe that was best.

"Paulette, you are magic," Christine whispered. "You are wonderful."

"I'm so glad I'm here," Paul replied.

In the candle light, Paul saw the woman lean over the far edge of the bed, then come back with a cigarette. "Want some?" she asked.

"No, thanks," Paul said, thinking of the battle he waged so long ago to stop smoking.

And then he realized, from the way she inhaled, that it was marijuana. He decided he'd rather revel in his feelings than alter them. Christine took three long drags, and each time she slowly exhaled the smoke at Paul.

"What's your schedule tomorrow?" he asked. He didn't like the idea of missing an 8 AM class, but he was at Christine's mercy for transportation.

"I'll drop you off at UNO when I go to work," she said, dreamily. "I get up at 6:30." Paul saw her clock. It was 2:15.

"It's worth it," he smiled at her. "You're worth it."

"I love you, Paulette," she said. She lay on her side, facing Paul, and closed her eyes. In no time she was asleep.

Paul lay next to her with a huge smile on their face. He wanted this to happen again, and again and again. He wanted Amy to be okay with it. If Amy could share her body and her time, then Paul could be Paulette for a night or two every week. He never wanted to feel stuck in the back of her head again.

Eventually, sleep claimed him.

⌇ 28 ⌇

Friday, October 15, 2021 -- West End section, New Orleans

The sound of Christine's alarm clock woke Paul with a jolt. "Make it stop!" Amy said out loud.

The buzzing ended, and Christine leaned over to look down on him. "Good morning, Paulette," she said, and kissed him gently on the mouth. "Rise and shine."

"Wait," he said. He sat up on the mattress, then hugged the woman, tightly. "This is real," he whispered. "You're real. It really happened."

She rubbed his back. "I love you, Paulette. It's great to wake up with you." She gave him another soft kiss, then released him and stood up. "I've got to shower. There's not much in the kitchen, but you're welcome to anything." A smile, and she was gone.

"Good morning," he thought to Amy.

"Bah! Humbug!" she said out loud. "My head is killing me. How much did you give me to drink last night?"

"Paulette? Are you okay? Who are you talking to?"

"Yeah, I'm fine," he yelled to her. "I'm talking to my other me."

"Oh. Okay."

He thought to Amy, "Two margaritas, and then a bunch of wine."

"You owe me," she said out loud.

"Agreed. Did you have a good time?"

"I think so," she said. "Did we really lick her? Down there?"

"Boy howdy, did we!"

"You are an animal, an absolute beast."

"But did you have a good time."

"It was okay. When my head stops pounding, we need to talk."

"Christine is taking us back to campus. You can go back to sleep, I'll take notes in class."

"Thanks." Paul heard her yawn. She moved their right hand to pat him on the left forearm. "Thanks."

When Christine returned to the bedroom, she was wearing the clothes she had left in the bathroom the night before. Except, she said, "I'm wearing your underpants," and she giggled. It made Paul smile. "I guess I get to wear yours."

She held out a hand to help Paul stand up. "Lovely," she said, looking at Amy's naked body. "You are so --" She hugged Paul, holding their nakedness against her clothed body. "I want you so much!" she sighed.

"You got me," Paul said. "My turn for the shower?"

"Oh! You've got fifteen minutes before we have to leave. Otherwise I'll be late for work."

Paul held his left index finger to Christine's lips. With a smile he said, "Give me ten," and went to the bathroom.

The shower woke Amy. "Arrrgh! My head! I'll get you for this!" Paul tried to hide his smile from her. "I'm hurrying," he thought to her.

"Please, hurry faster."

He joined Christine in the living room, where she was sitting on a futon, leafing through a magazine. She looked up with a smile, and then laughed. "Your skirt," she said. "Doesn't the zipper belong in the back?"

Paul began to slide it around their hips. "I never get this right," he laughed.

"Are you sure you're not the boy?" she asked.

He took a deep breath. "No, I'm not sure I'm not the boy," he answered.

There was a heavy silence. Finally Christine said, "You are the only boy who will ever touch me."

A wave of relief washed over Paul. He had noticed his worry over the way he had blended himself and Amy in talking to

Christine, but until he felt it lift he didn't realize how guilty he had been feeling. "You are a smart woman, Christine," he said. "I am honored."

"When do I meet the girl?" she asked.

"She's sleeping off a hangover right now," he said. "How about Saturday?"

"I still -- what is your real name? What do I call you?"

"Paul. Please, keep calling me Paulette. I like it when you do that."

"Paul. Paulette." She seemed to be weighing them. "I love you, Paulette," she finally said. "I never thought I would want a boy to touch me again."

He held a hand out to help her up from the futon, and they hugged again. "I'm glad I met you," he said, and felt her nod.

"We gotta go," Christine exclaimed. "Come on."

She stopped her car outside Amy's dorm building. "I'm running late, you have to go," Christine frowned.

"Roll down your window," he said as he got out of the Smart Car. He walked around to the driver's side and leaned in. He held Christine's face in both hands and kissed her on the mouth. "See you tomorrow. I'll pick you up at noon, okay?"

Christine gave him another kiss. "I love you, Paulette," she said, and waved as she drove off.

"Amy?" he said. No answer. He went upstairs to change clothes, but he kept Christine's underpants. He was happy.

❦ 29 ❧

Friday, October 15, 2021 -- UNO campus Cove, New Orleans

Paul was the one talking to Florence in The Cove at dinner time on Friday. Amy was awake, but felt wretched with a hangover from the combination of liquor and wine. She also was coming to grips with what happened with Christine, and her mixed feelings. Every now and then she'd think something to Paul; mostly, he was on his own.

"I have a date!" Florence bragged. "I met a guy in the TV room of the dorm. He was watching the Saints game. He hates the Panthers' quarterback as much as I do."

"Glad to hear it, I've been worried about you."

"Nah, I'm good. I just like to bitch about men."

"Don't we all," he said, thinking about the exception that Christine had granted him. "So, what's he look like?"

"Tall, dark, and handsome. If you squint." She laughed. "He's taller than me, so he meets the height requirement. I think he's a looker. His name is Pete Croix."

"When are you getting together? What are you doing?"

Florence leaned back in her chair, with her hands locked behind her neck. "Hot date Saturday night. We're going to a dance at some club in town."

"I didn't know you danced," Paul said. "Have a good time. You know," he looked down and fished one last french fry out of an ocean of ketchup, "I've got some plans for Saturday, too."

"What are you doing?" he heard Amy think to him.

"Oh? What are you doing?" Florence asked.

"Climbing a tree with a gal pal. You know LaSalle Park?"

"Sure, that's where the Zephyrs play."

Pretending to be Amy, he said, "I grew up near there. My sister and I used to climb a particular tree. They don't let you do that anymore, but I'm going to do it anyway. Try, at least."

"I have to top off my Sprite," Florence said, standing with her drink cup. "Can I get you anything?"

Paul held up his cup. "Limeade. Thanks!"

He heard Amy moan.

"Still in pain? Is it time for more aspirin?" he thought to her.

"Not yet. And -- Paul, I'm starting to not like you pretending you're me. You did it with Christine, and now you're doing it with Florence."

"Uh-oh."

"Yes, uh-oh."

"Do you want me to go to the dorm? How should I talk to Florence?"

"I don't know. Ow, ow, ow, my head. Just --" he heard her sigh, "just be you, I don't know. But you're not Amy, remember that."

Paul was smiling when Florence returned. "I didn't know they had limeade," she said. "Here you go."

"Thanks." He waited until Amy had drained the cup.

"Do you dance?" Florence asked. "If we ever both have dates on the same night, we can do it together."

"I haven't danced in a while," and he thought of Amy dancing at a fraternity party a few months earlier. He came to a dead stop: Amy didn't want him to pretend to be her, but he knew he couldn't admit that the last time he, Paul, chose to dance was sixteen years earlier, at a friend's wedding.

"You okay?" Florence asked. "It's not like you to be speechless."

Paul opened and closed his mouth silently, trying to turn it into a joke. Finally he said, "I may have run out of words. Can I get some at the bookstore? Hey, tell me more about -- is his name Pete?"

"Don't know much yet. Ask me on Sunday, I should know more then."

"I have to go," Paul said. "I need to have another one of those conversations with myself."

"Are you sure you're not crazy? Possessed? A portal to another dimension?"

"I keep telling you I'm the craziest person you know --" and mostly in unison with Florence, he added, "except for your sister, yes, I know. I wouldn't mind that other dimension business; that might be fun."

"Send me a postcard from Gallifrey," Florence said. "I'm going to call one of my gay boys and see what he's up to tonight."

As he left The Cove, Paul thought, "Do you want to lead?"

"No, I'm too pissed," she thought back.

"Uh-oh. Did I do something wrong?"

Amy didn't answer, but he could feel her anger.

"Okay, what's wrong?" he said out loud, and sat down on a stone bench along the walkway to the quadrangle. He sat with their back to the path so passersby would be less likely to notice them. Light was fading, but dusk hadn't quite fallen.

"I'm not sure," she whispered aloud. "But I'm angry, and I'm sad. And I'm scared."

He wrapped their arms around themself and squeezed to hug her. "Tell me," he thought to her. "You know you can tell me anything. Talk to me."

Paul felt a burst of anxiety because he had no idea, none at all, what might be wrong.

"Hold me some more," she thought. Paul squeezed their arms tighter, then rubbed their right arm with their left hand. When she remained silent, Paul whispered, "I love you, Amy. You know that, don't you?"

Paul rubbed their arms and rocked, waiting for Amy to talk to him. Finally she said out loud, "Let's go home. Stay with me."

"Of course. Always." He stood up and repeated, "Always." He grabbed Amy's purse, and set off for their dorm. "I'm here. It's going to be okay, really..."

When they got upstairs, with the door closed and locked behind them, Amy seized the lead. Tears sprang from their eyes immediately, and she yelled, "I'm so angry!" She grabbed her pillow and threw it across the small room, then began pacing around it.

"What can I do?" Paul asked.

"Go move in with Christine!" she shouted. "Pack your crap and go live with her if she's such a big deal!" She sat on the bed and buried their face in their hands.

"Oh, Amy. I didn't --"

"Suddenly it feels like she's more important to you than I am. And you're pretending to be me to make her like you! I hate it! I hate her! I hate you!" She sat with her arms around her stomach, leaning forward and rocking.

"I had no idea," Paul said. "No one ever will be as important as you are, Amy. Without you, I don't exist. Literally."

She sniffed and snurffed.

"Please don't hate me. I -- I couldn't live if you really hated me. I'd just die."

Amy lay back on the bed, with their legs bent over the side and their feet still on the floor. "I actually like Christine," she said. "But I feel ignored. Like you're picking her over me. And then, and then, you're doing it by pretending to be me. Telling her about my life as if it was yours."

Paul used their left hand to touch and fondle their right arm, trying to comfort her.

"I know it shouldn't," Amy went on, "but it made me mad. I feel like I'm losing you." She snurffed again. "I hate it!"

"It's okay that you're mad. It's okay that you're sad. It's even okay that you're scared."

"Easy for you to say!" she bellowed. "What are you going to do about it? Tell me what, Paulette."

He continued to rub and touch their arm. "I am always going to be with you. Amy first. Always Amy first."

Amy dried her eyes on the shoulders of her shirt, not wanting to move her arms and break the contact she felt from Paul. "I'll tell you what scares me," she said. "It's giving you an evening or a day when you lead, and I'm in the background. I'm afraid --" she coughed and sat up, and reached for the tissue box on the desk "-- I'm afraid you'll lead and then never let me out again. Oh," and she hid her face in their hands. Her voice was muffled, but Paul heard her clearly, "Is that what I've been doing to you all this time? I'm so sorry. I guess I don't deserve you. Please, please..." and she began to hiccup.

Paul said, "Is that it? Are you worried that I'll see the lights of the city and won't come back to you on the farm?"

He felt her nod amid the hiccups.

"Is it because I told you I want to spend time leading? Being a real person?"

She nodded again.

"But -- what if I am a real person and I choose to be with you? Would you like that? Because that's what I want."

Another nod.

He tried to say her name, but the hiccups kept interrupting. Instead, he thought, "Amy, Amy, Amy. I swear, I will never leave you."

He felt her smile, until the hiccups interfered. "Damn (hic) it! (hic)" she shouted, and lay down on their side. She brought their legs onto the bed, then pulled the pillow in front of her so she could hold it like a teddy bear. Their face was still wet, but she wasn't crying anymore. She thought, "See that you don't!" and began to smile.

In the shower the next morning, Amy thought to Paul, "Was I awful yesterday? I'm so sorry."

"You weren't awful, you were angry," he thought back. "I'm glad you talked to me about it."

She turned to reach for her shampoo, and gave Paul a look at another woman showering. He made a noise; it took Amy just a moment to connect cause and effect. "You like that, huh?" she thought to him with a smile.

"Yes, please."

She turned away and thought, "You get plenty of that with Christine."

Paul laughed and thought to her, "There are never enough naked women. Never!"

"So -- is this how you felt when I was going out with that guy last year?"

"Yup. Plus, watching you and feeling you having fun, it made me feel like I was stuck in a cage." Amy nodded. "And I felt like you were neglecting me. In fact, I remember bitching about it repeatedly."

She rolled her eyes at the memory. "You know something?"

she thought as she rinsed her back under the shower head. Paul got the briefest of looks at the woman in the next shower. "I need to find a guy who hears voices but is as together as Christine. That's why she's not freaking out about us, she's used to voices. We could double-date."

"I don't know," Paul thought. "I hope for the best, but I'm afraid Christine may not be all that together. We've seen each other twice and she's saying she loves me?"

"Yes, she is a needy little thing."

Amy turned off the water, and began drying their hair. Once she got the towel wrapped around their head, she put on her terrycloth robe, and headed back to her room.

"Let's talk about the sex thing," Amy said when the door closed.

"I like what you and I do," Paul said.

"Good. I do, too. But that's not what I meant."

"I know."

"We're both hetero --"

"But I'm stuck in a hetero woman's body!" Paul interrupted.

"Shhh, not so loud," Amy laughed. "But yes, you don't want to sleep with men and I'd rather not touch tits with women."

Paul felt a spark of fear. "No. Oh no. You mean I don't get to be with Christine anymore?"

She was trimming her toenails while they talked. It still amazed Paul that Amy could do that so easily and quickly; before he lost his body, it was a five minute expedition for him, one that required beer and aspirin. Amy was done in no more than ninety seconds, and their back didn't hurt.

"Yes, no, maybe," she said. "If you can put up with me and a man, then I will put up with you and Christine. But if you can't, I won't."

"Well, that's fair," he said. "I don't like it for shit, but it's hard to argue."

Amy shook her head as she dressed, muttering "garbage mouth."

Paul did not like her arrangement. Before he met Amy he spent fifty five years as an old fashioned manly man, hating and fearing homosexuality in equal measure. Sure, he had had a few acquaintances who were gay, but none had expressed any sexual feeling for him, and Paul considered them exceptions from his cultural training that a man getting naked with another man was awful, if not downright wrong. And now he was told it was the price he had to pay in order to get naked with a woman again.

Paul thought about it for several minutes while Amy finished dressing. She was leaning in to the mirror, working on eye liner, when Paul said, "Christ, you drive one hard bargain." Their right hand slid over their face, leaving a heavy black line across the cheek. Even so, she smiled. "Yes, I do," she said, and she dipped a cotton ball in baby oil to remove the stray mark. "Do we have a deal?"

"I may cry," Paul said.

"I can live with that," Amy said. "Deal?"

"It may kill me, you know."

"That's a risk I'm willing to take. Deal?"

"Any way I can talk you out of it?"

"Nuh-uh! Deal?"

"Look over there! A squirrel!"

She laughed. "Nice try. Do. We. Have. A. Deal?"

"Only because I love you, Amy."

"Works for me. Now let's head out so you can introduce me to your girlfriend."

ঔ 30 ঔ

Saturday, October 16, 2021 -- West End section, New
Orleans

Amy parked her twelve-year-old blue sedan at the curb in
front of the triplex where Christine lived in West End. She walked
up the driveway, past the tricky steps, and knocked at the side
door. It was ten before noon.

The door opened and a red-eyed Christine stood there. A
smile spread across her face; without a word she stepped forward
and hugged her. "Paulette!"

Amy retreated, leaving Paul to lead. He enjoyed the hug,
rubbing their arms over the woman's back and arms. He closed
his eyes and felt his insides relax. "I'm here," he said, softly.

Christine looked down, sheepish, and said, "Uh, come on in.
You didn't have any trouble finding the place, did you?"

When they were inside, Paul took off their jacket. He peered
at Christine and said, "Have you been crying?"

She shrugged. "I was afraid you wouldn't come. I'm sorry."

"If that's all, everything's going to be okay. I've been looking
forward to seeing you again."

Christine took him by the hand and led him to the futon.

"There's someone I want you to meet," he said. "Are you
ready?"

"I think so."

"Good. Now, you know me. I'm Paul, also known as
Paulette."

Christine nodded.

"I have a kind of twin. A different kind of twin. Her name is

Amy. Amy, meet Christine."

With the same voice, of course, Amy said, "I'm glad to meet you, Christine."

"What?" Christine said. "Paulette, please don't tease me."

"It's real," Paul said. "We have the same voice just like we look the same. I live inside Amy's body."

"You're making fun of me! I should never have told you about my voices. You're like all the others." He could see the woman withdraw, almost as if she were getting smaller.

"No," Paul said. "I'm serious about this. Let me prove it to you."

Christine sat with quivering chin and a runny nose. She was close to tears. Paul said, "Amy, please think hello to Christine."

Amy did that, thinking a greeting to the woman. Christine's eyes grew big and her mouth -- no longer quivering -- fell open. "But -- but -- how do you do that?" she asked.

Amy thought to her, "I don't know. Paul and I stumbled on some things, but I have no idea how any of it works. I'm just glad it does. So, hello, Christine. I'm glad to meet you. You've made Paul very happy."

"You're a girl, right?"

Amy laughed. "Last time I looked. Yes."

"And Paulette is, is a man?"

She thought to her, "He thinks so."

Christine stared at Amy, absorbing the words she heard in her head and the image of Amy's closed mouth. "Can Paulette do this, too?"

Softly, Paul thought to her, "Yes, Christine. I can do this, too. I hope you're not disappointed."

She lowered her head onto their lap, with one arm around their thighs. "You're real!" she whispered.

Paul petted her hair as he thought to her, "Yes. I am real. And so are you." He felt Christine tighten her arm around them. "I told you!" she shouted; then, quieter, she said, "My voices said you were fake. I defended you. I told them you were real, that you had to be real, that I needed --"

"Yes, I'm real," Paul interrupted. "It's all right, Christine. Amy and I are real. Amy told me she wants to be your friend, too.

Is that okay?"

Christine sat up. She wiped her runny nose on her sleeve, then looked at Paul and gently kissed him on the lips. He put their arms around her. "Amy?" he thought to her, "Help me hug her." And so the two people in the one body held and comforted and welcomed the confused but happy woman next to them.

Paul said, "If I think to you like this, Amy can't hear me. Is it okay if I talk out loud? Even though I'll sound like her?"

She nodded vigorously, but didn't speak. Her eyes were huge, her mouth open slightly.

"You okay?" Paul said out loud. "We've got a tree to climb."

"Yes, yes," she said and even clapped her hands. Her eyes remained riveted on Paul.

"I know a cafe near the park, we can get some lunch. And then we will climb a tree higher than any girl has ever gone before."

Amy thought to Paul, "She breaks my heart. Part of her is like a little kid. But she is crazy about you."

"She makes me feel good. Needed. You know?"

They got in the car and Amy headed toward the park. Christine sat close to Amy, with her hand on their right leg. At stop signs and red lights Paul would nuzzle her, and Christine smiled. Along the way, the three of them talked about the things new friends talk about. Paul and Amy both thought it was odd that Christine had no curiosity as to how Paul ended up in Amy's body; apparently, she just accepted it, as she accepted the hallucinatory voices in her own head.

After lunch, they pulled into the Airline Drive entrance to the park. The main lot was almost empty. Paul said, "It's Paulette -- think we'll fit in the playground? I used to love those crawling tubes."

"I like the slides," Christine said. "Let's play."

They took a path that avoided the horse paddocks and performance areas, then cut through some trees to the playground. Paul thought it was exactly the same as the last time he and Amy had played there, when perhaps she was thirteen. But Amy said, "It shrank! I swear, all these things used to be twice as big. Three times."

Christine ran to a chute. She climbed the ladder quickly, then sat and let herself go down the metal slide. She was giggling by the time she got to the ground, and she ran around to the ladder and did it again. Paul thought to Amy, "I don't see why she should have all the fun," and he climbed up behind Christine. He sat on the staging platform, and Christine got on their lap. They all were laughing by the time they got to the ground.

Next they played on the swing set. It was easy to talk as they sat in adjoining swings. Paul pumped their legs and leaned back to get as high as he could. Christine was more sedate on her swing, sometimes shouting so Paul or Amy could hear her when they were at the top of their arc.

Paul thought to Amy, "This is like being at home with your folks. We can just be ourselves. I love this!"

Amy said, "You're right." She shouted to Christine, "Thank you!"

"Who's that? For what?"

"Amy. Thanks for letting us be us."

"What are you talking about? Who else would you be?"

Paul let their legs down to scrape the ground as they swung, bringing them to a stop after two or three passes. Christine did the same.

"There are only five other people in the whole world who know about Amy and me," Paul said to her. "With you now, we don't have to be careful and watch what we say. I don't have to hide with you."

"It's Amy. Usually it's only with my parents that we can relax like this." She thought to Paul, "I can't believe I'm saying this," then out loud added, "I'm so glad you and Paul have met."

"Yaayyyy!" Christine cried. She jumped off her swing seat and hugged Amy and Paul where they sat.

Paul thought to Christine, "Thank you. What a gift you are."

"Come on, I want to see if my tree is still there," Amy said. They walked holding hands, as Amy tried to remember the path. Then it was there -- a distinctive live oak, every bit as tall as she remembered it. "This is the one," she said

"I believe you're right," he said. Then to Christine he said, "Amy and her little sister used to climb this. We were excited when we got up to the sixth branch."

"What are we waiting for?" Christine asked.

"They don't let you climb trees here anymore," Amy said. "Let's go around to the other side, no one will see us." Paul tip-toed around, with an index finger in front of their lips. Christine smiled and tip-toed after them. Amy stopped when she thought they were hidden, and Christine put her arms around her.

"Wait a sec," Amy said and withdrew, leaving Paul to receive Christine's hug. And kiss. And grope. He heard Amy think, "Get a room!" but she was laughing. He returned Christine's caresses. While they kissed he thought to her, "I'm glad we're doing this."

Christine leaned back and said, "How do you do that while you're kissing me?"

He pulled her back to him and kissed her again, while he thought to her, "Damned if I know."

They both heard Amy thinking, "Okay, lovebirds, we've got a tree to climb."

Amy recognized a comfortable first limb, not one foot off the ground. As she pulled themself up to a second branch, Christine followed to the first one. Amy stayed close to the tree trunk, where there were fewer leaves in the way; it also would make it harder for anyone on the ground to notice her. "How are you doing?" Paul called to Christine.

"You're a brave girl, Paulette," she answered from below, "but this is fun."

Live oaks are easy trees to climb. When they reached the seventh branch, Amy paused and said, "I think this is the highest we ever got."

Paul thought back, "Let's keep going." Then out loud, he said, "We're headed for the toppermost." He heard Christine laugh.

Amy got them to the ninth level, and hauled themself up to sit on the branch. "I can see past the road. I didn't know there's a train yard over there."

A moment later Christine was standing on the branch below, her head even with Amy's knees. "Are we going any higher?" she asked. "This is getting spooky."

"It's Amy. Make sure you have a good grip, then look down."

They were about forty-five feet up the tree. The few people in the park looked like toys. At one of the paddocks a woman was standing in the center, lunging her horse in a big circle. The Zephyrs' stadium was empty, but the infield grass was a vibrant green.

"Make way!" Christine said as she pulled herself up to sit next to Amy and Paul. She put her arm around them, as much to steady herself as to show affection. The woman turned her head in every direction and said in wonder, "We've got the best view in all of New Orleans."

Paul kissed her on the cheek. "I sure do."

She smiled, but still gazed south. "There's the river, and the bridge to the west bank. This is great!"

"When's the last time you climbed a tree?" Paul asked.

"Oh, jeez, it's at least a million years. I still lived in St. Louis. Fifteen, maybe? How about you?"

"The last time we were here, I think Amy was thirteen."

"My MeMaw lives on a farm in Tennessee," Amy added. "That was the last time I climbed a tree. Maybe I was, what, sixteen? I think I was trying to impress that boy from the next house."

Paul volunteered, "Me, I was in my thirties. I let my roommate's friend dare me into climbing a ladder to get to some huge pine in his backyard." He shook their head at the memory. "It was totally insane. I think the kid was impressed that I did it, but it cured me of tree climbing for a long time."

Christine said, "Your roommate's friend was a kid?"

Paul was embarrassed, but he laughed. "They were the same age. I've always had a soft spot for you sweet young things."

"How old are you, Paulette?"

Paul turned his head to look at her, and he kissed her cheek again. "I am a notorious cradle robber," he said. "My next birthday is in April, and I will be 68 years old."

"Geezer!" Amy laughed.

Christine's eyes bugged out. "What?" she shouted. "Are you making fun of me again?"

Paul thought to her, "It's not a joke. I haven't told you how I ended up inside Amy, but honest to God, Christine, I was born in 1953."

Christine stared, open-mouthed, for what seemed like an

hour. "My mother wasn't born yet in 1953!" she exclaimed.

"Oh, great," Amy thought to Paul. "First you turn out to be a man, and now you could be her grandfather. What else could possibly go wrong?"

Paul thought back, "I really wish you hadn't said that."

And then Christine moved her arm to wrap it around their midsection, and she hugged Paul tightly. "I've never known anyone like you. Not even close. Tell me everything!"

"Not here," Amy said. "The story is too strange. We all might fall out of the tree." She smiled. "Can Paul and I help you with dinner?"

"I forgot!" she blurted out. She let go of Amy and brought both her hands to her face, and she wobbled. Paul threw their left arm around her, while Amy grabbed the tree trunk next to them with their right. They stabilized Christine. Paul kept his grip until the look of terror drained from the woman's face. He thought to her, "I've got you. It's okay."

"I think -- is it okay if we go down now?" Christine asked.

"Sure. We probably should scram before anyone notices us up here anyway."

Christine led the trip down. After her scare on the ninth branch she moved slowly and carefully until she was on the ground. As soon as Amy alit, Christine hugged her. Amy withdrew to let Paul lead, and he hugged her back. "You okay now?" he asked softly.

Christine nodded silently, her head against their chest. With one hand she was patting the back of their neck.

Amy thought to Paul, "She's a darling. She's adorable. But she's so fragile." Paul nodded, then whispered to Christine, "It's okay. Let's go."

Amy's phone rang. The caller ID said it was Riordan. "Excuse me, Christine, I have to take this call." She took the call, and said, "Clear. What?"

"Good, you're up."

"Up, hell. If you'd called five minutes ago, I'd have been 50 feet up a tree."

"I do not know what that means. Look, there's news."

Amy turned away from Christine, and held her right hand over the non-phone ear. "Please don't tell me there's been another body."

"Worse," the detective said. "Your lover boy's father is a hotshot lawyer and alderman wherever the hell he's from. We're letting Reggie out on bail this afternoon."

"Crap. I'll have to deal with him in a math class on Monday."

"He's still charged with assaulting you. He's supposed to stay fifty feet away from you. I'm worried about the mood on your campus. While Reggie was locked up the deans thought we were making progress. The partial lockdown may get more intrusive."

"Why? We know Reggie can't be the killer."

"Listen up, Sweetheart. The deans'll be concerned that we don't have a clue who the killer is. They're not going to be worried about lover boy."

Amy sighed. "Are you ever going to stop calling him that?"

She heard him laugh, "Introduce me to some other hunk you're seeing." And she heard Paul laughing inside; "Are you sure we can't tell him about Christine?"

"One more thing: Jermaine finally got me the details on the autopsies. The last one, that Megan girl, was different; she was suffocated by strangulation. No sign of sexual assault, he thinks the shirt was torn by accident. The other two women were killed by jugular vein stoppage. Maybe it's because all the bodies were outdoors, but he said there were no fibers, no DNA, no fingerprints, absolutely nothing. We got three dead bodies and we're no closer to solving this than the day you met me."

"So, now what?"

"I'm betting the dean will hold a press conference Monday afternoon. If he does, you may as well come watch. But you have to promise you'll keep your mouth shut. You're a great help, but it'll look like we're unprofessional if anyone finds out you're working with me."

"You know just what to say to a woman, don't you?" Amy said, annoyed. "I'm supposed to shut up and --"

"Get over yourself, Clear. The only thing that matters is finding the killer. I'll let you know when I hear about the press conference. And -- damn, my other line is going off. Talk to you later," and the detective rang off.

Paul said aloud, "You didn't get to ask him how his tooth is doing."

She replied, "Maybe it's infected his brain."

"That was fascinating," Christine said. "Uh, what was it?"

Paul said, "Amy, you tell us about it."

"Whoa, boy," she said, shaking her head. As they started to walk back to the parking lot, Amy told Christine about the series of murders at UNO, and how she had elbowed her way into working with the detective. "Paul's been a big help," she said, "but Riordan doesn't know about him."

Christine took their hand as they walked. "You two are amazing," she said. "You're like spies."

"Yeah, aren't we," Paul answered. "Amy's the brave one. I'm just along for the ride."

"I've heard the news stories. A serial killer. Who's doing it?"

Amy said, "My guess is the stalker girl. She's got a motive, plus she's delusional. But there's no proof, no evidence."

"Maybe you should stay at my place," she offered, a shy smile on her face. "I don't want anything to happen to my Paulette. Or to Amy."

Paul squeezed Christine's hand. After a moment, Amy said, "If Steven calls, I have to answer my phone. I have to do what he wants." Paul added, "That was Amy talking. Hey, can Christine come with us if you get called away?"

Amy looked up, something she did often when talking to Paul. "I guess." To Christine, "How are you with dead bodies?"

She stopped walking. "You're not kidding," she said slowly.

Amy shook their head. "I wish I were."

"I don't know." She laughed. "Let's talk about dinner instead."

The few people they passed while walking hand in hand paid no notice to them. Amy asked, "Where do you shop? It'll be fun to get dinner fixings with you."

"Rouse's. Is there anywhere else?"

"What were you thinking to make?"

Somehow, she knew it was Amy who had asked, Amy who was leading, and said, "I was going to bake a roast. Uh -- do you eat meat?"

Amy coughed. Paul said, "That's what happens when we both try to talk at the same time. Yeah, we're carnivores. Vegetables are okay, but they are not food; they are what food eats."

"All the girls I meet are prissy," Christine said seriously, "about food, about what they say and talk about, about everything. They'd never climb a tree. I'm glad you're not like that. But there's not enough time to cook a cow."

"You like spaghetti?" Paul asked. "I make a killer sauce."

"He does, too," Amy added. "It's as good as my dad's."

"I usually open a jar of Prego," she smiled. "Teach me, okay?"

"It's a deal," Paul said as they got in Amy's car and headed for the store.

They were giddy in the market. Christine was excited to be with Paulette, and Paul was enjoying the freedom of leading. Amy participated, sometimes confusing Christine, but she found she liked the woman, and she continued to be impressed with the unexpected confidence that Paul showed; she also was relieved that Paul was thinking to her, including her as well as his new girlfriend. Today she did not feel left out.

They laughed up and down the aisles of the Rouse Market #25. A box of rotini and one of penne noodles. Cans of tomato paste and crushed tomatoes, two green bell peppers, a bag of yellow onions, a pound of white mushrooms, and two pounds of ground beef. "How are you fixed for spices?" Paul asked.

"I don't know. What do you need?"

"Oregano, basil, bay leaf, and garlic," he said. "And cooking oil."

"I've got oil," she said, "and garlic powder."

He shook their head. "Nope. Fresh works better." They went back to the produce section for a small garlic bulb, then found the right bottles of McCormick's.

"Cheese!" Amy said. As they sped around the store, Christine put a fat baguette in their bascart. Paul suggested ice cream for dessert. Then there was wine, two bottles.

Paul thought to Amy, "This is a pile of stuff. Is it okay if I offer to help her pay for it?"

"I'm glad you asked, since it's MY money," she thought back, "but you're right, there's a ton. Offer to split it with her."

"It's Paul," he said out loud. "Can we help you pay for this?"

Christine shook her head. "I want to do this for you."

"I appreciate it. But look, this cart is overflowing. Please, we'll help cook, we'll help pay, we'll help eat. We might even help wash the dishes."

"Why are you so nice?" she asked. "I thought boys quit spending money after the girl said 'yes.'"

"I'm nice because I like you, Christine," touching her arm. "And only part of me is a man."

The serious look on the woman's face turned into a smile. "Sure," she said, "thanks. But you have to show me how to make this incredible sauce."

Paul grasped her hand, then made some silly hand gestures he had made up as a kid, a secret handshake he used to share with two best friends in West Virginia. "Solemn secret vow," he said. "Come tonight, you will be a master spaghetti chef."

Christine laughed and said, "You silly."

Amy thought to Paul, "When's the last time I told you -- I love you. This woman is good for you."

Paul stopped and looked up, and quietly said out loud, "Thank you."

At Christine's triplex they discovered exactly how tiny her kitchen was. "Good thing there are only two bodies in here," Amy said. They emptied the grocery bags, covering almost all the counter space.

Christine retrieved two cutting boards from a cabinet, and two knives. "Oh, great master chef," she said, "tell your respectful acolyte what it is you wish of me."

"Okay," Paul laughed. "Disciple Amy and I will work on the onions. How about you rinse the mushrooms and cut them? I usually go for chunky, what's your preference?"

"Chunky it is, chef Obi-Wan."

"And whichever of us finishes first gets to work on the peppers."

As they started peeling and chopping, Paul said, "Christine. Let me tell you how all this happened." He explained about coming to New Orleans for business and getting stomped into a coma in a street mugging, and about his personality getting transferred into Amy when fluid from a bedsore on his dying body was accidentally splashed on her at the hospital where her father works. Amy gave her perspective of being eleven years old and waking up with Paul in her head, and how they gradually learned to tolerate each other, and then cooperate.

"The only people who know about me," Paul said, "are Amy's family and two of the doctors that helped James figure out what happened."

"It's Amy," the voice went on, amid the sound of chopping onions and peppers. "I told one friend about Paul when I was in middle school. It didn't work out, and that made us gun shy. You are the first person we've told in what, six years?"

Christine responded, "This is so neat! I've never known anyone like you. You two."

Paul said, "This may be hard, but please, don't tell anyone that there are two of us. We're still worried about getting thrown into a wacky ward."

"I understand that," she muttered. "It's a good thing you said that though, otherwise I might have bragged to everyone I know."

"I'd like to meet your friends," Paul said. "You can introduce me as Paulette, that'll work."

"But if you meet any of MY friends," Amy picked up, "you have to call me Amy."

"Now I feel like I'm a secret agent," Christine said. She thought for a moment and said, "If I mess up, Amy, can you pretend your middle name is Paulette?"

"If I have to," she said.

"It's Paul. Are you okay with this?"

"Sure. Uh, why wouldn't I be?"

"Most people would think it's not possible. You know, for me to be real but living inside Amy."

She shrugged. "I've got my own voices," she said. "You and Amy are a lot nicer."

Paul put down his knife and hugged Christine. "Thank you," he said, and kissed her behind the ear.

"Down, girl!" she laughed. "Dinner first, then we play!"

Paul pronounced the sauce completed, after Christine and even Amy had paid close attention to the recipe that came out of his head. "I had a summer job at a café in Lewisburg. The owner was a one-armed freedom fighter who scared the crap out of me, but his wife, Mama Rienzi, she's the one who taught me." He brought their thumb and first two fingers together and lifted them to their lips to kiss, "*Buoni*," he finished, "*sono buoni*."

Christine boiled the pasta and put the garlic bread in the oven, then opened a bottle of the cheap merlot they'd picked up at Rouse's. She got three wine glasses out of a cabinet, and filled them all. Amy thought to Paul, "She remembered me! I love this girl!" then said out loud, "It's Amy. I appreciate you giving me and Paul our own glasses. We need that to gauge how loaded we're going to get."

Christine said, "I saw Paulette drink a lot the other night, but she was fine. How does that work?"

Amy explained that she came to the lead for each sip, swallow, and gulp, and that whichever one of them was leading would feel the most impact. "Tonight, we'll all get mellow."

Christine stopped, looking confused. "Uh, how many plates do we need?"

Paul laughed. "One for you and one for us. I expect we'll go back for seconds, though."

Christine and Paul loaded up bowls with pasta and sauce, and placed them at the living room table. They had to make a second trip to bring the three wine glasses, and the open bottle.

As they sat, Paul raised glasses in each hand. "To friends, old and new," he toasted, and they clinked glasses. Amy took a sip from the right hand glass, then Paul tipped the glass in their left hand. Christine took a sip from hers, but with eyes wide on her dinner guest. She wore an enormous smile.

Amy and Paul coughed over the first bite, both trying to say how good the sauce was. Christine said it for them; one bite and she called, "Hot spit! This is great!"

Amy thought, "Well done. I think you've impressed her."

"Tell me about your family, Christine. You said you're from St. Louis?"

She nodded, and swallowed the piece of garlic bread in her mouth. "Yup, born there. My mom is still there. I have a big brother -- he's a lawyer now -- he's there, too."

"Your dad?"

She shook her head. "I never knew him. He left before I was born."

"That's tough," Amy said. "Did your mom remarry?"

She shook her head again. "He got killed in a factory accident a little later, so there was insurance money and a pension and some kind of settlement. I don't know that she ever looked at another man. Except my brother, of course."

"Are you close?"

"With Mom? Yeah. She's been so good -- she was there when I got sick, and she tells me I'm always her sweetie. And when I told her that I liked girls, she said she didn't care if I liked flying saucers, just as long as I was happy."

"Wow. I don't know how my mom would take it if I did that."

"Oh, you mean you haven't told her?"

"There's nothing to tell!" Amy said sharply. "I like men. Paul says I'm boy crazy." He nodded their head.

Christine put down her fork, carefully finished chewing her food, and swallowed. "I don't understand. If you like boys, how -- I mean --" she gave up and repeated, "I don't understand."

"It's Paul. I'm the one who likes women."

"But -- but -- how did Amy, you know --"

"Amy was drunk," Paul laughed.

Amy continued, "I was sick as a dog the next day. It was the worst since my dad fed me beer at home to make me understand what a hangover was." She shook their head.

Christine had not gone back to eating. "Paulette, what do you do when Amy is with a boy?"

He sighed. "I cringe. I hate it."

"But you do it?"

He shrugged. "We're still figuring all this out. Either each of us has to put up with the other's sex life, or we'll have to go into a convent."

"I couldn't do that," Christine said, shaking her head. "It would --" she stopped abruptly, then shouted, "She does too! Paulette does so like me!" She dropped her fork, and huddled in her chair, shrinking into herself. "She does so," she whimpered, "and so does Amy, so there."

Paul got up and knelt by Christine's chair. He opened their arms to the woman, and she turned to him, let them envelop her.

"You see?" she whispered, "She does. She does. Now go away, please."

Paul rocked her and caressed her back and her arms. "I'm here," Paul thought to her, softly. "You are right, and the voices are wrong. I'm here for you." He felt her exhale deeply in their arms. Paul didn't know Amy was thinking the same sort of thing to her.

"I'm sorry," she finally said. "I'm okay, they're quiet now." Paul leaned back on his heels, his hands still touching her arm. "Paulette. Amy. I'm sorry. I -- I need to take one of my pills." She smiled weakly, and stood up and went to her bedroom. A moment later she was back with a brown prescription vial.

"Tell me about the medication," Amy said. "My dad is a doctor."

"I'm supposed to take one in the morning and one at night," she said, and she took a gulp of wine to get it down. "Sometimes they make me foggy inside, though. I didn't want that today. I wanted to be close to you."

"I'm right here," Paul said, "and I feel very close to you. Take care of yourself."

"They're gone, they won't be back tonight," Christine said, "Good! What sort of things do your voices say?"

"I forget your voice isn't like mine. Mostly, they tell me I'm no good. They say no one will ever love me. When they're real bad, they tell me I should kill myself, but I don't listen."

"Oh, Christine," Amy sighed. "Do the pills help?"

"When I take them, yeah," she said. She picked up her fork and went back to the spaghetti. "I hope I remember how to make this, it's so good."

Amy thought, "I'm not hungry anymore."

"Not even ice cream?" he said back, out loud.

"What about ice cream?" Christine asked.

"Amy's full, I'm trying to talk her into dessert."

"Oh, am I eating too slow? I'm sorry."

"No, you're fine. I'm pleased that you like the sauce so much. You eat, we'll talk."

"Good," Christine said, "I don't want to stop. So what do you do, Amy, about boys?"

"Lust from afar, mostly," she said. "I seem to have bad taste in men. I'm insecure about them. I can't imagine being close to someone and not telling them about Paul, but that's not the sort of thing you do on a first date."

"Paulette told me about you -- well, she hinted pretty quickly. If I were a boy -- oh no, I'm not going there." She laughed.

"I only see Amy through her eyes," Paul said. "I think she's smart and pretty. I think all the cool men should be drooling all over her."

"Euuuuwwww," Christine said, between bites.

Amy said, "Paul amazes me. He is so self-confident, he can talk to anyone. At the club he was chatting up the bartender, he was comfortable with you, and on the way home he talked to a hooker at the bus stop."

"You go to prostitutes?"

"No," Paul said, "a lady walked up to the bus stop and we chatted. She said she was on her way to work, that she was a whore. It was not a professional conversation."

Amy added, "He's so nice, though. Paul told her that with her looks, he was sure her business was great."

"I think I understand it," he mused. "Somehow, I must come across as available. People say 'hello' because there must be something about me that makes them think I'll respond, I won't be rude or snotty."

"Wait a minute," Christine said. "How can you look anything when Amy is what you look like? Especially since I think you're saying Amy doesn't look available."

"Hmmm. I don't know, maybe the expression on our face, posture -- attitude, I guess. I know it's not what we're wearing. Good point, Christine. Amy, what do you do when strangers say hello?"

"I don't know, get sweaty palms, I guess. If some hunk I think is dreamy sits next to me in class and says 'hello,' what should I do to look available? Unbutton my shirt? God, I hate slutty."

Christine laughed. Paul answered, "No, all you have to do is say hello back. Look at him and smile instead of looking away. Tell him your name and ask him his. That sort of thing."

There was a long silence. Finally Amy said, "Really? That's

all it takes?"

"That's what I did when Christine said hello. You see how well that worked."

"Paulette was so friendly," she nodded. "I was a little scared about walking over, but I had to know the girl behind that tooth."

"Really. That's all?"

"As pretty as you are," Paul offered, "it'll work if you haven't had a bath in a month and there's a bird's nest in your hair."

"You really know how to sweet talk a girl, don't you?"

"You ready for ice cream?" Christine asked. She was clearing the table. Paul picked up the bowls of sauce and pasta and walked them into the kitchen.

"Let me help with the dishes," Paul said.

Christine turned and hugged him tightly. "They'll wait," she said, "that's what the washer is for." She moved her hands to their face, and kissed Paul.

It was a long kiss, as Paul and Christine soaked up each other, the physical warmth, the emotional comfort, the percolating desire. Paul thought to her, "I've wanted to do this all day." A noise came out of Christine, and her hold and kiss became more intense. When they stopped, they hugged tightly and leaned against each other. "Me too," the woman said. "You have no idea."

They smiled, and Paul said, "Show me."

"Aren't you the hot bitch?" she laughed. She took their hand and led them to her bedroom.

They were resting about an hour later, bodies entwined under twisted sheets. Christine said, "Amy? Can I ask you something?"

"Sure."

"Were you there for all of that?"

"The most I can do is shut my inside eyes. I'm always there -- it's my body. And Paul always is there."

"Did you like it at all?"

There was a long pause until Amy said, "I like you, Christine. And I like how much you care for Paul, and how good you are for him."

She wore a big smile. "That's not what I meant."

Amy went on, "I feel everything Paul does, and it felt good." She took a deep breath. "But it's hard to get past that it's another woman who's making those feelings. Those sensations. I -- I want a man."

"This is for you," she said, and she kissed them on the cheek. "You're part of Paulette, so I love you, too. I want you to like me, I don't want to turn you off or make you feel weird."

"You're a considerate woman. Thank you. And I have to say, I love your tooth."

She twisted her body to roll across Paul. "Your eyes are amazing. That gray. You are so pretty."

"Oh, thank you." Then, "It's Paul. I've been crazy about Amy's eyes since the first time I saw them. You're pretty, too. What was your hair like before you made it like this? What do you call it?"

"It's straight, I used to wear bangs like a little kid. I had a, uh, a girlfriend who took scissors to me one night and did this. After I stopped being mad I realized I like it -- it's all different lengths everywhere. I did the color myself. It's *le coif Christine.*"

"*Oui!*" Paul said, "*Magnifique!*"

For a long time they looked into each other's eyes. Christine saw a woman who wasn't afraid of her hallucinations like all the other girls were, because she had her own. She didn't know how real Amy was, but she didn't care -- Paulette was the girl she cared about, who liked her and was nice to her all the time. If Amy was Paulette's hallucination, at least Amy was an enjoyable one, supportive, fun. She didn't say the bad things that her own voices said.

Paul saw a pretty young woman, full of energy, but mentally delicate and in need of reassurance and support. When he was a young man, in a young man's body, such vulnerability would have sent him running away; but now, her need and her affection touched him deeply. He had spent ten years in the back of Amy's head -- good years, once he finally accepted that the alternative was having died along with his body on that gurney in her father's hospital -- but now, with Amy letting him lead and be a whole person again, he was parched for emotional and physical connection. Christine was giving herself to him. He couldn't remember ever feeling as alive as he did right then, holding the woman, and getting lost in her light brown eyes.

❦ 31 ❧

Monday, October 18, 2021 -- UNO Campus, New Orleans

Christine dropped Amy and Paul off a little after seven, on her way to work. Because of the UNO partial lockdown, she wasn't able to drive into the campus; she had to let Amy out on Elysian Fields, near the blocked main driveway. "Call me after work," she said to Paulette, "I'm worried about you with the trouble here." He leaned in the open window to kiss her goodbye, and he held their left hand against her cheek. "I'll call. I want to see lots more of you." She smiled that childlike smile and waved as she headed for her job.

Amy's Pontchartrain Hall dorm wasn't very far away, but police stopped her twice to see her student ID card. "This place is empty," she thought to Paul while a woman in blue uniform examined her ID. "Where is everyone?"

"Florence's roommates are staying off campus. Christine offered --"

The policewoman thought the smile was a thank you for returning her ID, but Amy interrupted Paul to think, "Sweet of her, but nuh-uh. I'm part of this now. I need to be here -- no, that's not right." She thought to herself as she walked, then corrected herself: "I want to be here. I will not miss a moment of this."

Safely back in her dorm, Amy opened the psychology book she should have spent the weekend studying. "What do I do with Reggie?" she asked out loud. "He's in my ten o'clock class." She looked at the textbook without reading.

"Riordan said he has to stay away from you. It might be fun to chase him."

Amy giggled at the idea.

"Did you -- was the time with Christine okay for you?" he asked

"Yes," she smiled. "I have trouble with the sex, but I guess it's easier for women. Girls dance with each other, we go to the bathroom together, it's not as horrible as it is for you. But I'm not exactly comfortable with it." She tickled their left arm -- Paul's arm -- with their right hand. "But I like her. She's nice, she's fun, and I know she makes you happy, and it's such a rush to see how happy you make her."

Paul leafed through the text book, hunting for Amy's bookmark. "It's not just me," he said softly. "She knows you, too. It's such a relief to be with someone who knows both of us."

"Well, ain't we the happy twins," she said, and finally began catching up on her class reading.

It was just before nine when her phone buzzed. When Amy saw who was calling, she took the call and said, "Clear. What?"

Riordan told her that the press conference would be at two-thirty outside the administration building, and she was not to talk to him there because the chief would be in attendance. She repeated his points to make sure she heard him correctly.

"I'll wave," she said, "but I won't blow your cover."

Amy slammed her text book closed. "I miss another Psych class, yippee."

Paul was laughing. "What are James and Tracey going to say when you come home with a 'D'?"

"Mom and Dad will give me hell, and then they'll say they love me anyway and will I try harder next term?"

"My father said the same things," Paul offered, "while he was wailing on my ass with a belt."

"Ouch. That would be called child abuse today."

"Funny, that's what I thought it was at the time."

She got a little more reading in before going to her math class. When she entered the classroom, she saw Reggie in the third row and headed for him. "Is this seat taken?" she asked as she sat.

He did a double take and said, "No! I mean, you can't sit there!" He dropped his voice to a whisper, "I don't want to go back to jail."

She smiled, and turned to a woman in the row behind them. "Hey," she said, "if anyone ever asks you, I was the one who insisted on sitting next to him. Okay?"

The woman frowned and said, "Whatever."

Amy turned her smile back to Reggie. "See? You're in the clear. I want to talk to you about --"

Just then the graduate student leading the seminar dropped his notebook on his desk and began the lecture.

"Leave me alone," Reggie whispered out of the side of his mouth. "First you beat me up, then you got me thrown in jail." He leaned to his right, away from Amy.

"But I did it with love, Sweetums," she hissed back.

When the instructor closed his book and left the room, Reggie looked at Amy as if he expected her to hit him again. His broken nose was still swollen and red from the beating Amy and Paul had given him when he accosted them in the dark hallway of her dorm. While the rest of the students filed out, Amy said, "Tell me about Megan Silver."

"No."

"No, what?"

"No way," he said. "I'm scared to be anywhere near you. That fifty foot restraining order is to protect me, not you."

She smiled, mostly because she thought it would upset Reggie. "Okay, I'll tell you about her. She was a kinky freak who liked to humiliate the men she slept with."

His jaw dropped. "How did -- I mean --"

"You're not the Lone Ranger; we've talked to some other men she went out with." He did not respond, so she went on, "Do you know a woman who calls herself Larissa?"

A head shake.

"Talk to me about Bruce."

"Who?" he asked, puzzled.

"You have a roommate; his name is Bruce Weeks."

"Oh, him." Reggie laughed, then winced with pain from his swollen face. "Not much to tell. He's a geek, total loser. I guess he's okay."

"What do you think Bruce would do if you asked him to kill someone for you?"

There was a long pause before he shouted, "What? What the fuck are you talking about?" Amy was glad the room was deserted.

"Just a thought. What do you think?"

Reggie shook his head repeatedly. "First, I'd never do that. And second, he's a nerd, but he's not a killer." He laughed, "Now that I think about it, that's funny. Are you a crazy woman?"

Amy thought a moment, holding her chin in her right hand. "I don't know about the detective, but I'm satisfied that you're not the UNO Strangler," Reggie began to speak, but she held her palm out to stop him and continued, "but you still seem to be the one thing that connects all the victims. Any idea who the killer might be? Is there anyone who might target your friends, the women you've gone out with? We're brainstorming here, I'm not asking for an accusation."

"You're serious," he said, and exhaled sharply. "Those cops were saying it was just a matter of time before they charged me with murder." He shivered. "But -- I've got some enemies, I suppose." A little laugh. "Shit, they'd want to kill me, not those girls."

"Alex Scruggs? I hear she's not completely crazy and you've spent some more time with her."

"My social life dried up. After Yvonne was found, girls said they wouldn't go out with me because they didn't want to be the next victim. Alex still likes me."

"Do you like her?"

"Yeah, she's okay. I don't want to bring her home to dad and marry her, but we have some fun together."

She slapped her palms down on the chair desktop and stood up. "Thanks, Reggie. If you think of anything, or of anyone, call the detective. No, call me." She left before he could ask her what just happened.

On the way to her noon class, Amy heard Paul think, "He can't be the murderer, because he was locked up when Megan was killed. And I believe him that Bruce is hardly Jack the Ripper material. So who targets the women that some slimy cock-hound has slept with? Uh, present company excluded."

"You think you know all my secrets. I've seen you eat peanut butter out of the jar, don't give me no guff." They both were laughing. "I don't know," she answered silently. "A jealous ex, maybe delusional, like stalker girl Alex?"

"Where's Reggie from?" Paul thought. "Maybe some enemy or rival of his high power father?"

"Possible, I suppose, but not very likely." Amy detoured off the sidewalk to tromp through a pile of yellow and red leaves that the grounds crew had thoughtfully left for her. "Or maybe Reggie has bedded so many women that that is not what connects them."

"Run that by Riordan," he replied. "As a man -- well, as a former man, I cannot comprehend such a thing, but it's no more far-fetched than a rival of his father trying to ruin the family."

"Are all press conferences like the ones with the President?"

It took Paul a second to catch up with Amy. "I guess. Some big shot or other, and a bunch of people with press cards. I like the ones where everyone ends up shouting."

She glanced at her watch. "I guess we find out in a couple of hours."

Amy was not the only UNO student milling around the administration building before the scheduled start of the press conference. The wind had picked up, and it was getting chilly despite the afternoon sun. Amy talked to Greta, her dorm resident advisor; and she asked Mikayla Washington about her sister's family funeral in Opelousas.

"Are you still in charge of this?" she heard Florence Draper say from behind her. Amy held her index finger to her lips and said, "Steven says I'm supposed to be invisible today. His boss is here somewhere."

"I like how easy it is to get around school now," Florence said. "My roomies aren't the only people who moved out for the duration."

"I got an offer myself," Amy said, "but I'm staying put." She was scanning the area around the building steps where a microphone had been set up, looking for the detective.

"Well, sure. A killer tries to get you and you'll just beat the living shit out of him."

"I don't think he's the killer. Besides, you know my motto: don't fuck with Amy." She smiled at her friend.

There was a burst of feedback, and someone at the

microphone said, "Is this thing on? No? Oh, it is, okay." Turning to face the couple hundred people waiting, the older man in the business suit said, "Thank you for being here today. I am Llewellyn Grimes, Dean of Students for the University Of New Orleans at Lakeshore." He motioned to one side and said, "With me today are Detective Steven Riordan and Captain John Ramirez of the Orleans Parish Police Department."

"I know him!" Amy exclaimed.

"How? Did you babysit for his kids?"

"No, it was ten years ago. Paul -- uh, my dad and some of his colleagues were involved in a case. He made me a Junior Commander." She heard Paul think, "He looks great! A Captain. Good for him."

"The Privateers of UNO are under siege right now. It's no secret that three of our students have lost their lives this semester. We welcome the police presence on campus in the hopes the violence stops while the culprit is brought to justice."

The dean continued, "UNO has sent messages to all students and their families about the sad incidents. We are complying with all the statutes and court decisions about keeping our campus community informed. The Women's Studies department will be holding a 'Take Back the Night' demonstration this evening at the amphitheater, and all Privateers are invited. Now I'd like the police to talk about the investigation, and to give us all advice on how to minimize the danger we face. Detective?"

There was a smattering of applause while Riordan went to the microphone. His suit was oversized -- Amy realized now it was so he could carry all the forensics tools -- and he held his fedora in one hand. "Thank you, Dean Grimes." Then, looking out at the audience, he went on. "In the five weeks since Laura Adams was found, we have interviewed dozens of students, friends, and staff members to find the information that will let us end this reign of terror. We have our eye on several persons of interest, and the investigation is ongoing. At the request of Dean Grimes, we are overseeing a partial lockdown of the campus to make it harder for evil-doers to come among you. I ask you, and you, and you --" he pointed randomly into the audience "-- to help us. If you see anything suspicious, tell us. If you see strangers, tell us. Any piece of information might turn out to be the clue that lets us return calm and safety to the school." He dictated his phone number twice.

"In the meantime, everyone here should take precautions for personal safety. Walk in groups, not by yourself. Stay in well-lighted public areas. Tell friends where you are going and when you will be back, and then call your friends when you do return. If you must walk at night and alone, call campus security and they'll send a guard to accompany you."

"I'm going to let Captain John Ramirez explain the campus partial lockdown that's underway. Johnny?"

The Captain came across the top step to the microphone, resplendent in the gold braid of his dress uniform. He was a little heavier than Amy remembered, and his face had some worry lines, but he looked healthy and in command.

"Thanks, Steven. I want to explain the inconvenience everyone on campus is going through now with this partial lockdown. Parish police are stationed in various places on the grounds. They will challenge everyone they see. Please cooperate and show your student ID when we ask. Tell us where you are going. We are not prying into your lives; we are trying to save them. The purpose is to limit access to UNO to students, faculty, and staff who belong here. By keeping outsiders away, we are preventing outsiders from harming anyone. At the same time," he went on, "by limiting the traffic on campus, it is easier for us and for you to notice anything unusual, suspicious, or dangerous."

"Let me repeat what Detective Riordan said. If you see anyone or anything out of the ordinary, tell authorities. Tell your professors, your dorm advisors, campus security, or uniformed police. All police work depends on the cooperation and good will of citizens like you."

He turned his head, and Dean Grimes walked across the steps, clapping his hands, to return to the microphone. "Thank you, Captain," he said. "Your presence makes us all feel safer."

Paul thought, "No, a nine-millimeter in our pocket would make us _be_ safer." He heard Amy think, "Shush. You and your guns."

With the press conference over, Amy headed toward the steps of the administration building. "I wonder if he'll remember me?"

she thought.

The Captain was standing with Riordan, talking quietly with Dean Grimes. Amy walked up on the Captain's side, behind the dean. She saw Riordan's look of horror, and saw his hands at his side, motioning to shoo her away. She smiled, then waited for their discussion to end. Instead, the dean noticed her and said, "Yes? What is it?"

"Actually, it's the Captain." He looked at her, while Riordan rolled his eyes. "I doubt you remember me, but I met you when you were a Sergeant. You made me a Junior Commander and you told me to go to the police academy."

Graciously, he said, "Goodness, you must have been just a child."

She smiled shyly. "I was. I was eleven years old. You told me I single-handedly helped you capture a killer, somebody-the-shiv."

His eyes went wide, and his mouth opened in surprise. "Hank Lattimer, how could I forget! That case made me a Lieutenant." He thought for a moment, then said, "As I recall, your father was a very brave man." Amy saw the detective smack his palm on the side of his head.

"He still is, Captain. He'll be flattered that you remember him. I'm Amy Clear," and she held out her hand.

The Dean looked annoyed. "That's all very well," Dean Grimes began, but Ramirez said, "No, no, I remember this girl. This woman, she was a girl when I met her. UNO is lucky to have her here." Then turning back to Amy, he asked, "When are you going to the police academy?"

"I'm a math major," embarrassed, "and I plan to get my Masters in statistics. I'm taking, uh, lessons in forensics, but I don't know that I'll make it to the academy."

"It's a delight to see you," he said. "If there's ever anything I can do for you, Miss Clear, you call me." He was beaming at her

She enjoyed the praise from the man who had complimented her ten years earlier, when Paul was a new addition to her life. She felt awkward, but she reached forward and hugged him. "Thank you, sir," she said, and backed away. The dean quickly reclaimed his attention.

Amy saw Riordan motion for her to follow him as he went around the corner of the administration building. The wind was particularly strong on that side, and the air was getting cold. When they were hidden from the dean he asked, "Why didn't you tell me you knew the Captain?"

"I didn't know I did. The last time I saw him was ten years ago and he was a Sergeant."

"Thank God you didn't say anything about working with me."

"You told me not to!" She stamped her foot. "I'm not a total lamebrain, you know." Meanwhile, she heard Paul think, "It was great to see Ramirez. I feel safer just knowing he's around." "Me too," she said aloud.

"You too what?"

"Are we talking about that ancient rock band?" She didn't know why Paul was laughing.

Riordan squeezed his eyes shut and held the bridge of his nose between his thumb and index finger. "Let's start over. How do you know my Captain?"

"I met him over something my dad did a long time ago. He was nice to me, I liked him. It was a treat to see him just now."

Finally, the detective smiled. "I still want to hide you from him, but maybe it won't be the end of the world if he finds out. I mean, maybe it won't be the end of my career."

"I'm against the rules, aren't I?" she asked, sheepishly. She heard Paul inside her head and Riordan in her ears: "Boy, howdy."

"Now we wait," he said. "Maybe the killer will send a message; sometimes they like to taunt the police."

It was Paul who said, "Or we wait for another body to turn up."

"One with clues," Riordan responded. "That's about it."

"And meantime it takes an act of congress for me to get to my classes."

"Sweetheart, I don't want to hear that you pulled any 'But I'm working with the detective' crap with the officers. When they ask for your ID, show it and smile."

"Yes, Your Majesty," and she curtseyed.

"Go on with you," he said, smiling. "Get to class or whatever you college kids do. I have to check in with the Captain and that

God-awful dean of yours."

When Riordan left, Paul thought, "You still have four chapters of Psych, plus today's math."

"I know," she said aloud, "I'm going to find Florence." She walked to the front of the administration building, but the crowd had dissipated; all that remained were Ramirez, Riordan, Dean Grimes, and some campus workers dismantling the sound system.

Amy was stopped three times on her way to Florence's dorm. First, two police outside the business school asked for her ID and wanted to know where she was going. She thought to Paul, "At least they're nice about it. He said 'please' and 'thank you.'"

He thought back, "That pistol on their hips says '...or else!' to me."

When she walked across the large parking lot, an officer left his post at the Alumni Center to interrupt her, also politely. "This is getting old fast," she thought. She was rubbing her upper arms to keep warm.

Finally, two uniformed police stopped her before she entered the Privateer Hall complex. She smiled, as Riordan had told her to, but thought to Paul, "If we don't solve this fast I'm going to scream at these cops."

She heard him laugh and reply, "You and another ten thousand students."

Once inside the dorm apartment complex, she was not challenged. As they walked up the stairs, Paul whispered aloud, "This doesn't make sense. If the killer is a student, this partial lockdown gives them free reign inside the dorms. If I were in charge --"

A policeman was standing in the hallway as they left the stairway. "May I see your ID, miss?" he asked.

"You're Mullinax, aren't you?" She handed over her swipe card.

"Do I know -- Oh, right. You're the one who walked that creep into a door. How are you doing?"

"Enjoying the kind of reputation every girl dreams of," she said. "I appreciate you showing up with Steven to empty my trash that night."

"Steven? Oh, Riordan, right." He returned her ID. "You be

careful, miss."

She heard Paul think, "For once I am glad to be wrong."

As usual, Florence's door was standing open. She was looking through a pattern book while she talked with one of her roommates. Amy knocked on the door frame and called, "Paging Florence Draper!"

"Well, well," Florence said, standing up to greet Amy, "I didn't expect to see you again so soon."

"What did I tell you about locking your door?" she said, "There's a killer out there. And what are you working on?"

She reached around Amy and closed the door. "Oh, just a tailored shirt. I promised one of my gay boys I'd make one for him."

"Still hanging out with them? Sorry you haven't found some guy to like."

She shrugged. "I do like these men. And you know, it's kind of a relief not to worry about sex for a change. You want to go for a walk?"

"And get stopped by the police every ten feet?" Amy said.

Florence's roommate slammed a closet door and lay down on her bed with a text book.

"Oh. Let me borrow a scarf. It's turned into winter outside."

Florence tossed a bright red knit shawl to her and grabbed her coat. "See you later, Consuela" she said as they left.

"Domestic problem?" Amy asked.

"She's a lovely woman," Florence said, her voice dripping with sarcasm. "Gracious, flexible, open to new ideas -- just lovely."

"I thought she and your other roommates were staying off campus."

"Yeah," she frowned, "they kicked her out after two nights."

When they were outside, Florence said, "You're right, it is cold! Cove or the library?"

"Cove has french fries," Amy said. "And coffee."

"Talked me into it," as the first set of police stopped them.

"What blew up with your roomie?"

"Don't ask. If I just threw her through the window, I'd get a letter of commendation from the resident advisor and from her sorority sisters." One of the cops peered at her, then shook his head.

"Whoa," Amy laughed, "aren't the walls perpendicular? Aside from that, how's things?"

"I keep seeing you on the TV news," she said. "You're always in back, somewhere near that detective with a hat. I could teach him how to buy a suit that actually fits."

"Uhh, his suit is too big because of all the stuff he has to carry with him. Florence, I am having the time of my life!" Amy said.

"Good for you. How's school?" Another pair of uniformed men, another challenge.

"Somehow I'm keeping up with everything but Psych. Not only this investigation, but I told you about my friend Paul? He's got a new girlfriend, I've spent some time with the two of them."

When the guards returned their ID cards, Florence pushed the door open to the Cove and said, "Heat! I need BTUs!" She shivered, but began unbuttoning her coat as they headed for the inside vestibule door. "You told me he's not your boyfriend, but I didn't believe you."

"Would I bother to lie to you?" Amy smiled. "I really like the woman, she's a sweetheart. They're cute together."

"What do you do to not be three's a crowd?"

"We had a good time at LaSalle Park, going down the slides and climbing a tree. Then we had a blast making spaghetti together. I learned Paul's recipe. It's as good as what my dad makes."

"Better!" Paul thought to her.

"I'm glad your friend is getting some, but how about you?" She threw her coat on an empty chair and headed for the bottomless coffee urn. Amy followed.

"I'm too busy to worry about men. Although it was fun to hassle that guy I beat up. They let him out of jail and he's back in my math class." Amy laughed, "He's scared of me. Terrified. It's really neat."

Florence turned to stare at her friend. "You are the strangest creature I have ever known."

"Is that a bad thing?"

"Probably not. Ask me again in a year."

Paul took the lead and said, "I like Paul's girlfriend. She's becoming my friend, too." He heard Amy scream silently, "Don't do that!"

"Fuck, I'm impressed," Florence said. "I hope these gay boys turn out to be half the friends this Paul is for you."

Paul laughed inside. Amy thought to him, "You shush. Don't make this harder."

Florence went on, "You know, men I don't have to dress up for, or undress for, just to be buddies." She went on, "When's the last time you had a date?"

"That guy I beat up. Ugh, he was such a jerk."

"Most of them are, but I keep looking for a keeper."

"Are you seeing anyone now?" Amy asked.

"No. Dammit, no, I'm not, I'm making do with these gay men. Actually, I like them, they can be so funny." She sighed. "Sometimes I want to take a flame thrower and kill all the guys in the world. The straight ones, anyway."

"Somebody you want to ask you out?"

"Not even! I rule out a lot of men because they are such obvious mooks."

"Paul says --" Instantly, Amy wished she hadn't begun the sentence that way. "My friend says that girls and women are always more mature than guys the same age. We need to find some older men."

"Too bad your friend has a new gal pal, otherwise I'd ask you to introduce me. He sounds like a very cool guy."

"Yes, he's very cool."

Paul bounced their legs in their chair. "Yay me!" he thought to her, "Go Paulette."

Florence said, "The last date I had was three weeks ago. Robbie, he's a junior I met at a party somewhere. God, he was so good looking, I couldn't keep my hands off him! We went to an Italian place uptown, and when he got the check he told me how much I owed him! I still couldn't keep my hands off him, but I wanted to strangle him. And he still expected me to sleep with him!"

"Did you?" Amy asked.

"Well, yeah!" Florence answered. "If he wasn't going to buy me dinner, the least he could do was show me fireworks."

Amy was uncomfortable with Florence's direct discussion about sex, but she admired her friend's lack of inhibition. She said, "Well, did he?"

Florence laughed. "For a day and a half, he sure did!"

"Whoo-hoo!" Amy yelled, and joined Florence's laughter. "When are you seeing him again?"

The laughter ended. "Son of a bitch said he'd call me and of course he never did. Mook."

"On-field violation of the three day rule?" Amy volunteered.

"Yup. Waited three days and I called him. Left a message on his cell phone, asked him if he wanted to go out and play. Did I say he never called me?"

The two women sat silently in The Cove. Voices from other students reverberated around them. Suddenly Florence cried, frustrated, "What the hell am I doing wrong?"

Paul thought to Amy, "Is it okay if I talk to her for a minute?"

"Be careful!" she thought back, and retreated.

"College may not be the place to look for true love," Paul went on. "A zillion women here, we're all the age where we look prettier and sexier than we ever will again. We're just cookies in a jar to the guys. They'd be crazy to do anything but sleep their way through school."

"Fuck true love. I just want some men to be nice to me."

"And after three dates you dump them?"

"Woman's prerogative."

Paul sighed. Softly he said, "The things you're complaining that the guys do? Aren't you doing the same thing?"

There was a long pause. Amy thought "Paul!" and elbowed her way past him to lead. "I'm sorry, Florence, I didn't mean that."

Florence shook her head. "No, you're a good friend to be honest with me. I tell myself all sorts of stories, but I don't trust the men I meet. None of them. It's like I need to hurt them, and it makes me angry if they don't call because then I don't have a chance to beat up their precious little egos. Christ, maybe my sister's not the crazy one in the family."

Amy hissed to Paul, "You are so lucky you didn't just ruin my friendship with Florence, I'd have killed you dead."

Paul said out loud, "I don't think you're crazy, and believe me, I know crazy. But is this what you'll do forever? Break hearts just to make yourself feel better? I --" he stopped, thought, and went on, "-- Florence, I'd rather see you happy."

Florence sat thinking, resting her chin on her right hand. Then she shook her head and said, "Mama Flo prescribes ice cream. Who needs to get laid when there are gay friends around?"

Paul thought to Amy, "Are you sure we can't tell her about me? Man, what a setup line that was!"

"Vanilla. With rainbow sprinkles. Come on, Florence, I'm buying."

ॐ 32 ॐ

"It's a relief to hear from you, Paulette," Christine said. "I'm worried about what's going on at your school. It's all over the news."

"It's great to hear your voice, too," he said. "Busy day at the agency?"

"Oh, sure. But it's just a job. You?"

"We were at the press conference today. Turns out a sergeant we met ten years ago is the police captain now. I feel a little better knowing he's on the case. Amy, too."

"I'm glad. Are you sure you won't stay at my place until they catch the killer? I worry about you."

"It's Amy. You're a sweetheart. But I'm part of the 'they' that is going to catch the perp. I want to stay here. But thanks." Then Paul took back the lead, and said, "There's a cheap movie Wednesday night in the University Center. Want to run the gauntlet and come up here?"

"Sure thing, Paulette. If the movie's bad, you can show me your dorm room."

"I like the way you think," he laughed. "Look, there are police all over the school, so call me when you're on the way and I'll meet you just off campus. Come up Lakeshore Drive, there's a big parking lot you can use."

"Oh boy," Christine said enthusiastically, "it sounds like an adventure!"

"I am so looking forward to being with you. Look, Amy's got some homework. She can't do it while I'm on the phone, so I have to go. We'll talk Wednesday. I'll see you for the movie."

"I love you, Paulette," she said. "Don't forget me."

"Never," he said.

When the call was over, Amy said, "That woman breaks my heart. 'Don't forget me'? What kind of life has she led?"

"I am crazy about her," Paul said. "She makes me feel needed. And all the emotion she has -- I can't get enough."

"Wow. Do you love her?"

"I doubt it. I've seen her, what, three times?" He paused, thinking. "Still too much lust and gratitude to be able to tell."

"Teach me to tell the difference." Amy was sitting on the bed in her dorm room. "When I like a boy, I get so confused and scared. If he likes me, I'm happy, and if he doesn't I'm not."

"Me too," he said. "That's what I mean about too many other feelings to know if I'm in love or in lust. Sometimes the best you can say is 'I don't know yet, but I'm having a great time.'"

"Do you remember Rhonda from St. Pius?" Amy asked.

"And how! She was your, uh, well-developed friend."

"You're impossible," she smiled. "Rhonda married a boy from Edward the Confessor. I think they actually did it the week before graduation. She's miserable now. The guy is real good looking, but he drinks and he's such a goof-off that his father fired him from the family business. She's stuck with him and with two kids."

"Sorry to hear that. She was your friend; just for that she deserved better."

"I think she could have used your advice. Wait a while to see what you feel after the dust settles."

"I hope you don't think I'm telling you how to live your life," Paul said.

"Oh, I'll let you know, believe me," she answered. "This is just good advice. Great advice. I wonder if I'll remember it next time I need it?"

✆ 33 ৡ

Wednesday, October 20, 2021 -- UNO campus, New Orleans

"Why did I take psychology?" Amy said out loud, dragging her textbook onto her desk. "I've got four more chapters just to catch up, and there's a test on Friday."

Paul looked forward to Amy's reading, because it meant he could read the novels he enjoyed so much. "You'll do fine," he said, "I won't let you stop studying until --" he looked at the red LEDs on the desk clock "-- until five o'clock, okay?"

"Hard to say 'thank you'. What are you reading now?"

"Trollope. *The Warden*. Funny and sad at the same time. I'd love to visit Barchester."

"Maybe this weekend," she said. "How far away is it?"

"Umm, the Atlantic Ocean is kind of in the way."

Amy shook her head, but laid out Paul's novel beneath her Psych book. For most of the next two hours they took advantage of their peculiar ability to read different things simultaneously. Amy forced her way through her textbook, highlighter in their right hand, while Paul periodically turned the pages in his novel with their left.

At one point Amy said, "What do you think this means?" and she pointed to a paragraph in her text. Paul put their left thumb on his place in the novel, and switched his attention to her book. He read the sentence twice, then again, out loud.

"One can explore dimensional vibrations that cross traditional boundaries of algebra, string theory, post-Einsteinian physics, holonomic brain theory and Jungian concepts of the collective unconscious and synchronicity. The result is abstract, and yet, in a very real sense, particular.

"I know what all the words mean," Paul said, "but not in this combination. This is a pile of shit. What are they teaching in college these days?"

Amy smiled grimly. "Thanks. I'm glad it's not just me." She took a pink highlighter to the paragraph and went back to studying. Paul returned to Barchester, Hiram's Hospital, and the gentle story of Septimus Harding.

They were still reading when Amy's phone went off. "Hey!" Paul said, "that should be Christine," and he took the call.

"Paulette, they won't let me drive in. Help!"

"Where are you?" he asked.

"I think I'm on Lakeshore. There's a roadblock at some traffic circle. Is Technology Park part of your school?" He could hear her breathing fast, and her voice was higher pitched than usual.

"Ask the cop where you can wait for me to get there. I'm maybe five minutes away."

"Okay. Wait." He heard the ambient noise increase as she rolled down her window, and heard the campus guard tell her to wait on THAT side of the circle. "Paulette, he says I can wait here for a while. Please come get me; I'm scared of all these police."

"Five minutes, Honey," he said. Amy grabbed her jacket with their free hand as Paul ran out of the room and down the stairs.

Paul walked up Elysian Fields, the eastern border of the campus. Looking toward the river, he saw a display of flashing red and blue lights worthy of July 4th fireworks. "You heard her," he said, "she's getting freaked out by all this." He started to run again.

"Over there," Amy thought to him when she recognized Christine's yellow Smart Car at the curb on the far side of the traffic circle. Paul ignored two policemen who called to him, and he knocked on Christine's side window.

The worry and fear on her face dissolved into a smile as she rolled the window down. "There you are!" she said. He leaned in and kissed her just as one of the guards caught up to him and pulled on their elbow.

"I told you to stop," the guard barked.

Paul said, "I'm sorry. My friend was waiting for me. She doesn't know what's been happening here and she was frightened. What do you need? My ID?"

"Next time law enforcement tells you to stop, you'd better do it," he said as he took Amy's swipe card. "We're all a little on edge here."

"This is my friend Christine," he said, holding her hand at the sill of the car window. "We want to go to the campus movie tonight. If I ride with her, can she park in the Privateer Hall lot?"

He handed the ID card back to Amy, then bent over to look in the window at Christine. "What's your business here, honey?" he asked.

"Uh, like my friend said. We're going to the movie. I think it starts at seven."

"When will it be over? When do you plan to leave?"

Paul bent down to the policeman and whispered, "If I'm lucky she's staying overnight."

When the officer stood up to look at him, Paul tried to wear the little-girl-innocent face he'd seen Amy practice in the mirror for occasions just like this. He heard Amy think, "Great. The whole campus is going to think I'm a lesbian. No guy is ever going to ask me out," and he fought the impulse to smile.

The policeman shook his head and said, "Whatever. Get in. You know where she can park," and he walked away.

Paul got in the passenger side. Christine reached out to grasp their left hand, and asked, "What did you say to him?"

Paul let the smile take over their face as he told her.

She smiled at him, and started the car. "I love you, Paulette."

"I'll let Amy navigate, okay?" A moment later the same voice said, "It's Amy. Campus is a zoo with the police here."

"Oh, hi, Amy," Christine said. "I thought you were part of the investigation. They still make you show your ID?"

"It was explained to me in words of one syllable I was not to pull rank. The whole thing is a nuisance."

"I hope you solve the mystery fast."

Amy heard Paul think, "She thinks you're running the entire case." She thought about explaining, then decided to leave it at, "Me, too. Thanks."

Amy showed Christine where to park, and they made their way to The Cove for a fast dinner. "Are you getting to help Amy?" Christine asked.

"Some, yes," Paul began. "Of course, the detective doesn't know about --"

"You two," a guard's voice boomed, "I want to see some ID."

Paul showed Amy's swipe card, while Christine fumbled in her wallet for her driver's license. "Where's your campus card?" the guard asked.

"I'm not a student, I'm --"

The guard took her by the shoulders and spun her around, pushing her to one side of the walkway. "You stay right here," he said, and flicked a button on his walkie-talkie.

"Excuse me," Paul said, but the guard held up his free hand, palm out. Louder this time, Paul said, "I said, 'excuse me.'"

"I'm busy," the guard growled.

"So are we."

Christine looked back and forth from the guard to Paulette, becoming more and more agitated. "It's okay, Paulette," she said.

The guard turned to Paul and said, "You're interfering with police business."

Amy jumped to the front. "How would you know?" she said, "You're not a cop. You're a sixteen-dollar-an-hour crossing guard. Get Mullinax over here."

"And who the fuck do you think you are?" he said, threateningly.

"Watch your mouth, big boy," Amy hurled back. "I asked you to get Mullinax. Do it." The guard hesitated, taken aback by Amy's forcefulness. She added, "NOW!"

"Okay, you and your friend can go," he said, then turned to find other students who might be easier to bully.

Paul thought to Amy, "You're getting great at that."

"If what they're doing made any sense -- but it doesn't!"

Paul took Christine's hand and she walked close beside him. "Was that you? Or Amy? You made that troglodyte back off."

"That was Amy," he said. "I'm learning from her. The other

day she said her motto is 'don't fuck with Amy.'"

"You're both amazing," Christine offered. "This --" she waved her free hand at the campus partial lockdown "-- would make me hide. I'm glad I'm with you, Paulette."

He squeezed the girl's hand.

They were stopped at another check point by real police, who behaved professionally and were unperturbed by Christine's status as a visitor. As they came up on the doorway to the Cove, another policeman hailed them. "Excuse me, I need -- Oh, is that you, Miss Clear?"

"Officer Mullinax, what a pleasant surprise. This is my friend Christine. She's a townie, but we're going to grab a bite and then see the movie. Can I bring you anything from inside?"

"A cup of coffee would be a Godsend," he said, and he nodded at Christine.

"Chicory?"

"Is there any other kind?"

Amy waved and they walked inside The Cove. "Amy?" Christine asked. "You really know him?"

She laughed. "Let me get his coffee first. Do you want to take a table and wait?"

"I want to stay with you and Paulette."

Paul squeezed her hand again, and led her to the counter so Amy could get the coffee for the officer. He thought to her, "It's a shame the campus is in police state mode, but you're safe with me and Amy." Christine smiled and leaned her cheek against their shoulder.

"You were serious!" Mullinax cried when Amy gave him the big styrofoam cup of New Orleans chicory.

"You have no idea how glad I am you're here," she said. "This is the least I can do. How goes the war?"

He took a long chug of coffee, then put the plastic lid back in place. "A lot of scared people. A lot of pissed off people, uh, excuse me. No killers, though."

"I haven't talked to Steven since Monday," Amy went on. "Any developments?" He shook his head.

Christine arched her neck to whisper in Amy's ear, "Aren't you hungry?"

Amy laughed, "I hear the dinner bell. See you later," and the women went back inside The Cove.

"How are their burgers?" Christine asked.

Paul said, "Not bad, with enough ketchup. Or are you a mustard person?"

"People put mustard on hamburgers? On what planet?"

Amy let Paul lead to place their orders, and to pay. They claimed a table and waited to hear her name called.

"What's this 'take back the night' thing?" Christine asked, looking at a poster by their table.

"Three women have been killed and a lot of people are scared," Paul commented. "The rally is a useless feel-good thing, but I hear they're giving out rape whistles. That might help."

"It's Amy," the voice continued. "I think the rally is a good thing. It teaches people to pay attention to their surroundings."

There was a smile on Christine's face as she softly said, "You really are two people."

A cough, and then she heard Amy think "Yes" and Paul think "Yup" to her. Her smile grew.

"I have never known anyone like you," she said. "Like either of you."

Amy and Paul each put a hand on Christine's. "You are a delight." Somehow Christine could tell when Paul took the lead to say, with the same voice, "I'm so glad you were brave enough to introduce yourself."

When the PA system aired Amy's name, Paul told Christine to hang on to the table while he got their food. When he returned, Christine was leaning forward with her face down and her arms spread out to keep anyone from using the table. "That worked great," Paul said, as he unloaded the tray.

"I don't want to share you," Christine said. "Either of you."

Paul ignored it when Amy thought, "Please don't"; he leaned over and kissed Christine on the tip of her nose. "All yours," he whispered.

Amy said, "Oh no, I'm going to be on the front page of *The Driftwood*. I can see the headline, 'Dykes Invade UNO.'"

"It's Paul. As femme as we are, no one will care."

Christine started to dress her burger. "My mom is like that," she said. "She says PDAs are bad, but then she's always hugging me and kissing me wherever we go."

"So that means PDAs really are okay?"

"Totally." She looked up and grinned at her Paulette, then went back to her meal.

The path from The Cove to the University Center for the movie went across the campus, from near the London Avenue Canal to the now blocked entrance driveway off Elysian Fields. Three times they were stopped by pairs of campus guards or Parish police. Paul muttered, so Christine could hear him, "This is such a waste! They're barely paying attention, and it doesn't seem to matter that you're not a student."

"Oh. I'm sorry," she said softly.

"No, you're not doing anything wrong. And the cops are just doing what they're told. It's the premise, the, the, concept behind this partial lockdown that's wrong."

"It's Amy. I think Paul is right." She smiled at an officer as he handed back her ID card. "What we need are clues. The necklace."

Unconsciously, Christine reached for the pearl pendant around her neck. "What necklace?"

"You can't tell anyone," Amy began.

Christine laughed. "I already can't tell anyone about you two; what's another secret?"

"The medical examiner thinks all three women were strangled by the same necklace, with a distinctive pattern." Then, "It's Paul. The public can't know, because the police don't want the murderer to know that we know."

Christine put her arm through Amy's and said, "I feel safe with you. You're going to fix everything, aren't you?"

With a smile, Amy said, "Or die trying."

When Paul invited Christine to the movie, he was merely looking for an excuse to be with her; he had no idea what the film was. When they got to the screening room, they found the brochure that the campus film society had prepared for a documentary called *Inside Australia*. Christine began reading it and said, "This is great! I've always wanted to go to Australia."

Paul thought for the first time in his life that he'd always wanted to go there, too. "What's the attraction?" he asked.

"Kangaroos," she began, and ticked items off on her fingers. "Ayres Rock. Aborigines. Beer. Cave paintings. It's summer there when it's winter here. And they speak English."

"When are we going?"

"Don't tease me, Paulette," she smiled. "I've wanted to go since I was thirteen years old. I'm so glad you asked me to see this."

"It's Amy. Have you ever gone out of the country?"

Shaking her head, she said, "Mom and my brother and I went to Yosemite when I still lived at home. That's the biggest travel adventure I've had. So far."

"We used to take vacations every summer. We went to Mexico one year. We all took turns getting sick. Bad water."

"It's Paul. My sister and I made it to Canada a couple of times. Australia would be a great place to go. Amy, is your passport still valid?"

Amy answered, "What passport?"

The head of the film society stood in front of the screen. "We're doing something different," she told the twenty or so people in the room. "Usually we feature third world films that teach us about the race, class, and gender-based issues of social justice that plague people throughout the world. But Barney Olsen, the society VP, landed an exchange student slot at the University of Wallamaloo, so he insisted on something more personally relevant today." She signaled an assistant who turned off the lights and started the DVD.

Paul and Christine leaned on each other as they sat, holding hands in her lap. And even Amy enjoyed the film.

"The movie was great," Christine said afterwards, "but I just wanted it to be over so we could come back here." They were lying in the skinny single bed in Amy's single dorm room. "I wanted to get undressed with you. I love you, Paulette, I always want to be touching you. Like this," and she caressed Amy's breasts.

"And I love it when you do it," he said. He hugged her as they lay next to each other. The room smelled of their excited bodies.

"Will you stay?" Paul asked.

"I have to be at work so early."

"I'll get up with you. It'll be easier to get through all the cops if I'm with you. You can drop me off once you're off campus."

"You'd do that for me?" she asked as she felt Amy's arms and chest and neck. The touch wasn't so much erotic as it was exploratory, getting to know Paulette.

"Yes," he said, "Yes, yes, yes!" and he rolled toward her and licked her ear. Christine gave a happy shout and snuggled against them.

After awhile she said, "Amy? Are you okay?"

"I sure am."

"And, it's okay what Paulette and I do?"

A laugh. "I'm sure I'll get used to it. Paul still has trouble when I'm, you know, with a man."

"This is for you," she said, and kissed them on the cheek. "I love Paulette. And you're part of her, so I'm just going to love you, too."

Paul thought to Amy, "There was a time when I'd have run screaming from a woman saying these things. But now, I just can't get enough."

"You are a dear thing," Amy said. "And you make Paul happy. I mean, he and I get along pretty well, but," she shook her head, "you make him happy."

Christine giggled. "What can I do for you, Amy?"

She turned her head to stare at the woman. They both had a crooked front tooth. "Be my friend," she replied. "Paul is your lover, but let both of us be your friend."

"I'd like that. I told you, I don't have a lot of friends. Paulette is so open with me, and you, too. Do I really matter to you?

"This is Amy speaking," she said, and put her hand on the woman's naked shoulder. "Yes, you matter to me. You make Paul happy, and that matters to me. And I like you, you're fun. That matters to me. And I -- we -- can be ourself around you. There are only a handful of people who know that Paul and I share this body. It can be exhausting to always watch what we say, to remember to say 'I' when what we both think is 'we.' We don't have to do that with you; we can just be -- us. Yes, you matter to me."

Christine threw her arms around them. "I love you, Paulette! I love you, Amy!"

"You want me to lead?" Paul thought to Amy. "I know you don't like that touching tits thing."

"In a minute," she thought back. "I told her the truth. She matters to me, too."

"Good." Then, "Am I going to be jealous of you?"

"Only if you're going crazy. I like her, but you're the one she touches."

Paul took back the lead and continued the hug. "It's Paul. And you matter to me, too."

She squeezed them, then suddenly moved down the bed to lick their stomach. Paul let his hands play in her multi-length hair, feeling content.

Christine's voice was muffled, her face still pressed against their abdomen. "Paulette, what do you do when Amy is with a boy?"

He laughed, and he heard Amy laughing inside. "Mostly I wish I weren't there. I have to close my inside eyes. I think I understand why you don't like men. They've got this penis, and they poke you with it, and then it --"

"Stop!" Christine interrupted. "Don't remind me!" She licked their stomach again. "If I wanted to get poked with a prick, I'd be with a man. Uh, who had a man's body."

"I have to be devil's advocate," Amy said, "I like that poking prick thing."

"You know how you can tell when a boy is lying?" Christine asked. "His lips are moving. For most of them I think there's a chip in their head that short circuits when a girl talks. They are not capable of hearing what a girl says."

"Not Paul," Amy said.

"Well, he's hardly your typical boy. For one thing, I love him."

Amy thought to Paul, "I'm so glad she does."

"Thanks," he said out loud, of course with her voice.

"For what?" Christine said, lifting her head to look at Paul.

"For being friends with Amy."

This time she kissed them on the stomach. "She's a part of you. I have to love her, too." She lay on her side, elbow bent, head resting on her hand. "I'm a lucky girl to know you. Both of you."

Paul closed their eyes and let the wave of gratitude and security wash over him. He knew he could not tell exactly what his feelings for the woman were, only that they were very positive and very strong.

She leaned over and kissed him on the mouth, then rested her head on his chest. She liked the view of Amy's breasts, with their freckles. She liked how warm Paulette was. She liked that Paulette cared for her, and seemed to know how to make her voices go away when they started talking their trash. And Amy was like the sister she never had.

"I try to pretend the guy Amy's with is really a woman," Paul said. "As long as he's just using his hands, that's easy. If he'd shave first, I might even be able to pretend his mouth is a woman's. But you taste better." He kissed the top of Christine's head, and she curled her toes.

"When Amy's boy starts that poking," Christine said, "think of me. Think of me doing this," and she began to play with Amy's labia, and beyond. "Does that feel good?"

Paul sighed; an "Ummmmm" came from their mouth. With a mischievous smile, Christine took a long time arousing them. After awhile it was Amy, unannounced, who gasped and said, "Oh, oh. Yes, that feels good."

Christine kissed their breastbone, then retrieved her hand and licked her fingers. "Good. Just think of me; it'll be all right."

Amy thought to Paul, "Why would I want to think of her when I'm with a man?"

He thought back, "She was talking to me. She's telling me how to keep my end of our bargain."

☙ 34 ☙

In the morning, Paul led and shared a chaste shower with Christine in the dorm's communal facility. Amy lent her a clean shirt so it wouldn't be too obvious at her job that she had not gone home overnight. The three of them talked about their barely remembered glimpses of sleep dreams. When they walked to the parking lot, only one set of police stopped them, and it was just a cursory look at IDs. When they were clear of the officers, Paul said, "Even the cops are bored with this partial lockdown."

"Next time, come visit me," Christine said. "I feel safe with you, but everyone is so tense here."

"Amy?" he said aloud.

"Psych exam tomorrow. I'm still four chapters behind." She led Christine through a narrow gate that opened on the parking lot. "How about Saturday? What's the club like on a weekend?"

"That would be great," she replied. "I want you to meet my old girlfriend. We're still buddies, and I like her new partner. Uh - - Paulette, I'll introduce both of you as Paulette. Is that how it works?"

"It's Paul. That'll work. In your world we're Paulette. On campus we're Amy. But it's both of us."

She shook her head. "How do you keep it straight?"

"We just do." Then, "Paul's right. We have no idea how any of this works. Welcome to the grand experiment."

Paul got in the passenger side when they got to Christine's car. "If you go out this way," pointing, "you'll be on Elysian Fields and you can drop us off."

"I'm glad --"

Amy grabbed her phone and said, "Clear. What?" Paul thought to Christine, "It's the detective. I hope there's no trouble. We may as well start going."

She drove slowly toward the exit and the looming check point, listening to Amy's half of the conversation. "No! Tell me you're joking. Okay, then tell me you're lying. Oh, shit! Where? There? But there's no dorm near there. Yes -- yes -- okay, ten minutes. When will you and Jermaine get there?" They heard Amy laugh, and she said, "I'll do my best, Your Majesty."

"Your Majesty?" Christine asked. "Amy, is everything all right?"

"No," she said, turning off her phone and sliding it into a pants pocket. "Another body. It's behind the chemistry and science buildings." She looked at Christine. "I'm sorry that call wasn't five minutes later, you didn't need to hear this."

"Paulette, Amy, you be careful! I just found you, I don't want to --" as she stopped speaking, she pulled to the side of the ramp. She was staring straight ahead, gripping the steering wheel with white knuckles.

"It's Paul," he said, and slid closer to put their arms around her. "We'll be okay. I never let Amy do anything too dangerous." He touched her cheek and felt tears. "Really. Amy's with the police, nothing bad is going to happen to us."

Christine finally turned to look at her Paulette. "I worry. It's what I do. I love you. I'd be crazy if anything happened to you."

"Sshhh, sshhh," Paul cooed, bringing his left index and middle fingers to her lips. "I understand. We'll be okay. Just for you. There's so much more Christine I want."

They looked at each other for a long moment. "It's Amy," finally came from their mouth. "I hate to be insensitive, but Riordan needs me to supervise the crime scene until he gets here. I'm sorry, Christine, it's an emergency."

"You do such important work, Amy," she said, and she resumed the drive. "I'm sorry."

Paul put his hand on her shoulder. "We'll get together this weekend. The detective may postpone our plans, but I won't let him cancel them. I'll call you.

At the check point, the policeman ignored Christine's wet face when he asked for her ID. She handed over her driver's license, and said, "I'm not a student; I was visiting." From the other side of the seat, Amy called, "I'm a junior in Pontchartrain North." The officer looked up, then returned Christine's license and waved her through the traffic circle.

Paul trotted to the open window in Christine's door to say goodbye. "I had a great time with you," he said. "I can't wait to see you again."

She wiped her cheek with her shoulder. "I love you, Paulette. You be careful. And take care of Amy."

Paul kissed her on the mouth, and lingered, until Christine pushed back. "I can't be late for work, I have to go. I love you!" and she was gone down Elysian Fields.

"Now what?" he thought.

"Dead girl number four. Riordan wants me to run the rent-a-cops again. We gotta go."

Despite the scattered officers and guards, the campus seemed calm. "Nobody knows yet," Amy thought. "What will Dean Grimes do, make us stay locked in our rooms?" They went through two check points with bored police before they came up on the area behind the chemistry building. The usual two campus guards were there, as well as the one Amy had challenged the night before.

"There she is!" one of the guards shouted, and waved her to come faster.

"They were easy to train," Paul thought as they began to trot to the guards.

"Your detective called. He said you'd make sure we did things right." He stepped aside and pointed to the latest victim of the UNO Strangler, some thirty feet away.

"You've kept everyone away?" The guard nodded. "But you did check to see if she is alive?" Another nod.

Amy tried to take in the details while Paul asked the basic questions: Who found the body? When? Anything obvious and suspicious? Do they have a name for the deceased? It was the guard himself who found the dead woman on a routine patrol, around 6:45. "I thought someone dropped a coat on the grass, so I went to pick it up. As soon as I realized it was a person, I checked for pulse, then called command, and I backed away from the body. I hope I didn't mess up your evidence like I did last time."

"No, you did good," Paul said, with Amy's voice. "Not everyone learns from mistakes. I appreciate it." The guard beamed at the praise. "Keep anyone away from the body. I want to size up the area."

As Amy began to walk the perimeter, looking at the grass for any sign of a killer's point of entry, she heard a familiar voice say, "Who the fuck do you think you are?"

She straightened to see the same campus guard who had confronted Paul and Christine the night before.

"I told you once to watch your mouth," she said. "I'm Amy Clear. I work with Steven Riordan. What's your name?"

"You gave me a hard time yesterday," he grumbled.

"I asked you your name."

"You're just a kid. I don't have to pay attention to you."

Amy smiled and took a step toward the man; immediately, he backed up. "Yes, I'm just a kid. I'm the kid who is in charge of this crime scene until Riordan gets here with Doctor Jermaine. Either help the other guys keep anyone away from the area, or go over there and sit down." She turned away without waiting for his reply, and went back to the task at hand.

She thought to Paul, "Steven would look for clues showing how the girl got here. How a killer got here and away."

"So, we're looking for what? Bent grass? Footprints? Cigarette butts?"

"All of the above," and she slowly paced the sidewalks that framed the large grassy area where the body lay, looking for anything. When she finished a circuit, she moved a pace closer to the dead girl, and walked the perimeter again. On the third lap, she thought to Paul, "Here we go."

She crouched to get a better view of an irregular area of flattened grass.

Paul thought, "What if she already was dead? What if the killer was carrying her and dropped her here?"

Amy tried to be careful not to disturb the area, but she wanted to see it from different angles. "I wish I had some of Steven's orange markers," she muttered. She was surprised to feel Paul take her keys out of her left hip pocket and drop them alongside the point of interest.

"Clear!" She heard the detective yell her name. He was getting out of the unmarked car at the far end of the parking lot. She waved and stood up to wait for him. "He'll be able to tell us what this grass pattern means," and then she felt Paul nod.

Riordan came down the paved walkway, with Jermaine a few steps behind, struggling with his medical bag. "What do we have?" he shouted as he got closer.

"Tell me what this is all about," she said, and pointed at the disturbed grass.

"That's convenient, the killer left their car keys."

"Uh, those are mine."

He grinned, "So you're the killer?"

"I don't have a pocket full of those orange markers like you do. I was afraid if I didn't mark the area, I'd trample it later when I looked for it."

"Got to admit, that's clever. But a word of advice: never introduce any personal items into a crime scene."

"Oh." She looked down, embarrassed. She retrieved the keys.

"Who's the victim?" Riordan went on.

"Don't know. One of the rent-a-cops found her. I told them to make sure nobody came up this way, and I guess they've done a good job."

"Any ID?"

"I haven't gotten to her yet. I was doing that spiral search thing to try to find a point of entry."

He raised his eyebrows. "You're a quick study, Clear. But --"

She heard Paul wince, "Here comes the 'but'."

"-- never take somebody else's word for it that a victim is dead. Always check yourself, and that's always the first thing you do."

Amy's stomach sank. "You mean she might be alive?"

"I mean she might have been alive when you got here. Why would Fontenot and Claiborn know if she's dead?"

Her shoulders fell. She looked down and shook her head. "I killed her?"

Riordan put a hand on her shoulder and patted her. "Let's go look." He led her back down the paved walkway until he saw a clear path through the grass to the body. They knelt on either side of the woman, who was face down with one arm pinned beneath her. The detective gently pushed her thick black hair aside and felt her carotid artery for a pulse. "She probably was already dead," he offered gently. "Those guys aren't total doofuses. It's just something to remember."

"Steven, look!" For some reason her keys were still in Amy's hand, and she used one to point to the dead woman's neck.

"Garrote. What?"

"The necklace marks are smooth around the back of her neck. The killer was in front of her when he strangled her."

The detective slowly said, "Shit." He glanced up at Amy, then looked back at the marks on the dead girl's neck. "And looky, a blood stain. If the ligature broke her skin, there's blood on that necklace, whenever we find it." A broad smile broke on his face.

He fought the temptation to turn the body over, and instead stood up and waved to his colleagues. Amy stood beside him, a step behind. "Lawson, get pictures of everything. You know the drill -- overall, medium, and close-ups. Get IR and UV of the body closeups, and make sure you get that dried bloodstain. Clear, spiral search, but start here at the body. I'll get to work on the sketches. Jermaine, make sure you save that blood for the lab, it's our first decent break in this case. Go, go, go!"

Riordan began sketching the scene in his notebook. Amy asked, "Can I have some of those orange markers?"

Without looking at her he said, "Come get me when you find things. You're still an intern." A glance, "The captain is right. You should go to the police academy."

It was Paul who said, "BAAAAAAP. Beulah the Buzzer says 'that's not right'." As Amy turned to her search, she heard Paul think, "If Riordan's talked to Ramirez about you, we're in. We're as official as a civilian can be."

When he finished the rough sketch, Riordan went to talk to the campus guards to make sure they kept the area behind the four buildings secure. Amy saw him talking to one, pointing at a clipboard, and using his fingers to number tasks. He went to the second for a similar briefing, but she noticed the guard point to her and then both men laughed. Finally he approached the third one, the new one, the guard who had given Paul and Christine a hard time the night before. Amy stopped to watch; she couldn't hear them, but she saw they were arguing. Riordan pointed to the main campus, almost like an umpire throwing a player out of a baseball game. She saw him fold his arms in front of his chest, and watched the guard slink away.

Almost immediately, Amy saw marks in the grass like the ones Riordan had found near Megan Silver, showing something had been dragged. Before she had a chance to call to him, the detective was back at the body and laughing. "Clear, you going into politics?"

"What? No. What are you talking about?"

"Claiborn there says he's going to vote for you for President."

"Ah, The United States of Amy, I like that. Want to be my Attorney General? Good pay, and I'll let you arrest anyone you want to."

"He says you gave him a gold star."

She thought a moment. "I told him not everyone learned from their mistakes, like he did."

"Yup. These guys make sixteen dollars an hour and everybody they deal with gives them shit. They're like puppies -- if you're nice to them they'll be loyal forever." He shook his head, still laughing. "It's not my style, but looks like it works for you."

"Say 'thank you,'" Paul thought, and mechanically, she did. Then, "What's with the new guy?"

"I sent him home. Asshole. He didn't see why he should have to listen to some kid. I told him I didn't see why my assistant had to put up with his shit. Hey, did you see this?"

He looked at the marks in the grass at her feet. "I was going to show it to you. Killer drag the body?"

He made notes on his sketch, and threw down one of his markers. "Be careful, but follow the drag marks out. We may find the point of entry."

The drag marks began about thirty feet away. There was a gap of ten feet or so, and then she was on the original trampled area she had found earlier. She hailed Riordan, and he shadowed her route, throwing down another marker at the start of the drag sequence, and another -- finally -- at the place where they thought something had been dropped.

"Tell me what you have," Riordan asked.

"I think someone dropped something large here," pointing to the initial area. "I think he picked it up, carried it to here, then dragged it there. The body."

"Possible," he said. The detective crouched and leaned this way and that, sizing up the first area of grass. "Maybe. If the perp dropped the body here, where were they coming from?"

Although they were standing fairly close to the science and chemistry buildings, the grass markings indicated the origin was in or on the other side of a narrow parking area. "That's Biology," Amy told him, pointing left, "and that's the Computer Center over there. There's a door on the back of the Biology building."

"Check for any traces between there and this marker," he said. He was aiming his LED tape measure at the body, and transcribing numbers to his sketch.

Amy walked a straight line from the drag marks and drop spot, across the paved parking area, on to the grass behind the Biology building. It was undisturbed. Paul said, "Let's mark this spot, then look at the grass that way toward the back door." Amy thought a quick "Yes;" heeding Riordan's warning, she took a stone from under a bush and scraped a big "X" in the edge of the pavement to indicate the radial from the body. Then she got on her knees and examined the grass back to the front door. "Damn," Paul said out loud, "nothing."

"Let's look in the other direction," Amy thought. She stood up and walked back to her scrawled "X", then went down on all fours to look at the grass behind the Computer Center. "Here we go," she said, then stood and waved to the detective. He was looking away. "Your Majesty!" she shouted, "Over here!"

He raised a hand to indicate she should wait, and then finished writing up notes. "Whatcha got for me?" he called as he walked toward her.

When he reached her, Amy pointed at the grass. It looked as if someone had walked through it recently, and next to it was a bright silver wafer battery.

The detective raised his eyebrows as he crouched to examine it. "Somebody came through here," he mused. "When we're done with this, I want you to see how far this trail goes." Then, turning his attention to the battery, "Now, what about you, my pretty?"

When he stood up, he called to the photographer. "Everything has to be documented," he explained. "Pictures, the sketch, and then the evidence grab."

When Lawson reached them, Riordan pointed at the battery and backed away. "He knows what to do," he said to Amy. "And he'll be a few minutes. See if you can trace a path in the grass. We'll meet back here."

Within three steps, the grass with its sign of someone having passed through turned to sand and pebbles. "You see anything?" she thought to Paul. She felt him move their head and look from different angles, then shake it. "So much for honorary Chief Tracking Dog, I don't see a damn thing. What's ahead up there, anyway?"

They stood up and walked farther. They were in a narrow alleyway between the Computer Center and the Biology building, at one point no more than eight feet wide. Eventually the path led to a broad paved courtyard and the fronts of the buildings. "Not much help," Paul said aloud. They began the return trip, but just at that narrow part of the alleyway, Amy pointed to the Biology building. "Door," she said. No knob or handle, no swipe pad or keypad, no sign.

"Huh," Paul responded, and turned them to face the Computer Center, where they found the same feature.

"Someone could have come out of either of these doors," she whispered.

"And toted the woman toward the parking lot," he continued. "Dropped the battery when he was struggling, then he dropped her."

"Picked her up for a bit, then dragged her to where he left her."

They stood between the closed doors, looking out at the parking area. "Okay," Amy said, "We solved it, now can I study for my Psych exam?"

"Let's run it by Riordan."

They emerged blinking into the broad daylight of the parking lot. "Just about done," Lawson said while focusing on a close up. The detective was impatiently waiting for the photographer to finish.

"The grass turned to dirt and pebbles after five feet. I couldn't see any marks," Amy said, "But we found some interesting doors." She heard Paul think, "We?" and she flinched.

"We?" Riordan said.

"Uh, yes, that's me, myself, and I. You know, the holy trinity of Amy. I'm going to incorporate as a tax-exempt religion."

"I'm too old to get circumcised, but let me know if you make any money at it. Where are the doors?"

Amy led him down the alley to see them. "Very interesting," Riordan admitted. He eyeballed each of them, trying to find any mark that might indicate if they had been opened recently. "Later we'll find them from the other side." They walked back to the parking lot, and he added, "That was a very good thing to notice, Clear."

Lawson was gone, so Riordan knelt by the battery, and Amy followed. "Let me see you get that into a bindle."

"Into a bundle?" Amy asked. "I don't understand."

"Bindle. I haven't shown you that yet?" When she shook her head, he reached for an inside pocket and pulled out an odd piece of paper with tape on its sides. "Bindle. Cheap, easy, and better than plastic bags for small pieces of evidence. Get your gloves on."

Amy dutifully donned a pair of blue nitrile gloves.

"Every piece of evidence you handle, you have to be wearing fresh gloves, remember that." He squeezed the outside edges of the thing he called a bindle, and pointed it at Amy so she could see it had opened into a pocket with a flap. "Store bought envelopes aren't sealed, so evidence gets lost or contaminated. With this doojimer, it's a tight seal of folded paper. Just don't stick your finger in it!"

She flinched. She asked, "Can I look?" and Riordan handed it to her. As she examined it she heard Paul think, "We used to call those 'wraps'. I used them for -- uh, never mind. I'll show you how to make one."

"Something funny, Clear?"

"Just amusing myself, Your Majesty."

"These are just copy paper. You fold it in thirds, then unfold it, then turn it ninety degrees and do it again. Then you fold over the outside thirds, and fold up the bottom third, and tape 'em." He crouched by the battery she had found, and continued, "There's a good chance there's a fingerprint on the metal. Something this size, I'd package it and let Jermaine look at it in the lab. If this were something big -- a car, or a store window -- we'd handle it differently."

Amy reached for the battery in the grass, but Riordan slapped her hand away. "One last thing. Because there may be a print, don't handle it. Not even with gloves." He took a business card from another pocket. "Use something clean to lift it, then slide it into our low-tech device. Here," and he gave it to her.

Amy held the open envelope alongside the battery, then slowly pushed the card into the grass, below the level of the evidence. She carefully slid it under the battery, then lifted and shoveled it into the bindle. She looked up at the detective to see if he approved.

"Well done. Next step, a slap of tape --" from another hidden pocket in his oversized jacket "-- and a felt tip pen to put the date, the time, and your initials over the tape." He passed a fine point Sharpie pen to her, and she did as he instructed. "Never use ballpoint. You'll poke a hole in the bindle and contaminate the evidence. And we're still not done." He stood up, and groped through a few of his pockets before he found a small mailing envelope. "Number 6. NOPD buys them by the boxcar load," he said, and held it on top of his notepad. "Here's where you do that date and time thing, your name, and a description of what the evidence is. You put the bindle inside it, seal it, and give it to me. I'll give it an item number and put it on the sketch. It has to match Lawson's pictures."

"Why? This seems so nit-picky complicated."

"Sweetheart, most judges and all defense lawyers are nit-picky assholes. All the stuff we write on evidence is called 'chain of custody.' Without it, the defense says someone tampered with it and the judge throws it out. I'll tell you, it's so frustrating when that happens, that after a couple of episodes you learn to do it right. Believe me; you remember the stupidest little rules real fast."

"What next?" Paul asked, of course with Amy's voice.

"Sketch, done. Pictures, done. Search, done. Jermaine's probably done, so let's let him tell us what we've got." They walked to where Jermaine was sitting in the grass, near the body. He was halfway through a bottle of Barq's, looking up and talking to a short man in a blue business suit.

"Hello," the detective said to the man. "Steven Riordan, Orleans Parish police."

The man extended his hand and replied, "I am Jonathan Kwang. I am the dean of exchange students."

"Forgive my bluntness, but it's been a long day." Riordan pointed, "Is she one of yours?"

The man looked surprised, and shook his head.

"Next question. Who might know who she is?"

"She appears to be Japanese," he said slowly. "I am Korean. We from Oriental culture often can tell us apart."

Paul thought, "Remember how I hated that diversity lecture they made you take?"

"Think about baseball or something," she thought back. "It won't help if you go ballistic on the dean."

Riordan said, "I'll take that as a 'no.' Okay, we'll do fingerprints. Her roommates will wonder where she is, her parents will think it's so unlike her not to call, but we'll run the search. Jermaine?"

The medical examiner grumbled as he stood up. "This would have been easier when we first got here. Now rigor mortis has set in. It's one thing to roll a finger to get a print, it's a bitch to roll the whole body." He went to get his medical bag that also held forms and ink.

The dean said, "We are anxious to avoid attention. We --"

"Four dead women," Riordan shook his head, "avoiding attention no longer is an option."

"I was going to say, the school has ID card photos on file, and the database is indexed. I have access in my office."

"Clear, what time is it?" he barked.

"Eleven forty-five, Your -- uh, Detective."

"No wonder I'm starving. Dean, I've got another hour's work here. You got a card? Let me visit you after lunch."

Dean Kwang gave him a business card, which he handed to

Amy. The man repeated the school's desire to avoid attention and left.

Jermaine was preparing to take prints off the body. Riordan put his hand on one shoulder and said, "Emergency over. You can do that at the lab."

The doctor looked up, annoyed. "Can't we hurry this up? My grandson turns five tomorrow. I need to find a present."

"Okay we'll hurry how's this for hurrying?" he said as fast as he could, which provoked the slightest hint of a smile on Jermaine's face.

"What do we have?" he asked, serious again.

"The girl is five two, I'm guessing she weighs ninety pounds. I would have thought she was foreign born, this is very small for Asians born and raised here. Net result is that our killer could easily overpower her and then carry her."

The detective nodded. "We've got some clues in the grass that she was carried, dropped, and dragged here. Overpower?"

"You pointed out she was strangled from the front. It was a confrontation. I expect there's something under the fingernails this time."

"Time of death?"

"Look at this," the medical examiner said, shifting his crouch and holding the woman's left arm above the paper bag that covered her hand. "An old-fashioned analog wristwatch. It stopped at twelve-fifteen when the crystal was smashed. It's only a guess," he dropped the girl's arm, "but the watch may have been broken during the struggle."

Amy heard Paul think, "If your digital watch breaks, it's lights out. You get nothing."

Jermaine shuffled in his crouch to move alongside the upper body. "It's possible this is just dust, but I think we've got some fiber traces to work with. Can you see the specks on the back of her shirt?" Riordan and Amy both nodded. "And there may be some more on the front. Strangulation is a close-quarters affair."

"When will you know what evidence is there?"

"I think I said something about my grandson. It'll be Monday. Sorry."

Amy said, "Yes. Family first."

Jermaine smiled and said, "That's not a very police-y attitude,

Miss. I like you."

"Yeah," Riordan said, "we all like Clear. Haul her away, doc. I'll release the scene. I'm going to grab some lunch before my stomach turns itself inside out, and then maybe Dean Kwang can help us identify the girl."

He turned to Amy and said, "Where's that hell-hole you took me to last time?"

"The Cove. This way, Chief. I hope you brought enough money to feed me, too."

The officers running the check points they passed recognized Riordan and waved him and Amy through. "How come a guard didn't see the dead girl going to wherever she was killed?" she asked.

"Probably one or two did. We don't keep records. The biggest value of a partial lockdown is the artificial sense of security it generates in management."

Paul said, in Amy's voice, "So that explains airport security. But how come a guard didn't see a killer with a dead girl on his back?"

"All girls your age are boy crazy," he replied, "but get the notion that the killer is male out of your head. We've pretty much ruled out lover boy, so right now it's stalker girl that's our prime suspect."

"Let me rephrase that. How come a guard didn't see a killer with a dead girl on its back?"

"She may have been on her front, just like we found her."

It was Amy who shouted, "Steven!"

"Yeah, okay. Two possible answers." He turned to look at her as they walked toward lunch. "First, a guard did see her, but he was an asshole and didn't call anyone then and I fired him this morning." Amy realized he meant the campus guard who had been such a pill. "Answer number two, the murder site was so close that the killer didn't pass a checkpoint."

"The doors to the Biology and Computer Center buildings?"

The detective opened the front door to let Amy enter The Cove. "Good places to start. If we eat fast we'll have a chance to look at the inside of those doors before we visit Dean Foreigner."

"Kwang," she corrected.

"What I said. Can I get a beer in here?"

After they placed their orders, they commandeered a large table. Riordan tossed his notebook down and unfolded his sketch. "C'mere," he said, patting the chair next to him, "help me go over this." He pointed at the big red X that represented the dead woman. "You found those patterns in the grass here," pointing to the drag marks, "and here," where it appeared something or someone had been dropped, "and here," just on the other side of the parking strip. "What does this tell us?"

Amy got the sense that this was not a lesson; that the detective was trying to brainstorm to make sense of isolated facts and a few suppositions. She was flattered that he asked her.

"Access to that area was limited only by the check points," she said. "But what clues we have point to those buildings across the parking area."

He held his chin in his right hand, stroking it as if he had a beard. "So," he mused, "it's possible our killer with the corpse slipped out of one of these three doors and left her there." A pause as he stared at the sketch. "Where would the killer go afterwards?"

Paul said, "Back to where the killing was done. To hide clues? Clean up? Finish a midnight snack?"

Amy went on, "We use our ID cards to get in buildings after hours. Isn't there a record of who went in Biology and Computer?

The PA system called Amy's name for the food, so she left Riordan pondering while she picked up the trays, one in each hand. At the condiment table she saw Florence and poked the top of her head against her friend's shoulder. "Whoa, careful," Florence began, then looked and said, "Hidy, neighbor. Let's sit together, I want to tell you about a guy who asked me out a second time."

Amy pointed at the two trays and said, "Can't. The detective and I are solving the murders. Can I visit this weekend?"

"Call me Sunday, although I hope I'm not home, dressed, or awake by then."

"You go, girl," Amy grinned. "Uh, can you get me some napkins and sporks?"

"Who's the redhead?" he asked as she spread their meals on their table.

"Spying on me, eh? A friend. One of the Amy Irregulars. I have my fingers in everything."

"Not in my sandwich, damn it."

"Oh, sorry. That was an accident."

"What you said about swipe cards. Who do you think has the data?"

She thought with a french fry in her mouth. "Physical plant? Campus cops? IT department?"

"Crap. I hope the nimrod I dinged wasn't the son of the chancellor or anything. These departments -- where are they?"

"Facility Services has a building by the canal. Rent-a-cops are across from Privateer Place, the lake side. And the IT department --"Amy took a big bite of her cheeseburger "-- Computer Center. Convenient, huh?" It sounded like "Cumpr cer. conf, mmm?"

He nodded absently. "Look, I have to check in at the station. I've got two other cases on my desk. Don't let anything happen to my notepad. And don't let anything else happen to my sandwich." She nodded, still chewing.

She heard Paul think, "I have to call Christine. She was freaked out this morning. Soon as we get done, let me call her."

Amy nodded. "First," she thought back, "we eat."

But Paul put down the burger and got the phone out of their back pocket. "Can't it wait three minutes?" Amy whined.

"No. I want to be done before Riordan gets back." He punched Christine's number.

"Thank you for calling West End Realtors, this is Christine."

"That's how you answer your cell phone?" Paul asked.

"Paulette!" she cried, excited and relieved. "Force of habit, I'm at work. How are you? Amy? Is everything okay?"

"What a sweetie," Amy thought, "she even remembered me."

"I'm fine, we're fine," Paul answered. "The detective and I spent all morning processing the scene. We're in that place I took you for dinner. Going over notes while we eat lunch."

"I'm so glad to hear you're okay. I knew you would be, but, you know. It's always better to hear it."

"We haven't identified the victim yet; she was a little Japanese woman. Amy and I are learning so much. But look, we're still on for Saturday. I can't wait to see you. It'll be a relief to get off campus for awhile."

"I'm glad you're okay, Paulette. I love you."

"Me too, Honey. See you Saturday."

Riordan returned part way through the conversation. When Paul ended the call, the detective said, "'Amy and I are learning so much?' Who are you and what have you done with my Clear?" He was smiling as he sat back down.

"I'm me," Amy said. "It was that me, myself, and I thing."

"Ah, I see. So, was it Myself or I that was talking?"

"Uh. I don't know. Let me ask." She waited a second, then said, loudly, "Hey in there! Who was that?"

She let Paul respond, of course with her voice, "Ain't nobody here but us chickens."

Riordan said, "Don't go crazy on me; you don't qualify for workers' comp." He went back to his sandwich. "Is your date with a murderer?"

"Hmm, I'll be sure to ask. Everything under control?"

He shook his head. "Meth lab in Terrytown. Probably won't blow up a second time, but there's two dead."

"I'd hate your job," she said.

Riordan raised his eyebrows as he took another bite. "You look like you're having a good time doing it."

"If I'm lucky I'll get a "D" in psychology. If I really had your job, I'd flunk."

"Yeah," he said, smiling, "you trade your social life and all human feeling for a paycheck when you're a detective."

Amy and Paul exchanged the lead with each bite of their burger; by holding it in their hands, they avoided giving the clue of moving a fork from one hand to the other. Silently they chatted while they watched Riordan finish eating. "If I don't pass," she thought, "Dad will tell me how disappointed he is. I hate that!"

Paul thought back, "Yeah. It would be easier if he spanked you."

"What if he says he won't pay my tuition anymore and I have to get a job?"

"Oh, that's easy, the world would end. Next question?"

Amy stuck her tongue out and blew, "Pttthhhhhh!" She heard Paul laugh, and Riordan said, "Christ, Clear! I told you not to go crazy on me!"

"Sorry, Your Majesty. Argument with my co-pilot."

"Was that Myself or I?"

She stuck her tongue out again.

"Here's what's going to happen," he said, tapping his notepad. "Jermaine will indulge in family pleasure, so it'll be Monday or Tuesday before he tells me if there is any physical evidence on the body. Maybe fiber or hair on her clothes. Maybe the perp's DNA under her nails."

Amy nodded.

"If it's green light, I'll have search warrants by the afternoon. We'll cut pieces of carpet out of lover boy's and stalker girl's places. Then --"

"Alex Scruggs has linoleum. Maybe she's got rugs?"

"-- Uh, okay, carpet or rugs. I'll probably be on the west bank for this meth lab case, so you'll get the samples."

Amy was giddy at the responsibility, excited and proud that the detective had so much faith in her. It was Paul who said, "In a wrap? Uh, I mean, a bindle?"

Riordan narrowed his eyes. "Junkies call it a wrap. Are you a secret junkie, Clear?"

Silently she screamed at Paul, "It's your fault!" Out loud, she said, "I have a friend who must have been a druggie a million years ago. He told me he never heard the word bindle before, that he used to call them wraps."

"I think I don't want to meet your friend."

"Don't worry, you won't."

"But the answer is no, not in a bindle. I'll give you some big evidence bags before I leave. Aren't you done yet? We have to get to Dean Foreigner's office."

Amy threw their meal debris onto a tray, and used the trash can by the doorway. "Kwang," she said.

They walked through three check points on the way to the administration building, again being waved through by guards and police who knew Riordan. It was Paul who asked, "Is it easier to order a partial lockdown when you know it doesn't apply to you?"

"I know an officer or two who insist on showing their IDs at stops. They call it leading from the front. I call it stupid. As stupid as your question, Clear. Of course it's easier this way."

Paul thought to Amy, "At least he's honest about it."

"Did I say something funny, Clear?"

"No, Your Majesty. It was Myself or I, I can't tell which."

"You want to share it with the class?"

"Umm, no thank you."

Mullinax greeted them outside the administration building. Amy said, "Good to see you again, officer."

"Same here, Miss Clear. That coffee saved my life. Steven," and he waved them through.

"Where's this guy's office?" the detective asked when they were inside the building.

She took the card out of her pocket. "207-F. Upstairs." She led as they made their way to the second floor, and she knocked on the door frame of Dean Kwang's office.

A slight Oriental woman was sitting at a desk so large that she looked like a child playing dress-up. In a heavily accented voice, she asked if she could help.

"This is Detective Riordan with New Orleans police," Amy said. She glanced at the business card and went on, "Jonathan is expecting us."

She nodded and pushed a button on her phone. They heard the Dean's voice say, "Yes, Sook-Joo?"

"Police, sir. They say you expect them."

"Ah. Show them in, please."

As she sat, the woman bowed to the intercom when the dean was done, then she stood up and said, "You please to come with me."

Standing, they saw the woman was barely five feet tall, and was skinny enough to make a super-model jealous. Paul thought to Amy, "What Jermaine said. Foreign-born Asian girls are small."

She led them into the Dean's sanctum, then bowed and walked backwards out of his room. Dean Kwang stood to shake their hands. "Let me slide some chairs over here so we all can see the computer screen." Riordan helped move them, and then he and Amy sat to work with the dean.

"This isn't the fastest search," he warned them. "UNO has more than eleven thousand students." He pulled up a search screen, and began to enter criteria. "We want female. We start with undergraduates. And I believe the woman is Japanese." He pressed the enter key and turned to Riordan. "Officer, what is going on here?"

"Uh, Detective," he corrected. "I believe we have a serial killer on campus, White, Black, Jewish, now Asian. It's an equal opportunity criminal. I would be surprised if it were a hate crime."

"That is a relief. Even in 2021, you would be shocked at the prejudice our foreign-born students face."

"Are you saying there are crime incidents here that you are not reporting to NOPD?" Amy took her notepad out and opened it to a fresh page, pen in hand.

"Of course not," the dean said. "Prejudice and bigotry don't have to manifest themselves in criminal acts. Often, it's just dirty looks, or being ignored when they ask for help."

Paul laughed inside. "I guess I'm a bigot because I don't understand Korean. And dirty looks? Has this man never heard 'Sticks and stones may break my bones'?"

"Ssh," she whispered.

Riordan heard it and said, "Clear?"

"I'm pretty sure that was 'Myself.'"

Results popped up on the computer monitor. The Dean explained, "UNO has 11,700 students in five colleges and forty-two graduate programs. We ignore the six percent who think it's cute to refuse to answer the EEO questionnaire. Our racial groupings lump all Asians with Pacific islanders, so this five and a half percent includes everyone from Pakistan to Pago Pago. There are --" he pushed his eyeglasses back up his nose and peered at the screen, "-- 644 students in this classification. But based on the self-identification form, there are only one hundred and sixty-three who are of Japanese ancestry, and ninety-nine of them are female. Let's look at those." Amy scribbled the figures into her notes.

When the Dean clicked the 'view results' button, a portrait came on the monitor, along with basic student information.

"Wait," Riordan said. He took out the death mask picture Lawson had printed for him, and put it on the dean's desk in front of the computer screen. Amy leaned to look at it because she hadn't seen the woman's face at the crime scene. "Okay, let's go through them."

It took twenty minutes and seventy six records before Riordan called, "Bingo!" They saw a young, alert, bright-eyed woman with thick, straight black hair. She had slightly slanted eyes, and sparse eyelashes. She was smiling. The information attached indicated her name was Ashley Probst, she was twenty years old, and she was from Beaumont, Texas.

"Can you print that out?" Riordan asked. The Dean nodded and pressed a print key. "And can I get her information? I need to know her parents' names and numbers, and where she lived, her roommates, her sorority, her major, all that." The Dean made a few keystrokes and pressed the print key again.

Amy said, "Is Probst a Japanese name?"

"I do not think so," said the Dean. "Nor is Ashley. I told you she was not one of my students. My guess is American-born, maybe only one-quarter ethnic, and completely assimilated." He frowned, "She probably did not speak a single word in her own language."

Paul said, "You said she's probably three-quarters non-ethnic. Wouldn't that make English her own language?" Immediately, Amy added, "I'm sorry, forget I said that."

"Let me guess, that was Myself again."

The Dean answered, calmly, "I work in the department of ethnic diversity. I think it is a shame when anyone with even a drop of ethnic blood does not know their ethnic language or culture."

Riordan stood up, which prompted Amy to follow suit. "The walls in here sure are perpendicular," he said. "Dean, thank you for your help. If I can get that printout from you, we'll let you get on with your day's business."

Amy hung her head and said, "Dean Kwang, I apologize. I did not mean to be rude."

"Apology accepted, young lady," he said, graciously. "You have what we call an "Iron Age" view of race, that to some degree racial identification is relative and voluntary. We no longer hold to that simplistic idea."

Amy nodded, even while Paul thought to her, "One drop. That was enough to let Massa call you a slave. Or Hitler call you a Jew. And he thinks he's so enlightened."

When they were in the hallway, the detective said, "For someone who's as smart as you are, you sure can be dumb." Amy began to puff, but before she could speak, Riordan said, "Just because Dean Foreigner is too stupid to realize he agrees with the KKK's idea of race is no reason for you to be stupider and point it out to him. People don't say 'thank you' for that sort of thing."

"Uncle," she said. "Didn't you ever make a mistake?"

"Most every day of my life, Sweetheart. I'm not trying to bust your chops, I just want to make sure you learn from them."

"I'm getting a Ph.D. in mistakeology." When she heard Paul laugh she thought, "You hush. I'll deal with you later." She heard him laugh more.

Riordan handed the computer printout to her as they began to walk back to the Biology and Computer Center buildings. "You said there's a communications person who gets to give the Probsts the news?"

"Yeah. God, that's a job I hate, and I've done it enough to know." In a silly sing-song voice he said, "'Hi, I'm the misery fairy and I'm here to ruin your life.'" He shuddered.

"We talk to roommates? Boyfriends? Sorority sisters?"

"Yeah. But we can probably speed this up by visiting Reggie and stalker girl."

Amy was unprepared when they returned to the place where Ashley Probst had been found. Although a cool day, the sun was bright in a cloudless sky. Students were using the area for shortcuts between buildings, the yellow tape was gone, and there no longer was any indication that a murdered woman had been found there seven hours earlier. When Riordan said, "Tell me about the doors you found," it jolted her back to reality.

"I showed you the ones between these buildings," she said, pointing to the alleyway. "The ones with no knobs or swipe pads." Then she led him to the door to the back of the Biology building, facing the open area where Ashley had been dumped by her killer. "We can get in this way."

When the detective saw the swipe pad, he stepped back and said, "Open Sesame, Clear." Amy dutifully waved her student ID card, and pulled the door open.

It took a moment for their eyes to adjust to the indoor

lighting. "Where are we?" he asked.

"I never had a class here, let's explore." The doorway was at the end of a stairway landing. They went up the one flight, and let themselves in on the top floor of the building. A quick walk along the hallway showed lecture halls, laboratories, and offices for instructors.

"Very interesting," the detective said. "Only the second floor has direct access to that doorway."

A different stairway took them to the hall and rooms on the ground floor. There were more classrooms, another lab, two instructor offices, and the departmental office. Riordan mused, "There's supposed to be a door somewhere along here."

"Right. The one with no handle. Or swipe pad."

They entered two vacant lecture rooms but found nothing. They looked through the glass square in the door of another room that was in use, and Paul said, "There. It's in here." The detective looked over their shoulder to see it, then pushed the door open.

The instructor -- a graduate assistant, maybe twenty-three years old -- stopped in mid-sentence, but Riordan and Amy walked past him to the far wall. "Can I help you, please?" he shouted at them.

"No, we're good," the detective said, looking at the door to the outside. "Keep calm, carry on." In big red block letters a sign read "Door Is Alarmed." Paul said, "Maybe if we sing a lullaby the door will relax?" Riordan threw himself at the panic bar to open the door, but nothing happened: no alarm, and no opening.

"That door is sealed," the instructor shouted. "What do you want?"

Riordan examined the edges of the door. They were caulked, and there were no indications it had been opened in years. Meanwhile Amy called back, "We're from the power company. Want to make sure no electrons are leaking in or out through this, you can't be too careful. Nice door you got here." Riordan tipped his fedora as they walked behind the instructor and back out into the hall.

"Our killer didn't get out that way," Amy said, and the detective nodded. "Clear, in your notes, put a big star and write, 'Sealed door under Exit sign in room --" he stepped back to read the little plaque "-- room 112. This is Biology?" Amy dutifully opened her notepad and did as Riordan ordered. "They need a visit from the Fire Marshal."

A few doors down, Riordan stepped into the department office and asked the receptionist, "Can I talk to the department head or whoever's in charge?" He opened his badge holder for the woman.

"That's Doctor Brinker. I'm afraid he's not in his office." She was in her mid-twenties, dressed very businesslike in a print dress with high bodice and low hem.

He smiled. "So who's in charge when he's gone? You, I'll bet."

"How did you know, you sweet-talking stranger?" she said playfully. "I was just about to double my salary and close the office for the day. Why don't you give your daughter a dollar for the movies and let's you and I discuss heavy philosophy?"

"If only I were not on duty," he grinned. "You and a bottle of gin and the phone off the hook -- sounds like heaven on earth." He sat on the edge of her desk and leaned close to her. "There was a murder out there overnight. Do you have the swipe card access records for the building?"

"Aw, you don't want to play?"

Amy tugged at Riordan's sleeve and said, "Daddy, I hav'ta go potty."

The detective patted Amy on the head, then tugged her to him. She stuck her thumb in her mouth. "Who does have the records, Sweetheart?"

"Wow. I think Building Services."

"Thanks," he smiled. When he stood up he pretended to look at a section of floor hidden from the secretary by her desk. "Oh, Amy," he said, wagging a finger under her nose, "couldn't you hold it in for a minute?" He turned back to the secretary. "Better get a mop." He tipped his hat and pushed Amy out the door in front of him.

Both of them were laughing even before they got outside the building. "Did she ever make a pass at you!" Amy cackled.

"Some dames love cops. God bless 'em. Okay, let's see how things look in the Computer Center." They walked to the right, past the head of the alleyway between the buildings, and into the front door of the Computer Center. They stayed on the main level, looking through classroom door windows to try to find the doorway to the alleyway.

"A-ha!" the detective cried, and opened the door to an empty, dark room. He flicked on the overhead fluorescents. The door to the alley looked just like the one in the Biology building -- gray, panic bar, and sign warning of an alarm. "Clear, remember where I parked?"

"I think so."

He tossed his keys to her. "There's a satchel in my trunk. Get it like a good little intern."

"Why?"

"Because I asked nicely."

Amy laughed. "I mean, what's in it that you need?"

"Fingerprint kit. I want to dust this panic bar before I test drive it."

She nodded and trotted out of the building, down the alleyway to the parking area in the back, and then over to the detective's unmarked car. "Another Psych class down the drain," Amy thought.

Paul thought back, "Please, let's read those chapters tonight or tomorrow. I'll be cranky if I can't hang out with Christine on Sunday."

"Oh, we're staying over, are we?"

"I hope so. Hey, she likes you, too."

Amy unlocked the trunk. She saw the big briefcase Riordan wanted her to bring back. "Oooh, shiny!" Paul said out loud when he saw the two shotguns, "Can I touch?"

"No!" Amy shouted. With her right hand she slapped the back of her left, by their convention Paul's hand. "Steven's waiting for me to bring back his bag." She continued silently, "Ask him if you can handle it, but I don't want any part of it."

She heard Paul think, "Mumble, bitch, gripe" on the way back to the Computer Center. Then he thought, "So I can talk to Riordan?"

"No!" she cried again. "Crap. I'll ask for you. Double crap." Paul laughed.

When she presented the satchel to the detective, he said, "There you are. I was about to send the Marines out to find you.

What took you so long?"

She heard Paul think, "Pretty shotguns, oooohh," and she said, "I was dazzled by the light reflecting off the shotguns. Do you want to take me pigeon shooting?"

Paul thought, "Huh?" at the same time Riordan said the word aloud. "I hope you mean skeet shooting," the detective said. "That's where you shoot at clay pigeons. You really want to do that?"

She was torn. She heard Paul pleading "Please, please, pleasepleaseohplease," but she felt skittish about the guns that Paul remembered from his independent life before coming to her. She told Riordan, "Part of me does. I think it's Myself, maybe it's I. It's hard to tell them apart." She made herself smile.

"That kind of talk, Clear, I don't know that I'd trust you around a shotgun. Ask me when all of you have more of a consensus about it." He opened the satchel, and took out several bags and boxes, a portable klieg light, and a camera. "C'mere, hold the light," he said as he turned the unit on and aimed it down at the front flat surface of the door's panic bar. He bobbed his head up and down, and side to side, and ordered Amy to move the light, until he finally saw what he was looking for. "Flip that switch on the handle," he said, "let's see what we've got under UV." The light turned a cosmic blue. Riordan took two pictures.

"Now we get to work," he said. "Hold that light steady, go back to regular white light." He pulled on a pair of blue latex gloves, and then opened a jar of black print dust.

"My dad has something like that," she said. "He puts shaving cream on his face with it."

"This brush uses squirrel hair. The squirrel doesn't like it, but we're bigger than he is, so that's that. You can't clean a brush, so keep track of what color and type of powder you use it with. Purchasing absolutely hates to pay for new brushes." He dipped just the tip of the brush in the black powder jar, then gently twirled it over the area where he saw the print. Gradually it became visible to Amy. Riordan worked the brush in the other direction, now following the whorls and swirls in the print. It turned out there were three prints together. "Okay, that's developed nicely."

He dropped the brush into his satchel, and pulled out a small pink plastic bulb. "Puffer bulb," he said, "It's one way to get excess powder off the print. Never blow on a print to do this."

"Uh, why not?" Paul asked.

"Hold the light steady," he said. "Because you'll spit all over it and blow the whole thing away. that's why not." Satisfied, he took two more pictures of the prints.

"Now we lift the prints," he said. He took a pack of white transfer cards and a shallow plastic case from the satchel, and put them on the seat of a nearby chair desk. He pulled one transfer card out and set it on the desk part. As he unscrewed the lid of the plastic case, he said, "Lifting tape. I like the two-inch size, which means you like the two-inch size. Tell me, Clear, what size lifting tape do you like?"

"Sir, I like two-inch tape, Sir!"

He smiled, but cautioned, "Hold the damn light still." He pulled about three inches of tape loose, then started to stick it to the door panic bar a few inches away from the prints. Amy watched him pressing firmly as he pulled more tape off the roll, until he had covered the entire treated area. "You press to keep air bubbles from getting in, they fuck up the print. And you don't cut the tape yet." Still holding the body of the roll in his right hand, he rubbed the applied tape with his left hand.

"Now comes the fun part. Start pulling up from where you're holding the roll, and make sure you keep tension on the tape or else it'll stick to itself and ruin things. There's no second chance to do this right." Amy watched closely and saw him pressing his left index finger against the tape an inch from the end. "Hold the free end with your other hand so when you finally peel it off it doesn't whip around." She nodded.

Carefully keeping tension on the tape, Riordan turned to the white transfer card. He stuck the first inch of the free end of the tape to the desk, then positioned the transfer card below it. Slowly, he began sticking the tape to the card. "Keep pressing, we don't want air bubbles here, either." When he finally had the prints adhered to the card, he took a knife out of the satchel and cut the tape off the roll. He put the roll back in its case and screwed the top down, then went back to the card. He freed it from the desk top, and wrapped the excess tape before and after the prints around to the back.

"Ta da!" he said, and held the card up for Amy; "We're done with that light." She could see two complete prints and part of a third. "Looks like someone opened the door by pushing their fingertips against the bar," she observed.

"All this may be a waste of time," he said as he put his equipment away. "This is an active classroom, so lots of innocent people probably touch the panic bar every day. If the door is sealed like the first one was, it's all moot. And even if the door opens, these prints may have nothing to do with the perp."

When the satchel was repacked and secured, Riordan said, "Moment of truth. You want to do the honors?" He pulled off his latex gloves.

Amy stood before the door. Suddenly she was self-conscious about her own finger prints. She bent her arms and pressed the door release with her clothed forearms.

Despite the warning sign, there was no alarm. Instead, what they heard was the sound of students walking between the buildings outside the open door.

℘ 35 ℘

Thursday, October 21, 2021 -- UNO Campus, New Orleans

"I am so tired!" she said aloud. It was eleven-thirty and Amy was finally lying on their bed, still wearing their clothes. She had gotten up with Paul at six in the morning to see Christine off, and then their day was commandeered by detective Riordan and the fourth co-ed strangling on the UNO campus.

The two of them in her body went over the events of the afternoon: Riordan's trip to Facility Services, where he flashed his badge and left with two boxes of printouts of the security card swipes from the days of the four killings, from the dorms and other buildings near the murders. When Amy told him she had a Psych exam Friday afternoon, he said he'd go through the data over the weekend. "He said there were a bunch of nulls on one of the pages," Paul thought to her. "Somebody has a card that opens doors but doesn't leave any user information."

Then there was a visit to Llewellyn Grimes, the Dean of Students. The dean was explosively angry, finger pointing and spittle flying, shouting his displeasure at the way the Parish police had handled the case. Riordan had stunned him to rationality by standing up and saying, "Fine. We'll withdraw. Let me know how that works for you."

Then an unsatisfying interview with the Second Vice President, because the President and First VP were out of town on fund-raising missions. Riordan had to explain -- twice -- why a full lockdown was not an appropriate response. However, he did get her to understand he might be seeking search warrants, and got her permission to cut up carpeting and other potential evidence.

Riordan asked Amy to call Reggie Young so they could find and interview him. "I'm sure he's blocked my number," she told him, and dictated Reggie's phone number to the detective. He was asleep in his dorm room, it turned out. Riordan said, "Put on some clothes and hide the girl in a closet. I'll be there in ten minutes." Once there, the detective had to assure Reggie he was not there to arrest him for violating the restraining order against being in the same room with Amy. Reggie told them he had gone out with Ashley Probst a few times in April and May, and that they remained friendly. His last contact with her was two weeks earlier. "She said she was asking everyone she knew for help on some computer project. I told her I didn't know much more than how to turn them on and off." In addition, he confessed that he was spending more time with Alex Scruggs, his former stalker. "No one else will go out with me!"

The last chore of the day was the sad meeting with Ashley Probst's two roommates. They met in the women's dorm room in Privateer Hall, along the canal. The first roommate they met was June Sato, born in Florida, the daughter of a Japanese man and an Anglo woman. "That June woman, she was so pretty," Paul said. "Do you think some mixed race people end up with exceptionally good looks?"

"Not just her looks. She seemed so self-assured and outgoing. Even though she was upset about Ashley."

The contrast was Utako Nakamura, an exchange student from Kitakyushu. "I felt so sorry for her," Paul sighed. "I don't know if she understood a tenth of the words she heard. So timid. So small. And so scared."

"I didn't expect we'd hear from Dean Kwang again. He told Steven the two women would move to a different dorm room."

They learned that Ashley Probst was a well-liked woman, completely Americanized but with pride in her Japanese ancestry. June told them the woman had gotten a terrible score on a history test, and her computer project was to hack the school website and change her grade. Neither of the roommates had known Ashley the year before, so neither had any insight into her relationship with Reggie Young.

Riordan impounded Ashley's cell phone, wallet, and laptop

computer for the lab techs to examine.

"I hope I remember everything he taught us," Amy thought to Paul. "Fingerprints. Bindles. Fooling secretaries and suspects into talking too much. My head is overflowing."

"Sure was fun. Does your back hurt?"

"That would be 'our' back, and yes, it hurts. I'm so wiped out. And all that psychology waiting for me in the morning. I told Steven I absolutely must be in class at two for this exam."

She unbuttoned her pants and pushed them off, then rolled onto their side. "I need your help studying," she went on. "Would you please read the Psych with me? That way between us we'll still remember everything on the test."

"I'll make a deal with you. I'll read with you, and we'll take the test together. Then on Saturday when we're with Christine we won't talk about psychology."

"Sold," she said aloud, and closed her eyes.

One of them yawned. "Hold me, will you?"

He wrapped their arms around themself. Paul said, "I'm proud of you. Riordan's a fan, you two work together well."

She let herself enjoy the comfort of the hug. It wasn't the same as another person doing the hugging, but Amy and Paul had learned to make the most of their peculiar life. "When we're done with this," she said, "do you think he'll ask me out?"

"Would you like that?"

"Yes. I'd like that a lot. He's good looking, in case you can't tell."

"I'll take your word for it. Maybe we could double date with Christine."

A laugh, "Oh, please."

Paul smiled and tightened their arms around themself. "Christine showed me how to survive you being with a man. May as well bring it on."

"Why, Paul! You've always put up a fight before." They both laughed. "Do you finally understand I'll never leave you?"

"Yeah," he said. He knew it was true, that he and Amy were dyad for life. No matter how important Christine might become to him, he would always owe his very existence to Amy, the actual owner of the body where he lived. And if Amy married and had a dozen children, he'd always be closer than husband or progeny. They were one.

And then they were asleep.

✍ 36 ✎

"Hurry up," Amy said out loud, "We have to study!" She was in the safety of her dorm room, where she and Paul felt free to speak instead of think to each other. Her Psych textbook was open on her desk, with another four chapters left to read.

Paul punched in Christine's phone number and pressed send. Two rings later he heard her voice, her broad alto, and he began to relax. "There you are!" he said.

"Paulette, yay! How's your day?"

"Dull compared to yesterday. Amy and I are studying for an exam she has this afternoon. Want to hear what we just learned about Karen Horney?"

"Um, that's okay. As long as you remember it until after the test. How about the detective? Any news?"

"We don't expect to hear from him until Monday. And when we're together tomorrow night, I'm going to turn Amy's phone off."

"You're going to what?" Amy interrupted. "Hi, Christine, it's Amy."

"Yeah, I can tell. You're going to solve everything, aren't you?"

"I'm working on it. Paul's a great help. And the detective is a wizard."

"It's Paul. What's up with you?"

Christine told him about some things at work, and some news about her old girlfriend Gina, with whom she still was friends. "I want you to meet her. Her lover is very strange but really sweet, I think you'll like them."

"I'd love to meet your friends. Will they be at the club tomorrow?"

"I'll call them. They want to meet you."

"Is that good or bad?"

"Oh, you silly Paulette!" she giggled. "I have to get back to work, but I'm glad you called. Good luck on your test, Amy. I love you, Paulette."

Paul held the phone for a few seconds after ending the call. He heard Amy say, "Hmmm?"

"I like her. And I love leading. Let's ace this test and put it behind us." They went back to the desk and the textbook.

Later, as they walked to the Psych class, Amy and Paul quizzed each other silently. Paul thought, "Maslow." She replied, "Hierarchy of needs. Psychological, safety, love and belonging, esteem, and self-actualization."

"Examples of safety?"

"Physical security. Financial security. Health and well-being. And... and safety net, like insurance."

He said aloud, "Piece of cake."

Amy quizzed, "Skinner."

"Behaviorism. Schedule of reinforcement. Skinner box. Daughter won't say if she was raised in one."

When she took a seat in the lecture hall, the graduate assistant who was proctoring the test came to her in the third row. "You're Amy Clear?"

She replied, "That depends. Does she owe you money?"

"I forgot what you look like," he said. "As much class as you've missed, why did you bother to show up?"

"Is being a graduate assistant so crappy that you have to go around sniping at students?" Paul said, and he heard Amy respond silently. "Careful. He's probably the jerk who'll grade the exam."

"Actually, yes, it is crappy," the grad student said. "I get $600 a semester and lose my social life. But I get to boss around plebes like you."

"We all have problems," Paul began, but Amy elbowed to lead. "I may not get an A, but I've studied to make up for missing class. Tell you what -- if I fail, you buy me lunch. If I pass, I'll buy you lunch. Fair?"

"Are you trying to bribe me?"

"You can be bought for a sandwich and a Coke?"

He turned away and went back to the desk at the front of the lecture hall.

One of them put a smile on their face as they prepared pens and blue books for the exam. Paul thought, "I love what a pretty girl can get away with. Will you marry me?"

"I thought you'd never ask," she whispered; then silently, "We've got a test to pass."

Ninety minutes later they were exhausted but giddy. "A 'B'," Paul thought, "definitely a 'B'."

Amy agreed, and wondered if the proctor would let her buy him lunch. "He was a jerk, but a deal's a deal, right?"

"Now what?" Paul asked.

"I think... I think a nap is in order. Then I'll call Florence and see if she's available for some company. I wonder if she's throttled that roommate from hell yet."

"Ouch!" Paul said aloud, then continued silently, "Not even in jest. Not until we nail the UNO Strangler."

❦ 37 ❦

On Saturday afternoon Amy opened her closet and said aloud, "What shall we wear to titillate your girlfriend?"

"Jeans. It's too cold for a skirt."

"That's what pantyhose are for." Amy started grabbing clothes.

"As a man, I think the purpose of pantyhose is eternal frustration."

"You know, they make them with an open crotch."

"And you just happen to have how many pair like that?"

Amy laughed, "Okay, we'll think of something else."

Eventually, Amy dressed themself in an updated version of her old St. Giles school uniform: dark knee socks, plaid pleated skirt to just above the knee, a white shirt with a gray necktie, and a dark blue blazer. She stood in front of the mirror and watched Paul's smile fill their face. "I am in love with me," he said.

"*Pièce de résistance*," she said, and slipped a wide white band into their hair.

"*Mais* fucking *oui!*" he shouted. Then, "Wait. Do women like this? I know every man we see tonight will want us, but women?"

She replied, "I'm betting the kind of woman who likes women will like it as much as a red-blooded man like you."

Paul turned from side to side, admiring themself in the mirror. "This is my idea of reincarnation," he said. "Coming back as a beautiful woman." He turned and preened some more.

Amy admired her handiwork in the mirror. "C'mon, let's go break some hearts!"

Amy let Paul lead to drive down to Sappho Rising. Stopping at red lights, using the turn signals, all the little things of everyday life; Paul was happy, ecstatic. He had adjusted to life in the back of Amy's head -- after all, the alternative had been remaining in his body that was now long dead -- but he missed the delight of leading and participating in reality. Tonight was a treat.

The plan was to meet Christine and her friends at seven o'clock. As they walked into the club and paid the cover charge, they heard two women let out wolf whistles. Amy said, "See?"

One of the whistles came from Christine, who was standing at a table in back, waving. On the way they were intercepted by waitress Ashley, who said, "Let me comp you, please? A margarita?" Paul nodded at the distraction, then ran to the table and lifted Christine in a big hug.

Christine cradled their head and kissed him on the lips. "And I'm glad to see you, Paulette," she smiled.

When he let her down, Christine said, "I want you to meet my friends. Paulette, this is Gina Gales --" "Hiya!" and this is Shawna Mallory --" "Good to meet you." "Gina, Shawna, this is my lover, Paulette Owens."

Paul thought to Christine, "I like the way that sounds." She smiled as if there were nothing odd about hearing Paul's masculine voice in her head.

"You look adorable," Gina said. She was a tall, attractive woman, with sandy hair in an old fashioned hairdo; she was dressed very conservatively, in a severe black dress with long hemline.

"Oh, thanks," Paul said. "You look like you came from work. What do you do?"

Gina nodded. "I'm a case manager at Touro Infirmary," she said. "Have to look professional for the clients and their relatives."

"You do," Paul said. "Very responsible, very reassuring."

Shawna said, "Do you think I'm ugly?"

Paul blinked. The kindest description would be 'interesting,' but ugly was more accurate. Shawna's eyes were not level, and she held the lids in slits as if she were fighting bright light. Heavy braces on her teeth, a mouth that was extraordinarily wide. There were moles with thick black hairs on her chin and one cheek. Only her nose seemed symmetrical, but it was overwhelmed by the rest of her face.

There was silence at the table. Paul could almost see the huge chip on Shawna's shoulder. "You're asking the wrong question," he finally said. "I don't care what you look like because you're Christine's friend. That's what matters to me."

Christine grasped Paul's hand, and leaned over to whisper, "You're wonderful." Gina smiled, gazing at her girlfriend with pride. And Shawna allowed herself a smile. "You pass," she said, and added, "I'm an artist, I spend most of my time in a studio."

"I like the piece you're working on now," Gina offered. "How do you think up those things?"

"What's your medium?" Paul asked.

"Everything. I paint a lot -- canvas, found objects, even the side of your garage."

"Are you showing anywhere?"

"You're a sweetheart," Shawna laughed. "No, not yet. But one day..."

Ashley appeared with a margarita for Paul. "On the house," she announced.

"Why?" he asked.

"'Cause I really want to do you."

Paul heard Amy laughing inside. "You can look but don't touch," he said. "My heart belongs to Christine. And the rest of me. And when you get a chance, I need a Diet Coke chaser."

"Can't blame a girl for asking," the waitress said. Abruptly she leaned forward and gave Paul a peck on the cheek, then went away. Christine smiled broadly and hugged their arm.

"You really look sweet," Shawna said.

"Thank you," he said. It had been ten years since anyone had complimented Paul's appearance, since he didn't have his own body anymore. He had heard many men tell Amy how pretty she was, but this was different; even though it was still Amy's face and body, he was the one leading. He was embarrassed, but he was proud. He heard Amy think, "I told you."

"What do you do, Paulette?" Gina asked.

Paul was stumped, and he sat with a stupid look on their face. Amy didn't like him to pretend he was her, so he didn't want to say he was a student. Should he talk about the market research work he used to do?

Christine solved his dilemma. "She's at UNO. Majoring in math. Isn't she smart? And she's solving those murders."

He thought to her, "Thanks," and he saw her smile and nod.

"I see numbers in some of the things I paint," Shawna said.

"I hear them in music," he responded. "I think it's the ratio of frequencies, either cycles per second of sound or the wavelengths of colored light."

"Yes!" Shawna said, banging the table with her fist. "Yes, exactly!" She turned to Christine and then Gina, and said, "You've heard me say the same thing, right?" Back to Paul, "You're brilliant."

Paul smiled shyly and looked down. "If I'm lucky, I'm as smart as you are."

Ashley brought the soft drink for Paul. She looked wistfully, then left the table.

Gina said, "I've heard about those things at UNO. It's horrible. Christine says you're involved with it all?"

He heard Amy think, "Drink!" and he let her lead for a long, long sip of margarita.

"My friend and I are working with the police," he replied. "A detective took us under his wing. He's teaching us all the procedures. It's a lot tougher than it looks on TV." He took a sip of his Coke.

"Uh, isn't that strange?" Shawna asked.

"Hmmm?"

"Tequila and coke?"

"Oh," finally understanding what she was referring to. "Yeah, I guess so."

Christine offered, "She drinks like she's two people." Then a double-take look at Paul, "Oh, that came out wrong."

Under the table he patted her on the thigh. "Catch me on a good night and I do drink as much as two people."

It was after eleven when Paul announced, "It's been a tough week. I really have to go." There were polite protests, met politely. Paul liked Gina, and he was impressed with Shawna. But he was wired from Thursday's investigations and from Friday's preparation and exam. Besides, all he wanted was to be with

Christine.

They hugged in the parking lot, a long and passionate hug. "Your friends are great," Paul said, "but I've been dying to be alone with you."

She touched his cheek with her hand and stared into his eyes. "I'll meet you at my house?"

Paul kissed the tip of her nose. "You bet."

Christine released him, then instantly hugged him again. "I love you, Paulette," she whispered. Then, smiling, she went to her car.

At home, Christine gave Paul a glass of wine while she took a few puffs from a joint. They sat next to each other on the futon, leaning against one another, relaxing. "How long did you and Gina go out?" he asked.

"Just a few months. I was so in love with her. Isn't she great? I'm glad she still likes me. Shawna seems to have cast some spell over her."

"I like Gina," he said, "and Shawna impresses me. She's like Yoko Ono."

"Like what?"

A verse of Steely Dan's "Hey 19" went through Paul's mind. "An old performance artist," he said. "She's smart."

"I guess," Christine said, and she began to undo Paul's necktie. "You were so diplomatic when she asked about her looks. She asks everybody that."

"What happens if someone points out the obvious?"

Christine laughed. "As far as I know, I'm the only person who ever said, 'Yes, you're ugly. So what?' We get along fine."

Christine sat back on the futon and said, "No."

A chill ran down Paul's back. "No, what?" he asked.

"I'm not going to undress you. You look so yummy in that outfit." She stood up and held out her hand. "Come with me, okay?"

"Anywhere," Paul said. "To the gates of hell."

"Will the bedroom do?" She led him in. As they stood by the bed, she said, "Paulette, I want you to stand very still for a minute. Close your eyes."

He did. He heard some sounds that he couldn't identify, and

something soft falling. Then he felt Christine slide her hands under their skirt and pull down their underpants.

"You can open your eyes now," she told him.

Christine was naked in front of him. In her right hand she was twirling their underwear around her index finger.

"You look so good," he told her. He reached out, but she stepped back.

"Not yet. I want to look at you. Paulette, you are so pretty. You make me feel so good, that you like me, and you're so much fun, and Amy likes me too. I want to be special for you." She wore that childlike smile that once unnerved him, but since came to fill him with happiness.

"Special? How could you be any more special than you are?" Again he reached for her, and again she took a step back.

He gazed at her, her bare skin exciting him as much as touching it would. Thick thighs and thin forelegs, covered in pale skin. A dark patch where her legs met, a healthy midsection, a stud in her bellybutton. Breasts bigger than Amy's but not large, her dark nipples erect and set off by the pale skin. A weak chin, a delightful smile that showed off that wonderful crooked front tooth, light brown eyes, and her multi-colored, multi-layered, multi-length hair. Paul was enchanted.

Christine said, "I always want to remember what you look like right now. I can't believe you're mine."

"I am. I am your Paulette. I -- I am yours, Christine."

She smiled. "I will make you so glad." She fell back on the mattress, then sat up. Paul began to feel for his buttons, but she said, "No. Come to bed like that. I want to love you with those clothes on."

"I need a refresher about what to do when Amy's boyfriend starts poking."

"We'll think of something." Then she whispered Paulette's name and embraced him.

Later, Paul lay against Christine, her arms around him and her hands playing with the skin on the side of their neck. He heard Amy think, "You really love her, don't you?"

"Still can't tell," Paul thought. "I'm in heavy-duty lust, leaning toward infatuation, that much I'm sure of." After a moment he added, "You know I love you, right?"

"Go ahead. Touch her and touch us."

Paul moved one arm. Still in Christine's embrace, he moved his left hand to one of the breasts he shared with Amy. "I love you, Amy," he thought to her.

He heard Amy giggle inside. "How do you do it? You don't even have a body, and you're in bed with two women who love you."

"I have always said I am the luckiest man on the face of the earth."

On Sunday morning, Christine shyly asked Paulette to keep her company at the laundromat. Much to Amy's amusement, they learned Christine shared Paul's enjoyment of Jane Austen, although more the movies and TV dramatizations than the novels. "No more than one in a sitting, okay?" Amy laughed. "Please don't make me endure an Austen marathon." Christine began to apologize, but Paul stopped her and said, "We put up with each other. Amy likes crappy formula mystery novels." He shook their head, "Brrrrrr."

"Some of them are so life-like," Christine observed.

Amy said, "Thank you!" and Paul followed by saying, "Those aren't the crappy formula ones."

They made plans for Paul to visit on Thursday night. With the partial lockdown and sense of danger on campus, they wanted to steer clear of the school when possible. "I've got to get home," Amy said. "A ton of my own laundry awaits. And now that I've caught up on psychology, there's a pile of statistics waiting for me."

"I understand," Christine said, with a forced smile.

"Come here," Paul ordered." She stood in front of them, and leaned forward, her forehead resting against their chest. He put his arms around her and inhaled the smell of her hair. And again. "Please hold me," he asked, and Christine threw her arms around them, just above the waist.

He heard the woman sniffle. "I. I'm." He kissed the crown of her head to prod her. "Go ahead," he said. "I like to hear you talk to me."

"Even when --"

A pause. "Yes, Christine. Even when."

He felt her tighten her embrace for a moment. "You're sure?"

He nodded against her, and started petting her hair with their left hand.

"Okay," she said, "you asked for it." Before Paul could feel a burst of dread Christine stepped back -- hands still on their sides -- and said, "Whenever I leave you I'm afraid I'll never see you again." Abruptly she hugged them close.

Amy thought, "She is a needy thing. Sad."

"Then I'll have to see you again. And again. And again after that."

A sob broke from the woman, just one.

"You're a brave woman to admit that's how you feel. I admire you for that."

Her voice was muffled against their chest, "You don't hate me for it? You're not scared?"

"I'm not afraid of your feelings. I'm flattered that I mean so much to you." He felt her tighten her hug again.

They stood together in her living room, just being together. Paul thought to Amy, "I love the sex, but this -- this is what it's about."

"It does feel good to feel loved," she thought back.

Finally Paul stepped back and held their left hand against her cheek. "I've got to go, Amy has stuff we have to do. But I'll be back," he said, and watched a real smile come over the woman's face. "I'm nowhere near done with my Christine."

She held their hand when they walked into the alleyway and back to where Amy's blue sedan was parked. "I love you, Paulette," she said. "And I believe you. You -- you really will be back for me."

He kissed her on the mouth and thought to her, "Yes."

When the kiss finally ended, Amy said, "That was intense."

"Oh, I'm sorry," Christine said. "I don't want to make you uncomfortable. I like you, too."

"I don't think you realize what you do to Paul. Uh, Paulette."

He thought to Amy, "Wow. Or to you."

"You drive," she said as Paul got behind the wheel of their car. Then, to Christine, "We'll all talk tomorrow. Thanks for a fun weekend."

"It's Paul. Thanks for a GREAT weekend. Talk to you soon!"

Christine stood in front of the car, her right arm bent and fingers waggling to wave as he backed out of the driveway. Through the open window they heard her say, "I love you, Paulette!"

On the drive back to campus, Paul waited for Amy to explain her assessment of their kiss with Christine. He did not know what she was thinking, and her feelings weren't strong enough to be evident to him. But he knew her well enough to know that her cryptic comment was significant. He waited.

Finally, she said aloud, "You really like her!"

"Haven't I been saying so?"

"What you were feeling, it was so strong I could feel it. You weren't just turned on. It was..."

Paul smiled, "Hmmmm?"

"Gratitude," she finally said. "And, uh, contentment? Is that a feeling?"

He turned onto a side street so he could pull over to a curb. "I guess. She makes me feel good." He wrapped their arms around themself. "She's the first woman to know me and like me romantically in years, since back when I had my own body and was married. You bet I feel grateful."

There was a long pause as they petted one another's arms. "I know you," Amy said. "And I like you. I love you. And it's romantic, kind of."

"Yes, sometimes it is. Nothing's changed -- it's Amy first. Always Amy first."

They were quiet for a few moments. Then Paul drove down the street to make a NOLA U-turn across the neutral ground and resumed their drive back to campus.

"After we nail the UNO Strangler, let's find me a guy who hears voices and is as cool as Christine. Wouldn't that be great?"

Paul laughed, "That has possibilities. I'm still looking for the perfect double date."

When they got back to the dorm room, Amy ran a mental inventory. Three fifteen. "Laundry. Statistics. Maybe dinner with Florence. And more detectivizing tomorrow." She let Paul whistle while she filled her clothes hamper to drag downstairs.

Afterwards, Amy forced herself to read her math textbook, but she was too anxious to keep at it. "Hey! Hey!" Paul shouted when she abruptly stood up, knocking his paperback out of their hands and losing his place.

"I'm too restless to sit here," she said. "We were so busy with Riordan, then that exam that we aced, or at least B'ed, then a nice weekend with your girlfriend. Suddenly I feel caged." She paced the room.

"Florence!" she barked in her phone. "Dinner? Now? How's pizza? No, I'm buying. See you."

She closed her phone. "Sixteen seconds and I'm feeling better. Canadian bacon and onions okay for you?"

On the walk to Florence's dorm, Paul thought, "Are you finally going to tell her about me?"

"I want to. I love how comfortable we are with Christine. I'd like more of that."

"You know I'm a people person. If you can tell Florence about me, I'm all for it."

Because of the series of killings, Florence's door was uncharacteristically closed. Still, when Amy knocked, Florence opened the door without looking; she was concentrating on slides in a lightbox.

Florence held up a finger as she finished examining something through a loupe. She wrote down some notes, turned off the lightbox, and smiled up at Amy. "Hey, you," Florence said. "I haven't seen you in so long, I think you've grown two inches."

"Gained three pounds, and lost five IQ points," Amy said. She hugged her friend. "You ready for food?"

"Sit for a while," she said. "What's up with you? Have you caught the killer yet?"

"Perp still at large. I hope I spend tomorrow collecting evidence samples, Steven is asking for search warrants." She plopped down on the edge of her friend's bed.

"And how about Amyland? What's going on there?"

"Aside from being Nancy Drew? I managed to pass a Psych test. The proctor pretty much bet me I'd fail. And I've been spending time with Paul and his girlfriend. She introduced me to a very strange artist lady. It's been a lot of fun. Hey, have you ditched your problem roommate?"

"Ah, Consuela, where do I begin? I'm this close to drawing a line down the middle of the room to keep her away." She shook her head. "How can such a cute woman be such a screaming jerk?"

It was Paul who said, "Are those mutually exclusive traits?"

"I expect attractive people to be together people. Florence and Amy kind of people."

"I'm in," Amy laughed.

Florence picked up her jacket. "Not to be too much of a pig, but there was this promise of free pizza. Where's this Italian place?"

"Not far, but I'm driving. Come on, and tell me about Pete."

On the walk to the student parking deck, Florence told graphic stories about her weekend romp. It wasn't until they were driving that she added, "I don't know if I'll see him again."

"Why not?" Amy asked. She didn't understand how Florence could be so casual about sex. "Obviously you two get along pretty well."

"If I ever want a fourth date with a man, I'll be trying on wedding dresses. I told you, I get bored. Been there, done him."

Amy shook her head. "I don't work like that," she said, trying not to sound as judgmental as she thought she was being.

"Does that mean you're having issues over your fling with what's-his-name?"

"God, no. Even I can recognize a hopeless situation."

Paul thought, "Are you going to tell her about me? And Christine?"

"Oh, pipe down!" Amy said out loud.

Florence said, "I swear, I only thought it!"

"Thought what?"

"You really need to detail this car."

Amy laughed. "I guess you're right. But first, we're going to order dinner, and I am going to tell you a story that will either bond us as friends forever, or you'll be calling the guys with butterfly nets on me."

"Can't be crazier than my sister."

"Keep thinking that," Amy said as they got out of the car.

Pizza Milano was not too crowded on a Sunday evening. The young woman who greeted them steered them to a booth surrounded by diners. Amy said, "Could you put us over there," pointing, "so we can talk?"

The woman walked them to the more private area and said, "I'll send Eduardo over."

Florence called after her, "Tell him to bring a couple of Dixies."

"Amaze me," Florence said as they sat across from each other.

She smiled with her mouth closed, while Paul thought, "Hi, Florence. I'm Paul. I've heard so much about you."

Florence turned her head to see if the voice came from behind her. When she turned back to her friend, Amy's smile had become mischievous. Florence asked, "Have you learned ventriloquism?"

"No, no, no," Paul thought. "I live inside Amy's head. I'm not crazy. Amy's not crazy. You're not crazy, although I hear your sister is."

"What is this shit?" she said.

Amy thought to her, "Welcome to my life. This happened when I was a kid. Paul is real. He's not me, but he's stuck inside me."

"Crap. Maybe my sister isn't as crazy as I thought."

Amy spoke out loud. "Florence, I need you to keep an open mind and listen. You know those arguments and discussions I have with myself? They're with Paul. He really is my best friend. My family knows, and a couple of doctors from when it first happened. And Christine knows, Paul's girlfriend."

"Why was I hearing voices when you weren't talking?"

"It's something we can do. That's usually how we talk to each other, and then we discovered we can talk to other people that way. Directly."

"This is crazy."

Amy nodded. "Absolutely impossible. I know."

Eduardo brought glasses and two bottles of Dixie. "Good evening, what can I get you lovely ladies for dinner?"

Florence whispered, "Tell him what we want like you talked to me."

"Florence!" she laughed, then told Eduardo out loud what they wanted on a pizza.

When the waiter left them, Florence said, "Does this mean

you're a schizo? A split personality?"

"No! Paul told Mom and Dad about his life, we checked it out, and he was real. We even met his sister. She thought it was weird that her brother looked like a teenage girl, but she came around."

"You are not kidding?"

Amy shook her head. "Look, this is not something I tell everyone. I need you to do two things: Never tell anyone else about it, and believe me."

"Yes. And maybe. I'm going to need some convincing that you're not making this up to distract me from your unforgivable behavior, ignoring me while you turn into Sherlock Holmes."

Amy took a deep breath, then said, "My life is complicated. Paul is seeing Christine, I almost failed a Psych test, and yes, I'm learning how to be a detective. I'm juggling all this stuff, plus trying to keep up in math, and just -- there aren't enough hours in the day."

"Wait a minute. Wait a god-damned, pea-picking minute. If Paul lives inside you, how is he seeing this woman?"

Elbows on the table, Amy balled their hands into fists and wedged them under their cheekbones to hold their head up. "The only body Paul has is mine. So for him to be with his girlfriend, I have to be there." She was vibrating with anxiety from the risk of admitting this.

There was a silence as the passing looks on Florence's face showed she was thinking, trying to make sense of the incomprehensible. "So -- so -- Let me get this straight. Paul lives inside you. He's a man?"

"He thinks so. He was when he had his own body, before I met him."

"So...no, this is crazy."

Eduardo showed up with the pizza. Amy said, "Please hurry, we're talking. But bring us more Dixie." The waiter left the pie on the metal stand, and disappeared.

Florence tried again. "So you think you have a guy inside you. And obviously he likes women. Did he... you know --"

"How unlike you to be so shy," Amy smiled grimly. "Do Paul and Christine have sex? Yes. What does that mean? It means Paul borrows my body to do it."

"You're a lesbian? No, there's what's-his-face. You're bi? Did you and the guy and the girl, you know..."

"No threesome. And I'm not a lesbian, I don't want to touch women. Paul doesn't want to touch men, either. We're still figuring out how to do this."

"This is fascinating," Florence said, stuffing a folded slice of pizza in her mouth. "Ips jst fathntng."

"Your beverages, ladies," Eduardo said, bringing more beer. Florence, with a mouth full of hot pizza, said, "Ha -- tks!"

"You know I'm not crazy, we've spent a lot of time together. I don't talk in tongues, or flop on the floor, or howl at the moon. Please, Florence, please believe me. Christine knows, and Paul and I have gotten used to being able to be honest with her."

"I want to know every bit of this story," Florence said. "Do not leave out so much as a jot or a tittle. When did this happen?"

Amy explained about Paul's appearance, her father's investigation to prove Paul was real, and his struggle to keep Amy safe and out of institutions. She told Florence how she and Paul became friends, and how they still worked at figuring out how to live as a dyad.

The pizza was long gone, and they were on their fourth round of Dixies when Amy finished with, "Now do you believe me?"

Florence was smiling. "Not a word of it. But it's fascinating. You ought to write a book, call it something like *A Different Kind of Twin*."

"Damn!" Paul said out loud. He continued, "Florence, this is Paul. When I talk I sound like Amy because all I have to work with is her body, and her throat." Then he thought to her, "You'll only hear my real voice when I think to you."

"I don't know how you do it, Amy," she said, "but it's great."

He shook their head. "Still Paul. Please, like Amy asked, please never tell anyone about me. If you don't believe I exist, please don't tell anyone that Amy does. Okay?"

Florence was on the verge of laughter.

"Okay?" he thought to her, as ominously as he could. Then, aloud, he said, "If the wrong people hear about it, Amy and I will spend the rest of our lives in a mental hospital. You know Amy-- do you think there's anything wrong with her?"

"Of course not," Florence said.

"It's Amy now, good. You don't believe me, okay. Can you do something for me? Even though you don't believe this, please let me talk to you about it. You're my best friend; I need to be able to talk to you about all this stuff."

"Even though I think it's all a fairy tale?"

"Suit yourself," Amy said, "but the view from my castle is spectacular. I'll share if you let me talk to you about it."

"When's the last time I told you I've never known anyone like you?" Florence asked, still smiling.

Amy shook her head and laughed. "I can't remember. In all honesty, I've heard that before."

"Yeah, right."

"Seriously. Christine is crazy about both of us because we treat her as normal."

"'Both of us'?"

"Sure. Me and Paul. But she calls him Paulette. She knows he was a man, but she prefers to think of him as a woman."

"Do you have any idea what this sounds like?"

Amy drained her beer. "Yes, I do. It sounds exactly like my life. You ready to go?"

℘ 38 ॐ

Amy was scribbling notes frantically on Monday morning, trying to catch up in her statistics class. As the graduate assistant talked about Z-scores, she heard Paul -- who had been a market researcher when he had his own body -- think, "Old news." She thought back, "It's new to me. I need a tutor."

Her phone's loud ring told the entire room she had forgotten to put it on vibrate. She ran from the class while enduring frowns from students and lecturer alike. In the hall she said, "Clear. What?"

"I'm tied up in Poydras on a new case," the detective said. "I need you to do some things for me."

"Sure, Boss. What's the new case?"

"There's one of those fancy new ATMs out here that uses fingerprints. This morning someone called to say there were two human fingers lying on the machine."

"Euuuwwww!"

"Yeah, I expect, I'm on the way there. Look, the judge approved search warrants for lover boy and stalker girl --"

She laughed, "I don't believe that's what the warrant says."

"I can't get over there, so you're going to have to collect evidence. Jermaine will call you in a while and meet you to drop off supplies, but then he's got to hightail to some body they found upriver."

Paul thought, "Hey! We're in charge! Not bad for an unpaid intern. This'll be fun."

"Yeah, right," she said to Paul, but out loud. Then, "What am

I doing?"

"You're going to cut samples of carpet or rug, then process them. Shoot for twelve by twenty-four, it's okay if they're a little bigger or a little smaller. Take more than one sample from each place. Label them immediately or else you'll forget which sample is from the doorway and which is from the window. And you have to make sketches."

"I can't draw!" she said, thinking of the tidy sketches Riordan gave her to work on.

"Clear, listen. You're at UNO. They have a book store, right?" A pause. "Right?"

"Uh, yes, right."

"Buy some graph paper, Doofus! Quarter-inch squares. You'll do fine."

"Okay, I --"

"And every piece of carpet you cut out, use new gloves, and wash down your knife with alcohol and a lint-free cloth."

"Check. Listen, I --"

"Don't bend or fold the samples when you put them in the evidence bag."

"Okay, I --"

"The only private areas where you can snoop are what's in the warrants, that's for Young and Scruggs."

"Yes, okay, but --"

"Any public area that looks worthwhile, take samples, I got us permission from the 23rd vice president in charge of not knowing anything."

"I got it --"

"If anybody asks what you're doing, tell them it's official police business. Don't answer any other questions."

"Your Majesty, will you --"

The detective screamed, apparently out the window of his car, "Hey, you! Chase that mutt away! You hear me?" Then, "Fuck me, a dog has one of the fingers, I gotta go. Jermaine'll call you soon. Hey, pooch! Poochie, come--" and the call ended.

As she put her phone away, she thought to Paul, "I've heard the best way to teach someone to swim is to throw them in the deep end."

Paul thought back, "The hard part is getting out of the canvas sack."

Amy spent another seven minutes taking notes before her phone went off again. This time she muttered, "Sorry, sorry, excuse me," as she took the call and went back to the hallway. "Clear, what?"

"Miss Clear?"

"Oh, Doctor Tallant. Steven said you'd call."

"You know my name?"

"No, that was just a guess. How was your grandson's birthday?"

She heard a hint of a laugh, "You are entirely too nice to do police work. It was a delight, thank you for remembering. But you can call me Jermaine. Everyone else does."

"Okay. Jermaine. You've got supplies for me?"

"Yes, a bunch of material. Let's see... a box of gloves, evidence bags, evidence tape... It's more than you can fit in a pocket."

She said, "I've got a backpack, will that work?"

"May I recommend a suitcase with wheels and a handle?"

Paul said, "How about a steamer trunk on a hand truck?"

"That might be overkill. And you don't want to contaminate any evidence or controls."

"Behave!" she thought to Paul. "When do I meet you, where?" she asked the medical examiner.

"I can get to the parking lot by the lake," he said, thinking. "Twelve fifteen? Twelve thirty?"

She glanced at her watch. "I'll be at the entrance off Lakeshore. What are you driving?"

"It'll be hard to miss," he said soberly. "It's a hearse."

When she tried to sneak back into math class, the lecturer stopped in mid-sentence and said, "Will you please turn off your phone?" It was not a request. Amy held it up and dramatically pulled out the battery. When she sat, a man next to her leaned over and said, "You're a hoot and a half."

She stuck her tongue out at him and went back to her notes.

Shortly after noon Amy was standing by the driveway that led to the campus streets and the Privateer parking lots. "I feel silly with my suitcase," she thought to Paul.

"Nah," he thought back, "we look like we're going away for the weekend."

"It's Monday."

"Okay, for a long weekend."

The doctor's hearse was unmistakable. Large, long, black, and with NOPD insignia on the doors and the hood. Amy stuck out her thumb, and the vehicle came to a halt. The driver's window slowly lowered to an electronic buzz, and Jermaine called, "Get in, we need more room than this." So she wheeled her case around to the other side of the car and let herself in, holding the luggage in her lap.

"Thanks for the lift," she said. "Make a right up ahead. I'll get you to the parking lot."

The medical examiner deliberately took up four spaces, giving him lots of room to transfer the supplies Amy would need. When they let themselves out of the vehicle, Amy lay her suitcase down and opened it.

She flinched when he opened the back door, but instead of the vehicle's intended cargo there were several large boxes. He began handing things to her, saying, "Latex gloves, two boxes. Use them like water, and never use the same glove twice." She put the boxes on the pavement next to the suitcase.

"Denatured alcohol, swab things down," two bottles. "Lint free cloths," a huge bundle wrapped in plastic. "Disposable knives for cutting samples," a cardboard box that claimed to hold two dozen. "If you must use one over again, wipe it down with alcohol and let it dry." She tucked them away in her suitcase.

"Evidence envelopes," he said, "Riordan said you'll need the large economy size for carpet control samples."

"He told me to aim for twelve by twenty four."

"Good rule of thumb. Put the samples in flat, we don't want the fiber surface rubbing against itself. Did he tell you about hygiene?"

"Uh, hygiene?"

"Yes, Miss. Fresh gloves each time. If you cross-contaminate the samples, they're worse than useless. Now, here are a bunch of regular sample envelopes. You put the bindles inside these."

He rummaged around the back of the hearse and pulled out a

black plastic case. "Take this; with luck you'll need it. I'd like hair samples from our suspects, if you see them."

"I have scissors in my room," Amy said, "or should I just use the knives you gave me?"

Jermaine stood up and stretched, hands on his lower back. "Ideally, hair samples include part of the follicle. There's clean paper in the kit, you spread it on a table and sit the suspect in front of it. Then you have them brush their hair forward a bunch. You'll be surprised how many hairs will fall out, even people as young as you are. Then turn them around and have them brush their hair back a few times. Pour the hair into a bindle and label it. And throw out the piece of paper, do not try to use it again." He thought for a moment. "For this case, you don't need to know about collecting pubic hair."

"Damn," Paul said.

He handed over another black plastic box. "Fingerprint kit," he said. "Better safe than sorry." She placed it in the suitcase.

Jermaine closed the hatch. "A few more things," he said. "This is for you." He handed her a plastic ID badge on a lanyard. It had an odd picture of her, probably taken by Lawson with a telephoto lens when she was doing a spiral search at the Megan Silver crime scene. The badge misspelled her name as 'Aimee,' but labeled her as 'Orleans Parish Police Employee.' "This should cut through any crap you get from the school or from the suspects."

She thought to Paul, "He likes me. Riordan thinks I'm good." She was filled with pride and pleasure.

He took some folded documents out of his inside jacket pocket. "These are the search warrants. This is important, so pay attention." He hunkered down. Automatically, Amy sat on the pavement so she was still at eye level with him. "First, knock loud on the door. If the door is open, knock loud on it anyway, do not enter the room." She nodded. "You're an employee now, so you yell, 'New Orleans Police to serve a search warrant.'" Again, she nodded. Paul could feel how excited she was at being trusted with the task.

"Give them about thirty seconds to respond. It doesn't hurt to announce yourself a second time; it's not like this is a drug case. If they open the door, you hand them the warrant and ask to be let in. If they refuse, you enter anyway -- once the warrant is served, they don't have a choice."

"What if no one answers the door?"

"You knocked, you announced yourself, and you waited a reasonable length of time. Let yourself in."

"Jermaine," she whined, "what if the door's locked? Or what if they're twice my size and they say no?"

"You're on the team now," he smiled. "Call campus security for backup, or grab one of the officers at these stupid checkpoints. We're actually allowed to break down the door, but that might mess up our relations with the Regents."

"If the suspect is not there, leave their copy of the warrant behind when you're done. In any case, the last page is a blank form for a receipt, you write down what you take away. We don't have permission for secret searches." He stood up.

Amy felt the thick, heavy wad of papers. Until that moment a search warrant was just an expression from TV shows. Suddenly they felt very real.

When the doctor climbed back into the driver's seat, Amy said, "Can I ask you something?"

"Of course, Miss."

"Steven. Does he always use helpers like me?"

He swung the door back open, and turned in his seat so he was facing her. "Hardly anyone calls him that. Everyone calls him 'Riordan'. Just like everyone calls me 'Jermaine.'" He shrugged. "Don't know why, that's just how it's worked out. No, he doesn't always take on helpers. He does sometimes -- he has an eye for a pretty face, you know. But the real reason is NOPD is so short handed. There should be six officers on our response team, but there's just him, me, and a photographer. He needs the help. And from what I've seen, you are a very smart young lady with an excellent work ethic. He's never had a badge made for a helper before."

Amy felt Paul rub her right arm and think, "Well, ain't you hot shit!" "How can the police be so under-funded?"

"I've been with NOPD for sixteen years. I've watched the city population drop after each hurricane, each flood, each oil spill. Somehow the crime rate keeps going up. For all the tourist trade, New Orleans is an impoverished city. Low property tax base, high unemployment, and a new body fished out of the river every two days." He shook his head. "If I were younger I might go back into private practice, but now I'm just hoping my pension is still waiting for me in 2035."

Still holding the badge and the search warrants, Amy asked, "Any advice?"

He stared at her. "You ignored me when I told you to go home that first day."

"I do that a lot. But I'd rather ignore good advice than be ignorant of it."

He nodded with eyebrows raised. "Fair enough. Okay. I advise you to get started on this right away. Bring the samples to the Rampart Street station. And say as little as possible. If a suspect asks you what you're going to do next, make an obvious point of not answering them. Here, try me. Ask me what I'm going to do after taking a hair sample."

"Uh, okay." She took a deep breath. "Now that you've made me mess up my hair nine ways from Sunday, what will you do next?"

"Thank you for the hair sample, Miss. We'll be in touch." He smiled.

"Not very satisfying."

"Exactly. Call if you run into anything. Otherwise, do the best you can. I'm sure you'll hear from Riordan this evening." He started the engine.

"You can find your way out of here?" Amy asked.

"I think so. If I have to, I'll plow my way out. Hell, this hearse is so big it would take a Bradley tank to stop me." He waved and raised the window.

Amy stood in the parking lot by her suitcase on wheels. The sun was bright, but it was a chilly October day. She slapped her upper arms for warmth, then thought, "So, now what do we do?"

"Savor the moment," he thought back. "We have a steenkin' badge and we don't have to stop for any more check points."

She wheeled the suitcase behind her as she headed for Pontchartrain Hall South and stalker girl, Alex Scruggs. "What if no one's there and the door's locked?"

"I never got around to it," Paul said, "but I always wanted to learn how to pick locks."

"My econ teacher last spring would have said, 'Evidently not.'"

He thought a mental raspberry to her. "You've got a badge now." He considered it for a moment, then thought, "If Reggie or Alex refuse to let us in, we go get one of the cops from a check point. If the door's locked, we call the rent-a-cops. What's the one who wants to vote for you for President?"

"A plan!" she said aloud as she wheeled her case toward Alex Scruggs' dormitory. "I feel better now." She grinned as she presented her new employee badge at three different check points.

"Welcome aboard, Miss Clear," one uniformed man said.

"Thank you, Officer Mullinax, I'm glad to be here."

"You can call me Woody now." He pointed at his uniform name tag. "The W is for Woodrow."

She smiled as he let go of her badge. "I'm honored, Woody. You can call me Amy." He tipped his hat as she wheeled past him.

Amy thought, "If Alex is a jerk, we come get Woody." She felt Paul nod.

Outside stalker girl's door, Amy wiped her sweaty palms on her jeans and knocked. Before she could announce herself, Alex Scruggs opened it. Paul smiled to see her.

"Oh, it's you again," the woman said. "I guess you can come in."

Amy held up the warrant. "This isn't a social call, Alex. I'm here as an employee of the Parish police. May I come in to execute this search warrant?"

Alex took it, read the front, then swung the door wide. "Yeah, sure, I've got nothing to hide. What are you looking for?"

Amy wheeled the suitcase in front of her, practically chasing the woman down the hall to the living room area. "Flooring samples. It's spelled out in the warrant."

On the near side of the living room, Amy laid down the valise and opened it. She thought to Paul, "What am I doing?"

He spoke, with Amy's voice, "Is there any carpet in your suite?"

"Nope." Alex sat on her sofa, her legs under her butt, with one eye staring at Amy and the other looking at the far wall.

"Rugs?" She was donning blue latex gloves.

"One in the bedroom," she said.

"I'll start there. Please come with me." Amy was ill at ease in Alex's suite and the idea of removing the rug without her knowledge made her more uncomfortable. She pushed her wheeled valise behind Alex and followed her.

There were fresh piles of clean clothes against one wall, and the bed was not made. The rest of the room seemed in good order.

The rug was brown, two by three feet, with an intricate gray and silver design of Celtic knots. As she began drawing on the graph paper in her clipboard, Amy thought, "I'll cut it and take all of it."

As Amy guesstimated the size of the bedroom, Alex volunteered, "I have to thank you."

"Huh?" She was sketching the bed, the rug, the windows, the door.

"Reggie has been spending a lot of time with me. He practically lives here now. That wouldn't have happened without you. I never thought I'd thank anyone for putting my boyfriend in jail."

Paul thought, "Why does 'boyfriend in jail' sound so trashy to me?" But Amy was paying attention to the woman. "So when you first told us that he was your honey, that wasn't true then, was it?"

She shook her head. "I just wanted it to be true. I wanted it so bad." She looked up, at least with her good eye. "And you made it happen."

"You're happy now?" She put aside the clipboard, and positioned herself on the floor by the throw rug.

"Yeah. Yeah, I am. Reggie treats me nicer than he ever did before."

Amy nodded absently as she positioned the knife and began to cut.

"What are you doing?" the woman shrieked. "That's wool!"

Amy finished the cut. "It's still wool. I'm sorry, Alex, but now it's wool evidence in a murder case." She slid the cut piece into the paper evidence bag and sealed it. Then she wrote the date and time and her name on the outside, and '1/3 of rug, bedroom, side nearest closet.'

"Who's going to pay for that?" she demanded.

"I don't know," Amy said as she began her second cut. "I'm just the courier."

Alex jumped at her, knocking the knife out of her hand. "Stop!" she shouted, and flailed harmlessly.

Amy grasped the woman by the shoulders and ordered, "Sit!" She was on the floor next to her. Softer now, Amy said, "I can't imagine what this is like, but acting up is only going to make it worse. Do you hear me?"

Alex nodded, one eye on Amy.

"It's a court ordered warrant. A judge signed it and you don't have any say about it. I don't know if the police or the school or anyone will make restitution. But I'm here for evidence, and I have to process it a certain way." She looked at the woman. "Okay?"

When the woman remained still, Amy retrieved the knife and finished the cut, then bagged the two remaining pieces of rug.

"I'm done in here," Amy said, looking around the bedroom. She heard Paul think, "Maybe we should sweep the living room floor? Since there's no carpet in there." She nodded, and said, "Right. Alex, do you have a broom? I want to sweep your living room."

"Please do the whole suite," she said as she went to get the broom.

Amy peeled off the gloves as she walked back to the suitcase, and stuffed them and the used knife in an outside pocket. "First I have to clean the broom," she thought to Paul. When Alex presented it, Amy beckoned her down the hallway and outside the suite. There she took the broom and began massaging the bristles, trying to rid them of as much dust as possible. She even ran the broom across the textured wall surface in the public area.

"I dunno," Paul thought. Amy said, "I've got an idea," and walked past Alex, back to the living room.

"What's your idea?" the woman asked.

"Oh, thinking out loud. I'll show you, though." First she put on a new pair of gloves. Then she opened the hair kit Jermaine had given her, and took out one sheet of clean white paper.

"That's huge," Alex said, interested.

"It's 33 by 46 inches" Amy said, pretending she had always known what she had just read on the side of the box. She folded it in half on the short width, then bent an inch or two of the edge over. With a piece of evidence tape she sealed the flap. "Can I get you to steady this?" she asked.

While Alex held the broomstick, Amy positioned the folded paper over the bristles. She folded the open end and taped it, making a paper envelope over the business part of the broom. Finally she taped the paper to the stick.

"There we go!" Amy said proudly, and she changed gloves again. She used the device to scrape and push the dirt and fibers and maybe clues across the linoleum floor. Finally, she brushed the debris onto another sheet of paper from the hair kit. She bent the makeshift dustpan and carefully tapped the accumulated detritus into a bindle.

"Here's your broom back," she said. Amy folded the bindle closed and taped it, then wrote her initials and the date over the tape. She slipped it into a paper evidence bag, and sealed it, and labeled it. She tossed it in her valise.

"One last thing. I need a hair sample."

Alex put her hands on the sides of her head. "No, I won't let you cut my hair. I finally got it looking good for Reggie."

Amy held up her empty hands. "No cutting. Please clean off your desk; we'll do it there. And if you would, can you clean your hairbrush and bring it in here?" She waited while the woman retrieved her brush. She was still pulling stray hairs out of it when she returned to the living room.

Amy put on fresh gloves and spread a large clean sheet of white paper on the desk. "You sit here," she told Alex. "Now, lean over the desk, and brush your hair forward from the back of your head."

"That's going to make a mess of my hair!" she complained.

"Yup, it will, but we'll finish up brushing it properly. I need you to start -- brush it forward. The sides, too."

Amy was surprised that what Jermaine told her was true -- twenty or thirty hairs drifted down to the paper. She hoped they had part of the follicle that he had said was important.

"Okay. Now let's turn your chair around." When the woman had done so, she said, "Lean back and brush your hair back. Sides, too."

More hair fluttered to the paper.

"Great. Well done, Alex. Give me a minute to process this and I'll be on my way." She prepared a bindle, then folded the paper and tapped it to coax the hair to the evidence container. She sealed it, signed it, put it in a brown paper evidence bag, and filled out the form on it.

"When are you going to see Reggie?" Alex asked.

"Thanks for the hair sample," Amy replied. "We'll be in touch. Oh -- let me fill out the receipt on the search warrant."

Alex handed over the warrant, but sternly said, "I asked you a question."

"And I gave you as much of an answer as I'm going to." She indicated the rug and the hair sample on the receipt form, and returned it to the woman.

"I'm not happy about this."

Amy zipped up her suitcase and pulled it upright. "The next time I see you," she said, "I hope I'm just Amy and you're just Alex and we can be friends. But today I'm the police and you're a suspect. I will not answer your question. I -- well, have a good day."

Amy heard the door slam behind her as she wheeled her way down the public hall, away from Alex Scruggs' room. Paul said out loud, "That was amazing!" and then silently, "How did you think up that broom business? I have to say, I'm impressed."

She smiled at his praise. She bumped the valise down two flights in the stairwell. "I knew the broom was too dirty," she thought, "I don't know where the idea came from to wrap it up."

"Good instincts, just be grateful for them. That's why Riordan and Jermaine trust you for this job. I am so excited!"

Amy wheeled her way to her own dorm room to unload the evidence samples before heading for Reggie Young's place.

"Yes," she said out loud, "me too." In the safety of her room, she sat at her desk and awkwardly, she with their right hand and Paul with their left, they high-fived themself. "Let's get a drink to celebrate."

"We've got a little more work to do," he counseled. "Reggie."

She dialed the detective's phone, but was surprised when he said, "Riordan. What?"

"I want to check in, Your Majesty. Got the samples from stalker girl, and next stop is Reggie Young's dorm. Did you ever get the finger?"

"Several times a day," he said, "usually. Do you have any idea how hard it is to get a half-chewed index finger out of a dog's mouth?"

Paul answered, "That depends if the finger is still attached to your hand." He heard Amy giggle.

Riordan said, "You have a strange sense of humor, young lady."

"So I've been told. Hey, this morning you didn't tell me about the computer printout. What did you find?"

"Oh, important," he said, then, off the phone mouthpiece, "No, that's okay, you don't have to wrap it. Really. I'd rather -- oh, sure." He muttered, "Damn clerk charges me too much, puts mustard on it, and then insists on putting it in styrofoam. Someone on your campus has a get-out-of-jail-free card."

"Say what?"

"Their swipe card. It lets them in but doesn't stamp the system with who it is."

Amy thought. "So, is it someone in building maintenance?"

"Good guess. It's possible. The interesting thing is when and where the card was used." It sounded like '...whr th rd s st.'

"How's the burger?" she asked.

She heard him swallow. "They'll rot your innards. This is a fish sandwich. They make 'em for you fresh instead of leaving them under a heat lamp for hours."

"Mustard on a fish sandwich? Ugh!"

"You ain't kidding, Sweetheart. Look, the printout says this blank card was used in Laura Adams' dorm an hour before Jermaine says she died. Used in Privateer Hall maybe two hours before Yvonne Washington went toes up. Again a few hours before Megan Silver turned up dead."

Paul said, "Circumstantial but damning." Amy took the lead to ask, "What about before Ashley Probst --"

"I was getting there," he interrupted. "Nothing in the Biology building, but that card was used maybe a dozen times in the

Computer Center. And according to the guy at school who runs the program, it's used over there every day, bunches of times."

Amy was pacing her dorm room while she listened. "That lets out Reggie, he told us he barely knows how to turn a computer on. And I think Alex Scruggs is an education major."

"Oh, she's going for her M-R-S degree?"

"Hey, my mom was an education major!"

She thought she heard him chuckle, but she couldn't be sure over the phone. "I've got to meet Jermaine upriver. He says I'll love some clues that are lying around. Go ahead and get those carpet samples from lover boy. I'll call you tonight."

She sat back down as she turned off the call. "He is never going to let me forget I slept with Reggie."

"How about you?" Paul asked out loud. "Are you ever going to forget it?"

"Probably," she said. "Someday I'll be head over heels happy in love and will forget every other man I ever knew. Except you. Until then, though --" she thought for a moment "-- I'll remember. I had a good time. He wasn't a jerk until later."

She slapped their thighs with both hands and stood up. "I wonder if I'll be a Corporal by the end of this. Or a Sergeant. That'll impress dad." She cupped water from her sink for a quick gulp and set out for Privateer Hall.

She passed another three checkpoints on her walk, and each time her plastic employee badge got her waved through. "I must be some kind of hot stuff," she thought. "You'll make sure I don't forget all the little people who got me here, right?"

"Oh, I promise," he laughed.

Amy let herself into the dorm complex with her swipe card, and dragged her suitcase up to the second floor. She knocked on Reggie's door and shouted, "Police! I have a search warrant!" Two different doors on the hallway opened, but not his. Amy waved at the man seven doors down who was sticking his head into the hallway. She waited half a minute, then knocked and shouted again, still with no response.

Paul reached out for the doorknob. "Damn," he muttered. It was locked.

"No problem," she thought and opened her phone to call

campus security. The businesslike voice on the other end said, "Security, this is Claiborn."

"Officer," she lied, "This is Amy Clear. I'm Detective Riordan's assistant?"

"Oh, sure," he responded, now in a friendly tone. "Uh, please don't say there's another body."

"No, nothing like that. The detective wants me to execute a search warrant, and nobody's home and the room is locked. I need you or maintenance to help me with a master key."

"A search warrant? We don't see many of those."

"You're welcome to read it. Look, I'm also a little worried that if the suspect comes back while I'm taking evidence there might be a problem. Can you stay with me until I'm done?"

"You bet! Uh, I mean, yeah, I can do that. Where are you?"

She gave the guard Reggie's room number, then ended the call. She put the suitcase on its side and sat on it, waiting.

Paul thought, "That's the guy who's going to vote for you for President?"

"I don't know which one is which. Now that I got them trained, they're okay."

"What if Reggie shows up?"

"We beat him up before," she smiled, "we can do it again. Besides, he's scared of me. And unless he's got a minion, I'm pretty sure he's not the killer." She snorted aloud, "He doesn't have anything to worry about. The only problem is that he might not realize that."

They were idly playing rock paper scissors when the campus guard showed up. "What on earth are you doing?" he asked, incredulous.

"Umm, waiting for you," Amy said, and stood up. "Here's the warrant, you said you wanted to read it."

The man leafed through it, keys dangling from a big D-ring on his belt. "Wow," he muttered, "this is just like on TV. Wow."

"It's pretty cool," she agreed. "Can you let us in?"

The third key he tried opened the lock. Amy shouted over his shoulder, "Police! Search warrant!" There was no response.

The guard tipped his cap, and Amy felt a moment of panic. "Can you stay with me while I do this? In case he comes back?"

"I guess so, Miss," he said. He took off his cap, and sat at a desk chair.

Amy wheeled her valise in and prepared to take samples. She thought to Paul, "Three or four from the living room, and a couple from his bedroom."

"Sounds good. Let's get to work."

The guard watched with fascination. It wasn't just the crush on Amy; he considered himself a would-be policeman, and he thought of Amy as a current one. He wanted to see how real police did the things he saw on TV.

"Where did you learn to do this?" he asked after she had processed and labeled the first piece of carpet.

"The deep end of a swimming pool," Paul said, while Amy took a fresh knife from her case.

"That doesn't make any sense."

Amy noticed the man sounded hurt, so she stopped and looked up at him. "I'm sorry, that was rude. What is your name?"

"Roy Claiborn," he said with a sudden smile.

She nodded. "I'm still learning. Detective Riordan and Doctor Jermaine have been tutoring me. You want to be a cop?"

"Yeah, I do," he said eagerly.

"People tell me I should go to the state academy," she said. She put on a new pair of gloves, and began hacking a second carpet sample.

"That sounds so hard," he replied. "I didn't do so good in school." He started a monologue about still living at home, about fights with his father, about wanting his own place, and wanting to start a family. Amy and Paul took turns nodding and saying a non-committal "uh-huh" from time to time.

At one point, Amy said, "Can I get you to move, Roy? I want to get a sample from where our suspect sits." He wheeled the chair back a few feet, then stared at the few inches of bare skin on her back, below her shirt and above her jeans.

As she started a new cut, the guard said, "Are you seeing anyone?"

Since her back was to him, he did not see her eyes spring wide. Paul thought, "Oh, shit!" then he said -- with Amy's voice, of course, "Yes, I am. You're sweet to ask. Thank you." He thought of all the times as a young man that women fibbed to spare his feelings, only to leave him feeling worse later. He heard Amy think, "I'm glad you took care of that. He's a nice guy, but..."

"So, you don't have a girlfriend?" Paul went on. He thought the sound from behind him was the guard shaking his head.

"Nah. I don't date too much. It takes money to take a girl out."

"I understand," Paul said. "The people we like, we want to treat them nice." Amy finished cutting and bagging the carpet sample. She stood up and pulled off the latex gloves. "I need to get some samples from the bedroom; then I should be done." She wheeled the valise into the next room and went to work.

"It's just --" Roy began, "-- I don't know, you're really pretty, and you're nice to me. You actually listen to me."

Amy cringed. "Please make him stop," she thought.

Paul asked, "Your family doesn't listen to you?"

"Nah. My dad says I'm stupid and I don't have the sense God gave a rock. He's always telling me to shut up."

"You've got friends?"

"Oh, sure. But we don't talk about -- you know, about important stuff. Personal stuff."

"But they like you? They accept you?"

He started describing his crowd, the four or five people he'd known since high school, still friends, still drinking together, still waiting for anything to happen.

As she began the last cut, Amy thought, "I'm going to scream if I can't get away from him."

"Then don't listen," he thought back. "Maybe it's because I'm happy about Christine; I feel sorry for the guy."

"Whatever," she muttered out loud. She slid the carpet sample into the big brown evidence bag and labeled it.

When her phone rang, Amy wriggled it out of her back pocket. "Clear. What?"

"Paulette?"

Paul thought, "It's for me," and he took the lead. "Hey, Christine. What's up?"

"Does Amy always sound so mean on the phone?"

He laughed, "No, she's just caught up in this police work. How's your day?"

"It's over; it's almost five o'clock. I want to see if I can come visit."

"Let me check," he said. Amy thought, "We're just about done here. And I'm hungry. Sure."

Paul said, "Yeah, come on. We can get some dinner, maybe drive into town to drop off some things at the police department." He noticed Roy was staring, open-mouthed.

"I was hoping you'd say yes," she said. "I'm at that traffic circle place. Come get me!"

"It might be half an hour. Amy is wrapping things up here. See you soon!"

"I love you, Paulette," Christine said, and ended the call.

"Thanks for keeping me company," Paul said as they stood up. "I'm glad Reggie didn't appear, but you'd have been a life saver if he had." They wheeled her case back to the living room to take a final look around.

"What -- what was that?" Claiborn asked.

"I got a phone call. No big deal. Why?"

"I don't know. It just seemed, I don't know, weird somehow."

Paul flashed a big smile and put the evidence bags in the suitcase.

"What's going to happen to the rest of the carpet?" the guard asked.

"My guess is the school will pull up what's left and put down some cheap new builders' grade. I think it looks pretty *avante garde* like this, but that's just me."

Amy sat down at the other desk to fill out the receipt page of the search warrant and froze. "Paul!" she shouted inside her head, and pointed.

"What?"

"The necklace!" she thought back, pulling her right index finger forward and back to point it out.

"That's not a necklace. That's -- Oh. My. God."

There on Bruce Weeks' desk were seven or eight heavy-duty computer cable wraps. They were linked together to make one strong, plastic string about thirty six inches long. The square heads, where the tails were inserted, looked like little white diamonds sitting on the dark blotter paper desktop. There was a brown spot on one of the ties.

Paul reached for it with their left hand, but Amy slapped the hand away with their right. "We can't take this," she said out loud. "It's not in the warrant."

"What is it?" Roy asked, walking over to look.

"Don't touch it," she said. "That string of tie wraps -- we've been looking for it for weeks." She pulled her phone out of her hip pocket and took a series of pictures.

"You solved it," Paul thought to her. "I looked at it and didn't see a thing."

"I guess I've got one more stop to make," she said out loud.

"Can I -- I mean, do you still need security?"

Paul looked at the man. He was feeling happy about Christine waiting for him, he was ecstatic about Amy finding the mystery ligature; he was in love with the entire universe. "No, that's okay," he said to the guard. "Look, there's a girl out there for you. She's cute, she's fun, and she wants to have your babies. Don't give up, you'll find her." And to Amy's surprise and horror, Paul stretched up on tip-toes and kissed Roy Claiborn on the cheek. "You'll do fine," he smiled, then started to wheel the suitcase out of the dorm room.

Amy used her new badge to breeze through more check points on her way to the traffic circle on Lakeshore. She thought, "You are going to ruin my reputation. First you kiss Christine in The Cove where half the campus can see us, and now you plant one on the campus guard? Who are you and what did you do with Paul Owens?"

He laughed. "I'm in love with the universe. It's all good."

"No, it's not all good. I don't like kissing guys I don't like. And I thought you didn't like it when I kissed men, period."

"I felt sorry for Roy. You don't think he'll ask you out again, do you?"

"God, I hope not. I mean -- he's okay, but he doesn't do anything for me. And his father may be right about the rocks."

"Our conversation with Christine confused him."

She thought about it. The guard must have heard Paul say 'Wait,' then a few seconds later -- after he and Amy discussed it silently -- say something to Christine. And Paul referring to Amy by name. "Probably did," she admitted. "If I weren't in here with you, it would have confused me."

"Christine can keep us company when we get the samples from the computer lab, right?" he asked. "Then dinner. And then take the samples to the cop shop."

"Oh, I want to tell Riordan about the necklace." As they walked she punched in the detective's phone number and got his voicemail. "Your Majesty, I found the necklace. Computer cable ties linked together. I'm attaching the pictures I took. Uh, I'm on my way to get more samples. Call me, okay?" Then she forwarded the photos.

When she put the phone back in her pocket, Paul took the lead to wave at Christine in her smart car. She waved back with a smile, and Paul hurried, dragging the suitcase behind them. The woman rolled down her window and leaned out, with both arms outstretched. Paul bent over to accept and return her hug. "What a surprise to see you today," he whispered.

"I love you, Paulette," she replied. "Is Amy doing better now?"

"Yes, I am. Something came up after we talked. Can I get you to help me?"

"With your investigation? Oh boy, I'd love that."

Amy put her suitcase in the tiny excuse for a storage area behind the seats, then climbed in the passenger's side. "Up there, make a left, I'll get us to my parking lot."

"It's Paul. How was your day?"

She rested her right hand on their left leg. "I know it's you. I think I can tell when it's you or Amy talking." She stole a quick look sideways at them. "Anyway, it was okay. Not too busy at the agency. Oh, and Gina and Shawna say hello. They want to know if we all can get together this weekend."

"That would be fun," he said. "Amy?" In a moment, the same voice said, "I think so. We should be done with this job by then."

Paul explained about finding what they thought might be the murder weapon. "We're going to take some carpet samples from the computer lab, then drive them to the police station in town."

"I knew you'd solve it," Christine said. "You and Amy are such a great team."

Paul couldn't hear Amy think to her, "Thank you. You've

made Paul so happy he actually kissed a guy today."

"What?" she said, laughing.

"What?" Paul said.

"Amy said -- you kissed a guy?"

He laughed. "One of the campus guards was hitting on Amy. I told him there was a girl for him out there somewhere, and I kissed him on the cheek."

Christine joined the laughter. "How'd that go, Amy?" she asked.

Quietly, she said, "I told him I wish he hadn't done it." Then, "Okay, down that lane. You can park next to my car."

Amy pulled her suitcase out of the car, then turned to Christine. Paul immediately led to say, "Wow! You look great." She was wearing a full, white skirt that went just below her knees, and a light blue long-sleeved sailor blouse. Her hair was its typical multi-hue and multi-length, and her smile let the setting sun sparkle off her crooked front tooth. Paul stepped to her and hugged her. They stood together for several moments, until Amy said, "Sorry kids, we've got some evidence to procure. Not to mention dinner."

Amy and Paul explained their findings while they walked to the Computer Center. Christine was impressed when Amy's badge was enough to get them both through a check point. "Employee? When did that happen?"

"This morning. Surprised the hell out of me. We still haven't talked salary."

Paul said, "I think we'll be lucky to get a lunch out of this deal."

With her ID card Amy let them into the Computer Center, and they went down the stairs to the lab. A graduate assistant was at the front bench, busy with his tablet. The room was brightly lit with ceiling fluorescents; one bulb on the left was pulsing in a disconcerting way. "You need a computer?" the student asked.

Amy showed him her badge. "We need to take some carpet samples from the back," she said. "We won't be long."

He shrugged and went back to his own work. Paul wheeled the valise down to the area where Bruce usually was set up, then laid it on its side to unzip it. On the bench were pencils, a legal pad, a small metal box with wires sticking out, and a handful of individual tie wraps.

Christine sat on a stool a few feet away and continued to chat with her Paulette while Amy examined the area. She thought, "Is that a Coke stain? I'll get part of it on one of the samples." She donned latex gloves and took one of the disposable knives from her suitcase.

Amy was working on the second cut when she heard Christine say, "Uh, Paulette? Amy? Someone's coming."

From her position on the floor Amy didn't see anything, so she stood up. She saw the graduate student leaving, and Bruce Weeks striding down the aisle. Reflexively, Amy waved her right hand, which was holding the yellow plastic disposable knife. The man was not smiling.

"What are you doing here?" he demanded. "God, I am so pissed at you."

Trying to blunt his anger, Amy sat back down and resumed cutting the carpet sample. "What did I do?"

Bruce sat on a stool, ignoring Christine and watching Amy. "You're the reason that -- wait, what are you doing?"

Without looking up, she answered, "I got hired by the cops. I'm taking carpet samples for the lab."

"Oh. Whatever. I was saying, you're the reason I never see Reggie anymore."

Amy slid the carpet rectangle into the evidence bag, then stood up to throw it on the desk top and label it. "Bruce, this is my friend Christine. She's a buddy's girlfriend. Christine, meet Bruce Weeks."

A smile flew across his face and was gone in a second. "Why?" he asked Amy, almost begging. "Why did you do this to me?"

"I don't understand. What have I done to you?"

He stood up. "You're the reason Reggie moved in with Alex. I haven't seen him in two weeks."

She dropped to her knees to take another sample, then said, "Christine, can I get you to help me?" When the woman knelt by her, Amy thought to her, "Move a little to your right. I don't want him to see this."

"Oh, okay," Christine said, and repositioned herself. "What?"

It was Paul who thought, "We think Bruce is the killer." Christine inhaled sharply and said, "Oh!" "Here, take this. I hope you don't need it." He handed her one of the used disposable knives; it was eight inches long, bright yellow plastic, with a small but sharp metal tip.

He could see her hand shake as she took the weapon, but she slid it up her left sleeve, then made sure the cuff button was fastened. Paul let out a small sigh of relief -- if worse came to worst, Christine would not be helpless. He thought to her, "Don't let him get behind you." He saw her frown, as if she didn't understand what he meant, but then she mouthed the word, "Okay."

"Thanks, Honey," he said out loud, and let Amy start work on the next carpet cut.

"Why, damn it!" Bruce shouted.

"It had nothing to do with you," she said as she hurried with her work. "They arrested Reggie because he attacked me, then they let him out. Later he told me that all the girls at school thought he was the murderer and no one would go out with him. Except Alex."

"I know the girls like him," the man said. "I'm proud of him that he's such a stud and he's my roommate. But now he's never around. I miss him."

Christine said, "Oh, that's sad."

"What do you know about it?" he said harshly; it wasn't really a question.

"No reason to be ugly to my friend," Amy said as she pulled up the second rectangle of carpet. As she stood up, she slipped the used yellow plastic knife into her right front pocket. "Hey, I'm impressed with your programming."

He scoffed. "There's no way you could understand what I do. My professors are all the time amazed at my work."

"I believe it," she said as she bagged the carpet sample. "You jiggered your ID card to make you anonymous. Impressive."

"That was easy," he said, but smiled at the compliment. "Here, let me show you something better." He punched some buttons on his phone, and they heard a loud 'ka-THUNK' as the front door of the computer lab locked, and half the overhead fluorescents went out. Christine looked around at the noise and then the dimness, frightened.

Paul thought, "I don't like where this is going." He felt Amy nod.

She stood next to Christine, who whispered, "Amy? Paulette? I'm scared." Paul thought to her, "We'll think of something." She grabbed their left hand.

Amy tried to hide the fear she felt. "With this ability -- you said you wanted to build the best computer ever. I think you'll do it."

Everyone froze when Amy's phone rang. Bruce said, "Get rid of that call." She pulled the phone out of her hip pocket and saw it was Riordan. "I'll send it to voicemail," she said as she hit the button to accept the call. She was still holding the phone in her hand when she said, "So, Bruce Weeks, what brings you to the computer lab?"

Bruce jumped at Amy and slapped the phone from her hand. It hit the side of the work bench and pieces flew off it. "You really think I'm an idiot!" he shouted. "You think if you're nice to me that I'll do whatever you want. I hate you! I hate you! I hate all of you that keep Reggie away!" He stood not a foot away from her, glaring down at her, breathing heavily.

Amy groped behind herself until she grasped a stool, then slowly walked it backwards until it bumped the wall. "Sit there," she thought to Christine, "so he can't get behind you." While Christine moved, Amy tugged at another stool.

"You think you're so smart," Bruce began. He was standing by his work bench, and he picked up some of the tie wraps. "You bat your eyelashes at the detective and you think that makes you a policeman." Slowly, he fed an inch or two of one wrap's tail into the rectangular head of another. "And you think that if you beat up Reggie no one will ever stop you."

"Beat up Reggie?" Christine asked. "Who's Reggie? Who beat him up?"

"Shut your fucking mouth!" he screamed, and Christine shrank into herself, pulling her head back and wrapping her arms around herself. "This has nothing to do with you!" Then, quietly, he said, "This is between me and her."

He added another tie wrap to the string he was building, then grabbed the ends and tugged.

Sitting on the stool next to Christine, Amy tried to calm the man. "You're right. Why don't you let her leave? Then you and I can talk about things."

He slid another cable tie tail into the growing chain.

"Your friend here," he said to Christine, "is a world-class bitch. Ever since I started to get my roommate to spend more time at home, she's been getting in the way."

Again, Bruce held the string of cable wraps by the ends and flexed it. "Playing up to the police, holding the detective's notebook -- do you wipe his ass, too?"

Quietly, Christine said, "You're scaring me. Please stop."

A smile spread across Bruce's face and stayed there. "You have no idea. You're just starting to get scared."

He picked up another tie wrap and added it to the chain.

Paul stood up and said, "Leave her alone. She's just a bystander. It's me you want a piece of." He swallowed, but made himself walk to where Bruce was testing his plastic necklace ligature. Paul held their left hand against the side of their neck, palm out, hoping to fight the coming garrote.

"Oh, miss police woman, you misunderstand me," he said as he added yet another cable wrap to the chain. "I don't want a piece of you. I don't want anything to do with you. I just want you to pay for making Reggie go away."

Christine blurted, "Are you gay, too?"

He hurled himself past Amy, screaming "No!" Bruce grabbed Christine by her hair and pulled her off the stool. "There's nothing wrong with me!" he shouted. "You're just another one of those, those temptations!" He lifted her by the hair, then threw her against the back wall. Christine gave a cry of pain as her face hit; immediately there was a big red stain on the drywall, from her nose and lip. She was stunned, and it took her a few seconds to sit up against the wall, dripping onto her once-white skirt.

It was Paul who shouted at Bruce, and ran at him, shoulder first, like a football blocker. Bruce staggered sideways, toward a corner. Paul heard Amy think, "Knife in our pocket. Watch out for --" but before she finished her sentence Bruce had flicked the cable wrap garrote over their neck. He pulled the ends of the plastic ligature, tugging Amy until their faces were only inches apart. The only things she could see were his eyes, all pupil, enflamed with rage.

She began to feel light-headed, and dizzy, and her field of vision was getting narrower and dimmer. Amy struggled to work her hand to her front pocket, but her fingers were tingling and would not cooperate. She remembered Doctor Jermaine's evaluation, that Bruce's first victim was unconscious within ten seconds. She thought Paul's name, she thought she heard his voice in her head saying "I love you, Amy." Her fingernails were digging into the skin on their neck, desperate to ease the lethal tension of the weapon that was engraving marks into their flesh that would look like they were from a beaded necklace.

Everything was fading -- sound and sight and even the tingling in her fingers. She didn't hear it when Christine bellowed, "You God-damned boy! Leave my Paulette alone!" Amy and Paul barely felt the jolt from Christine leaping onto Bruce's back. They did not know the woman was reaching around to his face, scraping with her nails. When he opened his mouth to yell, Christine caught the corners with her fingers and yanked hard.

Vision and hearing were beginning to return when Paul realized they were lying on the floor by the bench. Out loud he called, "Amy?" and felt relief when he heard her respond silently. Feeling was replacing the pins and needles in their fingers and feet.

Paul saw Christine perched on Bruce's back, her legs wrapped around his waist. She had retrieved the disposable knife Amy had given her, but in her excitement she had grabbed the wrong end and was striking the man with the bright yellow handle; it had cracked, and the sharp plastic edges had torn into his scalp and pulled out small tufts of hair. "Leave her alone!" Christine screamed, "She's mine!" Bruce was snarling, too disoriented to dislodge her, or to think of anything but pain and anger.

Still groggy, Paul forced themself to their feet. He went beside Christine, thinking to her, "You are a life saver. Now, hang on." He summoned all their dizzy strength and shoved Bruce forward, into the same wall where Bruce had thrown Christine. This time it was his blood that stained the wall. "Paulette!" she shouted, "You're okay!" She jumped down to her feet, panting.

"Thanks to you," Paul said aloud. The enraged Bruce was slowed down only for a moment. Blood running from his smashed nose, he turned and came at Paul and Amy barehanded. Paul reached into their front pocket for the yellow plastic knife, with its little metal blade. As Bruce's fingers closed on their neck, Paul forced the knife point into the man's abdomen. His eyes flew wide, the rage replaced with shock and pain.

They felt warm liquid soaking their shirt and pants as Bruce slowly relaxed his grip on their neck. "If you are pissing on me," Paul hissed, "I swear I will kill you dead."

Bruce slowly slid down, trying to grab on to any part of Amy as gravity overtook him. Amy pushed against him with one leg and he fell to his knees, then sideways to the floor.

When Bruce was breathing heavily and holding both hands over the knife wound, Amy leaned forward with their knee on his neck. "What is it with you men?" Amy shouted. "I'll never get this blood out of my pants!"

She felt Christine's hand on their shoulder. Amy took a deep breath, then leaned toward Bruce and asked, "You did it? You killed all of them?"

"I was protecting myself," he said, voice distorted by pain and anger. "They were taking Reggie away."

"Even Ashley?" She glanced up and saw Christine's beatific smile.

"That was different," he struggled to say. "She wanted help on a scheme, but she caught me reprogramming an ID card." He coughed, then grimaced in pain. "She said she'd turn me in if I didn't help her."

"Help her do what?" she asked. Vaguely she heard noise from the front of the lab room.

"She wanted me to hack her grade in a class. I wouldn't do it because that would be wrong."

"So you killed her? Because hacking a grade would be wrong?"

Christine called, "Paulette, the police are here. How do we let them in?"

Paul poked the man in the stomach, setting off a wave of pain that was transparent on his face. "How do we unlock the door, creep?"

Panting, he said, "Key. Middle drawer, front desk."

Christine overheard, and got the door unlocked just as Riordan was explaining to Mullinax that a chair thrown through the glass would solve all their problems. "Are you all right, Sweetheart?" Riordan asked when he saw her bloody face, and red stains down her shirt and skirt. "And where's Clear?"

"Back here," Amy shouted. "We got a present for you."

The detective and the uniformed officer followed Christine down the aisle to the back of the dimly lit lab, where Amy was still holding Bruce down with their knee on the side of the man's neck.

Riordan crouched to look in the man's face. "Bruce Weeks, I presume?" He gurgled, so Amy let up her pressure on her knee and let the man croak, "Yeah." A smile creased Riordan's face. "Clear, you okay? When he looked at her, his hand went to the scratches and marks on her neck. "He almost got you!" he said.

"Christine saved us. She made him let go of us so we could take another whack at him."

There was a pause, then the detective asked, "Who's 'we'? Oh, Clear, don't tell me you slept with him, too!"

"No!" she shouted, but she was smiling. She thought to Paul, "I don't care what he thinks. We're alive, we're going to be all right."

As he stood up, Riordan accidentally on purpose kicked Bruce in the stomach. "Now, will you look at that," he said, "you got blood on my shoe." He nodded at Mullinax, who pushed a button on his walkie-talkie to request an ambulance.

Amy got to their feet, and put her arm around Christine. "I want to introduce you to a friend. Steven, this is Christine Hodges. Christine, this seems to be my new boss, Detective Steven Riordan."

"Pleased to meet you, Sweetheart," Riordan said, taking off his fedora. "You look like you had a hard time. I appreciate you rescuing Clear here."

"She's my friend. I had to help her."

Mullinax read Bruce his rights and handcuffed him on the floor while Amy began to tell the detective about the afternoon's events.

☿ 39 ♋

Monday, October 25, 2021 -- Great Wok restaurant, New Orleans

By the time the detective led the women into Great Wok on Mirabeau, Christine had washed the dried blood from her face, and left wet spots on her skirt from trying to get blood out before the stains set. Amy thought her jeans were beyond salvage, so she just left the deep red stains. When Paul saw themself in the ladies' room mirror, he thought of Jackie Kennedy after the JFK assassination -- minus the pillbox hat. They all knew Bruce Weeks was in a guarded room at Charity Hospital where his recovery was certain.

The *maître-d* greeted Riordan as an old friend and seated the three of them in a quiet booth toward the back. As they opened menus the detective announced, "I'm glad you weren't hurt, Clear. I'd never have been able to explain a worker's comp claim for you. And you," turning to Christine, "thank God all you've got is a fat lip. I don't even have a band-aid for you. What's your name, Chris? Christine? --" the woman nodded "-- Okay, Christine. Clear. On behalf of NOPD, please consider dinner as payment in full for some halfway smart police work."

"Halfway?" Christine said, defensive for her lover. "Paulette found the bad guy." She saw Amy flinch and heard Paul think to her, "He doesn't know about me. But I'm glad you're here." She smiled, and slid her hand on the bench seat until she poked Amy in the thigh.

"Who?"

"Amy. Amy did. She's the hero." Christine stuck out her

lower lip, belligerently. Riordan grinned, happy to have closed the case.

"Tell me how you spotted the weapon. We all thought it was a necklace."

"When I took the carpet samples from Reggie's room, the campus guard was sitting at his desk, so I sat at Bruce's desk to fill out the search warrant receipt page. And there it was, just lying there on the desk. It was so obvious once I saw it."

"Mullinax was supposed to get another warrant and collect it. Plus we've got the ligature he tried to use on you tonight." He thought for a moment. "Police work is a lot of detail, but without inspiration it's not enough. I don't say this very often, but you done good, Sweetheart."

After another bite out of a potsticker he went on. "That stunt with the phone. It worked -- you told me who the perp was and where you were. But I'm not surprised he broke your phone, and you're one lucky woman that he didn't throttle you on the spot."

"So, what should I have done, Your Majesty?" She was holding a half-eaten egg roll in her right hand. Even though Riordan was giving her a hard time, she was euphoric with the joy of having escaped death.

"Let's see. You could have taken him out with karate." Amy shook her head. "Okay, flip open your baton and wail on him." Another head shake. "Service revolver, two warning shots through his best liver." Amy and Christine were laughing. "What?" Riordan asked, "What's so funny?"

It was Paul who said, "I could have sworn I heard you say 'thank you'."

He stopped while the waiter brought their chicken chop suey, pork fried rice, and crawfish lo mein. He also put out three beers -- Dixies for Amy and Christine, and a Tsing Tao for Riordan. Christine said, "We were going to have dinner hours ago!" as she spread the cloth napkin over her damp, stained skirt.

"I want you to know that I talked to Captain Ramirez about what you did." Amy looked up while she sucked in a lo mein noodle. "He said he wasn't surprised. He thinks you'd be perfect at the state police academy."

"What?" Christine said, eyes as wide as her mouth.

"Not going to happen," Amy said, shaking her head. Paul put

their left hand on Christine's on the bench seat, where the detective couldn't see. "This was very exciting, but I don't know that I want to do it all the time."

"Clear, you said something about not breaking up the team. I -- New Orleans police -- can use some help. Your help."

"You're offering me a job?"

"Not really." He looked down and pushed his fried rice around his plate. "You don't have the credentials to justify a payroll position, and dinner is blowing my budget for the year." He looked up and met her eyes. "But I'm impressed, and Ramirez is impressed. Let me call on you when I need extra hands -- I'll pay you in moo goo gai pan and won ton soup. Or tacos and burritos if you prefer; I'm easy."

"If I can't get money," Amy began, laughing, "I want something on campus named after me. The Amy E. Clear Amphitheater. The Me, Myself and I Memorial Computer Building. Something like that."

"I'll take it up with the dean," he laughed back.

Amy thought to Paul, "I'm going to ask him out."

"Oh, crap. Well, let me warn Christine first." Paul thought to the woman to let her know what Amy was going to do. Christine shook her head and muttered something about 'Not another boy'."

"Tell you what, Steven. I'm a junior and I really want to get my degree and a masters. As long as you know school comes first, yes, it would be fun to do this some more with you."

He nodded.

"Oh boy," she whispered, working up her courage. "And after this, tell me something about you. Your life. You were a great teacher, I -- I want to know you better."

"You flatter me, Clear. And I guess you're flattering my wife's excellent taste in men. But I'm sure there's some man out there who's cute and fun and wants you to have his babies."

Her jaw dropped.

Laughing, Riordan came around to her side of the table and hugged her from the side. "Claiborn says now he'll vote for you for God."

"I'm sorry, Ste -- Riordan." She rolled her eyes toward the ceiling and said, "God, I'm so embarrassed."

"How many times do I have to tell you to get over yourself? It's okay." As he went back to his seat, he said, "We work together, and that's easier if we like each other. You're smart as a whip, you work hard, and you are the bravest college student I've ever seen. Almost as brave as your friend here." He lifted his beer and said, "To the future." Amy looked at Christine and Paul thought to her, "Yeah. To our future." The woman smiled and said, "Oh, yeah."

"Now, let me get this straight," Riordan said. "This Bruce guy had a man-crush on Reggie Young. So he started targeting the women Reggie slept with?"

"Or even was friends with," Amy said, "like Laura Adams. I didn't know what he meant, but after Bruce found out I beat up Reggie, he said he'd never mess with me. I guess he hadn't figured out yet that -- well, that I was one of the women keeping Reggie away from home."

"All because he missed having a very occasional beer with his roommate?"

"A roommate who thinks he's a total loser," Amy added. "So sad."

It was almost midnight when Riordan dropped Amy and Christine off on campus. The police presence had evaporated, and there were no interruptions as they walked to Amy's dorm. Paul was holding Christine's hand. "Can you stay over?" he thought to her. "I'm sure Amy will let you use a nightgown if you want one."

She said out loud, "Amy, Paulette invited me to stay tonight. Is that okay with you?"

"Yes," she answered immediately, then abruptly stopped walking. "You saved our lives tonight. I'm not ready to let you out of my sight."

"So I'm special to you?"

Hands on both of Christine's shoulders, Paul stared at her and said, "You're special to Amy, and you're special to me. To both of us. Without you, we'd both be dead. Never forget that -- I know I won't."

As they resumed their walk to the dorm, Paul went on, "There's some culture where if you save a person's life, you're stuck with them forever."

"I can't wait," Christine said.

❦ Coming Attractions ❧

What's next for our dynamic, dyadic duo?

Amy uses her college Masters in statistics to work at a market research company, with a specialty in demonstrating there is no such thing as Extra-Sensory Perception. A mysterious and somewhat creepy client asks Amy to find just such a subject -- someone with the ability of broadcast telepathy, to think into the minds of other people. Although she and Paul are amused to be exactly what the client is seeking, they set up rigorous protocols to earn a living with an honest project.

Soon the New Orleans police are fishing bodies out of the Mississippi River on a daily basis, including one of the subjects presented by Mister Creepy Client. Before they know it, Amy and Paul are risking their life to run down a ruthless drug baron, while trying to protect one of the subjects who is a mirror image of Amy and Paul -- a young man with a younger woman dyad in his head.

The Amy and Paul Saga continues soon with *Another One Like Us*. Look for it shortly at your favorite book retailer! And meanwhile, turn the page for a sample...

When Amy found Florence and Leon at her door again, he was holding a tool box. "Come in, come in," she said, and she hugged Florence as she passed. Amy ushered them to the sofa, where glasses of wine were waiting.

"It's so nice out," Florence said, "I want to play. It's a good day to be spies."

Leon was wearing a striped necktie on a blue pin-striped shirt, over black slacks. He looked like the accountant he was. "I think I'm ready." he offered. "Would you like to see my sketches?"

"You remembered, good. Let's see them."

The three sat with Leon in the middle, so they all could share the drawings. He had made them in pencil with a degree of detail that surprised Amy. There were three of them.

The first put Amy's hair under a fedora, and added a thin moustache. The second featured a hippie look with her hair in a mullet. And the third showed her hair in a short queue, and used shadowing to give her a menacing and masculine appearance.

"These are amazing," Amy volunteered. "I had no idea you were such a good artist. Do you draw or paint?"

Leon shook his head, but he shyly said, "Thank you. I do this for my costume designs."

"I like the first one," Florence said. "Something about the hat and the moustache, the drawing looks like how I imagine Paul."

Amy stared at her friend, her mouth open in surprise. She thought to Florence, "We don't talk about Paul to outsiders." Immediately, Florence's hand flew up to cover her mouth. When Leon turned back to Amy, Florence mouthed "I'm sorry!"

Amy held the first and third drawings, trying to make up her mind. Finally she decided, "The hat would fall off and I'd be dead meat. Florence, can you do that to my hair?" She pointed at the braid.

"Sure," she replied. "Your hair is so straight it'll look great. Last time I tried it on myself I looked like a frizz machine."

Amy sipped her wine, then said to Leon, "The shadows on the sketch look tough. How do you do it in real life?"

He bent over and opened the tool box at his feet. It contained tubes of greasepaint, a few dozen packets of foundation and clarifier, liquid latex, brushes, and sponges. Florence said, "And I thought my makeup kit was extreme."

"Do you have a junky towel?" Leon asked. "This might get messy. Will we fit in your bathroom?"

"Will this stuff make permanent stains?"

"If you leave it too long."

"Hmmm." Amy stood up and walked to her linen closet. "Yes, these will work." As she brought them back to the sofa she said, "Left over from trying to dye my hair."

"Those stains are pink!" Florence said.

"I did something wrong."

"But, pink?"

"I did something wrong, sue me."

Leon tried to placate both women. "The towels will do fine. But you may want to change clothes before I apply the makeup. I don't know that this disguise will go with a dress."

"Good thinking! Will you excuse me?" she said, and disappeared into her bedroom.

"This is exciting," Leon said. "I've only done this for science fiction conventions and Halloween. Do you think she liked the design?"

Florence replied, "I've known Amy a long time, and she has no problem saying if she doesn't like something. I think you've got a new fan."

Amy returned in blue jeans and a faded work shirt. She was wearing a sports bra underneath to minimize her bust. "How's this?"

Florence and Leon nodded. Leon arranged the towels to

protect Amy's shirt, and started opening tubes and packages. He looked confident and comfortable as he brushed kohl and latex, as he patted and sponged. He worked quickly and finished up with powder. "What do you think?" he said as he presented a hand mirror.

Amy and Florence were impressed. It worked. Even with her hair loose, the makeup made her look older, masculine, and tough. With her hair in a queue she might look like a roustabout.

Florence imagined she was looking at Paul, and smiled. She felt an itch. Leon might just get lucky after all.

"Why are you an accountant?" Amy asked. "You're an artist!"

"Do you like it?" he asked, looking down.

Amy reached out to put her fingers on his chin, and turned his head to look right at her. "Yes," she said, "I like it. I like it lots."

He looked down, blushing with pride.

"Here, let me braid your hair," Florence said. To Leon, she asked, "How robust is this? If she sweats, will it all fall off her face?" She was separating Amy's hair into thirds.

"Don't go swimming," he suggested. "And come in out of the rain. Otherwise, you'll need these to get it off." He put canisters of cold cream and baby oil on the table.

Loose, Amy's hair hung to her shoulders. Florence braided it into a queue that was four inches long. When she was done, Leon said, "I think the pink hair band undermines the look we're going for." He reached into his tool box and came up with something gray and nondescript. "Try this."

Amy took another look in the mirror. She heard Paul think to her, "Who are you and what have you done with my Amy?" She laughed and said out loud, "Oh yes. Yes, this will work." Then she put down the mirror and asked, "How about some dinner?"

Amy did not drink a second glass of wine, plying herself with coffee instead during the meal. The women talked over their plan with Leon. "We're going to break in to a warehouse," Amy said.

"We're just going to look around."

"Amy has met some of the people who might be there, that's why the disguise," Florence added. "It's one of her clients."

"You two sound like spies!" Leon said, his eyes wide.

Amy and Florence smiled at each other. "We feel like spies," Florence replied. "We want to find out if the client is legitimate, or if he's some kind of bad evil."

"Aren't you scared?" Leon asked.

Florence thought a moment and said, "Now that you mention it, yes. Amy?"

"Nah. I've done worse. Besides, when I was little my dad and a friend taught me that it's okay to be scared, as long as you still do whatever it is you need to do."

"That's it? That's enough to make you not scared?"

"God no, Leon," Amy said. "But it taught me that you can't let being scared matter. When I was little, the way I did it was pretending I wasn't scared at all. And it worked."

"If you'll pardon me," Leon said, "I think you ladies are very brave. And a little crazy."

Florence smiled. "Yeah, ain't we though?"

When dinner was done, Amy said, "Do you want to ride shotgun with us?"

Leon shook his head vigorously. "But will you call me when you get back so I know you're all right?"

"That's so sweet," Florence said, and she kissed him. Despite his retiring and dweebish personality, Leon accepted the kiss and returned it. Florence was pleasantly surprised.

He picked up his tool box, and the three left together. Amy drove by Florence's warehouse, where Leon had parked his car. "Good luck," he said, "and don't forget to phone me."

"Thanks, Leon," Amy called to him, "I like what you've done." He waved and unlocked his car.

The women drove downriver. It was dusk when they crossed the Industrial Canal, and turned down a side street toward the river. When the road turned, Florence said, "We ought to park here. Just in case, you know, there's a party up there."

They locked the car, and began walking up North Peters Street. Florence said, "That disguise is excellent, but you're walking like a girl."

Amy stopped and asked, "How's that?"

"Like this," Florence said, and took a few steps with a pronounced wiggle. "Your butt is on both sides of the street."

"I wonder if this is what Paul felt like when I used to rag him about wearing a skirt?"

Paul said out loud, "Yes, it is. Let me show you how a man does it," and he led. He walked slowly and carefully for a few yards.

Florence, watching from behind, laughed. "Hate to say it, Paul, but you're walking like a girl!"

Paul in Amy stopped, and turned to look at her. Florence was trying to control her amusement. "It may have something to do with walking in a girl's body, what do you think?"

"Ooops," he said, "does this damn emasculation never end? Back to you Amy." He retreated, but Amy felt him laughing.

"Paul finally did learn how to sit in a skirt," Amy said. "Maybe if I practice I'll be able to walk like a man." They walked on, then she added, "Like I'm really going to do this a whole lot."

Florence said, "If we're stopped, let's say we're looking for locations for a photography shoot."

Amy nodded. "I'm easy. We're NOT going to get caught."

As they walked on, Amy said, "You realize you have to do all the talking."

"What talking?"

"Any talking. If I open my mouth it will blow the manly man disguise." In an artificially high-pitched voice she said "Do you feel lucky, punk?"

"It's bad to over-plan," Florence said grimly. "I'll fake it."

Both warehouses were dark. With dusk and moonlight to

illuminate the way, they walked along the near side of the first building and tried a door. It opened.

The building showed signs of an urban campfire, with empty pint bottles of Golden Grain and generic vodka tossed around a makeshift fire pit. About one third of the roof was missing, allowing some illumination inside. Florence whispered, "I don't even smell anything. This seems abandoned."

Amy retrieved Paul's LED penlight and looked around the section under the roof. Cracked concrete floor, some rags, a clot of dirty newspapers. "Let's try the other one."

They left by the same door, but instead of going back to the road they walked behind the warehouse, on the river side. The lights of the naval base and the Aurora Gardens neighborhood shone across the river and twinkled off the ripples. The river breeze, with its faint aroma of fish and Mother Nature, was invigorating. When they got to the opening for the dual driveway, Florence peeked around the corner and saw nothing. They ran until they were behind the second warehouse, then walked around it and looked for a doorway.

It too was unlocked. With so little roof remaining on the building, the inside was as bright as the night outside.

And parked in the middle was a shiny black Escalade. Florence walked behind it and felt the cracked plastic lens over the driver side tail light. "Bingo!" she said.

They looked for the thing they couldn't identify in the satellite photo -- debris? A wall? A doorway? It only took a minute to find the structure. Surrounded by a wall just one cinder brick tall was a flat double door, like the entrance to a storm cellar.

Amy got on her knees and put an ear to it. She heard a loud mechanical throbbing. Florence stood by her and whispered, "There's light coming through the edges." Amy stood and they retreated to the small dark section of the warehouse, under the remains of roof. She hoped they were hidden because there was no place else for them to go.

A minute later, the flat wooden doors swung up and open with a bang. Amy recognized the driver, the mute chauffeur she and Paul had named Igor. A small woman was next; Amy remembered interviewing her at Anti-Junk a week earlier. In the back was Hyde. When he was topside, he threw the doors shut with another bang.

"We'll have you home in no time, Mrs. Williams," a voice said. "Is that acceptable?"

"This has been such an adventure," the woman said. "Thank you so much. But I'm looking forward to sleeping in my own bed now." Igor helped her into the car, then rolled up the warehouse doorway. He drove the Escalade outside, then put it in park while he returned to close the doorway. The women heard the car start back up and fade into the distance.

Paul thought to Amy, "Can we breathe now?"

Florence whispered, "I'm glad Leon didn't come with us. He'd have fainted."

Amy walked into the moonlight and looked around the warehouse. There were erector-set shelves lining the north wall, holding old car parts. "Let's get our money's worth," she whispered to Florence, and headed to the storm doors.

"Amy," Florence whispered back, "I'm trying to pretend I'm not scared. It's not working."

Amy put her hand on her friend's shoulder. "My dad says being scared just makes you more careful. Let's go."

She grabbed one of the wooden doors and lifted it up, then held it as she let it down to the ground, avoiding noise. "I love their arrogance," Paul thought to her. "Big old lock on the door, and they don't bother to use it. It doesn't occur to them that anyone might be on to them."

Florence hadn't moved. Amy took her friend by the sleeve and hissed, "You can feel as scared as you like, but I need you to behave as if you're not!" She dragged Florence behind her, and they walked down the brightly lit concrete steps.

The landing opened onto a broad hallway, with a ceiling about seven feet high. Floors, walls, ceilings, all were smooth sealed concrete. Everything was well lit by old fashioned fluorescent bulbs, with a cool, blue tint. The air smelled too fresh; there was a hint of ozone, as if the atmosphere were being artificially generated.

There was an office on the left. About twelve by twelve, two desks, several computer screens, some large filing cabinets. Opposite was a commissary, with microwave ovens and sinks and two refrigerators. Amy couldn't resist, she opened one of the coolers. "Flo!" she whispered, "come look at this!" When her friend was beside her, Amy pointed to packages of pork chops and steaks.

"No way! Solid meat?" Florence exclaimed.

"I know," said Amy, "I want to move in here."

Next they looked in cabinets. Dishes, tableware, plastic containers, some canned goods. In the blue fluorescent light the room was exceptionally clean.

Down the hall on the right was a closed door, but it wasn't locked. Inside, Amy whispered, "This looks like Uncle Charlie's office." There was a gurney with white paper over it, a high metal tray on wheels, lots of cabinets, and much of the stock of any physician's office: blood pressure cuff, stethoscope, jars of rubbing alcohol with cotton balls, syringes, viewing nipples, and the neon pink plastic jar for used sticks. On a counter was a shallow tray filled with alcohol that contained a variety of scalpels. Blue and white cylinders of gas were against a wall. Amy heard Paul think, "I wish James could see this. Can you take a photo?" Florence saw her friend smile and take out her cell phone. She took three pictures to cover the room.

Florence opened some cabinets and looked inside. One had a box with some objects that looked electronic rather than medical. "What do you think these things are?" she asked.

Amy looked and saw it was mostly full of thin plastic rectangles, with rounded edges, and a tail of four wires trailing. "I think these are the implants!" she whispered. She took two from the back of the stack and tucked them into her work shirt pockets.

They closed the examination room door behind them, then looked across the hall. Amy saw a dormitory, about twenty by twenty five, with four sets of neatly made up bunk beds. They walked in to look around.

"I'm so glad to see someone," they heard a woman's voice say. Startled, Florence nearly hit her head on the ceiling. Amy thought it sounded familiar, and turned to look. It was Marilyn something, a woman she'd tested at Anti-Junk two weeks earlier. A very pleasant woman, somewhat delusional, and bound to recognize Amy's voice.

Amy thought to Florence, "I've met her, you have to do the talking. Say hello, tell her how nice it is to see her. Ask her how she likes it here. Be chatty. Be friendly. Now!"

Florence said, "And it's so nice to see you! How are you today?" Amy and Florence smiled at the woman from across the room.

"Oh, I'm fine," the woman said. "It's just a little lonely here since Mrs. Williams left."

"When was that?" Florence asked.

"Just a little while ago, but I miss her already. She was very nice. We could see things, you know."

At Amy's prompting, Florence said, "Where did she go? Is she coming back soon?"

"No, they're taking her home. I say home, it's to the institute where she lives. She says her husband and her son sometimes visit her there."

"How long have you been here?" Florence prodded her.

"I think it's about two weeks. Hard to tell without windows, and there isn't a clock."

Amy looked around while Florence and the woman talked.

The walls were smooth sealed concrete, but were painted a pleasant pastel yellow. There were a few dressers and chifforobes in the room. A large flat screen TV hung in a corner, turned off. One wall sported a colorful abstract print, while an open doorway on another led to a bath. She touched one of the bunk beds and felt the mattress was in good condition.

Then she noticed a far lower bunk was occupied. While Florence talked to Marilyn, Amy slowly walked to investigate.

Robert Carr, originally introduced as Joe Reynolds, was stretched out. His eyes were open, but his entire body was rigid. Either he was drugged, or he was in rigor mortis.

Amy did what she'd seen her father do a hundred times, held her fingers against the carotid artery in the neck. She felt a strong pulse. Still, his eyes did not move, he barely seemed to breathe. She leaned close to him and thought, "Robert, can you hear me?"

She heard a female voice in her head say "Can you help me?"

"Vicky!" Amy thought back. "Oh, I'm wearing a disguise, but it's Amy. We talked last week?"

"I remember you, I recognize your voice. How did you know to rescue me?"

"You've been drugged, that's why you can't move. It will wear off."

"We have to pee so bad!"

Amy thought, "I'm sorry I can't help you now. But tell me, have you been able to talk to Joe -- uh, Robert?"

Vicky thought back, "Yeah, a little. I'm glad you gave me that advice. Less shrill and crazy, he's more open. If we live long enough we might be friends."

Amy thought, "Making friends was the best thing I did."

"I have to pee so bad!" Vicky thought again.

"I have to go now. Tell Joe -- uh, Robert -- that I was here, but he can't talk to anyone about it. Except you." Amy touched their body on the shoulder, grasped it firmly for a moment, then turned back to Florence and Marilyn.

Amy thought to her friend, "Tell her it's been nice talking to her, but we have to go." After Florence did, the woman replied, "I appreciate the company, it gets boring here sometimes. Could you turn the light off on your way out? I'd like to nap."

Amy thought to Florence, "Tell her we'd love to but we can't because we aren't real, and wave."

Florence turned to look at Amy, then faced the woman again. "We'd love to, Honey, but we can't because -- well, we're not real. Goodbye!" and she waved.

Amy thought a lullaby to the woman. "So, dear friends, it's time to go, / Good night, good night" she sang silently in her stunning voice. The woman smiled, but didn't act the least surprised to hear the song in her head. She lay down on her bunk and closed her eyes.

The friends backed into the hallway. Amy whispered, "I'd love to go through the office." Florence said, "Yeah? Well I'd love to go through the front door and go home."

Amy took a deep breath and sighed. "You're right. Let's go."

Down the hall. Up the cement steps. Amy quietly closed the storm door. Then the friends walked out the unlocked side door, and again turned toward the river.

"What's the deal with that woman?" Florence asked. "She seemed nice, but not all there."

"That's the deal," Amy replied. "I interviewed her at Anti-Junk two weeks ago. Sweet, no psychic abilities, and a little limited in the non-psychic stuff."

"Do you think she might tell Hyde we were there?"

"It doesn't matter. You heard her, she sees things. They won't take her seriously. And you told her we weren't real."

They sat on some debris along the wharf, behind the warehouse. Now Florence felt safe, and a wave of euphoria came over her. "I think I get that business of pretending you're not scared," she whispered. "I feel so alive right now, this is better than sex. I feel like Josophine."

Amy smiled at her friend. "You ARE Josophine. I may start calling you that all the time. You did a great job with that lady."

After a moment, Amy whispered, "Did you see the man on the bunk bed across the room?"

"Vaguely, I saw you go over there, but I was talking to Mrs. Not-All-There. Was he dead?"

"Drugged," Amy answered. "That's the guy like me and Paul, there's a woman living in his head. I talked to her a little."

Florence was at a complete loss. "How are they doing?" is all she could think of to say.

"She didn't recognize me. Hey, let's tell Leon his disguise worked. Uh, she said they had to pee."

They heard a car in the distance, getting louder. After a minute they could see headlights shine between the two warehouses, harmlessly illuminating the Mississippi River. The motor idled while they imagined Igor got out to roll up the vehicle doorway. Then the engine raced for a moment, until the sound disappeared inside the building. When they heard the door roll down, they walked upstream, behind the first warehouse, then over to North Peters Street, and up to where they had parked Amy's car. Neither spoke until they were in the car with the doors locked.

Amy said, "Call Leon. He sounded like he was worried about you."

Florence punched his number on her phone. "Leon, it's Florence. Yes -- yes -- yes, everything went okay. We're on our way back to Amy's house. And your disguise worked, someone Amy had interviewed didn't recognize her."

Amy felt the same relief and exhilaration Florence had talked about on the wharf. "Paul," she thought, "that went well."

"Yes. Florence found the implants. You thought to her what to say to the woman?" Not aimed at him, he had not heard it.

"I had a feeling she'd do good, she came through."

"I'm having a blast with both of you. I saw you check Robert out, so he was drugged, huh? Were you able to talk to him?"

"He was out, but I talked to Vicky a little. She said she's beginning to make progress talking to Robert. I told her making friends was the best thing I ever did."

"You did? You told a total stranger that you're a dyad host?"

"A total stranger who also is part of a dyad. Seemed like the right thing to do at the time."

Paul thought, "You want a beer?"

"I want something better, I'll tell you in a bit," Amy thought.

Florence put her phone away. "He was glad to hear we're okay. He feels like part of the team. I've never heard him so excited. And so confident. Usually he's a wimpy guy, but not tonight."

"I feel so alive!" Amy yelled in the car, and beat on her steering wheel.

Paul said out loud, "We are the Crazy Brave Three. We are going to figure this out."

When Amy parked, Florence offered her a high five. The women hugged before Florence got in her car. "Thanks for a fun evening!" she shouted as she drove off for home.

Amy let themself into her house. She locked the front door, and turned off the front light. "Dinner was good," she said, "but I've got to brush my teeth. Did you see those steaks?"

Amy went through her bedtime rituals, chatting with Paul. When he knew she was done, he said, "How about that beer?"

Amy said, "I've got something better," and she dropped their clothes to the floor.